Restoring a Life

A NOVEL

BY

MARK MACMILLIN

Narration Publishers
Newport Beach

Narration Publishers

1400 Quail Street, Suite 210
Newport Beach, CA 92660
www.narrationpublishers.com

Narration Publishers edition, August 2012

ISBN-13: 978-0615666341

For Alexis, Madeline and Justin—

the lights of my life

Forward

There was a time, before television, maybe before the scientific method, where men, women, boys, girls, and Duke – the family's old, lazy bloodhound – would retire to the front porch after the evening meal. In my fantasy, the eldest male is sitting in his hand–crafted rocking chair, lighting his pipe as the children beg, "Grandpa, tell us the story ..."

And thus, wisdom – *the art of skillful living* – was cultivated and shared amongst loved ones.

It's not often that we hear of wisdom these days. In fact, following supper, we're more apt to push for the completion of homework, "and then spend an hour preparing for the S.A.T.!" I'm opposed neither to intellectual pursuits nor the academy; I spent 30 years pursuing both. I'm confident however, that neither is sufficient for the *flourishing life*. Something more – and different – is needed.

MacMillin's Restoring a Life gets this. On one level this is just a good story about a guy, a girl, an old dude...oh, and *a bad–arse sword laddie*. Like grandpa, MacMillin has us asking, eyes wide and jaws agape, "What happens next?!"

And yet, as in grandpa's retelling, something profound is happening: our souls are *becoming*. Simply put, by inviting MacMillin's characters and story into our internal worlds, we will be confronting ourselves, both our beauty and brokenness. It really is true: we are shaped and formed by those we dance with. In Restoring a Life, we dance with relational wisdom and truth.

In the end, this is a story about MacDonald and Thomas learning to *love, and be loved.*

What else is there?

David Pickens, Psy.D.
Psychologist

Preface

I have loved to read books since I was an adolescent, and found writers such as C.S. Lewis, George MacDonald, Victor Hugo and Charles Dickens a joy to read. I most valued the tales they told, and it would be difficult to overestimate the impact these writers have had on the development of my mind, soul and imagination. I have long wanted to write stories that would have even a fraction of the impact these writers have had on me.

Growing up, my grandmother told me about two of my ancestors, one being the first governor of Vermont and the other being George Washington's drummer boy. I often fantasized about what kind of adventures they must have lived.

As an adult I researched the first governor of Vermont and found him to be Thomas Chittenden, of the same family name as my grandmother. Thomas became the governor of Vermont before it was recognized as an official state. He led the young state through its infancy, which included the Revolutionary War. He was known for his uncanny ability to size up peoples' characters and relate to them in just the way needed.

I've often wondered what kind of formative years a man like that must have had. How was his soul formed, what sort of upbringing did he have, and what prepared him for the role he would later play? Being a psychologist I'm naturally curious about such things. As a result of these ponderings, I've taken the liberty in *Restoring a Life* to imagine Thomas's adolescence. I've provided Thomas a strong, spiritual mentor to guide and help Thomas form the kind of character he would need as an adult trying to give birth to a new state. Trying people and challenging situations test Thomas's character throughout the novel.

My hope is that *Restoring a Life* will stimulate introspective adults and mature adolescents to be curious about their own character development, and think about the direction in which they would like to grow. As a psychologist I aspire to help others both to tell their stories and to expand their stories. My goal as a writer is the same.

I've based this story on the life of my colonial ancestor, Thomas Chittenden. The dates he lived, the town in which he lived, and some of the details of his family are all true to my story. It's also historically accurate that Thomas embarked on a rescue mission similar to the one in the story that follows. Thomas held several offices in the local militia before entering a career in politics.

Acknowledgments

I've had the privilege of joining numerous people in their struggles to tell their own stories. I have greatly enjoyed the adventure, and my own story has been enriched along the way. One of the best parts about working as a psychologist is being part of others' most personal journeys, from which I've learned the value of knowing our stories.

I want to thank Dan Meisel, who was the first to give me encouragement to keep writing when my first draft didn't have much to it. Dan's combination of gentle support and honest critique were most needed at that early stage when I felt unsure of my storytelling ability. My sister Kathleen O'Dell has given numerous hours to helping me find just the right words. Without her help, my words would be less refined and more fumbling. My good friend Dr. David Pickens has allowed the early ideas of this story to ferment within his mind, and thus has been able to give me invaluable reflections on both the characters and the development of the story. Dr. Sharon Lewis–Bultsma and Dr. John Barrett are both trusted friends who have taken the time to read early drafts and provide needed feedback. I'm grateful to Catherine Loquet for her help in revising the current edition. And I thank Justin, Madeline and Alexis for help with cover and photo design.

I thank Dr. Laird Bridgman for helping publish an earlier version of this novel, Granting Thomas: A Journey Beyond Adolescence. The story is essential the same, yet with some revisions, that I hope have improved the storytelling. I want to thank Barbara Chittenden, my grandmother, for telling me a story about my forefather.

Restoring a Life

May 4, 1753 - Salisbury, Connecticut Colony

Few ingredients need be present for life to flourish, yet life insists on these. Trees require resources from Mother Nature, and often flourish when added to the care of human touch. Thomas learned to give his own tree the care it needed to be of strong constitution, but it had not always been so. At one time his tree had been a vulnerable sapling doing well just to survive. Now as an adult, when Thomas looked at people, they had the experience of someone sturdy looking directly at them and being fully present.

Thomas bent down and rubbed his hand through the soil, and then he gently inspected the wheat stock. He stood and moved further east. He looked up and down the field. Thomas rubbed his jaw and saw Father and Ben, his elder brother by two years, walking toward him.

"How do the west field look?" asked Thomas.

"Seems alright, maybe a bit dry," answered Ben.

"Well the east field more 'an a bit dry, it be downright parched," said Thomas.

"That right?" said Father. "Let's just take a look o'er at the creek." Ben and Thomas followed Father up the path struck between the two fields until they reached the shallow valley through which the creek ran.

"Damn, just as I thought. Only one reason the creek oughta be low this time o' year. I'm headin' o'er to Fredrickson's an' straighten 'im out. Son o' bitch stealin' our water again! Come on boys," said Father.

"Naw, I'm gonna stay back an' look 'round a bit," said Thomas.

"Suit yaself," said Father.

Father turned toward the Fredrickson farm with Ben close behind him. Thomas watched them go and then walked upstream.

The stream continued to flow at a trickle as he reached the northern boundary of the Chittenden farm. He climbed the fence and continued uphill until he came across two large boulders. Thomas found a collection of tree branches, rocks and debris amassed together, which had formed a natural dam. No beaver would leave such a haphazard dam as a finished product, but just the same it created a growing pool of water behind it. Thomas waded into the pool and dismantled the dam in a few short minutes. Immediately the water returned to its normal flow. Thomas had removed his boots and sat down to put them back on when he heard loud voices upstream.

"Ya callin' me a liar, Chittenden?"

"Damn right I am, an' if ya don't fix the water right quick I'm gonna..."

"Ya gonna what? Ya best get yer facts straight afore ya off an' go accusin' honest men! Now get off my land, the both o' ya!"

Thomas sadly shook his head as he stood and headed back to the farm house. Liz swept the front porch of the house and Thomas stole up behind her and surprised her with a bear hug. Liz turned around and kissed Thomas with a twinkle in her eye.

"Come an' get a cool drink with me," said Thomas.

Liz grabbed Thomas's hand and leaned on him as they walked. They sat on the edge of the stone well and gazed at the beautiful green grass and mature trees they could see in almost any direction they looked. Thomas had always loved the densely wooded surroundings of his home in Salisbury, oftening retreating into the forest to play as a boy. No boy enjoyed his backyard more.

The Chittenden farm included two farmhouses, a barn, and a sizable piece of land. Their farm was a few miles north of Salisbury town on Prospect Hill Road. Father and Mama had bought the land when Thomas was still young, so he'd grown up on this land all but the first years of his life.

At the sound of cursings Thomas and Liz looked up to see Father and Ben walking up to the gate. Thomas groaned. Liz looked at him with raised eyebrows.

"I'll tell ya 'bout it later," whispered Thomas.

Pulling off his hat, he wiped his brow with his shirt sleeve and sighed deeply. Thomas hopped off the edge of the well on his way back to work when the glint of sunlight reflecting off metal caught his eye. He searched for the source of the light and at first didn't see anything. A moment later the glint reappeared. Off in the distance a rider galloped up the road toward the Chittenden farm.

"Now who could that be," Thomas said.

Liz shielded her eyes and squinted. The Chittendens often received visitors, but rarely did they have any that Thomas didn't know. When it became certain that the rider was coming their way, Thomas headed down to meet him at the gate.

"Captain Chittenden?"

"Yeah, that's right."

"Urgent orders from the governor," gasped the rider!

"Captain Chittenden?" Thomas repeated under his breath.

Rarely was he referred to by that title. Thomas had been the captain of the Salisbury militia for the past two years, although he was only addressed as "Captain" every fourth Saturday when the militia drilled. He'd started out as a private in the militia eight years ago when he'd turned fifteen years of age. That might sound young to be in the militia, but at the time, most young men joined at fifteen to seventeen years of age. There simply were not enough available older men.

Thomas found the militia duties partly burdensome and partly enjoyable. He overworked himself on the farm as it was, without anything extra. He often groaned when he realized drill day had again arrived. For Thomas it meant putting off work demands and having to catch up around the farm later. However, whenever Thomas did arrive for drill, he enjoyed his time with the other men. The other men were mostly farmers as well. A few were merchants, and one worked the town's mill.

Thomas's hand shook as he reached up to receive the message from the courier. He thought through what it might be, but couldn't imagine what the governor would want with him. He'd never even seen the governor, much less had any correspondence with him. As Thomas opened the letter, he tried to remember the name of the governor of Connecticut. He drew a blank as he unfolded the letter and read the following:

3

Thomas Chittenden
Captain of the Fourteenth Regiment of the Colony of
Connecticut,

We have confirmed reports that a band of men have apprehended and taken prisoner an unconfirmed number of residents from the northwestern town of Litchfield. The identities of the captors are unknown, although it is suspected they might be Yorker militia. Their present whereabouts is also unknown, although they were last seen being led out of Litchfield, north toward the general vicinity of the eastern portion of the Housatonic River. What is known about the prisoners is that they were living in the general Litchfield area, and may have been in the process of establishing a settlement in the New Hampshire Grants.

Since Litchfield is without the benefit of a militia of their own and Salisbury has the closest full regiment, I hereby order you to assist them. You are to dispatch the full strength of your regiment with all haste, and to intercept and free said prisoners as soon as possible. I wish I could provide you with more information, but this is all that is known. God be with you.

Governor Thomas Fitch

Captain-General and Commander in Chief of His Majesty's
Colony of Connecticut in New England

Thomas reread the letter, dumbfounded by its contents. His mind spun, his palms perspired, butterflies formed in his stomach. Realizing abruptly that the messenger waited to be dismissed, Thomas absentmindedly thanked him and said there would be no reply.

"Well, what's all the fuss 'bout anyways?" asked Father. Thomas handed the letter to his Father, and Ben peered over his shoulder as he read.

"What's the Gov'ner doin' sendin' you? He oughta be sendin' a man with some grit, like myself," said Ben.

"Do this mean ya leavin'?" asked Father.

"Right away. I figure I best be headin' out just as soon as I can muster the regiment."

"What 'bout the farm? Who's gonna do your part?" asked Father.

"Don' know. Guess ya'll have to figure it out then. I'm headin' o'er to John's," said Thomas.

Lieutenant John Jackson, the second in command of the Salisbury militia, had earned Thomas's respect and trust. More than these, he had earned Thomas's friendship. John worked the mill a couple miles upriver from the Chittenden farm. Thomas trotted his horse over the rise and looked down at the Jackson property. The river shone in the afternoon sun as Thomas approached the mill. The Jackson house and barn were situated on the near side of the river, with the river curving around behind the house. A small crop field lay on the far side of the water, which produced just enough to feed them. A few chickens ran around in the yard in front of the house, pecking at the ground here and there. John was down by the mill talking with his father. Both looked up and waved as Thomas dismounted and tied his horse to the front porch. John Junior ran out of the house in his bare feet toward John, but Papa scooped him up before he could get to John. Papa scrunched up his face and gagged, holding John Junior at arm's length and looking around for his mother. Samantha turned her head away as she took her son.

John stood well over six feet tall and met few men taller. He had developed a barrel chest and tipped the scales at over two hundred pounds, without an ounce of fat on him. John and Samantha had married a year before Thomas and Liz. They had met in the school house when John was eight and Samantha seven. Before they'd known one another long, there were already comments about them marrying some day. They say the comments started with Papa, but no one knows for sure. Early on, everyone in Salisbury expected them to end up together.

Thomas and John became friends a year after John met Samantha. The first few years they only saw one another at school, but during their late teens, they came to spend more and more time together. Since they both worked long hours, the opportunities were hard to come by.

"Got news," said Thomas as he held up the letter. John gave Thomas a curious look and hesitated before reaching out to take the letter. He looked down at the signature first, his eyes growing wide at seeing the name.

"Figure ya must be pretty important to be gettin' a letter from the Gov'ner," said John with a grin.

"Well, maybe we been friends since way back," quipped Thomas.
John punched Thomas in the arm, a little harder than he'd intended, and then read the letter.

"Damn, can it be that things' gotten as bad as that? I been worried it'd come to somethin' like this," said John.

Thomas just shook his head.

"What do they want with the prisoners?" asked John. Thomas pondered the question awhile before responding.

"Been thinkin' on it, but I just can't figure it," said Thomas.

"Well, I know factions been formin' up out in the Grants. We been talkin' 'bout it more an' more at the General Assembly. There been reports o' more an' more disputes over land. Some folks got grants from Gov'ner Tryon o' New York, while some folks hold grants from Gov'ner Wentworth o' New Hampshire; sometimes for the same land if ya can believe it. It's becomin' more an' more of a problem. Don' know what's to be done. Don' think anybody knows yet. Though there been talk o' formin' up militias out there. I din't know it'd come to that yet," said John.

"Ya sayin' different folks holdin' grants for the same piece o' land from two different Gov'ners?" asked Thomas.

"That's right."

"Damn! 'Bout how many grants bein' issued out there?"

"Just heard Gov'ner Wentworth issued o'er a hundred o' 'em already. Don' know how many Gov'ner Tryon done. The problem be that the land's square between the New York and New Hampshire colonies," answered John.

"Damn, that's gonna cause a war."

"Maybe that's what we got on our hands here. Ya see, there ain't no recognized authority out there yet; both sides 're claimin' it. Last thing I heard New York requirin' folk with New Hampshire grants to come and pay New York as well," said John.

"We'll be damned whatever the cause. Inform the rest of the militia to meet up in town tomorrow morning at first light. We maybe got a long journey ahead o' us. I'll tell Chambers to prepare food an' water. I'm off to see 'bout Scout."

"Scout?"

"Sure like to have 'im along on this one," said Thomas.

Thomas mounted his horse and rode beyond the Jackson house to meet the river as it bent to the west and then to the north. The road ended at the Jackson mill, and the woods became more densely packed the farther he got from town. Thomas attempted to stay as close to the river as possible, but at times he had to leave it to ride around brush too thick to get through. Much of the time Thomas couldn't see the river, but he kept track of it by the sound of the swift moving water.

He rode through a clearing on the west side of the river. Up ahead he saw an impassable stand of trees and brush, and turned west to go around it. Thomas was thinking about the mission and suddenly stopped; something was different. He sat still trying to figure out what it was, and at first couldn't discern the change. Then he realized what it was: it was quiet. He'd lost the sound of the flowing water. Fearing he'd get lost, Thomas backtracked to where he'd left the river. Thomas looked across to the east side of the river and it also looked impassable, which only left one other option. He neared the river's edge and tried to assess its depth. Thomas wasn't sure he could ford the river, and he wasn't sure how comfortable his horse would be swimming, since neither of them forded many rivers.

Thomas tied his horse to a tree and stepped out into the river. A few steps later, he found himself at waist depth, with the middle of the river several yards away yet. The river was moving fast enough that he thought he might get swept well downstream if he attempted to go much farther. Small splashes of white water could be seen here and there. He went back and mounted his horse, and before he entered the water, pulled tight on the reigns to keep her head up and prevent her from seeing the moving water. Thomas figured he had a better chance of keeping his horse calm if she couldn't see the bottom. He led her into the shallows of the water. Thomas decided to walk his mare as close to the edge as possible. Thomas kept the reigns in one hand and soothed his mare with the other. Both horse and rider relaxed a bit as the water travel began smoothly.

The river swept to the right, and overhanging branches leaned out beyond the shallows. Thomas halted and eyed the deeper water. His hand tightened around the reigns and his stroking of the horse's neck quickened. The mare moved around the branches into the deeper water. Just as the horse prepared to swim, she lost her footing on a slippery rock. She panicked and lunged into deeper water. The swift current rolled the horse and rider over, and both went underwater. Thomas did retain enough presence of mind to take a deep breath just before the water ran over his head.

The horse rolled onto Thomas, pinning him to the bottom of the river. Rising panic has a way of sapping oxygen at a faster rate, and soon Thomas's lungs burned for air. He pushed against the back of the horse, which accomplished little. The horse's frantic turning and kicking rolled it upright and off of Thomas. Thomas pushed off the river's floor and gasped in air. His mare began swimming at full speed for the near shore. The reigns jerked out of Thomas's hand. He spun around and pushed off a rock with his legs, just reaching the reigns in time. Now the horse pulled Thomas through the water, and he coughed as water filled his mouth and lungs. He fought to get his mouth above water. As he inhaled, another wave washed over him. Thomas's involuntary gasping underwater refilled his lungs with water.

Thomas struggled to maintain consciousness as his legs flailed to find something firm to push against. Finally his legs found solid rock, and he kicked himself up out of the water to a standing position. His mare started running out of the river, dragging Thomas off his feet. Once she reached the shore, the horse faced a solid mass of trees and brush, bringing her to a stop. She spun from left to right, searching for a way out of the water. At this point Thomas regained his footing and pulled down on the reigns, bringing his face close to his mare's. Thomas made her look him in the eye and calmed her enough to get her to stand still.

Thomas walked her downstream fifty yards until he found passable dry land. He spent several minutes soothing his frightened horse, all the while trying to calm himself as well. Thomas's heart pounded so loud he could hear it. He kept to a slow walk, not wanting any more adventures. At the first clearing he stopped, tied his horse, and pulled off his boots, dumping out the water that had collected inside them.

A hundred yards to the east rose a low hill that was sparsely wooded. Thomas rode slowly up to the crest of the hill to try to spot his destination. It had been so long since Thomas had been out this way, he couldn't remember much of the landmarks. After straining his eyes for a good while, Thomas finally spotted something. A thin stream of grey smoke filtered its way up from between trees on the western bank two or three miles upstream. A weary smile made its way about the corners of Thomas's mouth.

Thomas was relieved to finally have his bearings and made careful note of a large boulder near the source of the smoke. Then he descended to the river and made his way toward the fire. He stayed on the east side of the water and picked his way through the wood until he arrived at another spot of high ground that he'd noticed from the first hill.

He left his horse and walked up the hill. The hill wasn't high enough to get him above the tallest trees, so he had to peer through them. However, he was able to make out the campsite across the river. Sure enough a fire burned with some kind of game cooking above it. Sitting beside the fire on a log was Scout Stone. Scout wore a coat of fur, boots of leather, and had his long hair held in place with a piece of cloth tied behind his head. The man looked rougher than Thomas remembered. Scout stood up and turned the meat over and then sat back down to work at something in his lap.

The last thing Thomas wanted to do was surprise him. Scout had been known to shoot first and ask questions later. Cupping his mouth with his hands, Thomas yelled across the water.

"Scout, hey Scout!" Scout quickly went down on one knee, raising a musket to his shoulder. Thomas waved his arms over his head and yelled again.

"Scout, don' shoot! It's Thomas - Thomas Chittenden!"

Scout lowered his musket and waved Thomas over. Scout's home consisted of a wooden lean-to that was built into the side of a cliff where a natural cave existed. The cave provided him with protection from the elements, and he only had to watch for trouble from one direction.

Thomas had met Scout six years ago, shortly after he'd first joined the Salisbury militia. Scout had been hired to train the new recruits. He'd been offered a commission as an officer, but Scout had turned it down; he didn't want the responsibility. Not knowing what else to call him, the militia's captain called him Scout. Right off Thomas had recognized Scout's experience and soaked up as much as he could about the use of muskets, pistols, hand-to-hand combat, and military strategy. Scout tried to teach Thomas a little tracking, but Thomas didn't take to it.

Scout Stone had been born in Philadelphia to wealthy parents. He had received the best education that Philadelphia could provide, with private tutors that lived at the Stone residence. His father owned a fleet of ships and did well in trade between the colonies and several countries in Europe. His father had expected Scout, as an only child, to help run the business at his side when he turned seventeen, and eventually to take over. His mother had social aspirations for Scout. She began negotiating an arranged marriage with another wealthy and socially respected family. Mrs. Stone had even settled on terms of a dowry by the time Scout was fifteen.

Scout went along with his parents' plans for him at first. At his seventeenth birthday celebration, many guests attended a festive meal with dancing. A few of the friends were Scout's, but most of them were his parents' friends.

Right after being introduced to many business associates by his father, Scout was taking a breather and sipping wine. His mother came and whispered in his ear that tonight would be the appropriate time to formally ask Lucille to become betrothed to him. Scout turned and looked at his mother blankly. Then he followed his mother's pointed finger and spotted Lucille across the room sitting with her mother, and felt nauseated. Scout actually thought Lucille fairly attractive, but found her blue-blooded manners unappealing. The next morning when Scout didn't show for breakfast, the house was searched, but Scout could not be found. He had made a run for it.

Scout traveled north for many days, staying at inns under assumed names. He eventually hired on with a fur trapping company and left the large cities for good. Scout found himself helping settlers who were being harassed, truly becoming "Scout" as his moniker depicted. He hated seeing folk being forced to do anything, whether to abandon their land, sell their land, or be strong-armed out of the produce of their land. Scout often tracked and hunted down thieves and ruffians who stole from folk unable to defend themselves. He hadn't set out to get involved in such disputes, but found a fire burning inside when he heard these stories, and he couldn't remain aloof.

On the whole Scout had a gentle spirit and a good sense of humor, unless folk were being strong-armed. Thomas had not only learned much from Scout, but he had been taken by his gentle manner right off as well.

Thomas forded the river, which was shallow at Scout's abode, and was greeted by Scout's strong grip. Thomas was glad to see Scout as well, but preferred his hand with no broken bones. Well built to begin with, Scout had become stronger yet from his hard life in the wild. Scout had many creased lines across a well weathered face and piercing eyes that reminded Thomas of an eagle. His skin was darkly tanned and had a leathery appearance that seemed to fit with his ungroomed hair.

"Thomas, looks like you came all this way for a swim," greeted Scout.

"Yeah, funny. Seem like you be more 'n need o' a bath than me," Thomas retorted.

"You gentle folk have such particular noses," said Scout with a good-natured grin.

Thomas laughed at being referred to as gentle. Scout pulled out his knife and sliced off two pieces of meat, handing one to Thomas. Both sat down and began chewing on the tough meat.

"Ya still like livin' out here all by yaself?"

"Yep. I had my fill of folk taking from me till there's nothing left. It seems like everybody wants something. Out here folk mostly just let me be," said Scout. "So, it wasn't a swim or my good company that brings you out this way; what's on your mind?"

"I need ya help," began Thomas. "Well, ya might o' heard I'm captain o' the militia now." Scout nodded.

"Well, we got a mission, an' I figure to need ya help with it," said Thomas.

"Naw, I'm done with the militia. I'm not interested in doing any more training. I prefer my life out here."

"I'm not talkin' 'bout training. I need a good tracker," explained Thomas.

"Tracking who?"

"Some Litchfield folk 're missin', an' the Gov'ner asked us to go find 'em."

"Oh come on, you're off to find folk that wandered off?" asked Scout.

"No, these folk been taken prisoner."

"Go on," prodded Scout. "You got my interest now."

"We don' know much more, just that some Litchfield folk were probably gettin' ready to take a plot out 'n the Grants, an' somebody took 'em away prisoner. That's 'bout all we know," said Thomas.

"Who took them?"

"We don' know for sure, but the Gov'ner thinks it was Yorkers."

"Damn, I've heard of such doings," said Scout. "Where'd they take them?"

"The Gov'ner thinks north."

Scout got up and paced back and forth. His gentleness disappeared, and a stern look came over him. He appeared deep in thought.

"Well, I have to think on it. I had my fill of such work, but I have to admit you got my interest some."

"We set out for Litchfield tomorrow first light," explained Thomas.

"I might be there and I might not, don't count on me. If I come I might bring another tracker; maybe you heard of Frank Haskins?"

"Can't say that I have."

"He's the most famous bounty hunter in these parts."

"We could use all the help we can get; bring 'im if ya want. Sure hope to see ya tomorrow," said Thomas.

September 1744 - Salisbury, Connecticut Colony

The town of Salisbury was located in the northwestern portion of the Connecticut Colony near the Housatonic River. Prior to settlers coming onto the scene, the northwestern portion of the Connecticut Colony grew darkly forested, virtually without natural clearings. The earliest settlers of the town, Dutchmen, hacked out many small clearings in the 1720s to create what later became Salisbury. Walking almost any distance from one of these clearings left one in dense, dark woods. In 1732, the Connecticut Colony's General Assembly commissioned a special committee to create the towns of Salisbury and Sharon, although it wasn't until 1741 that Salisbury was officially chartered a town.

The original owners of Salisbury land plots comprised an interesting mixture of land prospectors and families looking to settle. Many of these prospectors held the property for only a few years before selling at a substantial profit. The early settlers of the Connecticut Colony coast had abundant land. However, property became scarce not only because of the influx of additional settlers, but due to the exponential expansion of the families having many offspring.

The Chittenden immigrants, Thomas's forefathers, initially settled in Connecticut Colony in the town of Guilford and then moved to East Guilford as land became harder to obtain. Both Guilford and East Guilford are situated along the coast. Once land in East Guilford became scarce, Thomas's parents, Ebenezer and Mary Chittenden, purchased land in Salisbury. They certainly weren't alone; by the third generation of settlers, many families found their young adults moving inland once again, looking for more space.

The Chittendens were not original landowners, but rather bought their plot of land from one of the original land prospectors.

Not long after the family arrived in Salisbury, it was home to over 200 families totalling about 1100 people. Due to the young and large families settling in Salisbury, the average resident was sixteen year of age. Expansion away from the coastlands was well underway by the 1740s.

Thomas absentmindedly walked out of the schoolhouse. The Salisbury schoolhouse was located on the far side of town. Thomas sometimes walked home with his older brother Ben, and other times walked home on his own. Only this year had Thomas been permitted to walk home alone. He was now fourteen. The schoolhouse contained the one-room school all Salisbury children attended. Salisbury could only afford one school teacher. This meant that the Salisbury school had kids anywhere from age six to sixteen. Sometimes Miss Mayberry divided the kids into two groups, older kids on one side of the room and younger kids on the other. Dividing the kids seemed to only alleviate the chaos a little. It's not that Miss Mayberry was disorganized; it's just that trying to oversee 38 kids of different ages and teach them something at the same time was quite a challenge.

School didn't particularly interest Thomas. Even though he was plenty smart, Thomas sometimes had trouble following the teacher's lessons. Partly it was the classroom's disruptiveness, but mostly he simply had little time for school studies and often couldn't keep up with the teacher. By age fourteen he'd given up trying to do well in school. Chores around the farm seemed to dominate Thomas's time, although Mary and Ben Sr. made sure their children attended school regularly. How much their children learned in school mattered little.

Robert MacDonald stared out the window of his store, noting that once again Thomas walked past with his chin on his chest. MacDonald hated to see the boy looking so glum, as it was clear to him that Thomas was struggling. MacDonald wanted to help the boy and had tried to reach out to him many times, only to be rebuffed. MacDonald regularly called out to him whenever he saw Thomas walk past his store. Thomas would just grunt in response, or maybe flick his wrist in a quick wave. MacDonald had been content to be patient and give the boy time to come around. He knew Thomas didn't have any reason to trust him yet, and could see the suspicion on Thomas's face.

Thomas heard Mr. MacDonald call out to him as he walked past the Feed 'n Seed, Mr. MacDonald's store. Robert MacDonald had weathered more than fifty winters and wore a full grey beard, sprinkled with a few isolated spots of brown hair. He had penetrating clear-blue eyes, and a short, stocky build.

"Thomas, come visit wi' me, lad."

At first Thomas was inclined to ignore Mr. MacDonald and just keep walking. He thought about it for several uninterrupted paces, before he reluctantly walked over to the store. Thomas wondered what he wanted. Mr. MacDonald had often been friendly with him, but he didn't know why. Thomas didn't see much purpose in visiting with others, especially adults.

"How do ye be, lad?"

"Just fine thanks," responded Thomas.

"That what I be 'fraid of, lad." Thomas shot MacDonald a suspicious glance.

"An' where do ye be off to, then?"

"Oh, I'm in no hurry to get home."

"An' what awaits ye at home?"

"Just tendin' to my chores."

"Don't ye get much time t' play wi' other lads?" MacDonald asked.

"Oh, not much. There never seem to be time once chores 'r done."

"Aye, it's no good for ye t' be workin' all the time lad," said MacDonald.

Thomas thought about that. It seemed like chores had always eaten the lion's share of his time. He'd always thought that's just life on a farm. He had not thought that it might not be that way for others.

"Weel lad, maybe ye'd like to be out there havin' a bit o' fun." Thomas looked up at MacDonald and then back at the ground. He didn't know what to say. With the exception of playing with his brother, the only fun he had was in his fantasy. He loved to daydream, especially about being a hero.

"Cat got yere tongue, lad?"

"Uh, well, I guess I best be goin' now," said Thomas.

"Aye lad, an' ye come an' visit wi' me again now."

Thomas left the Feed 'n Seed and continued on his way home. Many thoughts came to mind. Why's he tryin' to talk to me? What does the old man want? Maybe he wants help with chores 'round his store? Maybe the old man needs more help than his daughter can give him? Thomas had seen a girl about his age working around the store, and maybe the old man wanted a boy strong enough to do some heavy work. Who knows, and with that thought Thomas dismissed the subject, making a mental note to be careful around the old man.

Thomas enjoyed kicking the dirt path on his way home, partly because it made Mama mad and partly because it was fun. Mama often complained of Thomas not listening to her. She'd tried to teach Thomas to clean his boots before coming into the house many times. Mama misunderstood why he rarely remembered to do this. Thomas could not explain to his mother why he forgot, but if someone suggested to him that he was angry with her, he wouldn't know what to say. Thomas just figured he had a bad memory and should try harder to remember.

For many years Mama'd noticed that Thomas seemed unhappy, but she hadn't known why. Mama wanted Thomas to be happy, yet was at a loss to know what it would take. At times she would search her mind to understand the reasons for his sullenness. On one or two occasions, Mama had talked with her husband about her concerns. Father would quickly dismiss them as a mother's fretting that didn't amount to much. Mama would just sigh in response and hope her husband was right. Maybe she worried too much.

At times Mama was worried it was her fault Thomas was unhappy. She wondered if maybe she and Father worked Thomas too hard on the farm, or maybe she hadn't helped him to have enough friends. A couple times she'd arranged for Thomas to spend the day at the Oldhams', hoping time with other boys would help. Each time Mama watched to see how much he smiled after his day at the neighbors. Sometimes he smiled more and she'd get her hopes up that she was being a better mother. However, his newfound joy never lasted long.

The only things Thomas seemed to take any pleasure in were Ben and Sally, his brother and younger sister. Thomas especially loved his older brother. The boys had always played together the few moments that they were neither in school nor working on the farm. She didn't know much about what they did, as it usually involved playing outside the house. Mama pressured Ben to spend more time with Thomas, wondering if time with his older brother would help. Ben happily agreed but wanted to know when that would be.

Mama just sighed. Nothing seemed to help. Eventually Mama had given up trying, figuring there was nothing she could do for Thomas. Maybe she was just a bad mother.

"Thomas," Mama called, "your father's waitin' for ya down 'n the lower field."

Thomas inwardly groaned. "Father's always waiting for me to help 'im on the farm. I hate the stupid farm. I wish we'd get rid of it," he said under his breath. Outwardly Thomas replied, "Yes Mama, I'll be out right off."

Thomas took off his school shirt and put on one of his older, worn farm shirts. He liked to save his two nicer shirts for school. He took turns wearing them every other day. As Thomas walked slowly out to join his father in the lower field, he picked at the calluses on his hands. One of the calluses oozed fluid and hurt.

Thomas found Father and Ben already at work in the lower field. Hugo, Father's dog, lay at his side as always. If you found Hugo you found Father. The dog insisted on following Father wherever he went. Father had even talked Mama into allowing Hugo to sleep on the end of their bed. Mama wasn't too keen on having Hugo in her bedroom, not to mention in her bed, but after she saw her husband's persistence she reluctantly relented.

While his master worked away at the hay, Hugo took the opportunity to get some rest. He had lain down in the grass as near to Father as he could be without being in danger of being stepped on or hit. Hugo looked up as Thomas approached.

"Oh, there ya are Thomas. Give us a hand with tyin' up the piles o' hay. We gotta make sure there's 'nough hay for the whole winter, ya know. I think we gonna need a whole lot more 'an we got. This hay here has already dried long enough, an' we have to get it in the barn."

"Yeah, I know," mumbled Thomas as he reached for the ties.

"When ya done with that, I need ya to mend the fence 'n the western slope," Father called as he walked off to cut some more hay. Hugo alertly noticed Father moving and jumped up to follow.

Ben was already tying up hay when Thomas arrived. Ben looked up at Thomas and rolled his eyes. Thomas took some comfort in Ben being out in the field with him, but not much. Ben had more of a long and lean build like Father, after whom Ben was named. Ben was two years older and two inches taller than Thomas, although Thomas weighed about as much on account of his stocky build.

If you'd suggested to Thomas that he might be downtrodden he might have agreed, although he wasn't sure what downtrodden meant. What Thomas did know is that life seemed boring. There were brief moments of fun with his brother or sister, and even with the other kids at school, but these amounted to brief islands of joy in an ocean of boredom. Thomas wished for something to look forward to, yet he rarely seemed to be able to think of anything. It just seemed like life went on the same, day after weary day.

Sometimes he'd dream about having his own farm and how it would be fun and different. At times he'd fantasize about going off on a great adventure, an adventure where he'd save the day in a skirmish with Indians. He would also imagine saving a pretty girl from the hands of an outlaw or a cattle rustler. These dreams didn't last long, and he usually told himself he was just being silly. However, they returned repeatedly just the same. He never thought of talking with anyone about his dreams. The make-up play he and his older brother Ben engaged in came the closest. Sometimes they would pretend to be soldiers in the militia, fighting off the French or Indians to save the colony and the townspeople. These rare moments of excitement Thomas savored and often thought about.

Thomas felt relieved to see that Father had finally stopped cutting hay for the day, which meant there would be an end to the hay to tie up. Father and Hugo appeared to be heading off for the house. An hour later, Thomas had finished with the hay and tiredly walked off toward the western slope to look for the damaged fence father about which had spoken. He wiped the sweat from his brow and breathed a weary sigh.

As he approached the fence, Thomas noticed the Oldham kids playing on their farm on the other side. The Oldham farm butted up against the western edge of the Chittenden farm. They waved him over to come join them. Thomas glumly waved "no thanks." There was no chance Father would approve of him playing while work remained to be done. He stood and watched the Oldhams' play for several minutes. Thomas sighed and bent down to inspect the broken section of fence.

A couple hours later Thomas was heading back to the house, having mended the fence. As he neared the house he saw Father waiting for him. Thomas immediately felt nervous butterflies in his stomach. He knew that look on Father's face. He swallowed hard.

"Thomas, come here!"

Thomas hurried up to Father, not wanting to further provoke him.

"Yes, sir?"

"I thought we hadda clear understandin', son."

Thomas had no idea what Father meant.

"Sir?"

"Don't "sir" me, son. Ya know damn well what I mean. Din't I make myself clear that you an' Ben were to finish tyin' up all the hay 'fore supper?"

"Uh yes sir, ya did."

"Then why in the hell wadn't it done!" Involuntarily Thomas took a step backwards and took off his hat, holding it between his hands. He looked down at the ground waiting for what may come.

"I uh, I thought we did, sir," Thomas stammered.

"Come on son, do ya take me for one o' them idiots? Ya call that done! Come over here an' show me how done it look!"

Thomas responded only by following Father over to where he and Ben had been cutting hay. In moments such as these Thomas had learned to say as little as possible. Soon they arrived at the site of the hay.

"Now, tell me that look done to ya," bellowed Father as he pointed to a single pile of hay left untied.

"Uh, no sir, I guess it's not."

"You damn right it ain't. Now you finish that up right 'fore I see ya at the supper table, ya hear me? I already had ya brother finish up 'nother pile o' hay you boys left undone. Damn it boy, don't play me for a fool! When ya do a job, do it right!"

"Uh, yes sir."

Father huffed off back to the house, muttering under his breath something about having to do everything himself around the farm. Thomas exhaled heavily, not realizing he'd been holding his breath, and then bent down to tie up the remaining pile of cut hay. He couldn't believe he and Ben had been careless enough to overlook the last pile or two of drying hay. Normally Thomas double checked to make sure anything Father asked of him was done right.

Thomas didn't notice that his arms trembled as they worked. Few things, if any, bothered Thomas more than Father's anger.

Thomas couldn't stop shaking and vowed that he'd never be angry. Never did he ever want to be like that.

Thomas finished his work, and took a thorough look around to make sure there was nothing overlooked this time. He walked two hundred yards in every direction. The last thing he wanted was for Father to find something else. Then he walked over the entire area again. Being satisfied, he headed for the house.

As he walked, Thomas folded his arms across his chest to stop them from shaking. In spite of folding them tightly, they wouldn't stop. He pondered where else he might live if he had to. Thomas thought about each of the other boys in school, and thought maybe John's family might take him in. He couldn't picture living with anyone else. He uttered a pray under his breath.

"Please let me be able to stay. Don't let 'im send me away."

Thomas cleaned up at the wash basin before he sat down with the family for supper. His sister was already in the kitchen helping Mama get supper on the table. His brother was just sitting down at the table himself. Thomas cautiously eyed Father as he sat down. He kept an eye on Father while trying to appear unconcerned. Father glanced at Thomas with a placid face. Thomas immediately relaxed some, although his shoulders remained tense. He kept looking at Father every couple of minutes, yet was careful to avoid eye contact.

Supper was uneventful, with the usual polite conversation occupying the meal. Thomas took no interest in what Mama served for supper, as all the food tasted the same to Thomas. He didn't think much about the food, but just ate what he needed to fill his stomach.

After supper Thomas prepared for bed. He and Ben shared one of the bedrooms in the loft. Since the room was small, Father had built bunk beds right into the wall to save space. Thomas slept on the lower bunk, while Ben occupied the upper. He knelt next to his bed, folded his hands, and said his prayers. Thomas prayed for the usual things: a good year's crop, good health for every member of the family, and that little Sally's leg would get better. Sally, three years his junior, had broken her leg during an accident on the farm. The leg had never been the same, and she now walked with a limp. Thomas hated to see his sister cry during the cold winters. Her leg would stiffen up when it got cold enough. Thomas hoped her leg would get better. He prayed for her every day. Lastly, Thomas

prayed that he'd do his chores well enough to never anger Father again, and thanked God that he could still live at home, at least for now. When
Thomas finished his nightly prayers, he blew out his candle and climbed into bed for the night.

Sometimes he went right to sleep. Other nights Thomas would lay awake dreaming about some exciting adventure. These dreams are the kind that kept Thomas awake for awhile. At times he felt too excited to sleep. On other nights the dreams just wouldn't come. Some nights he just felt weary and bored and went right to sleep.

Sundays brought a bit of welcomed relief for Thomas. The Chittenden family all attended church together. Thomas didn't welcome church because of anything about church per se, but because church gave him a valued gift - the morning off. Thomas worked on the farm every other day all day, all day after school that is. Really the Chittenden boys had more than a half-day off on Sundays since they ate their midday meal before any work got done. The Chittendens normally ate quickly, but for some reason it always took longer for Ben and Thomas to finish eating after church.

Mama insisted all of the Chittendens wear their best cloths to church. She also went to extra trouble to see that all three of her children had their hair done nicely. Mama wanted them looking their absolute best. Sally and the boys never really understood these extra measures, and wondered why church required more primping than any other occasion.

When questioned about these extra preparations, Mama simply said we all want to look our best for God.

Thomas had never seen God at church and didn't know why He would care how he looked. Thomas wondered if God got extra cleaned up on Sundays. Rushing around to get ready in time regularly characterized Sunday mornings, not only due to Mama's primping, but also because Father insisted on them sitting in their pew exactly ten minutes before the service began. He said promptness showed respect for the Reverend, and Father wouldn't allow any disrespect from a Chittenden. Even though he didn't understand these things, Thomas just figured that what God wanted was for people to look nice and be on time. It didn't seem like too much to ask, and Thomas went along with the program.

The family rushed around getting ready, as usual. Father became impatient when his time to depart got close. Thomas hated when Father yelled and had long since learned to have himself ready on time. It wasn't as bad hearing Father yell at others. Church began at 9:00 sharp, and at 7:45 Ben and Thomas went out to the barn to
harness the family cart. At 8:00 Ben and Thomas were standing by the cart ready to go. Father was standing by the cart calling to Mama and Sally to hurry on out. Punctuality never had been Mama's best virtue, and she and Sally climbed into the cart at ten minutes after.

Because the family had left about ten minutes late, Father pushed the horse a bit faster than usual. Although it's not entirely correct to say faster than usual, since the Chittendens normally left about ten minutes late. The faster pace made for a bumpier ride and jossled their hair and clothing.

"Father, if ya don't slow down my hair'll be some frightful mess by the time we git to church."

"If ya'd been ready on time we coulda gone a slower pace," responded Father. "It's beyond me why ya can't get yourself ready by 8:00 sharp."

Father looked at his wife with disdain, never understanding her lack of punctuality. After all, being punctual came naturally to him. Mama never understood why the family had to be in the pew ten minutes early. Wouldn't it be fine to just be on time?

"Father, I'm sure we'll be in our pew before the service begins. Can't we just slow down a bit?"

Father just shook his head in response. He'd given up trying to explain to her the importance of being respectfully early. Realizing he wasn't going to ease the pace, Mama sighed and resigned herself to having to put her hair back together once she arrived. She'd tried many times to convince him to drive slowly, and she realized he would hear nothing to change his mind.

Once the Chittenden cart reached town, Father slowed the pace. He knew that if he hurried the horse all the way to the church, he'd just have to wait while she primped there; however, Mama could repair the misplaced hairs when he slowed the horse to a walk.

As usual, Father pulled directly up to the front door of the church, leaving Ben and Thomas to take care of the horse and cart. Father preferred to have the whole family in their pew by ten till, but resigned himself to being in the pew himself early. Father, Mama and Sally all breathed a sigh of relief as they finally sat in their pew, with no further need to rush. Thomas and Ben joined them a few minutes later. Thomas and Ben brushed Mama's hands away as she tried to tend to their hair and dress again.

While he awaited the start of service, Thomas looked around at the others coming into the church. He compared himself to the dress and personal hygiene of the others. Thomas noticed a couple of adults clearly dressed nicer, but took comfort in being as sharply dressed as almost any of the other boys. Actually, Thomas felt pride in comparing well with the other boys and girls. The Chittendens were one of a handful of families with their own pew. Only elders and important members of the church were permitted a reserved pew. The Chittenden's enjoyed high standing in the church, since Father occupied one of the coveted places on the elder board.

Thomas noticed a few families with shabbily dressed kids who even appeared dirty. Mother turned and whispered to her boys. "Now boys, look at them Johnson boys there in the back. Heaven alive!" Ben and Thomas looked over their shoulders at the Johnsons, who immediately noticed being stared at.

"Now boys, that would never do," continued Mama. "I do declare, I don' know how Mrs. Johnson can allow her boys to come to church like that; it's just a disgrace."

Father turned to shush them and pointed to the Reverend, who was just ascending the steps to the pulpit. The reverend beamed a broad smile as he turned and faced his congregation, having succeeded in ascending to his lofty perch. He lifted his hands, bowed his head, and prayed for the faithful followers as well as the unbelievers who were not in attendance. Next the reverend led his flock in singing a couple of hymns, before opening his Bible and sermon notes. Thomas couldn't have told you much about most of the sermons he'd heard. He normally began to daydream once the reverend began to preach. However, today he listened enough to gather that it had something to do with doing unto others as you would have them do unto you.

Father and Mama had long since taught their children to pay attention during church services, out of respect for God and the reverend. Thomas had learned to appear to attend to the service by looking up toward the pulpit; however, he found that he could look out the window behind the pulpit while seeming to be listening to the sermon. The window behind the pulpit was stained glass, yet the light colored portions allowed Thomas to see outside. Lip-synching also came naturally, as Thomas could move his lips in just the right way to give the illusion of actually singing the hymns.

A couple minutes into the sermon, Thomas's mind wandered. He slipped into his pretending-to-listen mode, and allowed himself the luxury of looking around at the others in attendance. He watched a couple of other boys elbowing one another in the ribs. Being momentarily off guard, Thomas was surprised at Father's stern look as he tapped Thomas on the shoulder. Thomas reprimanded himself for being caught and resolved to double his covert efforts.

On the ride home Thomas had butterflies in his stomach and kept looking at Father, trying to read his sometimes inscrutable face. Thomas wrung his hands as he bounced along in the back of the cart. No one was speaking, to make things worse.

"Father?" asked Thomas.

"Yeah?"

"So uh, what'd the reverend mean that we're to 'do unto others as we'd have done to us?' asked Thomas.

"It means we're t' not be selfish an' to think o' others first," said Father. Thomas screwed up his face in puzzlement as he pondered Father's answer.

"Do that mean 'tis selfish to think o' myself?" inquired Thomas.

"That's right, son. Take me for example, I work so hard for Mama an' you little ones. Ya think it's for me to work myself hard as I do? I ain't doin' it for me, I'm providin' for the family," said Father. "An' I look after my neighbors whenever I git the chance."

"So, do that mean it's not a good thing to git stuff?" Thomas further inquired.

"That's right son, we don' wanna be selfish now, do we?"

MacDonald would later tell Thomas that, "There be many different types o' trees in the forest, an' just as many types o' lads. Some believe they be made up only o' bark, havin' nothing else inside their tree. As though nothin' exists that nae be seen from a quick walk through the forest. In those rare times when they catch a glimpse o' somethin' inside their bark, these quickly push away any awareness of thar inner tree. Now all trees be havin' an inner tree, but many prefer to know nothing aboot it. Often these reinforce

25

their bark, makin' themself hardened an' nae easily penetrable to the softer wood beneath. They tend to be most happy when they be focusin' on thar surroundin's, perhaps even losin' themself in tasks, projects o' causes. If these were asked why they invested thar time an' energy as such, they might say somethin' aboot tryin' to get much done, the importance of stayin' on top o' things, or the great value o' thar causes."

May 5, 1753 - Salisbury, Connecticut Colony

Thomas had his gear spread out all over the bedroom floor as he thought through what he was likely to need on the mission. Having never been on an official militia mission, he wasn't sure what to bring. He knew he wanted his pistol and his sword. Thomas slowly ran his hand over the sword he had worked long and hard to wield well. He felt the familiar weight evenly distributed between his hands. The cold steel evoked a sense of strength and confidence, as well as a good memory of Robert MacDonald, from whom he had received it. The sword felt like an extension of his arm, and he knew it equally as well as the back of his hand. His sword was the last thing he'd leave behind on the mission. Thomas rolled it up in his bedroll for safekeeping as he didn't figure to need it right away, and then he changed his mind and strapped the worn leather sword belt around his waist. His hand went automatically to the sword hilt, assuring himself it was in its proper place.

As he was trying to figure out what else to bring Liz walked into the room. She stood in the doorway with her arms crossed. Thomas looked up and noticed the concern on her face.

"What's on ya mind, Liz?"

Her face momentarily changed as emotion burst through her veins. Liz searched Thomas's face and saw his kind eyes looking straight into her. His searching eyes were softened by the gentle smile that framed them, inviting her to open herself to him, yet without a hint of pressure to do so. Thomas's presence invited others to be honest about whom they are, as pretense seemed more and more foolish the better one knew him.

Liz eagerly walked over and sat on the floor next to Thomas.

"Thomas, I'm scared. I'm scared that after you ride down that road, I'll...I'll never see you again."

Liz's tears turned to sobs as the words came out of her mouth. She struggled to get the words out before her emotion choked them off. Thomas put his arm around her and pulled her close.

"Oh Liz, o' course you're afraid."

"I can't lose you, Thomas. I just can't lose you, not now. I don't know if I can bear to lose you ever!"

"Oh Liz, I'm comin' back."

"You don't know that," Liz shot back.

Liz' anger surprised Thomas. After thinking more about it, he realized that he didn't know for sure if he would be coming back, although he didn't want to think about that possibility.

"But you better come back, Thomas Chittenden! I'll never forgive you if you don't. Don't you do anything stupid, you hear! I don't care if the mission fails, you just come back! No foolish hero stuff!"

Thomas had recovered his initial surprise at her anger. "Look here, Liz. This whole militia thing is new to me, but I don' plan to take no stupid risks with my life, or anybody else's. I don' rightly know what to expect, an' ya right I can't know for sure, but I'm comin' home. Hey Liz, I know you're scared. I get that, okay?"

Liz looked cautiously at Thomas's eyes, looking for signs of sincerity. "Okay," she said. Liz threw her arms around Thomas.

"This whole thing seems unfair, taking men out of their homes to go after some folk who don't even live in our town. What about the wives that might be left alone? What about the farms left unattended in the meantime? What about those who have children left at home?" said Liz.

"I know, Liz; this whole mess don' seem right. Fightin' over grants, if that be what 'tis, to where folk are takin' other folk prisoner. It just ain't right."

At this point Liz felt a little better, getting her fears off her chest. Although talking with her husband couldn't take away the suspense of not knowing how long he'd be away from her, not to mention the possibility of him abandoning her for good. It was hard enough having him leave on a military mission, but even harder not having much idea when to expect him back. She wouldn't know when to really start worrying.

"Thanks for listening," said Liz. Thomas nodded with a smile.

"So are you worried?" asked Liz.

Thomas sighed deeply. "Yeah. This whole thing's got me worried some. I don't know if the men 'r ready for somethin' like this. Shoot Liz, I don't know if I'm ready. I've never done nothin' like this before. I'm worried 'bout how I'll handle things when the situation gets tense an' men 'r countin' on me. Damn, I'm supposed to be the leader here. How can I lead if I never done it before? I mean, what if I panic or somethin'? What then? Maybe other men might die if I crack."

"Thomas, look at me. I know you've never done this before, and I understand you being scared. And I know you are the right man for the mission. As much as I hate to let you go, you're the kind of man that knows how to lead others. Men will follow you. You're kindhearted and tough when you need to be. The men respect you. They'll listen to you. Even though you're afraid, you need to trust yourself in this. You're trained to lead men. You have the kind of tree for it."

Thomas at first eyed her with uncertainty, and then embraced his wife.

Thomas awoke just before daylight. As he slid out of bed he noticed the packed bag on the floor and remembered today would be a different day. Nerves shot through his stomach, erasing any hunger he might have felt.

Thomas went out to the barn to make sure his horse ate well before what might be a long ride today. He saddled his horse while she ate. She didn't seem to mind much of anything while she ate, which made it the best time to saddle her. Thomas walked back to the kitchen to grab a quick bite and a cup of coffee. He forced a biscuit down, and was just finishing up when Liz entered the kitchen.

"You about ready to go?" asked Liz.

"Yeah. Did I wake ya?"

"You mean you were going to leave without saying goodbye to me?" asked Liz.

"Shoot Liz, I din't think you'd wanna be woken this early," answered Thomas.

"How can you think that? Thomas, today you're leaving for God knows how long; maybe forever, and you think I wouldn't want to be woken to say goodbye to you? I can't believe you'd be that insensitive!"

"Well shoot Liz, if ya put it that way I guess so. I guess now I feel kinda foolish."

Thomas went over and embraced his wife, partly to say "goodbye" and partly to say "I'm sorry." As he held her, he realized that he didn't know when he'd hold her again. Thomas and Liz had not been apart overnight but once since marrying, and Thomas wondered how it would be to be away from her for days and perhaps weeks. His thoughts were interrupted by the sun peeking through the window, and he realized he had to leave.

"I gotta go, Liz."

"I know." Liz gave him one last tearful embrace and released him.

"I love you," said Liz.

"I know." With that Thomas grabbed his bag and hopped on his horse and was off for town.

Thomas rode the few miles into town to find most of the militia already assembled. Many had looks of apprehension on their faces, others looked excited, and a few seemed to have not fully awakened yet. The younger men appeared downright scared. These men, if you could properly call them men, were mere seventeen-year-old boys. Many of them had not even begun to shave. These soon-to-be men appeared thin and gangly next to the more filled out and muscle-bound older men. Thomas wondered how they'd fair on the mission. Thomas spotted John and walked over to him.

"John, what 're we doin' takin' boys into harms way?" John merely shook his head.

"Dear God, protect the men; 'specially the boys," pleaded Thomas.

"Maybe we'll be lucky an' settle this mess without a fight," John said.

"How many we missin'?"

"Just two. Wait, I see them coming up now. We got everybody, Thomas."

"Ya haven't seen Scout, have ya?" Thomas hoped aloud.

"Scout? I haven't seen 'im for years. You expectin' 'im?"

"Expectin'? I'm prayin' he joins us. We gonna need an experienced tracker like 'im," said Thomas.

"Well, we got Morse an' Johnson; they can track some," John countered.

"Yeah, but not like Scout. Now, let's do this right. From now on it's Captain and Lieutenant; at least in front o' the men, okay Lieutenant?"

"Yes sir, Captain," said John as he saluted.

Thomas scanned the assembled men, disappointed to still not see Scout. Thomas glanced over at the general store and spotted the portly Tom Chambers. Tom was one of the older men, being in his mid-twenties. He and his father owned and operated the town's general store, making him the obvious choice for grub master. Thomas walked across the street to inquire as to the state of the provisions. Second Lieutenant Chambers was responsible for all supplies, including weapons, ammunition, food and water. The Salisbury militia wasn't large enough to warrant separate officers for weapons and food. Tom was good about delegating responsibility to many of the enlisted men so as not to overburden himself. He had requested two men to be placed directly under his command, and Captain Chittenden had obliged.

The uncertain length of the mission had occupied Thomas's thoughts much of the time since receiving Governor Fitch's orders. Not only did Thomas not have experience on such missions, there was no way of knowing how far the prisoners had been taken by now, and how much further they might be before being overtaken. Thomas wondered if the militia would ever overtake them, or even find a trail to follow.

"Lieutenant Chambers, what is the state o' our supplies an' munitions?"

"Well Captain, we have enough food and water for two months."

"How much supplies can we carry with us?" inquired Thomas.

"Three, maybe four months worth, tops. 'Course we'll need fresh meat 'long the way."

"I hope we won't need that much, but plan for three months, Lieutenant."

"Yes sir," replied Lt. Chambers, "but I'll need more time to prepare provisions for 'nother month."

"Understood. Just make sure ya have a full three months o' supplies afore we march. What 'bout ammunition for the muskets?"

"To be honest sir, I don't know how much to bring."

"Bring enough powder an' balls for a two-day siege, plus additional supplies for skirmishing."

Chambers scratched his head as he looked off at the magazine stores. "All right, Captain."

Dr. Jacob Dickens fulfilled the post of regiment medic. He was a veterinarian by training, and the only other doctor in Salisbury. The town could not spare their only doctor trained to work on humans, as there was no back up. Thus, the regiment had to make due with Dr. Dickens. However, Dr. Dickens evoked confidence in others with his calm demeanor and good reputation in town for tending to the animals well. Thomas found Dr. Dickens talking with one of the other men.

"Pardon me. Dr. Dickens, got all the supplies ya need?" asked Thomas.

"I believe so, Captain. I've brought plentiful supplies for gun wounds, knife or sword wounds, and a few miscellaneous extras for whatever else I might encounter."

"Best to be ready for anythin'," said Thomas.

Thomas took a few moments to gather his thoughts, and then he told John to gather the men together. He wanted to address the men before leaving town. Thomas made an effort to use his best English in his address, as he thought it might instill more confidence in the men. Thomas could speak fairly well when he put his mind to it.

"Men, listen up. Most o' us are about to make our first march as a militia. This be an important day. For those who haven't heard, let me explain our mission. Fightin's broken out up in the Grants. Some Connecticut boys and their families were makin' ready to settle in the Grants. Before they could take hold of their land, they were taken prisoner by a Yorker militia, or at least that's what we figure. Our orders are to track down the Yorker militia and use whatever force is necessary to free the prisoners. The governor has placed his confidence in us by assigning the Salisbury militia this mission. Let's make him proud. Lieutenant, move out the regiment!"

Within the hour, the Salisbury militia had mounted up and ridden through town and south toward Litchfield. Thomas decided they'd begin the mission by inspecting the site of the capture. John trotted up next to Thomas.

"Captain, the entire regiment be on the move."

"Good, Lieutenant. How long for us to make the capture site?"

"I figure a day, maybe two."

Thomas privately hoped for closer to one day. He wasn't looking forward to sleeping on the ground, something he'd rarely done and didn't find particularly comfortable.

The militia had ridden a couple of miles out of Salisbury when they were overtaken by a horse and rider charging at a gallop. Thomas and John rode at the back of the caravan and turned around at the sound of fast moving hooves. Their curiosity was quickly satisfied as Ben Chittenden came into view. Thomas couldn't imagine why Ben would be riding after him.

Ben pulled his horse up next to Thomas and took a moment to catch his breath. He seemed to be reaching for something inside his coat.

"Thomas, a moment o' ya time," asked Ben?

"Yeah, what's up?"

"I mean a moment in private," said Ben.

"Oh yeah. Lieutenant, continue on with the men; I'll catch up," ordered Thomas.

John nodded and kept moving as Thomas and Ben pulled up their horses to a standstill. Thomas worried what news might have prompted Ben to go to such trouble to track him down. Ben watched until he was satisfied that John and the others were well out of earshot, and then he pulled an envelope out of his coat. The parcel was thick as it contained more than just a note. As he took it from Ben, he looked quizzically up at his older brother, misunderstanding the note to be from Ben. Ben merely smirked.

Thomas opened the envelope to find a note. Upon unfolding it, he immediately recognized his wife's handwriting. It read like this:

Dear Thomas,

I hate the way we said goodbye this morning. I feel badly about how I yelled at you; I was angry, but I think I'm actually mostly afraid. It scares me that you almost left without me having the chance to say goodbye. I understand that you were just trying to let me sleep. You mean so much to me, and I'm afraid to lose you.

I so wish I'd said goodbye to you differently. I guess I want to say goodbye to you differently in this note. I wish I had another chance in person, but I guess I'll have to settle for telling you in writing.

Please accept my apology for this morning. I love you and will think about you every day until you return, and I will pray to God Almightly that He will bring you back to me safely.

I love you,
Liz

P.S. I don't want you to forget me, so I've enclosed something for you to remember me by. Also, I gave Ben pen and paper so you could let me know you received the note and locket.

Thomas looked inside and saw something silver in the bottom. He reached inside and pulled out a silver locket. Liz always wore this locket around her neck and rarely allowed it out of her sight.

Thomas knew this to be the locket her father gave her for her fifteenth birthday. He carefully opened it and saw a miniature of Liz inside. Thomas noticed Ben looking over his shoulder and quickly closed the locket. It felt too personal to show it to Ben.

"It's a likeness o' Liz," Thomas explained. "So Liz gave ya somethin' for me to write back with?"

"Yeah, here ya go little brother."

Thomas scratched a response. As Thomas did not write well, his response took awhile to compose. The finished product read as follows:

My Deerest Liz,

I did git your note and lockit. I acept your apology. Liz, I know you was afraid and I understan why. Don't worry much about what you say in the morning.

I will keep this here lockit in my poket all the time.

By for now.

I love you,

Thomas

Thomas folded up the note he'd written, put it in the envelope Liz's note had come in, and handed it to Ben. Thomas wished he had more skill in expressing himself in letters, knowing his note didn't reflect all he wanted to say.

"Hey Ben, please look after Liz while I'm away."

"Sure thing little brother...Well, I s'pose I outta be gettin' back then," said Ben. Thomas nodded as Ben turned his horse about and headed back to the farm.

Thomas gently prodded his horse to a trot, being in no hurry to get back to the regiment. He wanted some time to think. It saddened Thomas to think about Liz's distress over the morning's parting, and he hoped his note would bring her some relief. Liz's ability and willingness to reflect on how she treats others and genuinely apologize when necessary evidenced the depth of character Thomas so loved about Liz. He silently thanked God for blessing him which such a wonderful woman.

Thomas knew of few people he deeply respected, and Liz was certainly amongst that small company. Her beauty emanated from the inside out. It was of the kind that only partly shows in the miniature likeness he held in his hand. Her beauty was enriched by the soul that occupies her body, like the greenish blue water that breathes life in an otherwise empty and barren river bed.

Looking through his pockets, Thomas searched for the safest place to keep Liz's locket. Thomas examined the stitching in each pocket and decided on the front, left pocket of his trousers. He found himself checking on the locket several times throughout his ride back to the regiment.

May 1745 - Salisbury, Connecticut Colony

By the age of fifteen, Thomas most enjoyed his time with his brother. He would play with the neighbor kids on occasion, but Ben and Thomas had long become best friends. They played when they were playing, and they played when they were working; that is, if Father wasn't around. When Father was around, work was work. Father considered their play a waste of valuable time.

Thomas walked into the barn to get feed for the animals. He noticed Ben bent over, milking the cow. Thomas immediately realized the opportunity before him. He slowly stalked his prey, walking cautiously and careful where he put each foot, not wanting to give Ben any warning. The straw on the ground was soft and soundless. Just one or two more steps and he'd be in position. He took one last step and flicked the back of Ben's ear with his finger.

"Damn you, Thomas!"

"Gotcha!"

Thomas ran off to get out of retaliation's reach. He looked over his shoulder to see Ben picking up the half spilled bucket of milk. Thomas was gratified to see that most of the spilled milk had ended up on Ben's boots. Thomas enjoyed successfully stalking his prey, but he knew such a deed was never left without repayment. Thomas looked over his shoulder to see that Ben had given up the chase, at least for the moment.

A grin remained on his face as he walked back to his work. As he thought more about the spilt milk, Thomas's grin turned to a grimace. The picture came to his mind of Father walking into the barn and seeing the wasted milk. Thomas looked back in the direction of the barn, searching for signs of Father or his accomplice Hugo. Although he didn't see Father, he walked back to the barn and put his ear to the door. Thomas's shoulders relaxed, as he couldn't hear any voices.

The day wore on without incident, both boys attending to their extensive farming chores. Thomas walked back into the barn to put away the tools he'd been using, tired and off guard. He was putting the tools away in the shed and noticed some rustling above him. He looked up, but didn't see anything unusual and went back to his work. Seconds later he heard a muffled laugh. Thomas looked up just in time to see the water falling on his head and the rest of him as well.

"Laughing heartily Ben called out, "gotcha back!" Ben didn't even bother to run. The brothers had an understanding that payback was payback, and they were even for now.

"All right, all right, ya got me."

Thomas dripped from hair and clothes, which actually felt pretty good after a long day working out in the sun. However, he didn't particularly like the feeling of the wet socks in his boots. Ben dumped more than enough water to completely drench him. Thomas headed over to the house to change, sloshing with each step. Ben continued to laugh and enjoy his revenge.

Ben walked into their room while he was changing.

"Hey Thomas, whats ya doin'?" Thomas gave Ben a put on evil eye.

"Hey, ya wanna head outta the cave? We got time 'afore Mama finishes makin' supper," asked Ben.

"Yeah okay."

The boys ran downstairs and out the door before Mama could ask where they were off to. As they ran off up the hill behind the farm, Thomas could see Father and Hugo down by the barn. Father threw a piece of leather for Hugo, and Hugo enthusiastically retrieved it time and again. Actually, Father had covered a stick of wood with leather covering to protect Hugo's teeth. Thomas felt relieved that Father didn't notice them run off behind the property, as he might have asked questions the boys didn't want to answer.

Father enjoyed playing with Hugo so much that he hadn't seen nor heard the boys. He focused on throwing the leather just far enough where Hugo had to run for it, but not so far that it got lost in the bushes. Father had practiced and perfected this skill for many hours. He had spent more than enough time searching for the leather in the bushes, helping him learn not to overthrow Hugo. Sometimes Father would fake throwing one way only to throw to the other, and would get a good laugh out of Hugo running off the wrong way. In spite of his laughing, Father truly loved him and treated him kindly.

Father grew up with a dog he'd loved. His folks had surprised him with a puppy when he was young. He insisted on having his dog at his side at all times, except when he was in the school house of course. The teacher wouldn't allow pets in school. Young Ben would squirm in his seat until it was time to run home and find his dog. He had spent most of his free time with Hugo. Every dog father had ever owned had been named Hugo.

Sally finished helping Mama with supper and wandered outside looking for something to do. She noticed Father and Hugo playing by the barn and limped over to see if she could join in the fun.

"Father, gimme a turn. Gimme a turn throwin' that thing."

"It's called a 'leather,' an' no, I don' want ya to get hurt. Sometimes Hugo gets excited, ya know."

"Oh Father, please. I'll be really careful. I promise."

"No, no Sally; maybe when ya older an' a bit stronger. I don't wanna take a chance o' you getting hurt again."

Sally's face fell, her head dropped, and she slowly turned and walked back to the house. Entering the kitchen, she noted that Mama had finished her work and sat knitting. Sally didn't bother asking Mama to knit, as she found it rather boring. She wandered to the window and watched mournfully as Father continued throwing the leather. Eventually she sighed and turned from the window.

She often had nothing to occupy her time. When her limited chores were completed, she usually searched about for someone or something to play with. Sadly, she often found no one. This time was no exception. She had a small room downstairs, as she had trouble climbing the stairs with her injured leg. Actually, Mama and Father forbade her to go up the stairs, fearing for her safety.

Father watched Sally hobble back to the house. He wished Sally would stop trying to do more than she could with that bum leg. He wished she understood that he was only looking out for her own best interests. He wished she understood that he was protecting her from getting hurt again. The silly girl didn't seem to appreciate him going to such lengths for her. Father picked up the leather and threw it again for Hugo to fetch.

Sally found her room the way she'd left it, with her dolls sitting at their table face to face. She often pretended to have tea parties or sleepovers with her dolls. Sally sighed and sat down to play with her dolls. She much preferred playing with another person. She wrapped a small bandage around one doll's arm.

"Okay Molly, ya have a broke arm," Sally announced to the doll. "Now Molly, ya don't have very many friends an' ya play by yourself. But sometimes ya get bored an' wanna play with a friend." Sometimes your friends are afraid to play with ya cause of your broke arm."

Sally made Molly dance around the room playfully and skillfully. Then she had Molly go find a friend.

"Hi Shanna, look at me dance. See how I can dance an' not be hurt at all. I know I have a broke arm, but it doesn't hurt when I dance. See! Look at me go! Sometimes other people think I'm a china doll, but I'm really a cloth doll. See how I bend without getting hurt. See, bend my other arm an' see how it goes right back. Sometimes my mama an' my father think I'm made of china an' that I break easy. But look, I'm cloth an' it's okay to play with me. Will you play with me, Shanna, or are you afraid I'm gonna break too?"

"Oh no Molly, I'm not afraid you'll break. I can plainly see that you're a cloth doll an' can bend in many ways without getting broke. I'll play with you."

"Oh thank you, Shanna. Ya know Shanna, God can mend china dolls that get broke. He heals broke dolls an' makes them into cloth dolls that have a new life, an' God made me into a cloth doll. I used to be a hurt china doll when my arm got broke, but God made me a cloth doll, an' I'm okay now. Not everyone believes in cloth dolls though."

Sally proceeded to have her two dolls play together and have fun. Afterwards, Sally took Molly to her home, because it was now time for supper. Molly gets home to find her mother preparing supper.

"Hi Mama. I'm home."

"Oh hi Molly. Where have ya been?"

"I was playin' with Shanna at her house."

"Oh. You din't get hurt, did you? I hope ya weren't playin' too rough."

"No Mama. I din't get hurt an' its okay for me to play a little bit rough. I'm made outta cloth, remember?"

"Yes you're made outta cloth, but you have a broke arm. You have to be careful with your arm. Girls with broke arms can't play the same as other girls. What if you weren't being careful enough an' ya hurt your arm worse?"

"I know Mama. But I'm not a china doll. Don't you know that I don't break so easy? I'm a cloth doll. I'm a cloth doll! See, watch how I can dance. See, I'm not getting hurt."

"Oh my goodness! You're not getting hurt, are ya?"

"No, I'm not gettin' hurt. You baby me, Mama. Stop babyin' me. I'm not a baby an' I'm not a china doll that you can only look at. I want to play like a regular girl. Let me play like a regular girl! Okay?"

"Oh Molly, I was wrong to treat you like a baby. I can see that you're not a china doll. I'm so sorry! Can you ever forgive me for treatin' you like that?"

"Okay Mama, I forgive you. Now we can play together an' do fun things together. Right?"

"Okay Molly, whatever you say. I promise I won't treat you like a baby no more, an' we will do fun things together. I promise."

Their cave was back up behind the farmhouse a ways. The brothers ran until they were sure they were beyond the range of eyes and ears. The boys slowed to a walk and caught their breath. They walked on mostly in silence. The path took them up through tall trees and small brush. Boulders lay here and there, as if someone had crumbled huge rocks in even larger hands and let them fall where they may.

The boys stepped off the path and into the creek bed, which was flowing briskly this time of year. Even though the rains had been light, there was still enough water to fully soak their shoes and the lower end of their britches. They had to brush past overhanging branches and bushes that crowded the edge of the creek. They normally returned home with a few new scratches in their skin and sometimes tears in their clothes. They rounded the final bend in the creek.

"There it is little brother."

"Yep, I hope nobody's found it still."

It was unlikely anyone would come across their cave, as it was on the family property and few others were allowed access. However, the boys worried about someone coming across it just the same. Dense foliage provided a front door to the cave, and rendered it almost impossible to see before running into it. The cave had been made by an underground portion of the creek, forged out of stone over years untold. The mouth of the cave was where the creek reemerged above ground.

The boys entered to find things just as they'd left them a week ago. Against the left wall were stored all their belongings. There were two medium-sized rocks to sit on, three or four blankets, some of Mama's preserves, a couple of candles, and two or three favorite books. They stacked everything on top of the rocks whenever they left to keep them dry, at least whenever they remembered. When the heavy rains came, anything that had been left out was washed away down the creek, never to be seen again. The boys had learned this lesson the hard way, having lost valuables on one or two occasions. They moved everything off their rocks and sat down.

"I tell ya Thomas, I'm not havin' that many chores on my farm. My farm is gonna run real good like, without havin' to work much. I'm even gonna have a day off!"

"I know Ben, me too. I hate all the chores we have to do, 'specially the extra ones like today. I figure Father just likes to work hard. He don' seem to wanna do much else."

"Ya, 'cept for smokin' his pipe an' playing with Hugo. That's 'bout the only other things he do."

"I wonder if Father worked this hard when he was a boy," wondered Thomas.

"I s'pose."

"My farm's gonna have hired men too," said Thomas.

"Yeah, me too."

The boys sat in silence for several minutes, pondering their own thoughts. "I don't know, Ben, maybe I won't have my own farm. Maybe I'll be a soldier instead. Ya know the colonies need people to protect 'em from Indians an' the French."

"That sounds dangerous to me. Ain't ya worried ya'd get shot?"

"Naw, I don' think 'bout that."

"Well, ya should; 'least a farm's safe. Nothin' bad's gonna happen to ya."

"Maybe," said Thomas.

Ben pulled his rock collections out and fingered through them. Thomas picked up one of his books and sat down with his back against the wall so that he could look out the opening. He read a paragraph here and there, but mostly just stared out the cave's opening. Thomas was a slow reader.

On the way back down to the house, the boys discovered Father standing by the stream that ran through the property. He paced back and forth, looking upstream and downstream. He frowned as he glanced up and saw his sons, his face red and furrowed.

"Walk with me, boys."

Thomas and Ben followed Father upstream to the northern border of the Chittenden land. Father bent down and examined the water. He stood and shaded his eyes on the left side of his face from the westering sun as he peered north. Thomas and Ben gave each other a searching look, and then waited.

"I jist can't figure it boys," began Father, "but one thing for sure, we ain't gettin' the usual amount o' water. I been watchin' now for a good number o' days, an' the creek just ain't the same. Maybe somebody upstream's usin' more water."

"Ain't that a new field up on Fredrickson's property?" said Ben. "I ain't noticed it afore."

"Damn! Don't think Fredrickson's ever planted that field afore. Damn, well that would do it! Old Fredrickson's usin' more 'an his share o' the water. Well, we'll jist have to do something 'bout that."

"What're we gonna do?" asked Thomas.

Father paused and stroked his beard while he thought.

"Glad ya asked, since this gonna involve you, son. You an' Ben 're gonna build us a dam!" Ben and Thomas exchanged a worried glance.

"A dam? Ya mean we gonna keep more 'an our share o' the water too?" asked Thomas.

"Ya damn right! We gotta fend for ourselves out here," said Father. "We barely gotta 'nough water as it is, an' we can't get by with none less. So, we gonna build a pond here to store up 'nough water for when the creek gits low."

"Can't we just pump more outta the well?" suggested Thomas.

"Oh, don't be stupid; that would take ya all day. I can't afford to have ya tied up doin' that."

"Maybe we could talk with Fredrickson 'bout it," began Ben. "Maybe he don' know we can't get by with less."

"No, no. You boys jist leave the figurin' to me. Ya ain't old 'nough yet to understand such matters."

"But ain't that gonna leave the folks downstream without 'nough water too?" asked Thomas.

"Now ya jist nevermind 'bout other folk. That ain't our problem. Ya see, we all gotta fend for ourself. Now first thing in the mornin' you boys start makin' a dam right here," said Father as he pointed. "An' ya'll need to dig it out right 'bout here to make for a big 'nough pond." Father picked up a pointed rock and drew a line around the creek on both sides. Then he tossed three or four rocks together in the middle of the creek.

It didn't take long for several of the downstream farmers to visit the Chittenden farm. They accused Father of diverting water, which he denied. When the farmers pressed him on it, he finally acknowledged he might be using a bit more water, but that technically he wasn't diverting any. Father impatiently heard them out, and then chuckled to himself that he didn't know what they'd do about it. He wished them luck and sent them on their way without a single concession. The farmers left uttering curses and threats, but Father merely dismissed them with a wave of his hand.

True to their threats, the water supply changed markedly soon thereafter. The downstream farmers evidenced remarkable resourcefulness, more than Father had imagined. They took their complaints to Fredrickson and found him quite sympathetic to their plight. From the vantage point of Fredrickson's high ground, they could see the new pond on the Chittenden property. With Fredrickson's permission and help, they diverted the creek to the west so that it completely bypassed Father's pond. While the original creek flowed across the entire Chittenden farm, the newly engineered creek bed bypassed half of the Chittenden property. The pond was reduced to mud.

Father and his boys stood on their northern boundary surveying the newly channeled creek. Thomas and Ben had their arms folded across their chests. Father stood with his hands on his hips and steam coming out of his ears.

"Damn them sons o' bitches! I ain't never seen the likes o' this manner o' selfishness in all my years!" bellowed Father.

"Ain't they just fendin' for themselves?" suggested Thomas meekly.

"That ain't nothin' o' the kind! Don't go mixin' up takin' care o' your own with downright selfishness!" exploded Father. Thomas averted his eyes from Father and toward the ground. Father stormed back and forth, looking from the old to the new creek bed. Finally he looked up at his boys.

"Well boys, we just gonna have to fend for ourselves best we can," said Father with less anger. "I want you boys to figure a way to get 'nough water to the eastern fields. I'll see to the western fields."

"But Father, we don't have any water on the east side o' the property," countered Ben. "All the water's on the west side."

"Well, ya jist gonna have to be creative then," said Father. "I'm holdin' you boys responsible for them eastern crops. At fifteen an' seventeen, it's 'bout time you boys started takin' more on ya shoulders. You'll be men soon 'nough, and'll need to take a man's share o' the work."

"What does that mean?" asked Thomas.

"That means you boys 're gonna have to find another way o' gettin' the money if ya ain't got no eastern crops to sell."

"How could we do that?" pressed Ben.

"That ain't my problem to figure," said Father, as he turned to leave. Thomas looked up at Ben, who shrugged his shoulders.

"I don' know what we gonna do, little brother. How can we water without water?" asked Ben.

"We can't."

Ben sat down next to Thomas on the edge of the dry creek bed, scratching his head. Thomas had his face in his hands, kicking at the creek bank. "Figure all we can do is hand water as best we can," suggested Ben.

"Hand water? That'll take us the whole day."

"I know. We'll jist have to get up a bit earlier to tend to everythin' else," answered Ben.

"How can Father expect..."

"Now jist knock that off, little brother. It ain't gonna do us no good to be complainin'. Let's jist get to work," pressed Ben.

In spite of the boys working extra hours every day, the eastern crops produced less than half of their normal output. At first Thomas and Ben tried hand watering both of the eastern fields. This turned out to be painstakingly slow work. To help their efforts, the boys created another smaller pond with a narrow channel leading water toward the eastern slope. It didn't help much, but they didn't have to carry the water as far. As Mother Nature helped out with rains much of the first month, their extra efforts seemed to be working. However, when the rains tapered off the next month, they initially doubled their efforts. Ready to drop with exhaustion,

45

at length they resigned themselves to letting one of the two eastern fields die. They kept watering the wheat field, the more valuable of the two.

"What're we gonna do, Ben? At best we only gonna have half the usual crop," said Thomas.

"I know. I been thinkin' on it, an' I think we only got one thing to do," began Ben. "We gonna have to get the extra from somebody else."

"From somebody else? Ya mean we gonna ask for help?"

"'Course not stupid! Who'd wanna help us? They all got their own farmin' to do. We gonna have to git it ourself."

"Ya mean steal it?" asked Thomas.

"Ya can't think o' it like that," countered Ben. "We'll get the extra from somebody that don't need it like we do."

"Naw, I don' wanna do that. Ya can call it whatever ya want, but it's still stealin' by my account," said Thomas.

"Now don't go an' get all religious on me, little brother. We gotta fend for ourselves like Father says, an' we gonna have to git it from somebody unless ya gotta better idear."

Thomas stood and walked a few feet away. He rubbed the back of his neck. He looked up at his brother and then out across to Fredrickson's. "I got it! I gotta plan. We hire ourself outta somebody needin' extra hands," suggested Thomas.

"Oh come on, little brother. When would we have the time to do that?" questioned Ben. "We can't even keep up with the work we gots already."

"Well, maybe Father would give us time off to go an' earn the make-up money."

"While ya dreamin' why don' we just go an' find a pot o' gold at the end o' the rainbow," laughed Ben. "Come on, when do Father ever let us off work?" Thomas shrugged his shoulders.

"Ya gotta accept it, we gonna have to get it from somebody that's got a little extra," said Ben.

"Like who?"

"Well, I been watchin' some at the Feed 'n Seed, an' they got more business than anybody else in town. I say we get the extra from them."

"Ya mean old man MacDonald," said Thomas. "I don' know Ben, he's a bit strange but he's been downright friendly to me."

"What that got to do with nothin'? Come on little brother, it's the only way. There ain't nobody else that seem to got extra that I can see."

MacDonald took a keen interest in folks in town. He often noticed when someone seemed to be struggling. MacDonald regularly observed Thomas walking past with head down and shuffling feet. He continued to feel for the lad and pondered what he might do to help.

MacDonald was no stranger to suffering, and it had almost been his undoing. He had waited until late in life to marry, and had finally settled down with Helen seventeen years back. MacDonald loved her deeply, and considered her his best friend. They talked regularly and didn't hold much back from one another, as best friends don't.

Four years after they were married Helen was returning home from visiting a friend. It had been a cold winter day and began to rain shortly after she left for home. Helen was used to walking a few miles here or there, since she and MacDonald just had the one cart and he needed it to make deliveries from the store. So she normally walked wherever she went, unless it was to help with a delivery.

The rain became heavy after a few minutes. Helen had thought of returning to her friend's home, but thought better of it when she realized she was already soaked to the skin anyways. She had to go home eventually, and she didn't want MacDonald worrying about her. By the time she arrived home, she was shivering and cold to the bone. MacDonald took one look at her and immediately felt her forehead. She felt okay at the moment, but her husband insisted on putting her straight to bed. He warmed water over the fire and filled two water bottles that he placed in bed with her.

In spite of the night in her warm bed, she was hot and feverish by morning. MacDonald rushed out for the doctor first thing in the morning. Doc came right away and got straight to examining her. After a careful examination, Doc realized there wasn't much he could do for her. She would fight the fever for her life on her own, and either master it or succumb. Doc and MacDonald could only offer comfort and keep her cool.

The doctor visited Helen every day. Each day he merely shook his head. On some days he wished out loud there was more he could do for her; other days he merely reminded MacDonald to keep praying for her and to keep her forehead cool. He could see that Helen grew worse as the days passed. MacDonald cursed his helplessness, wishing there was something more he could do for her.

MacDonald never spoke of his fears to Helen. He tried to keep her spirits up by speaking of what they'd do once she got out of bed. He downplayed the seriousness of her illness, not wanting her to lose hope and give in to the fever. Privately, MacDonald had trouble thinking of anything but his fear of her death. He often paced the downstairs floor, wringing his hands. Some days he would pace back and forth for hours at a time. MacDonald was always careful to compose himself before walking in to see Helen. Sometimes he stood outside her door at length, preparing himself to see her and hoping to see a sign of her returning health. Sadly, each visit she appeared either just as sick, or worse.

The next morning MacDonald arose at first light as he regularly did. He'd tossed and turned most of the night, as he had the past eleven days since Helen had been bedridden. He slowly folded up his bedding. MacDonald still felt strange sleeping downstairs alone. He picked up his Bible and sat in his favorite chair to meditate and pray for Helen. After staring at a passage in his Bible for some time, he dropped the book and fell to his knees. He pleaded with God to spare his wife's life. Tears filled his eyes as his pleading turned to sobbing. MacDonald awoke some time later, having fallen asleep in his exhaustion. He looked out the window at the sun's position and ran up the stairs. MacDonald slowed to a walk and took several deep breaths before opening the door to the bedroom.

Helen wore a hint of a smile that suggested peaceful rest. MacDonald felt his hope rising unbidden. He walked almost soundlessly over to the bed for a closer look. He wondered if she had slept more deeply. Yet something didn't seem right, but he couldn't put his finger on it. Almost not daring to, MacDonald touched her cheek: it was cold. He pulled his hand back quickly and stared in disbelief. MacDonald stood and took a couple steps back, wanting to run. However, he made himself kneel back down. He looked intently at her chest; it didn't move. It dawned on him what was wrong, and he collapsed onto the floor in a faint.

Toward the end MacDonald had known she would die, but he hadn't wanted to admit it to himself. He'd told himself that he was just holding onto hope. There's no way to fully prepare for that kind of blow. He felt like the life had been kicked out of him.

MacDonald didn't leave his home for days, might have even been weeks. He didn't remember. Those days seem like a blur now. He barely remembered to eat. Eating felt like a burden. Nothing seemed to matter now that Helen was gone. MacDonald often stared out the window for hours, not really seeing anything but his pain and the emptiness of his life.

Friends would come by to try to console him. They mostly found him staring out the window with a sword in his lap. He often mumbled words like, "nae again, no, nae again." At first he would not even talk to his friends, but seemed to take some comfort in their presence. They would stay a while, and then sigh, get up, and leave. After days of his friends' persistent requests, MacDonald began talking briefly to them. Later, he spoke at length with his friends, eager to have them share with him the burden of his grief. He would now probably say that his friends were the only things that got him through; his friends and the thought of his daughter Rachel.

Rachel had been with Helen's sister since she had taken ill. Maybe it was his fear of Rachel feeling abandoned that got him to finally bring her home. Maybe he waited until he was ready to resume being a father. Maybe both. Rachel responded coldly to her father at first. Later she reacted to him angrily, as if to say, "Where were you?" MacDonald regretted leaving her for so long. He could see he'd hurt his little two-year-old daughter by waiting for so long. It pained MacDonald when he realized that Rachel had lost both of her parents at the same time.

Even with Rachel home and MacDonald resuming his former work at the store, it was years before he was able to fully enjoy life again. MacDonald would be hard pressed to say when, but at some point, he began enjoying his time with Rachel. He brought her in to the store with him and let her help him fill orders for customers. Rachel delighted in helping Papa, which brought joy back to MacDonald's life. Her enthusiasm was hard to resist.

MacDonald lacked much formal education, and wasn't too sophisticated with words, but he understood a struggling soul. He knew what it was to need somebody to lean on. Since losing his wife, he found himself more aware of others' suffering, and wanting to help. MacDonald particularly felt for young Thomas.

MacDonald would later tell Thomas, "Every tree, like every lad or lass, suffer some sort o' bruise or blow, trauma or tragedy. Some limbs break off quite abruptly, while others be pruned quite regular. Some be burned by lightening, while others go withoot much nutrition in their soil. The winds blow all trees rough, some even withoot mercy. It be unusual to find a tree standin' alone, an' those that do have no shielding fro' the winds an' must bear the full brunt alone. Trees flourish when planted amongst others, although many trees prefer the illusion that they be requirin' no interface with others. It be the rare one that suffers a terrible trauma an' finds a way to not only go on livin', but flourish. Few can suffer the loss of a branch an' find a way to mourn the limb's loss withoot pretendin' as though no pruning happened." Thomas would later learn that MacDonald was one of these rare ones.

A couple days later Thomas walked home from school by himself. As he passed the Feed 'n Seed, he looked over to see if Mr. MacDonald was about. MacDonald worked in the yard and waved Thomas over.

"Hello there, lad. What 'r ye 'bout?"
Thomas reluctantly walked over to the store. He didn't particularly want to talk with Mr. MacDonald, but he also didn't mind too much. After all, Mr. MacDonald was an adult and seemed friendly.

"Hello," was all Thomas said.
MacDonald noted the lad's reticence, and thought that maybe he could get him to lower his guard a bit.

"Hey lad, come inside. I got somethin' I want t' show ye."
Thomas looked at MacDonald warily, searching his face for clues. After a pause he slowly followed the older man inside his store. MacDonald began to walk into the back of his store when he noticed Thomas was no longer following.

"What is it, lad?"
"Oh I don' know. I think I oughta be gettin' back soon. Mama will be worried 'bout me." MacDonald sat down on a box and smiled.

"Look 'ere, lad. Maybe ye're wonderin' what I want w' ye."
MacDonald saw that he had stuck a chord with his inquiry.

"Lad, level w' me. What'r ye thinkin' I want w' ye?"
"Look, I don' know Mister. I already got a plate full o' chores at my own house. I don' got time to help ya with yours."

"Oh, that be what ye 'r thinkin'," MacDonald said with a laugh. "Oh noo, lad. I ha'e no thought o' ye helpin' me wi' chores. I want t' show ye a treasure o' mine in the back. But if ye rather I can bring it out 'ere. Wait 'ere."

MacDonald disappeared into the backroom and came back with something long and narrow, carefully wrapped in blankets as if to protect it from harm. MacDonald smiled with a hint of melancholy as he held the package on his lap. Thomas lost some of his apprehension and moved closer with eagerness. His curiosity had gotten the best of him.

"What's that?" asked Thomas.

"Aye, ye'll ha'e t' wait an' see," said MacDonald with a gleam in his eye.

"Is it a musket?" pressed Thomas.

"Weel, 'tis in the same family, I s'pose." MacDonald slowly unwrapped his treasure with reverence. Once the blankets were off, a long wooden box sat in MacDonald's lap. If it were possible, with even more cautious movements, he lifted the lid. Thomas leaned forward to see what it was, although all he could make out was something black that might be made out of metal.

"What is it?" asked Thomas.

"That be a broadsword, lad."

"A what?"

"The broadsword be what every Scotsman learns t' wield." MacDonald pulled the sword out of the box and slowly pulled the sword from its sheath. In spite of the common and dirty outer appearance, the blade shone bright and crystal clear. Thomas gasped at the sword's brilliance. MacDonald looked at the sword with affection and pride.

"Whose sword is that?"

"It belonged t' me father, an' afore that it was me grandfather's."

"And what's it for?"

"For, lad? The broadsword be what ye protect yer family an' yer honor wi'."

Thomas shot MacDonald a strange glance before asking, "Ya honor? How do ya protect that with a sword?"

MacDonald laughed heartily, "Weel lad, besides yer loved ones, thar be nothin' better to guard. But a lad wi' honor rarely needs to pull 'is broadsword fro' the sheath."

MacDonald affectionately ran his hand across the blade and then put in back in the sheath. A couple tears slipped out of his eye and made their way down one of the creases on the old man's face.

"Weel lad, 'cuse an ole man for gettin' sentimental on ye. I didn't 'spect none o' that. But perhaps I can tell ye stories 'bout the old blade some time."

"Tell me one now."

"Aye lad, thar be a long family tale 'bout me sword. But maybe we best wait fo' 'nother day. Whole cart load o' deliveries be waitin' me. And din't ye say ye was in a bit o' hurry t' git home afore ye folks get worried?"

Thomas looked down and nodded his head. "Yes sir," said Thomas.

"Weel, ye be sure an' come 'nother time then lad."

May 7, 1753 – Litchfield, Connecticut Colony

Almost two days later, the Salisbury militia rode into Litchfield. The sun began to descend behind the hills to the west, leaving a reddish-orange background to the trees. Coming from the west, the men wore long shadows as they rode into town. Litchfield appeared smaller than Thomas had anticipated. The town square included a general store that doubled as a post office and a watering hole, and not the kind of water upon which children refresh themselves. This type of watering hole relaxes some and makes others crazy. Besides the two buildings already mentioned, the only other civilization in sight were a couple of farms off to the north and east of town. Litchfield was situated on a plateau, sloping down to a valley below. To the east was a small river, which was a sight for sore eyes. The river wound around to the north and the south. Thomas followed its course until the bend of the river took it beyond sight.

"Lt. Jackson, make camp along the river's edge. The men are free to go 'bouts the town once they set up guard duty," ordered Thomas.

"Thanks Captain, I wouldn't mind a little free time myself."

"I s'pose it's too late in the day for us to see much o' the site today anyways. But I want the officers an' scouts prepared to investigate the capture site with me at first light."

"Now by scouts ya mean Morse an' Johnson?" asked John.

"Yeah, for now."

The men groaned as they dismounted. Many stretched in various ways once on the ground, and sighs of relief could be heard throughout the militia. Without bothering to take the saddles off their horses, Thomas and John walked them down to the water's edge. Horses and men drank together, creating a symphony of various slurping and gurgling sounds. John splashed his face with water, not bothering to keep it off his shirt or hair. Thomas liked the idea and did the same to himself. The cool water dripping down his sweat-soaked back created the sensation of being both dirty and refreshed at the same time.

Thomas looked downriver and noticed two men crouching by the water. He couldn't see them well through the trees, yet they seemed to be filling canteens. John looked around and noticed the rest of the regiment had returned to camp.

"Hey Thomas, I think I'm gonna go swimmin'," said John.

"Ya go 'head, I'm gonna look 'round town," answered Thomas.

Thomas rode back up to the town and looked up and down the street running through town. He didn't see anyone. Then he dismounted in front of the tavern and went inside. Scout was known to enjoy spirits as much as the next man, and in some cases more than the next man. Thomas opened the door and scanned the faces sitting at the tables. He was disappointed not to see anyone he recognized and sat down and ordered a pint. Setting down his cup after the first long draught, he felt a sudden firm hand on his shoulder. Thomas turned to see a familiar face.

"Thank God ya come!" exhaled Thomas.

"I didn't want you to have all the fun," said Scout as he sat down. "I also figured you might drown crossing one of the rivers up north unless I was along to watch you. By the way, what happened to that eagle eyesight of yours?"

"What do ya mean?"

"Didn't you see me and Haskins filling our canteens at the river?"

"That was you?"

"Damn good thing I came, or them Yorkers would ride right up to you before you knew it. Anyways, this here is Haskins, Frank Haskins," introduced Scout.

Haskins had been standing in the shadow behind Scout, and Thomas hadn't noticed him till now. Haskins had a full head of ungroomed, dark hair, with a full beard to match. He wore a dark, stained coat with matching trousers made of some kind of hide. Thomas couldn't figure out what type of animal he got it from. Coming out of his beard was a scar across his right cheek.

"Pleasure," said Thomas as he offered his handshake.

"Pleasure's mine, I'm sure," said Haskins with a grin. "Figured you folk would need my unique skills on this kinda mission."

"Haskins loves to go hunting," offered Scout.

54

"Settlers 'n the Grants hire me to protect 'em from poachers or any other folk that wanna take their land. Figure ya ain't heard o' me?"

"Uh no, can't say that I have," replied Thomas.

"Well, maybe ya don't get out much," said Haskins pleasantly. "Anyways, here's my usual."

A wide knowing grin came over Haskins's face. He pulled a folded paper out of his pocket and pushed it to Thomas. Thomas scanned Haskins's face and then unfolded it and read the figures it contained.

"What's this?" asked Thomas.

"Those be my usual price for my valuable services, plus expenses o' course," explained Haskins. Thomas picked up the pencil on the table and wrote another figure underneath, and then pushed it back to Haskins.

"That's what I'll pay ya, same pay as for any scout," said Thomas.

Haskins glanced at the figure. Darkness instantly came over Haskins's face along with a furrowed brow, and a moment later his former knowing grin returned.

"I see ya must not be familiar with my reputation, Captain. Most folk 're more 'an happy to pay my modest fee for the unique service I provide. I'll overlook ya being unfamiliar with me. I think when I rescue them folk, ya'll be only too glad to pay me my due."

Thomas studied Haskins face for several moments, as if trying to decide on a response. "The terms o' your pay will be as I wrote on this here paper, if ya wanna take ya chances on somethin' else later, that's your business," Thomas responded.

"So what made ya come?" asked Thomas, looking back at Scout.

"The more I thought about folk being taken prisoner, the more angry I got. Before I turned in last night it was decided."

Thomas looked into his ale and noticed a swallow left, drained it and stood up. "Well, I figure I best be gettin' back to camp. Scout, a word on the way?"

All three men mounted up, and Haskins rode ahead to camp. Thomas and Scout walked their horses behind. "So what's with Haskins askin' three times the usual scout pay?" asked Thomas.

Scout laughed. "Thomas, you don't know this man's reputation. He's asking for a huge sum, but he can deliver. I don't know how many towns and families have been saved because of his help.

Haskins has more experience than me or any other man on this sort of mission."

"The Colony of Connecticut don' pay by experience or reputation; they pay by rank, an' you know that," reminded Thomas. "Enough 'bout that though. There's somethin' else on my mind. Look Scout, I don' mean no disrespect, I mean I know ya got more experience an' all, but I'm Captain o' this mission. The men have t' know that."

"Afraid I'm going to take over your party?" suggested Scout.

"Somethin' like that. I mean it do seem kinda weird with you trainin' me an' all. But I do need your help."

"I get it Thomas," offered Scout with a slap on the back.

Once his own camp had been set up, Thomas sat down to write a quick letter to Liz. He wanted to let her know he'd arrived safely. He'd made a mental note to write her as often as he could. Thomas wanted to do what he could to lessen her anxiety, although he knew he couldn't take it away for her. The finished product included several scratched out words and misspellings and had taken longer than he'd expected. He looked with dissatisfaction at the finished product, yet shrugged his shoulders and stuffed it into an envelope.

Thomas fingered the locket in his pocket as he slipped the note into his pack, planning to post the letter tomorrow. He took out the locket and smiled as he examined Liz's likeness. Thomas caressed the image of Liz's face. He thought back to the journey he and John had made to get supplies for the mill several months ago. That was the only other time Thomas had spent a night away from Liz since they'd been married. He'd missed her then too.

Replacing the locket, Thomas dug out his pipe and tobacco. He didn't like to smoke often, but he found it relaxed him when he was worried. This mission certainly qualified. The river looked inviting and he wandered back down and sat on a boulder overlooking the water. Thomas could feel the tension begin to leave his body as he sat and smoked and enjoyed the view. There had always been something relaxing for Thomas about water.

Thomas awoke before first light, as usual, but not of his own accord. Loud sounds he couldn't initially place startled him out of sleep. Shaking off his disorientation, he reached for his sword and pulled back the flaps of his tent. He saw most of the men gathered around Haskins. Many of the men reached out to shake hands with Haskins, and all the men wore smiles. A few men stood back at a distance and watched. Haskins told some sort of tale. Scout waited impatiently to head to the capture site. As Thomas watched Scout attempt to pull Haskins away from the scene, Haskins dismissed him time and again. Finally, the men went off in search of breakfast, and Scout succeeded in dragging Haskins away to their waiting horses.

"What was that all 'bout, John?" asked Thomas.

"Good morning Cap," said John. "I sent the scouts, make that the new scouts, to the capture site to get started."

"No, I mean with the men. What was all the fuss?"

"Come on Thomas, all the men 're excited to have the great bounty hunter with us," said John.

"So ya heard o' him too?"

"Ya pullin' my leg? 'Course I heard of 'im, everybody know o' Colonel Haskins," said John.

"He's a colonel?" asked Thomas.

"Well, I don' know 'bout any official rank, but that's what everybody calls 'im."

"I don' know 'bout 'im either. Guess I'm just gonna have t' trust Scout on this one. Anyways, where's the local guide?"

"Come now Thomas, this man's famous. I figure ya're the only one don' know 'bout Colonel Haskins," said John.

"Look John, if he can help us with our mission, I'm glad t' have 'im along, but his reputation, which may be deserved, don' help get those folk back. So, where's the local guide?"

"He left a map to follow. He left with the scouts."

"All right. Then let's finish our coffee at the site. Bring the most experienced with us," said Thomas.

"Ya don't wanna bring everybody?" asked John.

"Naw, they'd just track up the place and get in the way o' the scouts." John rounded up the three older men, meaning the men in their late twenties, and off they rode for the capture site.

John struggled to read the barely legible map. He studied it for a few minutes before nudging his horse forward. Thomas rode alongside John with the other three behind. They stopped again to consult the map for the third time before they eventually made their way up the road to the site. As they rounded a bend in the road, a small farm came into view. The land sat on the side of a hill on the western side of the road. A short ways up the hill stood a small, unpainted house with a porch on the front. A hundred yards to the right of the house was the barn, also unpainted. As the horses trotted up the path to the house, they could see the front door broken and lying on the front porch with the leather hinges hanging half off. The local guide and the scouts were standing just inside the door talking when Thomas and John walked in.

"Good morning gentlemen," said the local guide. "Ya must be Captain Chittenden?"

"Yep, a pleasure," Thomas said, as he shook the man's hand.

"James McClintock. I own the Litchfield general store, but please call me Jim."

"Okay Jim, so tell us what ya know."

"Well, there were two families living here, although it's hard to believe lookin' at the size of the place. Two sisters and their families lived here, to be exact. They had been stockpilin' provisions as they were fixin' to settle 'n the Grants. With the two families sharing the one farm, they was overcrowded an' was hoping for enough space for the both families out them Grants. They were buying more supplies from me than usual. I remember 'em tellin' me they was just 'bout ready to head on out before it happened."

"An' exactly what is it that happened?"

"Well, old man Stinson can best tell ya. He's the one that actually saw it."

"He saw the capture?"

"Yes sir."

"An' where can we find 'im?"

"Jonas Stinson's place is right 'cross the road over there. See that dark-wooded house on the hill there?"

Shading his eyes from the morning sun Thomas could make out a low, dark-wooded house about a mile away. "Okay, Lt. Jackson, send two men an' an extra horse to the Stinson house an' bring Stinson back here," ordered Thomas.

"Jim, do ya know just how many were livin' here?" continued Thomas.

"Yes sir, they was nine of 'em."

At the sound of approaching horses Thomas turned to see three men riding up at a trot. Stinson smelled as if he hadn't bathed in a month, with grease-matted hair held in place by a straw hat that likely had never met soap nor water. Thomas instinctively stepped back and positioned himself upwind.

"You Captain Chittenden," asked Stinson? Thomas nodded.

"What's the meaning o' you pullin' me 'way from work like that?"

"Thank ya for ya time, Mr. Stinson. We're investigatin' the missin' families that were livin' here. I understand ya know something 'bout that."

"Well why din't you says so right off? I woulda come right off if ya boys say so. And anyways, it's 'bout time you boys got 'ere. I reported this 'ere mess more 'an two weeks back. Them damn Yorkers gots a good two-week start on you boys."

"Now hold on, I want the scouts t' hear this. Where's Scout an' Haskins?" asked Thomas. Scout and Haskins appeared in the front door opening and made their way over.

"Okay Mr. Stinson, tell us what ya know 'bout the missin' folk," Thomas asked.

"They ain't missin'. Them Yorkers clean snatched 'em right out of their house. It was as if they was common cattle rustlers or somethin'. Thar ain't no mystery 'bout what happen."

"Could ya tell me exactly what you saw?" Thomas persisted.

"You bet I tell what 'em damn Yorkers did. I was up on the roof patchin' a hole. I was gettin' tired o' the damn rain coming on in however it like. Anyways, I'm up on the roof an' I see these Yorker boys ridin' up with guns drawn like they chasin' some criminals. So I says to myself, them boys 're up to no good. Well, it don't take long to figure it. They spread on out all over the farm as if they expectin' a fight. I guess they din't find nobody anywheres else, so they go 'n bang on the front door right there." Stinson points to the broken front door.

"Well these folks ain't no fools. Damn right they don't open the door or nothin'. They wadn't born yesterday. Then I hears somebody yellen' out somethin' 'bout openin' up in the name o' the New York law. I say to myself, New York law? Them boys is Yorker militia. I mean, who else is gonna say some fool thing like that? Well like I said, them folk wadn't born yesterday. They don't open the door. After a while them Yorker boys figured they'd waited long 'nough. They hauled off and broke in the damn door. Next thing I hears is a hollerin' an' a screamin' all over the place. It don't take 'em damn Yorker boys long a tie up them poor folk. They just tryin' a get ahead an' git thir own place out thar in the Grants. Folk got the right to git ahead, ya know. It ain't right for 'em damn Yorkers to haul 'em off like thar murderers or somethin'.

That the problem now days, everbody messin' with everbody's business. It jist ain't right, I tell ya. It jist ain't right."

"Stinson," interrupted Thomas, "tell us what happened after the Yorkers tied 'em up."

"Well, next thing ya know them damn Yorkers is leadin' them poor folk out the door with thir hands tied behind thir backs. They din't even give them poor folk time to pack nothin'. They left with nothin' but the shirts on thir backs!"

"Did you see which way they took 'em?" inquired Lt. Jackson.

"Damn right, I did. Damn Yorkers took 'em poor folk up north."
Old man Stinson pointed a crooked finger up the road.

"Do ya know how many strong they are?" asked John.

"Hell if I know. I din't do no countin'. I was too busy spittin' nails over what 'em damn Yorkers was up to. No good, I tell ya'!"

"Yes I'm sure of it, but could ya hazard a guess as to how many?" John said.

"Damn if I know, maybe twelve or fifteen. Hey, you boys heading after 'em? Cuz if so, I'm of a mind to git a musket down an' give 'em damn Yorkers what they gots comin'."

"I appreciate your offer, Stinson, but I think we're enough already. We won't give up till we free them folk," said Thomas.

"You damn right you won't. You give 'em what they got comin'!"

"Did you hear them say anything else," asked John?

"Oh just that bull 'bout 'em folk being in violation o' the New York law."

"There was nothing else?"

"No, nothin' else. What else do you boys need? Just git on your horses and go git 'em!"

"Thank you for ya help, Mr. Stinson. My men will take ya back to your farm. Lieutenant, take Mr. Stinson home. The rest o' you men, I want a complete going over o' the farm. I want to know everything there is to know. Scouts, over here for a word. Have ya taken a look at the trackin' yet?"

"We looked it over good before ya got here. It's hard to tell much, since others been all over the place messin' up the tracks. But I do make out tracks headin' out north like old man Stinson says," said Haskins.

"Okay, anything else?"

"Well, there's not much else really," interjected Scout. "It does appear there was some sort of struggle inside, although we don't see any signs of a gun fight."

"Okay, look around a bit more," ordered Thomas.

"I seen all I need t' see, Captain, it's a standard kidnappin'. I seen dozens of 'em. No disrespect to ya inexperience, but we done here. We best get on the trail of 'em right off," concluded Haskins.

Thomas wasn't going to leave until he'd inspected the capture site. He nodded to Haskins and Scout and then walked over and inspected the broken door. He could see that it had been forced off the leather hinges. The door was made of heavy wood, requiring some effort to lift. He walked past the door and wandered around the house, not sure what he was looking for. There were a couple chairs knocked over and a broken table just inside the door. He was walking about the kitchen when he heard shouts from the back of the house. John rushed into the kitchen to find Thomas.

"Captain, we've discovered a hidden room in the floor o' the house!" The two men moved quickly to the back part of the house and saw the others peering into a dark chamber underneath the floor.

John called out to Morse, "Quick, get a lantern over here!"

Morse hurried to retrieve a lantern from his pack, and upon returning, quickly put a match to it. The men all strained with anticipation to see what the light would reveal. The light first fell on earthen steps heading down to an unseen destination. The men looked at each other, wondering who would take the lead and walk down into the dark chamber.

After a few moments of awkward glances about the room, John broke the silence.

"Morse, Johnson, load your muskets. Ya goin' down with me."

John took the lantern from Morse and waited nervously while the men loaded their muskets. Morse spilled his musket balls all over the floor, apologizing under his breath for the delay as he put them back in their canvas bag. Johnson ended up with almost as much powder on his hands as in the musket barrel. John checked his pistol to make sure it was properly loaded. Seeing that the others were finally ready to descend, John took a deep breath and placed his foot onto the first earthen step. It held his partial weight okay. Taking another deep breath, he placed his full weight on the top step and descended into the chamber.

Six or seven steps later he stood on the floor of the chamber. John quickly examined the chamber with pistol at the ready. He held the light up higher to get a better look at the place. Nobody was in the room. He examined the walls and floor of the room carefully, looking for a door. Finding nothing, he exhaled a deep sigh of relief. The men had to stoop slightly to avoid hitting their heads on the wood beams that made up the ceiling, and John was bent over like an eighty-year-old man due to his height. The room had a cool and musty smell about it, like being inside a cave.

John called up to the others, "It's alright, ain't nobody here!"

Not that he'd expected anyone to still be in the room, but a man's imagination runs away with him when he doesn't know. The light revealed a fairly small room of about ten by ten feet. Along the near wall wooden shelves had been placed into dugout portions of the dirt wall. The shelves contained cans of food and jars of preservatives. A handful of partially-used candles and a box of matches occupied one of the shelves. Bags of flour and grain lay on the ground underneath the shelves. Several buckets of water sat on the ground in the corner. Two muskets leaned against the wall on the other side of the room. John examined them and noticed they hadn't been discharged. Next to the muskets were several piles of bedding. On the far side of the room was a makeshift commode with a piece of wood for a lid.

The floor appeared dark and wet. John thought it would be uncomfortable to sit on the ground for long, as there were no chairs. The room contained the bare essentials for survival in an emergency. A brief inspection told John that the hidden chamber had been used as some kind of safe shelter.

"Lieutenant, what have we down here?" Thomas had just come down the stairs.

"It appears the settlers expected trouble. The room has everything necessary to hide out."

"Yes. I wonder if the families ever made it down here."

"I would guess that they had based on the smell coming from that bucket," said John.

"Ah yes. Scout, Haskins, take a good look around down here an' report to me topside. I've had a nose full o' this room already."

Thomas ascended the stairs and wandered aimlessly about the house, not really expecting to find anything helpful. The house was left as if the families had merely walked into town for the day, except for the overturned furniture and the front door. Clothes lay in dressers, food and water in the kitchen, and the other belongings you might see at any farmhouse. The only thing unusual about the house was the stockpiling of extra supplies in the kitchen. John was examining something in the kitchen when Thomas walked in.

"Ya ever thought 'bout leavin' Salisbury for a piece o' your own land?" asked Thomas.

"Don't think so. Why?"

"I don' know, might be I could get used to havin' a spread o' my own." The scouts' approach interrupted Thomas's musings.

"Okay Captain, we finished our looking about," reported Scout.

"And?"

"Well, it appears these folk were only down there a short time. Only one candle had been burned, an' not burned that much. The can had been used, but even with the bad smell, there wasn't much to it. The bedding was all rolled up like it hadn't been touched."

"An' the food supplies don't appear to be used none," interjected Haskins.

"So the families din't have much warning then," observed John.

"I don't reckon so," answered Haskins. "Maybe only a few minutes. An' the house wasn't touched neither. Everything looks like it should, except for the extra supplies."

"I s'pose that's everything then," said Thomas.

"I believe so sir," answered Scout.

Thomas looked at Haskins, who looked back but said nothing.

"Okay then Lieutenant, let's get back to camp."

"Okay men, ya heard the Captain. Let's move out!"

Fall 1745 - Salisbury, Connecticut Colony

Thomas and Ben crouched in the bushes a hundred yards in front of the Feed 'n Seed. Thomas shifted nervously, while Ben maintained a steady bead on the store's front door. The door was framed by a wooden porch, unpainted and well worn with smooth spots made by many years of weather and boots trodden across it. A lone window overlooked the porch and entry into the store.

"I still don' know if this be a good idea, Ben."

"Oh come on, we been o'er this," said Ben.

"I mean, what if we git caught?"

"We won't. That why we waitin' till he an' his girl gone home."

"How will we..."

"Quiet!" whispered Ben. "Door's openin'."

The boys watched Rachel step out, close the door and hang a wooden sign that read "we gone for the day" on a nail on the front door. She picked up her coat and walked off. The boys watched her until she turned a corner and was out of sight. They looked back at the door, yet it remained closed.

"What 'bout Mr. MacDonald? He left too?" asked Thomas.

"What's this 'Mr. MacDonald?' Do ya know 'im or somethin'?" asked Ben sarcastically.

"Well..."

"Okay, ya wait here. I'm goin' in for a closer look," said Ben as he moved off toward the store.

Thomas watched his brother slowly and casually walk up to the porch, suddenly bending down to avoid being seen from the window. He made his way to the window and peered in, looking left and then to the right. Satisfied, he trotted back to the bushes in a crouched position.

"Okay, I think the old man's gone too. Can't see 'im anywhere," said Ben. "Let's move in."

Rachel headed off to spend time with a local girl with whom she was friendly. MacDonald stayed behind at the store to catch up on some work. He'd spent much of the afternoon talking with Rachel and hadn't gotten much work done. His mind began to wander away from thoughts about work. He found himself looking over at the box containing his father's sword. MacDonald set down his work and tenderly picked up the box. He slowly opened the box and removed the sword, filling with emotion as he touched the familiar metal of the hilt. The sword seemed to draw him to pull it out and look at it, yet something in MacDonald resisted. He feared what may be stirred within.

While MacDonald sat mulling over the sheathed sword, he heard sounds from the front of the store. He wondered who could be coming into the store at this hour, especially with the "we gone for the day" sign up. MacDonald heard slow, cautious footsteps. He soundlessly stood and went to the door to have a look. He saw a teenage boy crouched behind the front room counter looking through his drawers. Astonished, MacDonald realized he was being robbed! Nobody had ever tried to steal from him before. MacDonald stepped into the front room.

"Alright lad. What 'r ye up t'?"

A young man stood up. MacDonald recognized the boy as being from town, but couldn't place him at first. The boy pulled out a large hunting knife, brandishing it back and forth.

"Damn! So ya still here ole man. Ya should o' known what was best for ya an' gone home when it was quittin' time."

"Oh lad, ye don't want t' do this. Let's just set down me belongin's an' find oot what's brought ye t' such desperate times."

The boy appeared uncertain for a moment and hesitated. "No, ole man. If ya know what's best for ya, ya'll just go on home an' nobody gets hurt. Believe you me, ya don' want no part o' this here knife."

"Come now lad, there's no need fo' anybody t' get hurt now. Let's set down the knife an' hae us a talkin'."

The boy stepped toward MacDonald swinging his knife at him. The knife passed several feet from the old man two or three times. "Like I said ole man, go on ya way an' leave me to my work here. I don't wanna have to cut ya. An' drop whatever ya got in your hand."

MacDonald made no move for the door, but simply stood his ground. He still held the sheathed sword in his left hand. When MacDonald didn't move the boy decided it was time for action. With a determined look of anger he lunged at MacDonald with the knife. In one swift motion MacDonald unsheathed his sword and knocked the knife out of the boy's hand with the flat side of the blade, stepping out of harm's way.

The knife clattered to the floor several feet away. The boy, looking stunned for a moment, quickly regained his presence of mind and dove for the knife. MacDonald took a step or two and slapped the boy's hand with the broadside of the blade as he attempted to pick up the knife. The boy swore and grimaced as he held his injured hand against his stomach. The boy looked up at MacDonald in surprise.

"Hey ole man, how did ya do that?" The boy no longer spoke in belligerence, but in genuine astonishment. He hadn't even imagined the possibility of the old man getting the best of him in a fight. Still holding his sword, MacDonald wasn't sure the boy was done trying to fight his way out.

"Come now lad, let's sit down an' git t' the bottom o' this. Forget yer knife- there be no need t' make this worse for ye." The boy looked warily at MacDonald and then glanced over his shoulder back toward the counter. Seeing that the old man was determined, he obeyed and sat down on a box. Setting his sword on his lap, MacDonald pulled up a box and sat down opposite him.

"Now then, lad. Tell me..." Just then another boy stood up from behind the front counter with his eyes on the ground and his shoulders slumped. In his left hand he held a bag half full. It jingled with the sound of metal against metal. MacDonald's eyes darted to him. He rubbed his eyes and looked again.

"Thomas? Be that ye, lad?" Thomas glanced up sheepishly and nodded, returning his eyes to the floor quickly.

"Be ye intent on stealin' fro' me as weel, lad? I thought we was gettin' to be friendly."

"Oh, Mr. MacDonald, I'm so sorry! I don' know why I did this. I know it was stupid."

"Aye lad, that it was," said MacDonald softly. "Weel then, come an' sit wi' yer friend." Thomas readily obeyed, keeping his eyes averted downward.

"What 'as brought ye lads t' such desperation t' steal from another man's labor an' tarnish yer own characters?"

Both boys looked down in shame. All signs of bravado had disappeared from Ben's countenance. He looked hard at the ground, searching for a response, but none came to him. He hoped the old man would get the lecture over with and let him go. He underestimated MacDonald.

"Come now lads, loosen yer tongues an' oot wi' it. Don't think ye'll be leavin' till I hear all aboot it." Ben looked up, again with surprise on his face. Did the old man really just want to talk, and if so, whatever for? He waited, yet MacDonald merely held his gaze. Thomas glanced up from time to time, yet his eyes were heavily drawn to his feet as if by magnets.

"First o' all lad, let's start wi' yer name. What do ye call yerself?" Ben's eyes suddenly looked to the door, giving him some hope, as the boys had left it open. MacDonald followed his eyes and went over to close the door.

"Uh, my name's uh, uh Ben."

"Ben? Ye mean yer Ben Chittenden?" asked MacDonald. Ben reluctantly nodded his head slowly. Well, the cat was out of the bag now. All thoughts of running were dashed. There was no longer any point.

"So yer Thomas's brither then?" asked MacDonald. Ben nodded slowly.

"Oh lads, an' what hae brung ye to this?" Thomas was unable to speak. He shrugged his shoulders and looked to Ben. Different storylines came to Ben's mind. Should he offer a bold-faced lie? He considered a couple of possibilities, and then looked MacDonald in the eye. What he saw suggested to Ben that a lie was unlikely to work, and resigned himself to telling some version of the truth.

"Well, we was lookin' for ya till. We gots ourself in a bit o' a situation, an' we short on money," Ben admitted.

"'Tis clear 'nough yer lookin' fer a wee bit o' me money lad, but whatever for? What be yer situation?" Ben squirmed in his seat, trying to figure out how to say as little as possible. He glanced at Thomas, who imperceptibly turned his eyes toward Ben without moving his head.

"Look mister, I admitted we was gonna steal from ya, isn't that enough?"

"Oh noo lad, yer jist gettin' started. Ye see lad, want o' money can be an awful thing. It brings many a man t' do things he might otherwise not even think o'. But lads, as bad as going withoot be, tis a greater tragedy t' blacken yer character. Yer character's one o' the few things no man an' no poverty can take fro' ye, an' she's awful stubborn to restore once she's been blackened. I hate t' see ye both pay such a terrible price as that."

"Look mister, if ya wanna lecture me then go ahead an' do it. But let's get on with it."

"Not o' yer life, an' yer life might weel depend upon it. I can't let ye go withoot addressin' what ye been aboot lad," MacDonald explained.

"Ya know mister, ya jist ain't makin' no sense. I was tryin' to steal from ya since I got myself a debt I gotta pay up on, okay? Alright, we owe a bit to our father, okay? What else's there to say?"

"Let's just tell 'im," said Thomas, as he looked him in the eye for the first time. "The fields we responsible for din't do so good this year. The harvest only amounted to 'bout half o' the usual take. So, we gotta find a way to make up the rest."

"Aye lads, that be better. That explains yer want o' money. But how did ye decide to go after my till," MacDonald pressed.

"I guess we figured ya'd be an easy take," admitted Thomas. MacDonald just looked from Thomas to Ben without blinking.

"Come on, what else do ya wanna hear," Ben pleaded in exasperation.

"Weel lads, now for the makin' it right. What 're we to be doin' aboot that now?"

"I'm sure I have no idear what you're talkin' 'bout. Ain't what I said enough? Just lemme go home! I git that I did wrong, an' I won't do it again!" pleaded Ben.

"That's fine lad, but I be more concerned with makin' this right fo' yerself," explained MacDonald. Then MacDonald turned to Thomas.

"Hand me the money from me till." Thomas handed back the money, which MacDonald promply counted.

"Okay lads, ye were gonna take three days o' me wages. So, I want ye both to put in three days o' work fo' me. The only way I can think t' restore the stain o' yer character is t' hae ye work for the money."

"Ya want us to work for ya?" asked Thomas with widening eyes.

"Aye, lad." Ben looked incredulously at MacDonald, being unsure if his ears were failing him. The last thing he'd expected to hear was the old man wanting him to work for him.

"No way am I workin' for you, mister! Look, ya gave me a lecture an' now just lemme go!"

"Weel, I won't keep ye here any longer, but then I hae to talk wi' yer father."

"What! Ya can't talk t' Father!"

"An' why not, lad?"

"'Cause he'd kill me if he found out what I done," admitted Ben.

"Weel then, I s'pose ye hae to decide one road o' the other, lad."

"Uh, do I get a choice?"

"Thar always be a choice, lad. I'd be glad t' come home wi' ye an' make yer folks' acquaintance if ye don't take me offer. But ye see lads, yer character's at stake, an' either me o' yer folks need t' attend t' the restorin'o' ye both. So, what's it gonna be?"

Ben shifted in his seat. Then he stood up and paced the floor. He took a deep breath and resigned himself to take his medicine.

"Alright mister, I'll work for ya the three days, but that's it." MacDonald looked to Thomas. He nodded his assent.

"Now here's the way we're gonna do this, lads. I'll agree t' not tell yer folks wi' the understandin' that yer gonna come t' me store e'ery day fo' the next three days an' give me an honest four hours' work. If ye come e'ery day an' ye do an honest day's work, I'll pay ye what's right an' forget aboot tellin' yer folks. But make no mistake lads, if ye don't come an' make yer amends, I'll be pleased t' make yer folks' acquaintance. Do we hae an understandin'?" Thomas agreed at once. Ben stared at MacDonald. Then he slowly nodded his agreement.

Thomas and Ben shuffled into the house just as Father washed up at the water basin. He looked up as his boys walked in. They glanced at Father and immediately averted their eyes, pretending to have been on their way to their loft all along. Father watched them.

"Do ya think he suspects anything?" Thomas whispered to his brother.

"Shhh! He'll hear ya!" Ben whispered. Ben cautiously peeked over the loft long enough to see that Father had his back turned.

"Was he lookin'?" asked Thomas as he held his breath.

"Naw. We lucky so far."

Throughout supper Ben and Thomas tried to appear natural. However, they couldn't prevent themselves from stealing brief glances at Father.

"Now, what're you boys lookin' at over here?" asked Father. "Ya done somethin' I oughta know 'bout?"

"Oh no, nothing like that," said Ben quickly.

Thomas stared at his plate. He watched each bit all the way from plate to fork to mouth and back again.

"What 'bout you Thomas, ya got somethin' to tell me?"

"Me? Oh no sir," answered Thomas.

Thomas was just finishing his mathematics when Miss Mayberry rang the bell. Thomas put down his pencil and rubbed his eyes. He reached his arms back over his head and stretched. John joined him as he shuffled toward the door of the schoolhouse.

"Hey Thomas, let's go by the river on the way home an' skim some rocks. I wanna keep at it now that I'm gettin' it," invited John.

"Yeah, okay. Let's go," replied Thomas enthusiastically. "Oh wait a minute, I can't today."

"Why not? Come on, we won't be long."

"Naw, I can't. I got somethin' I gotta do," mumbled Thomas. "I'll see ya tomorrow."

Thomas opened the front door of the Feed 'n Seed and knocked on the door post. Looking around he spied Rachel behind the counter. She glanced up from her work.

"Oh, they be in the back; go on back yerself," Rachel said. Thomas presented himself in the door frame of the back room with his hands in his pockets and a wary look on his face. Just beyond the door to the yard, MacDonald instructed Ben on his work for the day. MacDonald wore his overalls and a blue worn work shirt underneath. Ben was lifting brown sacks into a cart. MacDonald noticed Thomas and waved him over.

"Hey Thomas, has Mr. MacDonald shown ya any of his sword tricks?" asked Ben.

"Sword tricks? What sword tricks?"

"When I showed up, he was doin' some sort o' maneuvers with that black sword o' his," explained Ben.

"Ne'er ye mind that, now. Come on lad, back t' yer work. Take the cart on o'er t' Jackson's mill. Get on wi' it; it'll be dark soon enough."

Ben opened his mouth to say more, but seemed to change his mind and hopped in the cart and off he went. However, Thomas wasn't so easily put off. Thomas figured he must be talking about the sword MacDonald got from his father.

"So, what 'bout the sword tricks. Ya never showed me anythin' on that sword o' yours."

"Come now, lad. Ye don't want nothin' t' do wi that ol' sword."

"Yeah, I do. Come on, show me somethin' with it. "

"Now jist let that sword be fo' now, lad. Ye don't be 'ere for sword tricks now, ye hae work t' attend to," said MacDonald firmly.

Ben returned from his last delivery. All the way back he'd been thinking about this being the end of the third day, but he wasn't sure how best to bring it up with MacDonald. He feared MacDonald might try to trick him into more work. Ben found Thomas in the front of the store and spoke with him in hushed tones. Then the brothers approached MacDonald together.

"So, I'm done with that last delivery," said Ben. MacDonald just stared at him. Ben kicked at the dirt with his hands in his pockets.

"We figure we done with our three days o' work for ya," said Thomas.

"Aye lads, 'course this be the third day. I almost forgot. I hae yer wages 'ere. Ye certainly put in yer three days."

"Mr. MacDonald, I don' expect ya to pay me, after what I tried to do an' all," mumbled Ben.

"That be the point, lad. We be workin' t' remove yer tarnish, an' I wan' to pay ye for yer honest work. Not only hae ye turned away fro' what ye did, but ye turned o'er a new leaf with yer honest work, the both o' ye. Now take yer wages an' I don' want t' hear another word o' it."

Ben and Thomas reluctantly took the money. They slowly put the money in their pockets.

"Now, hae ye lads found a way t' settle yer debts?" asked MacDonald.

"This should help," answered Ben as he fingered the money.

"Weel lads, oor business be done, but I invite ye t' visit as often as ye like. I'll keep an open door t' ye both."

"Oh I don' know, I think I had enough o' workin' for ya," said Ben.

"Oh no lad, I hae no thought o' puttin' ye back t' work," MacDonald said with a laugh. "I be invitin' ye t' visit o'er a cup o' tea."

"Tea?"

"Aye, lad. Ain't ye ever taken tea before?"

"Look mister, I know I did wrong by tryin' to steal from ya, but I paid ya back on that. Now I just wanna be left alone. I got nothin' to talk to ya 'bout. Why would I wanna talk to you anyways?"

"'Cause ye be in some distress," summed up MacDonald.

"Distress? How do ya figure?"

"Aye lad, it be as plain as day. It wouldn't be plainer if it be written 'cross yer forehead," laughed MacDonald.

"What's it to you even if I am in distress? That ain't none o' ya business, ole man!" At that Ben turned abruptly and ended the conversation. Thomas watched his brother walk out the back of the store. He started to follow him, and then hesitated. He turned back around to face MacDonald.

"I don' know if I can visit again after tryin' what I done to ya," said Thomas with his eyes averted.

"An' why would that be, lad?" Thomas cast MacDonald a strange look.

"Ain't it clear?"

"So ye'd let a wee bit o' guilt keep ye fro' gettin' what ye hungry for then?" countered MacDonald. Thomas laughed nervously.

"What be I hungry for? I don't git what ya mean."

"'Course ye don' lad. It be plain 'nough that yer in need o' some good talkin'."

"Talkin'? Talkin' 'bout what?"

"Weel jist hae to see, lad."

"Well, I gotta think on it. Ya sure gotta way o' puttin' things."

"'Course lad, it be entirely yer decision. My door be open to ye the same as t' yer brither."

As Ben and Thomas walked through the gate, they heard raised voices coming from the house. As they looked up they saw the reverend standing on the porch talking to Father. The boys couldn't make out the words, but they could see the reverend gesturing emphatically to Father. Father stood with his arms folded across his chest and his eyes averted down at the reverend's boots. Every so often Father nodded his head. The boys intuitively knew to remain at the gate for now. A few minutes later, the reverend shook

Father's hand, tipped his hat, and untied his horse. He climbed into the saddle and turned his horse toward the gate. He called over his shoulder as he left.

"Now, Ben. I'm sure I won't have to come back for 'nother visit. I got every confidence ya'll do right."

The reverend waved at the boys as he rode past them and out the gate. Then he halted his horse and spoke to them.

"You boys be sure an' help your Father fix everything up now." Then he turned and left.

Thomas and Ben cautiously approached Father, who remained standing on the porch rubbing his beard. After an uncomfortable moment in which he did not appear to notice their presence, he looked up at his sons.

"First light tomorrow I want ya both to get out to the creek an' put it back like it used to be. Take out the dam."

May 13, 1753 - Hampshire Grants

Several days later Captain Chittenden and his men wandered their way through the frontier of the Grants. The regiment had left the northern border of the Massachusetts Bay Colony yesterday midday. They'd left Litchfield immediately after inspecting the capture site, not wanting to give the Yorkers any more time to put distance between them. The inspection and interview of the local residents confirmed that the Yorkers probably headed north with the prisoners.

As he rode his horse along the faint outline of a trail, he noticed the earthy smell left by the recent rains. Thomas wondered if it rained year-round in the Grants as it did in Connecticut. He wondered if he'd like the climate. The damp trail yielded splashes of mud on his trousers. All around lush and green plants littered the landscape, having been well watered. Thomas liked that smell. It reminded him of many days back on the farm. John rode up next to him, interrupting his musings.

"Captain, the scouts have come across remains of a campsite. They figure a week or ten days old."

"Good," muttered Thomas. "Well, we must be makin' up time then."

"Yeah. If them Yorkers headed out two weeks ahead o' us, maybe we've made up a few days."

"I wanna see the campsite myself." John and Thomas followed the scouts to the site. They dismounted and looked where the scouts pointed.

"Whats ya got Scout?" asked Thomas.

"This is the seventh site we've found; that's seven sites in five days. I figure that means..."

"That means we gainin' on 'em," interrupted Haskins. "The pace I'm leadin's closin' the gap. Over here are bits o' jerky they left behind. I don't see any signs o' fresh meat, an' haven't at any of the camps so far. We figure they're living off smoked jerky, an' probably ain't huntin' any yet."

"They gonna have to slow down an' hunt eventually," said Scout. Thomas nodded.

The regiment remounted and resumed the trail. Thomas's thoughts now shifted in a more personal direction. Thomas didn't know the men in the regiment well, with the exceptions of Scout and John. Thomas was thankful to have his good friend with him on the mission.

"Lieutenant, let's drop back a bit for a spell." John nodded and slowed his horse, both men allowing the others to get a bit more ahead of them. John looked at Thomas with curiosity.

"What's up Cap?" asked John.

"I was just wonderin' how you're holdin' up on the trail?"

"Oh that," began John. "Well, I s'pose I'm holdin' up okay. I miss Samantha an' the little one a bit. I kinda hate to tell ya, ya know, being that us men ain't s'posed to be like that."

"Where'd ya get that idea? 'Course us men have feelings. Our trees might be a bit different, but we got 'em. Matter o' fact, some days I miss Liz somethin' awful; catches me by surprise at times," said Thomas. "There ain't no shame in missin' your loved ones like that." John laughed.

"Sometimes it still sounds kinda funny talkin' 'bout trees, but it sure has helped me," said John. "An' I s'pose you're right Thomas, it just ain't what I got told 'bout how a man oughta be."

"All right, that's fair enough, but maybe it 'bout time ya thought a bit different 'bout how a man oughta be," said Thomas.

John and Thomas had often talked about their trees and how to tend to them well. It had been many years since Thomas had introduced the idea of there being something beneath the skin. It had taken John awhile to get used to talking and thinking that way, as he'd never heard anyone speak of anything like it before. It had been well engrained into John's head his whole life that men don't think about, not to mention talk about, any kind of feelings. John learned that men work hard and provide for their families, and nothing else.

Thomas pulled out his locket, opened it, and handed it to John.

"Liz gave it t' me for to remember her by," said Thomas.

"Do ya look at it much?" asked John.

"Yeah, I figure 'bout every day."

"I wouldn't admit it till ya said so, but I started missin' Samantha real bad the first day," said John. "I wish I had somethin' o' hers to look at."

"Ya know John, I keep thinkin' 'bout them Litchfield folk tryin' to git their own land. I sure would like my own spit o' land...Damn, I wonder what kinda price they might be payin' for it though. Maybe it ain't worth it."

"Ya givin' serious thought to it? That be the second time ya mentioned it," said John.

"Maybe."

The scouts estimated they likely never would have caught up with the Yorker militia without the regiment being completely on horseback. Fortunately, the Yorkers were known to be partly on foot, which would slow them considerably. Not to mention the prisoners, who wouldn't be motivated to go anywhere very fast, and especially anywhere further away from their homes.

As Thomas wiped the perspiration from his forehead, he was thankful the heat of summer hadn't fully hit yet. In attempting to catch up to the captors, the regiment was pushing their horses to maintain a good pace. Thomas wanted to move quickly while the trail still yielded clear signs to follow. The spring rains diminished the tracks, but fortunately their scouts were skilled and could still make out enough of a trail to follow.

The next campsite they found was later that same day, just before dusk and along the edge of the Housatonic River. The Yorkers seemed to be following the river, at least for now. The site didn't reveal much, just a few rocks put into a ring for a fire and a few marks along the ground. Thomas noticed the scouts conferring over by some nearby trees.

"Find somethin'?" asked Thomas.

"Rope marks on trees," answered Scout.

"Means them prisoners bein' tied to trees," said Haskins.

"Damn! Back on the trail. Mount up!" ordered Thomas.

After another hour of riding the scouts located an adequate place to camp for the night as dusk was turning to complete darkness. It helped to have some light to pitch camp, and this time they didn't. Thomas had pushed them longer than usual today. They could still set up camp in the dark with a few lanterns lit, but it wasn't as easy and took more time. After a hastily prepared meal, the guards were set and the rest of the militia were free to do as they pleased.

Thomas smoked his pipe as he paced on the fringe of the camp. He kept picturing men and women tied up. He couldn't get it out of his head that the rope markings on the trees was several feet off the ground. Visions of people with ropes around their necks haunted him.

A number of the men gathered about Haskins's tent, including Scout. Haskins was teaching about wilderness survival, yet mostly he was telling stories of saving settlers from unsavory folk. Many clapped and cheered at the climax of each recounting. It was well after dark before Haskins reluctantly turned the crowd away and turned into his own tent. Haskins could tell such stories all night if his body's frustrating demand for sleep didn't interfere.

It seemed to Thomas that he'd only been asleep a few minutes when he heard shouting. At first he was only half awake and didn't understand the sounds he vaguely heard. As he became more awake he realized there was some commotion in the camp. Then a gun shot rang out in the night, which got Thomas out of bed. Thomas pulled his stiff muscles from his bedding, grabbed his sword, and went to see what the trouble was.

As he looked around, he saw light over near the mess tent and shadowy figures rushing about. He hurried over and saw Lt. Chambers bent over inspecting the mess tent with a lantern.

"What seems to be the trouble, Lieutenant?" asked Thomas.

"Someone or something done ripped a good-sized tear in the mess tent."

"Who would rip a hole in the mess tent?" Thomas asked.

"I think it might be more what than who, Captain," responded Scout.

"What, do ya mean an animal, Scout?"

"Yes, I do."

"What kind of animal would do that?" Thomas asked.

"I hate to say this, but I'm afraid it might be wolves. These markings on the tent are quite distinctive."

"Wolves?" Thomas's mind went numb. Wolves were just about the last thing they needed on this mission. Thomas groaned inside at the thought.

"Are ya sure, Scout?"

"Well I can't say I'm sure, but I wouldn't count on anything less."

By now Lt. Chambers had opened the tent and shined his lantern inside. He cursed under his breath as he saw the torn open supplies.

"Well, damned critters didn't take much, but they sure made a mess of my supplies," said Lt. Chambers.

"Did they spoil anything?" inquired Thomas.

"I'm not sure, Captain. I'll have to take a closer look at it in the morning light. They got at least one side of beef though. But one thing's for sure, we can't just leave our supplies sittin' in the tent for 'em to help themselves to any night they like, especially now that they know we're here," responded Chambers.

"Don't know what idiot left 'em supplies easy pickins like that, but one thing for sure is them marks is wolves," offered Haskins.

"Now wait a damned minute, if you be such the expert, then you set up the supplies the right way," retorted Chambers.

"Naw, I can't be bothered by such petty concerns," said Haskins with a sweep of his hand as he walked away.

By now John had joined the inspection and heard the assessment.

"Okay, extra guard duty. Who's next up for watch? I want the regular watch where they've been north and south of the camp and the next up standing guard over the mess tent, guns loaded," ordered Jackson. Johnson and Peters groaned aloud.

"Let's not have no grumbling, gentlemen. If those wolves get to our supplies, you'll be hunting for the rest of your meals," reminded Jackson.

Fall 1746 - Salisbury, Connecticut Colony

On his way into town for supplies, Thomas watched the fields
pass one by one. Thomas stared out at the clouds and the pale blue
sky and daydreamed. Now sixteen, Thomas loved to fantasize that
he was in the militia. He imagined himself to be a military officer,
bravely leading men into battle. Thomas could see the blue,
French-uniformed soldiers across the battlefield. Black smoke filled
the air from the volley of musket fire. Thomas looks down the line
of his men, seeing the fear on their faces as the French press closer.

With great courage he rallies his men to hold the line, avoiding a
disastrous retreat. Thomas runs up and down the line encouraging
his frightened men to stay in position, in spite of musket balls flying
over their heads. In some cases, the soldiers were watching the man
to the left or the right falling prey to one of the shots. On several
occasions Thomas jumps in and takes the place of a wounded man,
firing several shots to help his men hold off the attack. Thomas
sustains several wounds during the attack but refuses the medic's
attempts to treat him, insisting the wounds are minor and can wait.
His men respond to his actions with hope in their faces and renewed
courage in their veins.

The men stay in their line. As the French advance on their
position, Thomas's men fire on them at his command. After several
volleys the French are repelled again and eventually retreat. He and
his men have successfully held their ground and repelled the French
attempt to take their town. Thomas looks behind him to see
frightened women and children peering out from behind doors,
hoping to be saved. The men hail Thomas as a hero and
responsible for saving their town.

Coughing from the dust of the cart in front of him brought
Thomas out of his pleasant daydream. He was just entering the
outskirts of town. A few minutes later he stopped the horse and cart
in front of MacDonald's Feed 'n Seed.

"Hello, Thomas! I haven't seen ye 'n awhile. Where hae ye been lad?" inquired Mr. MacDonald.

"Mostly just workin' the farm as usual," muttered Thomas.

"What can I do ye for?"

"Oh father made out a list for ya," Thomas said as he handed MacDonald the paper.

Thomas waited several months after the stealing attempt before he approached MacDonald again. Although Thomas had allowed a number of brief conversations with him since, MacDonald sensed the boy wouldn't let him help much and had rarely spoken about himself. The only interest MacDonald noted came when he showed Thomas his father's sword. MacDonald had been content to be patient thus far, realizing Thomas might need more time to let him in.

"Thomas, I'm just sitting down t' a cup o' tea. Why don't ye join me?"

"Oh I don' know, I should be gettin' back soon," mumbled Thomas. "Mama an' Father will wonder what's come o' me."

MacDonald wasn't easily dissuaded and decided it was time to press Thomas a bit. "Come on, we won't be long. I'm nae acceptin' 'no' fo' yer answer this time."

Thomas looked carefully at MacDonald's face and weighed the invitation. Then he put his hands in his pockets and followed the old man into the back of his store. The back room served as a stock room. Along the far wall were numerous sacks of various forms of feed, most of which Thomas could name. The wall to the right contained shelves that held seed bags of all types, including everything planted in the northern colonies.

MacDonald pulled the steeping tea off the fire and handed a cup to Thomas before sitting down on the desk in the corner. He motioned Thomas to the lone chair in the stockroom.

"So tell me lad, how do ye be?"

"Oh, I'm okay I s'pose," Thomas replied.

"Come on Thomas, a lad don't walk 'round wi' shoulder an' eyes like yours if he's doin' 'okay.'"

"What do ya mean?"

"I mean yer body tells me somethin' different than yer words. Now level wi' me lad, what's weighin' ye down?"

Thomas paused and looked about the stockroom. "I s'pose I still feel bad 'bout tryin' to steal from ya."

"Aye lad, but I don' want that t' keep us fro' bein' friends. Maybe it's 'bout time ye let yerself off for that one. We all make mistakes, lad."

Thomas looked up at MacDonald, and then looked away out the window.

"Aside fro' yer guilt lad, there's more weighin' on ye. What do that be?"

"Well I don' know, things are as good as ever I s'pose. I mean nothin's really gotten worse."

"That's what I feared," MacDonald said. "I've thought fo' many a year that ye've been a burdened lad."

"Really?"

"Aye, lad."

"An' what do ya mean by 'burdened'?" asked Thomas.

"Yer shoulder's bow under a weight. I don't know what it be, but somethin's draggin' ye down." Thomas was surprised anyone had noticed.

"Isn't that how it is for everybody?"

"Noo lad, it's that way for many, maybe even most, but it don't have t' be so," MacDonald answered. "Don't ye ever talk 'bout these things wi' yer folks?" Thomas paused to think before responding.

"I don't like talkin' 'bout the chores with the folks. Mama jist feels bad for me an' Father gets mad."

"That's nae what I mean, lad. I don' be talkin' aboot the weight o' yer chores, I be talkin' aboot the weight on yer soul."

"Come on, nobody talks 'bout that sort o' thing with their folks," Thomas said.

"Sure thing, lad. Almost every day I ask me Rachel what part o' the tree she's in that day."

"What part o' the tree? Ya mean, Rachel climbs trees?"

"Noo, 'tis like this, lad. The top o' the tree means a great day; that ye're doing really well. The middle part o' the tree means you're doing alright, but maybe there's a thing o' two on yer mind. The bottom o' the tree means ye're havin' one o' those bad days we all hae sometimes. Whichever part o' the tree me Rachel's in, that tells me somethin' o' how she's fairin' that day."

Thomas looked quizzically at the old man, wondering if he might be crazy. Who talks about people like they're trees anyways? It was the most ridiculous thing he'd ever heard.

"Ya mean ya ask her 'bout trees every day?"

"Aye lad, ye probably think I'm pullin' the wool o'er yer eyes here."

"Well, ya have to admit it sounds awful strange talkin' 'bout trees," admitted Thomas. MacDonald laughed heartily.

"Weel, I hae t' give ye that much lad. Ye probably thinkin' I'm best be lookin' fo' me missin' marbles." Thomas merely smiled in response.

"So really, ya ask Rachel 'bout that every day?" Thomas asked.

"Weel lad, thar probably be a day here an' there I don' think to," MacDonald answered.

Thomas had never heard anyone ask how a person was doing, except maybe by way of a pleasantry. He was just trying to imagine Father or Mama asking him such a thing.

"So lad, what part o' the tree 'r ye in today?"

"After a long pause Thomas said, "I don' know sir. I never really thought 'bout such a thing. How would I even know?"

"Weel lad, it's a question that only yer innards can tell ye."

"My innards?"

"Aye lad, ask yer innards, the inside part o' ye. Ye may have t' wait a bit for an answer. Especially if ye're not used t' askin'. Many 're not aware o' what thar innards 're tellin' 'em. Most don't even know they hae innards."

"But what do ya mean the inside part?" asked Thomas.

"It be a listenin' that yer ears hae no part o'. Ye hae to learn to listen to yer spirit. Some call it thar heart, lad."

"I guess I'll have to think it over some. Don't be offended, but it still all sounds like hogwash to me," said Thomas.

"Aye lad, ye think it o'er, but I'll be askin' the next time I see ye. Ye might start by askin' what yer shoulders an' eyes 're sayin'.""

Thomas walked more quickly heading home from the Feed 'n Seed, leading the horse with her cart behind him. He took the longer way home, not being in any hurry. As he gazed out on the hillside full of trees and foliage he felt surprised at the beauty of the scenery. He hadn't really thought about it before. Thomas picked up and tossed the rocks he came across that were hand-sized. It seemed like he'd just left town when he looked up and saw the Chittenden gate.

Thomas quickly unloaded Father's supplies and walked into the house where Mama was preparing supper.

"Hey Mama, what do your innards tell ya? Do ya ever ask yaself?"

"What in the world are you talking 'bout?"

"Do ya have an inner tree?"

"An inner what?"

Thomas smiled and said, "never mind Mama, it probably just nonsense anyways." Mama turned and looked at Thomas through squinting eyes.

"That s'posed to be some kinda joke ya playin' on me?" Mama asked.

"Figure I'm just askin' how ye be today," said Thomas.

"How do I be? I got a pie in the oven that's 'bout to burn an' I ain't done cookin' the vegetables an' I best hurry on. Do that answer ya question?"

Thomas was already out of the room by the time Mama asked, and he didn't bother to respond. On the one hand Thomas thought it funny to surprise Mama with such a question, yet on the other hand he felt an empty feeling that she didn't know what he meant. He wondered if anybody besides Mr. MacDonald knew about trees. He thought of asking Father about his tree, but decided against it. Thomas felt like he'd been let in on a secret not many knew about. That idea excited him. At the same time, he didn't understand why he felt sad. He decided not to dwell on it.

On his way upstairs to his room, Thomas decided to look in on his sister Sally. He wasn't sure why he decided to talk with Sally, as he rarely had in the past.

"Hi Sally. What 'r ya up to?"

"Oh, hi Thomas. I'm just playin' with my doll."

"Have ya been playing with your doll long?"

"Yeah," said Sally dejectedly.

Thomas knew Sally didn't have many chores, but it had never occurred to him that it left Sally with idle time that no one else in the family had. Thomas hadn't ever thought about what Sally did with her day. Thomas had been standing at the door, and came into the room and sat down. Sally cast Thomas a sideways look, and then went back to her playing.

"Do ya often feel bored, Sally?"

"Yeah, I s'pose so. There ain't much to do."

"Do ya wish ya had more chores to do?" Thomas asked.

Sally laughed, "no don' be silly. I don' wish I had more chores, but I do wish I had somebody to play with. It seem like everybody else's always busy an' don't have time to play with me."

"Gosh Sally, I s'pose I'm one o' the everybodies that never had time for ya. I'm sorry." Sally quickly looked away. She pretended to be looking at something on her dresser as she wiped away tears. Thomas realized what was happening and felt uncomfortable. He politely got up and left the room.

Rarely did Thomas remember dreaming, but the next morning he arose with a clear memory of having dreamt. He dreamed he was out in the desert wandering around. All he could see in any direction was dirt and low rising hills with low rising brush. The brush appeared dead or at most half alive. He felt thirsty. After wandering about for what seemed forever, he spied a river of deep blue off in the distance. He made his way down to the river and found it brighter in color than it had appeared at a distance.

The azure water flowed gently from left to right with occasional areas of white water where rocks broke the surface. The river swept around a bend and out of sight a mile away. Several trees of bright green grew near the water's edge. The ground leading up to the river was fine sand, pleasant to the feet. He took off his sandals and found the sand both inviting and a bit painful to the touch. The hard dirt of the desert felt more comfortably familiar. The river seemed to beckon him, and he moved closer to the water's edge. However, once he came almost within touching distance he found the way barred by a sturdy iron fence. Thomas started at not having seen the fence before now. He shook the bars, but they refused to yield. He longed to get to the water, yet could not.

As he walked along the fence, he came to a gate. The gate was locked. He examined the lock and found it held fast. Looking up he noticed people in the water for the first time. Some splashed and played, some floated, and others rested near the water's edge. As he looked along the fence on the desert side, he saw many others nearby. Thomas was surprised to find there were far more on his side of the fence than on the river's side. Actually, very few enjoyed the river. On the desert side many leaned against the fence, some struck at the fence, yet few seemed interested in the gate. He tried to open the gate again, to no avail, and sat down in despair.

Some time later an older man in the river seemed to notice him and approached him at the gate. The older man offered a gentle smile set upon a firm jaw. He invited Thomas to come in. Thomas shrugged his shoulders and stood fast. The older man waited. Eventually Thomas asked for help. The older man reached through the bars and pulled a key out of the inside of Thomas's coat pocket. The man inserted the key in the lock on Thomas's side of the fence, turned the key and opened the door. He then held the door open for Thomas to enter. Thomas gazed at the old man, then at the river, and suddenly grew afraid. The old man patiently waited. Thomas turned away from the open gate and sat down against the fence. The old man grew sad, yet remained content to wait.

The next day Thomas awoke unsettled by the dream, and at first tried to push it from his mind. The dream kept returning to his thoughts, and he wondered what it might mean. He pondered it some, and then gave up trying to make heads or tails of it.

The next day Thomas was gathering his school things as he prepared to head home. As he walked out the door and down the schoolhouse steps, he noticed Sally sitting on the stairs looking glum. Normally Thomas would walk right past his sister and at times not even notice her sitting there. The truth is Sally sat on the schoolhouse steps every day after school waiting for Mama or Father to come pick her up in the cart and bring her home. This time Thomas decided to stop and talk with his sister, but he couldn't say why.

"Hey Sally."

"Oh, hi Thomas."

Sally quickly returned her eyes to the ground, expecting Thomas to continue on his way as usual. Thomas sat down next to Sally. She looked up in mild surprise.

"Are ya waitin' for Mama to come get ya?"

"Yeah."

"After thinking a moment Thomas continued, Well, I'm on my way to the Feed 'n Seed. Do ya wanna come with me?"

Sally's interest was immediate, "Yeah, could I?"

"Sure, why not."

"But, Thomas, how would I get home?"

"Oh, I guess ya couldn't walk, huh?"

"Probably not, but I could try," suggested Sally.

"Well, I could carry ya if need be."

"You would do that?" Sally's face lit up.

"Sure lil sister, let's go."

"Okay! Oh, but wait. What 'bout Mama. She'll worry if I'm not here waitin' for her."

"Oh uh, Thomas thought for a moment. How 'bout if we tell Miss Mayberry that I took ya home with me. Then Mama won't worry." Sally looked a little uncertain and Thomas pressed.

"Well maybe Mama will worry a bit, but it'll be alright. Come on, lil sis."

This was all the reassurance Sally needed. She bounded down the stairs ahead of Thomas and started off towards the Feed 'n Seed as fast as her stiff leg would carry her.

Minutes later brother and sister walked through the door of the Feed 'n Seed. He hoped MacDonald would ask him about his tree, but he also feared being asked since he still didn't know what to tell Mr. MacDonald. MacDonald had heard them walk in and stuck his head out from the back room.

"So lad did ye, hey, who did ye bring 'ere today?"

"Oh, hi Mr. MacDonald. This is my lil sister, Sally."

"Weel, hello there lass."

Sally just smiled in return. She was already exploring the store and was examining something off the shelf. Rachel worked in the front of the store and walked over to Sally. MacDonald motioned Thomas to the back room.

"So lad, did ye figure out where 'n the tree ye be today?"

"No, I still don' know what to tell ya."

"Weel lad, what came t' mind when ye asked yerself?"

"The only thing that came to my mind is that I'm bored a lot."

"Weel lad, there ye go."

"What'd ya mean? That ain't nothin'," said Thomas.

"Aye it don' be much, but 'tis a start, lad. Ye can be sure o' that."

"Ya mean me being bored has something to do with what part o' the tree I'm in?"

"Absolutely lad. It may not be sayin' a whole lot, but it tells us somethin' o' the nature o' yer leaves. I'd guess yer often feelin' bored. Be I right, lad?"

"Well, yeah I guess so. I don' know if there's much else."

"Weel lad, we'll see what we can do 'bout that."

"Really? What can be done?"

"I'm thinkin' ye don't rightly know much 'bout yer tree 'cause ye're not used t' bein' asked, lad. So we best start askin'." Thomas paused a moment, "Ya mean ya gonna be askin' me regular?"

"Aye, lad."

Thomas fidgeted with his hands. Then he stood and paced the stock room. He looked at the door and took a couple steps toward it, and then paused.

"I uh, uh, I don' know what to say," said Thomas.

"Aye lad. Talkin' 'bout trees be new for ye. Ye hae to give yerself time to settle in t' it."

"Okay, I'd better head on home. Goodbye, Mr. MacDonald."

"Good day, lad. Now ye be expecting my askin' now."

Thomas had to admit that he liked the idea of being asked about the condition of his tree, although he didn't understand why anyone would want to ask him at all, not to mention regularly. He wasn't sure he wanted the personal attention of having somebody paying him such notice. At the same time, Thomas hoped MacDonald would keep his word. He hadn't experienced such a thing before. Thomas also felt some pressure. He didn't know how he would regularly come up with something to tell MacDonald. Besides boredom, he couldn't imagine what else there would be to say. He thought on it all the way home. Nothing else came to him. Thomas also noticed that strange sadness again, yet he quickly brushed it aside as nothing. Strangely, he didn't feel bored right now.

After a half mile or so, Sally was tiring. Thomas put her on his back and carried Sally the rest of the way home. Her additional weight didn't bother Thomas much, as his mind continued to spin and whirl.

When brother and sister arrived home, Thomas set Sally down. He was exhausted by now, but he didn't want her to know.

"There ya go, lil sister."

"Thanks so much for takin' me with ya, Thomas. That was so much fun. Can I go again?"

"Sure ya can."

"Do ya visit Mr. MacDonald very often?"

"Oh I guess so; maybe once a week."

"When did ya start that?"

"Oh, I'm not sure when. Might o' been the last half year I been goin'."

"Well, what do ya talk 'bout with him?" Thomas laughed nervously.

"Uh, well I guess we talk 'bout whatever's on my mind that day."

"Whatever's on ya mind? Like what would that be? I don' get it. Do ya mean ya just talk; that's it?" Thomas laughed again.

"Yeah, Sally. That's it. Sounds kinda silly, don' it. Figure I'm still learnin' how to do it though." Sally peered at Thomas with wide eyes, yet with a light of curiosity as well. Mama walked into the room and Sally would have to wait to inquire further about Thomas's strange relationship with Mr. MacDonald.

Thomas didn't come across MacDonald the next few days, although it wasn't for lack of looking. He found himself looking for MacDonald every time he traveled through town now, which seemed strange after avoiding the old man for so long. It's funny how things change.

He'd been hoping to see MacDonald passing by. Thomas didn't like the idea of just walking right into the Feed 'n Seed too often, but it hadn't been working to just watch for him when walking through town. Gathering his courage, Thomas entered the front of MacDonald's store. He took a few steps into the store and, not seeing his old friend right off, he turned to leave. Thomas was just opening the door when he heard the familiar voice.

"Be that ye, lad?"

"Oh, hi Mr. MacDonald. Yeah, it's me."

"Weel lad, where were ye off t' so quick?"

Thomas looked down as his face turned a light shade of red.

"Oh, I uh, I din' see ya so I thought I'd come back later," he stammered.

"Oh lad, ye've been lookin' 'bout for me. I'm sorry if I been hard t' come by. Come sit down an' I'll make some tea."

"Well if ya have time to," Thomas responded quickly.

"Aye lad, certainly I hae time for ye. Pull up a chair." After a moment's pause, MacDonald grinned as if enjoying a private joke with Thomas.

"So lad, what question 'm I 'bout t' ask ye?"

"'Bout my tree?"

"Oh aye, ye got it!"

"I've been hopin' you'd ask," Thomas said with a sheepish grin, "'cept that I don' think I have much more to say. Not for lack of tryin' though. I thought 'bout it every day. I still think I'm mostly just bored."

"Aye lad, but ye're startin' to notice yer boredom," suggested MacDonald.

"Yeah I s'pose so, but what's that amount to?"

"It be a fine start, lad."

"A start of nothin'. Boredom is like nothin'."

"Is it, now?"

"Come on, ya don' mean bein' bored means somethin'?" asked Thomas.

"An' why not, lad?"

"Come on, Mr. MacDonald, bein' bored's like ya got nothin' to do," said Thomas a bit exasperated.

"Now there ye go lad, yer boredom might be tellin' us that somethin' be missin'."

"Missin'? Like what?"

"Weel, we don't know yet, lad." Both sat thinking in silence.

"Weel lad, hae ye noticed anything more than yer boredom?"

Thomas looked away awkwardly. "Well, there be one other thing. I uh, I do git excited some to see ya," admitted Thomas.

"Oh, that's great lad. Ye're developin' a healthy appetite."

"What? No, I don' mean I've been hungrier, I mean I think I wanna talk to ya more."

"That's just it lad. I think ye're hungrier, and not for food for yer body, but food for 'nother part o' ye. An' it took a good bit o' courage t' say so, I might add."

Thomas looked at MacDonald as though he were trying to decipher a hidden message, and a message for which he didn't have the code. "What other part o' me is there?"

"Yer soul of course, lad."

"My soul? Oh, I don' believe in that kind o' religious stuff, Mr. MacDonald." At this MacDonald laughed heartily.

"I mean we go t' church an' all, but I don' know how much o' it's right. Even if 'tis right, I don' git what it has to do with me anyways," said Thomas.

"That's fine lad, but fro' where do ye think yer desire t' talk wi' me comes? An' anyways, who said anything 'bout religion?"

"Din't you?" MacDonald laughed again, "Noo lad. I said nothin' o' the sort."

Thomas looked strangely at his old friend. He hadn't considered from where his desire to talk came, he just knew he felt it. "Don' the soul have somethin' to do with religion?" asked Thomas.

"I don' know lad. Honestly I don't concern meself wi' religion, 'though I do think o' God often."

"Ain't they the same?"

"Some may say aye, but I say nae. For many religion hae to do with right behavior, but yer soul hae to do wi' the very life blood o' ye. An' yer soul be awakenin' to yer God-given appetite."

MacDonald figured he'd said enough for now and waited to give his young friend time to take it in. Thomas looked like he was wrestling with a difficult arithmetic problem.

"Well, I figure I best be heading home, Mr. MacDonald. I'll see ya later."

"Oh, count on it lad."

When Thomas arrived home he went in search of Sally. He didn't have to look long, finding her in her room, her usual address. She was playing with her dolls, and looked up as Thomas entered.

"Hey, lil sister." Sally brightened to see Thomas.

"Hi, big brother."

"What 're ya up to?"

"Oh nothin', just playing with my dolls."

"Is it fun?"

"No, not really."

"Kinda boring?"

"Yeah I s'pose it is," responded Sally with dejection in her voice.

"Can I play with ya?"

"Oh come on, don' make fun o' me Thomas. I'm serious."

"No, I really would like to play with ya. Why don' ya start by tellin' me the names o' your dolls."

"And ya 'pect me to believe that after all your makin' fun o' me an' my dolls?"

"Look, I know I've been mean to ya at times, but I'm not playin' around now."

"Nice try Thomas, I'm not fallin' for that one," said Sally.

Thomas saw the look of firm resolve on his sister's face. Disappointed, Thomas left Sally's room. He hadn't expected her to rebuff his attempt to reach out to her. This wasn't going to be as easy as he'd hoped. It was as though he had eyes to see a whole new world, previously invisible to him. Sally too was just coming into focus.

Thomas thought about his sister much of the next day, as he went about his usual chores. He thought about how lonely she must be, spending so much time by herself. Thomas pondered never having given much thought to how Sally spent her time. He had been concerned about her leg and regularly prayed for healing, but that's not the same as being concerned about her tree. By the time he'd finished his work, he decided to give Sally another try.

Thomas washed up and changed his shirt, then headed to Sally's room. As expected, he found her in her room playing alone. On the way he'd wondered if there might be a better way to approach her, but couldn't think of anything. Unsure of the reception he'd receive, he hesitantly walked into her room.

"Hey Sally. What 're ya up to?"

"Oh, hi Thomas. Just the usual thing."

"Oh. Uh, are ya playing with your dolls?"

"I was, but now I'm reading a book."

"Oh really. Which one?"

"It's a diary of a early Connecticut Colony settler."

Thomas wished that Sally would make this easier on him, yet Thomas couldn't blame her for being suspicious of his motives. Sally waited, being content to see what Thomas would do. Thomas broke the silence by asking about her book. For several minutes brother and sister discussed the plight of the early colony settlers and the author's life. After a natural pause in the conversation, Thomas decided to dive in.

"So Sally, I get you not bein' eager to tell me 'bout your dolls last night. I haven't exactly been a nice brother to ya. Look, this ain't easy for me. I'm not good with words or anything. This might come as a surprise that I've been doin' some thinkin', an' I wanna change things with ya. Would ya give me 'nother chance?"

After studying Thomas' face for several moments, Sally sighed and relented. Sally was far from convinced of his sincerity, but decided to risk it. She then began to explain to Thomas each doll's name and who they were. She kept checking her brother's face for any signs of trickery. Not seeing any, she continued to slowly let Thomas into her world of dolls. Sally kept expecting his feigned interest to change to mockery at any moment.

Thomas asked questions about each doll, patiently listening to each explanation from Sally. Thomas felt surprised to find himself somewhat interested in her doll world. He hadn't expected such elaborate characters and well developed relationships as Sally had given them. Before they knew it, Mama was calling Sally to help her get supper on the table.

A couple of days later, Thomas prepared to run an errand for Father to the mill. He'd hitched the horse to the cart and loaded up, and was just about to leave when a thought struck him. He tied the horse to the fence and went to look for Sally. Sally was cleaning up after the midday meal with Mama.

"Hey lil sister, ya wanna come with? I'm headin' out to the miller's." Sally immediately looked at Mama expectantly.

"Can I go, Mama? Please, can I go?"

Mama glanced doubtfully at Sally, and then looked at Thomas.

"Well, I don' know. Thomas, you're not gonna have your sister help you carry anything, are ya?"

"No Mama, 'course not."

"Then why do ya want her to go," Mama asked?

"Oh Mama, I just thought Sally would like to come, seein' as she don' have much to do 'round here."

"I see. Well... I s'pose it's okay, as long as ya don't put her to work any."

"Oh, thank ya Mama," an excited Sally said as they gave Mama a hurried kiss.

Sally hurried out the door, leaving Thomas to catch up, not wanting to give Mama a chance to change her mind. Mama followed her daughter with an anxious look. The moment Sally and Thomas were off the property and down the road, Mama regretted granting her permission. What if the cart broke down, or what if Sally were bounced out of the cart? Many other fears plagued Mama.

Father was furious when he learned of Sally's whereabouts. Normally Sally was not permitted to leave the farm unless she was accompanied by one of her parents. School and church were the only places she ever went. He couldn't imagine what had possessed his wife to agree to such a harebrained idea. Father verbally lashed his wife in punishment of her decision. He didn't tell her how greatly he feared for Sally's safety. Anger seemed to be the one emotion Father displayed regularly, while his fear lay well disguished.

May 14, 1753 - Hampshire Grants

The rest of the night was uneventful. The wolves, if they were wolves, were smart enough not to try again that night with the camp on alert for them. Many of the men didn't sleep much, particularly the men sleeping nearest the mess tent. The thought of wolves nearby unsettled even the bravest.

The next morning brought a lengthy discussion amongst the officers concerning how to store the supplies where they'd be safe from predators. After much conversation, it was decided that the edible supplies would be placed in trees at the fringe of camp.

The next night John returned the guard duty to regular watches, thinking that the food was now safe. As usual, the two guards were stationed at the north and south ends of camp with the river on the west. The food hung about six feet off the ground, dangling from a sturdy tree on the east of camp. The night passed without incident.

In the morning Lt. Chambers and his assistants went out to the supply tree to bring the food back to the supply tent. The sight they found left them stunned. White flour littered the ground as if it had snowed, with partially emptied supply sacks, small pieces of bread, and the salt from two sides of beef strewn about. Lt. Chambers was utterly stupefied.

"How did them damned varmint get to my food?"
It was more of a rhetorical question. Chambers hadn't imagined animals would be able to get to the food six feet off the ground. Lt. Chamber's assistants merely gawked at the sight. They had placed the food in the trees themselves. Chambers assessed what was salvageable and what had to be discarded, and ordered his assistants to bring the remnant of the good food back to the mess tent. Having accomplished this, he turned in disgust to find the Captain. Chambers found Thomas on one knee before the coffee pot, helping himself to his first cup of the day.

"Them damned varmint got to my supplies again, Captain!"

"No! Were they up in the tree like we talked 'bout, Lieutenant?"

"Yes sir. I din't know them damned wolves could fly! I'd like to know how they got to my food six foot off the ground," Chambers replied.

Thomas just looked at him, bewildered. They'd had some trouble with wolves on the Chittenden farm, but it was always picking off animals left out and unprotected. Thomas had never known a wolf to get something out of a tree.

"Well Lieutenant, I guess we'll just have to figure something else out. So far the wolves, if they be that, 're outsmartin' us each step o' the way. We'll just have to be smarter. So how much o' the supplies did they get at?" asked Thomas.

"Best as I can figure it 'bout two days' worth of meat, and at least as much flour spilled on the ground, maybe more. I figure they was only interested in the beef; probably the flour was just in their way. Don't look like they got to much else."

"All right Lieutenant, gather the rest of the officers an' we'll meet at the mess tent."

Twenty minutes later Thomas was sipping his second cup of coffee as he walked up to the mess tent. The other three officers, who included Dr. Dickens, were already there. Thomas had walked over to the tree the animals had gotten to, and been even more impressed when he saw the height of the lowest branch. Thomas caught Chambers's eye and nodded to him to begin.

"All right boys, we got a situation here. Some damn critters 're takin' our food. Matter of fact they done it two nights in a row. We got to figure how to stash our food so them damn critters don't eat it before we can. So, we tried a tree. Got any other ideas?"

Thomas and John each looked the other in the face, hoping to find an answer neither seemed to have. Thomas quickly picked up that no one had anything to say right off, and decided to get the discussion started.

"All right, now who's had trouble with predators on their farms?" Each of the men nodded.

"An' what have ya done about 'em?" Thomas asked.

"We sometimes get wolves down at the mill. They come an' try to get to our meat. They don't seem much interested in anythin' else. A few times we heard wolves finishin' off meat left over from our supper. They can make a mighty mess of things. We learned to keep all leftovers inside the house," said John.

"Well I don't s'pose we could keep our supplies indoors here on the trail. We'll have to figure somethin' else," Thomas said.

The others nodded their assent and looked down at the ground as if it would provide a solution. Finally John spoke again.

"I guess our problem is that nobody leaves their food out in a tent back home, so we don't have much to go on here. I figure we all lock up our food supplies at home so critters don't get to it." Again there was a nodding of heads. Then after a pause, Chambers spoke up.

"Maybe I'll just sit up with a couple o' muskets loaded and welcome 'em real impolite like."

"Well ya can't do it alone, but maybe I can make a second rotation of guard duty for the mess tent," suggested John.

John received slow nods as the men thought through his idea. They realized the men would get half as much sleep with four guards on duty all night instead of two. Nobody could think of a better idea, so John's plan was agreed on by all.

John made sure each of the men in the regiment, since all non-officers participated in guard duty, understood how he wanted each guard situated to secure the food supplies. He wanted one man on each side of the mess tent, gun loaded and at the ready. The next night passed without incident, much to the relief of the men. No one relished the thought of coming face to face with wolves and only one shot to spend. The men speculated about how many wolves there might be. It was well known that wolves travel in packs. What would the guards do if confronted with more than two wolves and only two loaded muskets? To help alleviate their worry, the guards decided to each have a second musket loaded and readily available should more than two wolves appear. However, what if more than four wolves confronted them? And would they be able to react quickly enough even if there were only three or four? Many concerns went through the guards' minds, especially well into the quiet of night.

The men stood guard in two-hour blocks. It was thought that weary men would struggle to stay alert for longer than that in the middle of the night. The hard traveling took most of the men's energy. The first watch began at dusk, and the last one ended at dawn.

The next night began as the previous one had. The first two watches passed without incident. On the third watch, Haskins paced back and forth on the north side of the mess tent. Johnson guarded the south side of the tent fifteen paces away. Every so often Johnson would look over at Haskins just to make sure everything was okay. He felt reassured each time he saw an alert-looking Haskins. He didn't want to be out here alone.

Johnson still felt sleepy, even though he'd been awake for the better part of an hour now. He'd been on duty a good forty-five minutes. The guard currently on duty would routinely awaken the next guard to take his place a quarter of an hour before his shift was up to give the man a few minutes to shake off sleep and prepare for duty. Johnson paced as much to keep himself awake as to thoroughly guard his territory. He hadn't yet adjusted to being awakened from a deep sleep after only two hours of sleep, only to stand guard duty in the middle of the night.

A whistling sound off to Johnson's left caught his attention. He stared off in the general direction of the sound, straining to see. After a few moments the whistling sound came again, and Johnson decided it was only the wind. He felt reassured when he felt a slight breeze against his face. Johnson noticed his heart beating quicker. He figured he was just on edge and needed to relax. A younger and less experienced man might be on the edge of panic, or even beyond the edge. Johnson was amongst the most experienced men on the mission. At 26 years of age, only Haskins and Scout were older and more seasoned amongst the men in the regiment. They had the most experience facing the wilds of the open trail with nothing but stars above and dirt below their bedding.

In spite of his superior seasoning, his imagination ran wild with thoughts of bears, packs of wolves, and other unnamed predators. A man's mind creates all kinds of possibilities when afraid. Johnson kept telling himself that the animals would be foolish to attack two armed men, especially one as experienced as Haskins, but his fear wouldn't be allayed in spite of his best efforts. Things don't always make sense out in the wild. Tolerating and managing his fear was the best he could do in the present situation.

Johnson resumed his pacing back and forth. A few minutes later he thought his eye caught movement east of his position. He slowly went down on one knee to make less of a profile against the sky, as his training had taught him. Cautiously bringing his musket up to shoulder level he stared hard into the darkness, willing his eyes to see any movement. Johnson reminded himself to not make any sudden movements. He'd been trained to watch for movement when standing guard. Johnson quickly glanced over at Haskins, and was surprised to see him casually sitting with his back to a tree. Johnson wondered if he might be overly concerned and just needed to relax. He attempted to signal Haskins to look east, but Haskins didn't look his way. Johnson looked back to where he thought he'd seen motion, searching for signs of trouble. He thought he saw something out of the corner of his eye, yet nothing was there when he turned his head to look directly.

Johnson hazarded another quick look over at Haskins, who was still sitting against the tree. Only discipline kept Johnson from calling aloud to Haskins.

"Damn it Haskins, why won't ya look," he thought.

Then, as if from out of nowhere, a large animal bowled Johnson over onto the ground. Haskins responded automatically by raising his musket to aim a quick shot at the animal. Just as Haskins squeezed the trigger he was knocked off his feet as well, with his shot harmlessly missing high. As Haskins came to his senses, he saw a large wolf had hold of his left forearm.

The pain almost took away Haskins's consciousness as the wolf sunk his teeth deeply into the muscles of his arm. Although he was on the edge of panic, he had just enough presence of mind to realize he had to keep the powerful animal's jaws away from his neck or he was done for. Trying to ignore the searing pain in his arm, he grabbed the wolf's neck with his free arm and rolled over onto his side to get more leverage. Just as Haskins began to get some distance between the wolf's jaws and his own neck, he was struck from the back by a second wolf. It was as if the second wolf sensed the moment his brother required help. The second wolf's entire weight landed on Haskins's back and head, knocking his head against a rock. That was the last the scout knew of that night.

The next morning Haskins opened his eyes to the soft light of morning. A dull ache in his head came with consciousness.

Haskins moved his left arm to touch his head and felt agonizing pain in the arm. Confusion swept over him, as he had no immediate memory of why his head and arm hurt. As Haskins tried to remember what happened, he heard murmuring voices nearby.

"Looks like he's comin' to, Lieutenant." Haskins saw a couple faces looking at him with concern. He recognized John's face. John smiled as he saw Haskins was conscious.

"Ya lucky to be alive soldier," said John. Haskins only smiled weakly. He still had no memory of what happened. Sensing his confusion, John decided to fill in the gaps in memory.

"I don't know what ya remember, but you an' Johnson were standin' watch over the mess tent last night. At some point ya both were attacked by a pack o' wolves. Thanks be to God that Scout heard the commotion. It was only his quick thinkin' an' bravery that saved ya, Haskins."

Haskins took a few moments to take in what he'd learned and gather his slow moving thoughts. After searching for the words for a bit, he formed a question that he weakly voiced.

"What, uh, what did Scout do?"

John looked around for Scout, and not seeing him, sent Pumroy to fetch him. Pumroy walked west down to the river's edge. He looked downriver, and not seeing anything, looked upriver. Pumroy turned all the way around as he looked for any sign of Scout. Not catching any signs of Scout's camp, he walked down river for a good half mile, and then turned around to walk back upriver. He threw his arms up in the air as he cursed aloud.

"Damn Scout, where the hell 're ya," said an exasperated Pumroy.

"Is that what you're doing, Pumroy? I been watching you the last thirty minutes, and I kept wondering whether you were looking for a hot rock or your own arse," said a voice behind him. Pumroy turned to see Scout sitting with his back against a tree. With one tree to either side of him, Scout was well hidden. Pumroy made his way up to Scout's camp.

"Now why din't ya let on you was there, damn it! I been strainin' my eyes tryin' to find your hide," complained Pumroy.

"And miss all this priceless entertainment? Now why would I want to do that," said Scout with a twinkle in his eye. "You're more fun to watch than a bear in heat."

"Yeah, that be very funny," groaned Pumroy. Pumroy looked around and noted the isolated setting. He figured Scout's camp must be a good half mile from camp.

"So why do ya keep your own camp anyways? I never understood why you the only one that don't make camp with the rest o' us," mused Pumroy. Scout laughed as he nodded.

"Well, let's just say I can't stand to be too close to bears in heat," answered Scout. Pumroy gave Scout a sideways stare, and then shook his head slowly.

"So, you didn't come all the way down here to ask me about my camp," said Scout.

"Yeah, Haskins is awake an' the Lieutenant sent me for ya."

John looked up as he heard Scout and Pumroy approach. "Scout, come over here. Tell Haskins what happened last night, an' how ya saved his hide." Scout knelt next to Haskins so that he could see him.

"Well Haskins, there isn't much to tell. I wasn't sleeping much. We both knew the critters were wolves. I've seen those kind of markings before, and there isn't another animal in these parts that tears canvas like that. Anyways, I wasn't really sleeping and my instincts told me the critters were about. So I made my way up toward the mess tent and climbed up into a tree on the west side of the mess tent. I didn't have to wait long until I heard a snarl and a gun go off. I know that snarl; heard it more times than I'd like to remember. Good thing there was enough light from the moon for me to aim and fire. I was lucky to git one of them."

"Scout got the one on top o' you, Haskins," interjected John.

"Yeah," Scout continued. "I was lucky to git the one on top of you, and uh, the rest scattered before I could get another shot off."

Haskins shuddered involuntarily as he thought of what might have been. John noticed the paleness of his face.

"Can't believe I let 'em get me," muttered Haskins. "That never happens to me."

"All right men, let's give Haskins some breathin' room. Lay back down, Haskins, you're not going nowhere for now," ordered John.

Just then Thomas walked up to see how the patients were doing. Johnson had been torn up worse than Haskins, and was lying next to Haskins with both of his arms and his face bandaged. Dr. Dickens inspected his bandaging work as Thomas arrived.

"Doctor, how're the patients coming along?" asked Thomas.

"They just regained consciousness. We'll have to wait and see how the injuries heal."

"How bad are they, Doc?" asked Thomas.

"One thing's for sure, they're in no condition to travel for now. Haskins isn't too bad, but the wolves mauled Johnson pretty good. He's got lacerations across the face and both arms, and the muscle tissue may have been damaged on his left arm," Dr. Dickens summed up.

"All right, we stay put for today. I hate to give them damn Yorkers another day's march ahead o' us, but we have to tend to our wounded. We'll give Haskins an' Johnson a day o' rest, and we'll reevaluate tomorrow. I am to be awakened to take Haskins spot for guard duty," ordered Captain Chittenden.

"An' I'll take Johnson's spot. We're gonna have to rethink our strategy for protecting the supplies," interjected John.

"And we're gonna half t' find more meat. Those damn wolves stole another side of beef! I've only enough beef for two more days. I'll rip those damn wolves apart with my bare hands if I git ahold of 'em," said an angry Chambers.

"Those damn wolves aren't gonna be easily outsmarted," John said.

Thomas looked around the camp, spotted the man he looked for, and headed over to him. "Scout, take a walk with me." Thomas directed Scout to the edge of camp.

"Scout," Thomas began, "the one thing that's clear to me is that we need 'nother guard strategy. I'm not gonna sit back an' watch as those wolves pick us off one or two at a time. I don' know how we gonna do this, an' I believe ya have the most experience dealin' with wolves. What ideas do ya have?"

"I don't know, Cap. I certainly had my fill o' run-ins with the critters, but I don't know much about defending a food supply. Shoot them before they get their teeth in you."

"Come on," interrupted Thomas, "this is no time for false modesty. We need the use o' your experience. How can we defend ourselves from wolves out 'n the wild? I don' give a damn whether you've guarded food before. How do we best position ourselves with wolves?"

"I think you ought to ask the man with the most experience, and that would be Colonel Haskins."

"Damn it, Scout, don' do that to yourself. Ya puttin' 'nother man above yaself, an' ya gettin' the short end o' the deal. Now, ya got a good bit o' your own experience, an' right now we need it."

This was all the prodding Scout needed. With the Captain having stated his case like an order, Scout was ready to assume the role. "From a tree. The only position that could be defended out here is a tree. Anywhere else than a tree, they can get to you. And they will."

"Go on," ordered Thomas.

"Well, there ain't much else to say. I think we ought t' put the guards up in trees. Now of course high enough they can't get to ya like the food. That's the only way I know to not have to be watching your back all night."

"Of course, why din't I think o' that myself," said Thomas. Wolves can jump, but they can't climb trees. If we're high enough up, they can't get to us. Anywhere else, we're exposed. Then that settles it. Scout, I want ya to show every man in this camp how to do this right. Maybe, just maybe we'll be ready for 'em this time." Thomas waved John over to join them.

"Lieutenant, call the whole regiment over to the mess tent. In the meantime, Scout, I want ya to pick out the best trees to position ourselves in. I s'pose we're gonna half to start hunting soon as well," said Thomas.

By dusk every man in the regiment understood the new guard duty strategy. Scout placed each of the two guards in separate trees, one on either side of the mess tent. The trees selected by Scout were large, sturdy trees, situated several paces outside the camp yet close enough to the mess tent to see it. Each man equipped himself with a musket and plenty of ball and powder. From the vantage point of the trees, the men hoped to have time to reload if need be. There was a lighter, easier mood about the regiment after living in almost constant fear the past two days.

Thomas normally kept his sword down by his feet when he slept, but since the wolves appeared, he placed the prized sword at his left shoulder before retiring for the night. He thought he could most quickly draw the sword from this position. The entire regiment took more care for their weapons since the coming of the wolves. The smell of oil permeated the camp, gun cleaning oil that is. Thomas unpleasantly noted that his tent was amongst the closest to the mess tent. Well, there was nothing to do about that now.

It took several shakes to rouse Thomas from his slumber. He had to be told several times until he comprehended that it was time for his watch. Until tonight Thomas had enjoyed the luxury of not being awakened for duty, and took a number of minutes to rouse himself to stand guard. The first thing he did was fasten his sword to his belt. By now Thomas had trained with the broadsword many years. Even MacDonald showed surprise at how much mastery Thomas had developed, and openly expressed his pride. Thomas felt more protected feeling the weight of his sword at his side than holding any kind of firearm in his hands.

While climbing up into the tree, a branch scratched the side of his face. Thomas cursed under his breath and felt to see if he was bleeding. Fortunately the scratch had not penetrated far enough to draw blood. Thomas rubbed his red eyes and yawned as he settled into his position in the northerly guard tree. A secure location within arms reach was quickly found for the ball and powder. He checked to be sure the musket was properly loaded and laid it across his lap. Lastly, but certain not least, he situated his broadsword that he might quickly draw it. He kept the sword within its sheath to avoid dropping it.

Thomas hoped he wouldn't find himself in hand-to-hand combat with a wolf. Thomas had developed a quiet confidence, yet rarely overestimated himself. Certainly he did not expect to outmatch a wolf in hand-to-hand combat with only his sword.

Looking over at the other tree, Thomas took note of John's position. Thomas took some comfort knowing that his trusted friend watched nearby. It wasn't long before Thomas noticed his mounting anxiety. His heart began racing, his hands were soon moist, and a lump developed in his throat. He hadn't expected to be this anxious. He reminded himself that he'd never faced a wolf.

Any semblance of a sound captured Thomas's attention. After awhile, he concluded that he must be imagining some sounds altogether and tried to calm himself. He forced himself to take several deep breaths while he closed his eyes. Until he noticed his heart rate and breathing slow, he wouldn't allow himself to open his eyes. His eyes seemed to betray him. Many times he thought he detected movement in one direction or another. Each time he looked more closely, there was nothing there. It calmed him some to remember that a man's eyes can play tricks on him in the dark. Right now the only light was a lantern hung outside the mess tent to provide the guards with some light. Thomas also reminded himself that he was up in a tree, not as vulnerable as he might be, and that he didn't have to see the wolves quickly. He would know when they made an attempt on the mess tent, as that would be plain enough.

His muscles stiffening, Thomas repositioned himself more comfortably. In the midst of moving, he thought he heard something. He quickly dismissed it as his mind playing another trick on him, but then he heard it again. There was a familiar ring to the low sound, but he couldn't think of where he'd heard it before. Then, on the third time, it came to him; it was the sound he and John had used to signal one another since they were boys. Thomas looked over at John to see him waving, and breathed a deep sigh of relief. John signaled that their watch was over, and that he was going to awaken the next pair of guards.

Fifteen minutes later Thomas gratefully collapsed in his tent and was asleep almost immediately. The next thing he knew was shouts and musket fire. Thomas instinctively grabbed his sword, unsheathed it and stepped out of his tent. He straightened himself to his full height and was just turning to the left as he saw a wolf take his final steps before lunging at Thomas's neck. Fortunately instinct and training took over, for Thomas was in shock and no state to be thinking quickly and clearly. With a quick and powerful slash the sword flashed across the belly of the wolf, essentially eviscerating it. The weight and momentum of the beast carried it crashing into Thomas and knocked him to the ground. Much to Thomas's relief the wolf had died almost instantly.

He disentangled himself from the dead wolf and hurried to the mess tent. A flash of light came from his right along with the familiar sound of exploding powder. Black smoke filled the air, making it difficult to see clearly. Another musket fired and a loud yelp resulted. Several wolves lay on the ground, some still moving. Thomas scanned the scene, unsure of how to respond. On the ground was one of his men, wrestling with a wolf that had ahold of his right arm. Even amidst the chaos of the scene, Thomas realized the men in the trees couldn't fire on the animal, as they just as likely would kill the man. At the same time he knew the man had little time to live if something wasn't done at once. Thomas lunged and ran the point of his sword almost all the way through the side of the wolf, twisting the blade to make a quick death sure. Thomas heard another musket shot explode near him as he quickly swung his head around, scanning for more enemies. He saw the last of the wolves running into the darkness.

Thomas bent down to tend to the injured man, seeing that it was Pumroy. The wolf lay in the dirt next to Pumroy, clearly dead. Pumroy held his right arm, but otherwise seemed unhurt. One of the guards was climbing down from the tree.

"No, soldier, stay up in the tree till we're sure they're gone," ordered Thomas. The man looked down at Thomas with eyes wide as saucers, and then slowly remounted his post.

"Is anyone hurt?" yelled out Thomas. Several men called back that they were unhurt. Scout appeared at Thomas's side, having just reloaded his musket.

"Pretty sure they're gone, for now at least," assessed Scout.

"Okay, help me search for injured men," answered Thomas. "Dr. Dickens, over here, got a man hurt!"

Dr. Dickens knelt by Pumroy and examined his arm. In the dim light it was impossible to tell how deeply the wolf had penetrated, and Dr. Dickens wrapped it well to stop the bleeding. Pumroy's shirt was well covered in blood. Thomas looked up as John laid a hand on his shoulder.

"Two men hurt all told; Pumroy here and Slater on the other side o' the tent. Can't tell how bad Slater be," reported John.

"I'll be with Slater in a moment," said Dr. Dickens.

Thomas and John helped Pumroy back to his tent. They gave him a couple shots of whiskey for the pain and left him to catch whatever sleep the pain would allow.

"Damn, Thomas, them critters 're persistent," swore John.

"Ain't that the truth," Thomas responded. "I'm still shakin' pretty good myself."

"Yeah, ya ain't the only jittery one."

Once the regiment realized that no one had been seriously injured, hoots and hollers flowed freely. Much back slapping and congratulations were exchanged as the men sensed they had achieved a victory, and so they had. Having been unable to kill a single wolf before now, there hadn't been anything to celebrate until now. Four wolves lay dead near the mess tent.

During the celebrating, a couple of the men came across the wolves Thomas had slain. It was obvious from the wounds that the wolves had been killed by sword. As the captain was the only member of the regiment to carry a sword, the men immediately suspected whose work they were admiring. The two men, Morse and Pumroy, quickly confirmed their suspicions in a brief inquiry with their captain. Pumroy hadn't stayed in his tent long, as the cheering had brought him out. They quietly decided to make something of this. Pumroy waited for the majority of the raucous celebrating to die down. He then fetched a pint of ale for himself and Morse and called for silence as he proposed a toast.

"Gentlemen, hear me. I'll make a toast to our worthy captain," began Pumroy. Once he had succeeded in gathering the men's attention amidst renewed cheers, he continued. Pumroy placed himself behind one of the fallen beasts.

"Gentlemen, observe the defeated enemy at me feet," He pointed to the dead wolf with his pint of ale.

"Here lie the remains o' one o' two wolves our worthy captain courageously kilt. As ya can plainly see, this wolf has been kilt by sword across the belly. I'll have ya know the wolf was kilt as he was beginnin' to attack the tents o' sleepin' men."

A new chorus of cheers interrupted Pumroy's toast. He signaled for silence and continued. "It's hard to say how many o' ya worthy men our brave captain may o' saved by his defense o' our sleepin' camp. Many o' you may not be standing 'ere right now if it weren't for the captain's brave and quick actions. Join me in giving a cheer to our worthy captain, defender of our lives!" Pumroy received a rousing response as the men saluted Thomas.

Thomas grew increasingly uncomfortable as Pumroy's toast went on. He didn't mind a brief mention of his slaying the wolf, but this was too much. Thomas felt that he was being made out to be some kind of hero that he wasn't. To say he acted quickly and slayed a wolf or two was fine, but to suggest that he saved the lives of sleeping men seemed farfetched. After a moment's reflection, he decided to set things right. This became easy to do, as Morse had riled the men to egg on Thomas to give a speech. Thomas stepped forward and put his hands up to signal for silence.

"Gentlemen, I thank ya for ya generous toast, a bit too generous perhaps. We all have cause to celebrate tonight. However, tonight's actions be not the efforts o' one man alone, an' I can't take credit where credit ain't due. I will not have ya be led to believe that my actions alone saved the camp tonight. Yeah, I slayed two o' the wolves killed tonight. I wanna recognize Scout an' Bennett for also each killin' a wolf tonight from the trees. Their fine marksmanship was part o' repelling the pack's attack on us tonight. I further want to congratulate Scout and Lt. Jackson for creating a successful guard duty strategy. I believe their efforts are the main reason we be celebratin' tonight. Gentlemen, we are a regiment, an' each o' us depends on the others to watch our backs. None o' us can do this alone. Now, I want each o' ya to join Morse an' Pumroy in celebrating with a pint o' ale. Now off with ya!"

Thomas helped himself to a pint of ale, sat down by the fire and was soon joined by John. "So Captain, I guess ya didn't take to Pumroy's toast too warmly," John said.

"That obvious, huh?" John chuckled as he looked at Thomas to see if he was joking.

"Well, it seemed obvious enough to me, but then again I know ya better than most o' the others," answered John. If Thomas had joked earlier, a serious look came over him now.

"I won't have the men put me on a pedestal, John. I'll have 'em know me as a man with flaws, just as they be. I may be the rankin' officer, but I see myself as no better nor worse than any other man."

"Thomas, we been friends long enough for me to know ya got your feet on the ground an' aren't easily filled full o' hot air."

"An' that reminds me, ya been makin' a pedestal for Haskins along with Scout an' some o' the others."

"How do ya see that?" asked John.

"When Haskins toots his own horn with them stories he tells, ya right there cheerin' with the others."

"But ya gotta admit Haskins sure has some amazing stories o' what he done," said John.

"His experience ain't the issue. Yeah, he's a skilled scout. The point is that he makes himself outta be some kind o' hero," explained Thomas. "He don't got his feet on the ground." John rubbed his growing beard pensively.

"So what if I am cheerin' him on?"

"When ya put Haskins on the pedestal, where do that put you?" confronted Thomas.

"Well, I don' know."

"Well, think on it," suggested Thomas. John looked away and pondered Thomas's challenge.

"I'm not sure I get what ya sayin', but I do see that I been puttin' Haskins on a pedestal."

"Well good, maybe its 'nough to see that for now," suggested Thomas.

Both men were silent for several minutes, each pondering his private thoughts. "I'm thankful to have you with me on this mission, John. We've been friends a long time, an' now I need ya friendship more than ever. Bein' apart from Liz been hard on me. Bein' away from my old friend MacDonald been hard on me. I miss them somethin' terrible. I know all o' the men in the regiment some, an' Scout a fair bit, but you're the only man with us that I know well." John stood and slapped Thomas on the back as he headed for his tent.

The next morning Thomas stepped out of his tent and stretched. As he slowly became more awake, he noticed the sound of laughter. The laughter puzzled him, as the men normally didn't laugh much at dawn. The next time he heard the strange sound, he turned to see it coming from the direction of the dead wolves. Several men were crouched around the wolves, and appeared to be doing something to them. Curious, Thomas made his way closer. Surrounded by several men and two dead wolves was Haskins, standing with his back to Thomas.

"That's right boys," began Haskins, "I want souvenirs o' the victory I led you boys to. Cut off one o' the front paws from each o' the wolves for me, an' you boys can have whatever else ya want. An' don't forget..."

This was all Thomas needed to hear. He slowly shook his head and walked back to the fire for some coffee. The injured men didn't feel much better, even after some sleep. They were sore and in pain. Pumroy's injuries proved minor and wouldn't prevent him from traveling at any speed. Haskins seemed to be feeling just fine. When asked, he dismissed his injury as a mere scratch. However, Johnson turned out to be in significantly worse condition. Johnson could hardly bear to walk at a slow pace, not to mention riding at any pace. He tried to put on a brave face and told his officers he could travel, yet John and Thomas were not convinced. Thomas pulled John and Dr. Dickens aside for a private conversation.

"I don' know what we're gonna do here," admitted Thomas. "I can't bear the thought o' givin' the damned Yorkers another day's distance on us. Those poor prisoners. I hate to think what they might be goin' through. But, I don' know if Johnson can ride."

"I saw how Johnson winced when he even walked. I'm sure he made it sound as though he's better off than he is," said John.

"Johnson can travel slowly sir, but it will certainly slow his healing; might even delay his healing considerably dependin' on how much he's bounced around," said Dr. Dickens.

"There's no easy answer here. I too hate to give the cursed Yorkers another minute's lead on us. Look Thomas, I feel for Johnson, but we have to move on." Thomas pondered John's counsel.

"Ya probably right. We have to get back on the trail before it's too cold to follow. Damned wolves! They cost us time we don' have to spend. We'll ride as slow as we dare, but Johnson will have to travel for now."

The regiment resumed their tracking of the Yorkers. They had to travel slower than Thomas wanted, but at least they travelled. The men's spirits improved as they were now back on the trail and away from the site of the attacks. In spite of the setback of having two good men injured, Thomas could feel the increased confidence in the regiment after last night's success. These men needed confidence in their skill and training, as most of them had been untested beyond the confines of the weekend training sessions. It's one thing to perform well practicing hand-to-hand combat with your fellow militia or shooting at targets; it's another thing to be able to keep your head fighting for your life against man or beast.

Winter 1747 - Salisbury, Connecticut Colony

Thomas had little trouble convincing Father to let him run an errand to town for him. Father was only too eager to allow Thomas to take another chore off his hands and didn't trouble himself to wonder why. Just in case, Thomas left the farm before giving Father too much time to think it over, as he didn't want to explain his reasons. Soon he arrived at the Feed 'n Seed.

"Hello, Mr. MacDonald."

"MacDonald looked up from his work, Oh, hello lad."

"Here's Father's list o' supplies."

MacDonald took the list and looked it over and began gathering the items. He glanced up from his work to see Thomas watching him.

"So lad, how ye be today?"

"I figure mostly just glad to be here," Thomas said sheepishly.

"That's good, lad."

"Ya mean ya really don' mind?" asked Thomas.

"Noo, I like yer visits, lad." Thomas grinned. After a moment he turned away, pretending to look at the stock shelves.

"Weel lad, that be good 'cause it means yer lettin' yerself want more."

"I don' know. It jist seems selfish to me," said Thomas honestly.

MacDonald chuckled. "Noo, lad. Many consider it selfish t' want fo' their souls. There be many things worse a man could want. Many don' understand that we all try t' feed oorselves, and often withoot knowin' we be hungry. Ye see lad, when we don't know we be hungry, more times than not we feed oorselves wi' food that's no good for our souls."

"I don' get it."

"Weel lad, forgive me for gettin' ahead o' ye. Few understand there's more than one kind o' food. For now suffice it t' say that it's good yer lettin' yerself be hungry for food that's not for yer stomach. And I'm glad t' help ye get it."

Thomas shifted his weight back and forth while he fidgeted with his hands. His eyes wandered around trying to find a comfortable landing place.

"Uh, well let me help ya fill that order," he said.

"Sure 'nough lad, ye can grab a sack o' grain fro' the back. Ye know where they be."

Once in the back room, Thomas breathed a sigh of relief. He paced back and forth a few minutes once he was sure MacDonald couldn't see him. He wiped sweaty palms on his pants and took a few deep breaths. He waited until he felt a little calmer before returning to the front of the store with the grain.

"So, do ya git hungry t' talk some too?" asked Thomas.

"Sure thing, lad."

"Then who do ya talk with?"

"Weel, first there's my dove Rachel, an' a couple o' old souls 'round town. I find meself in need o' their company quite regular, lad."

"That right? How regular do ya figure?"

"Ooh, I don't find meself keepin' track, yet it be certainly at least e'ry hand full o' days."

Thomas picked up the items and set them into a box, taking his time. "An' do these old friends talk 'bout their trees with ya as well?"

"Sure thing, lad. I think they come t' rely on the regular time as weel," answered MacDonald.

After a pause Thomas added, "There's somethin' else. I don' know if it has anythin' to do with my tree, but sometimes my stomach hurts. Do that mean anythin'?"

"'Course it do, lad."

"Then what?" asked Thomas.

"Weel, let's see if we can make heads 'r tail of it. Ye see lad, when somethin's doin' in oor bodies, it means they be tryin' t' tell us o' something important. So, what might yer stomach be tryin' to say?"

Thomas stood and wandered about the store aimlessly while he thought. "I don' know. Maybe that I ate somethin' bad?"

MacDonald chuckled, "Maybe lad, but I think there may be a bit more t' it. Now yer stomach, do it seem t' hurt any particular times now?"

"Yesterday it started hurtin' when Father came into the barn when I was feedin' the animals."

"Aye, then likely yer stomach be tellin' us somethin' 'bout how ye feel 'bout yer father," suggested MacDonald.

"But I don' think I feel much o' anything 'bout Father."

"Noo, ye just don't know it yet. Do ye think ye might be afraid o' yer father, lad?"

"Oh, yeah! He can erupt like a volcano when he's mad 'bout somethin'."

"Thar ye go, lad."

Thomas screwed up his eyes as he said, "There I go what?"

MacDonald laughed. "Come now lad, the truth o' it be right before yer nose. Yere stomach's tellin' us ye're afraid o' yere father when he's angry."

"Really? Is that what my stomach says? It seem kinda weird that my stomach talks 'bout anything. Well, at least anything 'xcept for food."

"Nae lad, thar be nothin' more natural. I find meself makin' a regular habit o' listenin' t' me body. I don' understand all she say, but I hear plenty."

"Ya know Mr. MacDonald, you say some o' the weirdest things... but I s'pose I'm gettin' used to it. Well, I best be goin'," said Thomas.

Thomas reluctantly admitted to himself he'd like to see MacDonald every day. He couldn't allow himself to though. Yet he did want to let himself see MacDonald more often than the every couple weeks it had been. In spite of what he'd just been told, he still felt selfish wanting to talk with MacDonald so often. Thomas decided he'd permit himself one visit per week to the Feed 'n Seed and no more. Even once a week seemed overdoing it. He took note of today being Saturday and told himself he could go see Mr. MacDonald next Saturday, but not before.

The next week dragged on slowly. Thomas went about his farming duties faithfully, yet his mind was on Saturday when he could next see Mr. MacDonald. Thomas no longer had the distraction of school, having stopped a year ago. Father had lost his hired help about the same time and couldn't keep up with the work on his own, even with the boys' help after school and on the weekends. Father and Mama determined that the boys no longer needed schooling. After all, they could now read and write basic sentences and perform basic arithmetic. What else did they need to know that they couldn't learn on the farm? Thomas and Ben, now seventeen and nineteen, worked every day on the farm just like Father. Little Sally was the only one allowed to continue in school. She wasn't permitted to help on the farm much anyways.

Thomas began his workday by feeding the animals. Feeding had been his job as long as he'd been big enough to do it on his own. The family farm included four pair of oxen, a bull, two hogs, eighteen steer, eight heifers, eighty-two cows, five mares, ten colts, thirty-two sheep and a sorrel horse. Thomas also had a horse of his own. Mercifully, some of the animals could feed themselves, but most of them required some help from Thomas. The whole job took quite a bit of time if you didn't cut corners. Thomas had become more concerned about each animal getting the type of food it needed to prosper and be satisfied. As a younger boy, he hadn't thought much about the animals' needs; they were merely another chore to be completed. But now he liked to take a little more time and talk to each animal, or at least each group of animals. Maybe it was just in his head, but the animals seemed to respond differently to Thomas.

Thomas stared off in the distance, not looking at anything in particular. He was taking a break from work. Ben worked next to Thomas in the field. He noticed Thomas being idle and sat down in the field next to him.

"Hey little brother, what ya thinkin' on?" asked Ben.

"Huh? Oh, nothin' really."

"Seems like ya thinkin' quite a bit more. Ya din't used to."

"Yeah. That's probably right," acknowledged Thomas. After a pause Ben continued. "Ya know little brother, it seem like we don' play that much no more."

"Ya think so? Shoot Ben, I din't really notice. I'm sorry," offered Thomas.

"Oh, it's nothin' really; just wonderin' I s'pose," dismissed Ben.

He didn't want to tell Ben, but Thomas had been thinking about tomorrow being Saturday. Thomas had trouble concentrating on his work, as he wondered what he might talk to MacDonald about. Although it didn't really matter what they talked about, Thomas just wanted to see his old friend. He glanced over at Ben, who was already back to work, and put his shoulder back to the task.

Right after breakfast Thomas had the cart rigged up and was on his way to the Feed 'n Seed. He could hardly wait to see Mr. MacDonald. MacDonald understood him in a way that he hadn't known before. He seemed to understand Thomas better than Thomas himself. He was beginning to believe there was something to that whole tree thing. Thomas found he had more and more to say to MacDonald.

"Hey, Mr. MacDonald."

"Oh, hello there lad."

"What are ya up to?" asked Thomas.

"Weel lad, I'm just checkin' o'er the delivery brought i' this mornin'."

"Oh, I see. Do ya get deliveries regular?"

"Nae, lad. They get the supplies here whenever they can."

Thomas glanced over at Rachel, not feeling comfortable saying too much with her in the room. MacDonald followed Thomas's glance and asked Rachel to attend to some work in the front of the store. Rachel turned on her heels to leave the room; her eyes blazed briefly and her jaw clenched as she looked back at Thomas. MacDonald didn't notice her look. Thomas felt a knot in his stomach, yet quickly dismissed it.

"So lad, now what be on yer mind," continued MacDonald.

"I been thinkin' on Ben, my brother. He said somethin' 'bout us not playin' as much. I don' know, maybe we don' play like we used t'."

"An' why do ye think that be changed?" asked MacDonald.

"I don' know... Maybe 'cause I comin' here more."

MacDonald nodded as he sat down. "I can right see why yer brither might be upset."

"Ya think he's upset?" asked Thomas.

"Weel I don't know for sure lad, but why else would he be speakin' on it?"

Thomas took a seat on a box and sat with his hands under his chin. "So what do I do if he's upset?"

"What do ye wanna do, lad?"

"I don' know. I can't think o' anything; can you?"

"Weel sure lad, ye might jist talk with 'im.'"

Thomas scratched his head as he pondered that one. "But what would I talk 'bout?"

"'Bout his comment o' not playin' as much," suggested MacDonald.

"Oh no, I can't even picture Ben talkin' like that. He'd just act like it was nothin'.'"

"Aye lad, then there might be nothin' further to do."

"Ya mean I don' have to do anything?" asked Thomas.

"Aye, lad."

MacDonald and Thomas were silent for a few minutes. Thomas shifted in his seat. "I figure I feel bad 'bout Ben; probably he feels left out. I s'pose I'm hurtin' his feelin's... I don' know, it reminds me o' when we used to play all the time. Back then we was best friends. I remember the time we first found that ole cave. We couldn't o' been more 'an eight or ten. We was playin' hide 'an seek an' Ben was it. I din't know where to go, since Ben knew all my spots an' he'd always find me right off. I ran up the creek lookin' for something when I came across that big rock. I bent down behind it to hide. I figure I musta lost my footin' an' I fell back. I looked up an' saw some kinda o' opening. Just then I saw Ben comin' round a tree straight for me, so I ducked into the opening in the rock. It turned out to be this big cave. Well, 'course Ben never found me in there. Probably the only time he din't find me."

"Good memories, lad."

"Maybe I miss them times some," said Thomas.

"Aye lad."

Thomas wiped his eyes with the sleeve of his shirt; he stared down at the ground. "I also been thinkin' 'bout my sister. She doesn't really have anyone to talk with. I kinda wanna be somebody she can talk to."

"There ye go, lad. Now that yer lettin' yerself need to talk, yer seeing it i' others. That's quite a gift yer offerin' 'er."

"Really, what gift?" asked Thomas.

"Weel lad, yer offering the lass some food for 'er soul. There ain't many gifts more important than that, especially if she's goin' withoot."

"I guess our family's not really a talkin' family. I din't understand that before. She probably don't have anyone to really talk to, just like I din't; till I met you o' course."

"I'm glad for ye, lad. Maybe the scales 'r fallin' from yer eyes, lad. Yer seein' things ye din't hae eyes t' see before. An' thank God for it."

Thomas didn't see that God had anything to do with his new perspective, but he decided to not pursue the issue. He was more interested in talking about his sister. "Do ya think Sally's hungry to talk 'bout her tree also?"

"Tis likely, lad. Not many know they hae a tree, not to mention it bein' unwatered. The young lass hae likely been waitin' fo' someone t' see that she's been goin' hungry."

"Well, I just find myself wantin' to take more time. To be honest, I din't use to take any time to talk to Sally. I can't explain it, but I just wanna now."

"There ye go, lad. I'm proud o' ye."

"Really? How come?"

"Cause ye become a tree that's not only learnt to take in yer nutrients, but ye now 'r able to give 'em away t' others, lad."

Thomas smiled. Thomas felt good inside, yet also a bit strange. He'd never thought of himself as someone to help others before. "Figure I best be goin'. I'll see ya later, Mr. MacDonald."

On his way out Thomas stopped to have a word with Rachel. He felt guilty for pushing her out of the room. He wanted privacy with the old man, but felt selfish wanting MacDonald all to himself. As he walked up to her the knot in his stomach returned.

"Hey Rachel." Rachel looked up from her work and nodded.

"I din't mean for ya to be dismissed from the back room."

"Sure ye did, Thomas."

"Oh, I guess ya sore 'bout that."

"Aye I s'pose I am," Rachel responded sharply. "I know ye've come t' rely on me father, but I don't hae to like it. Ye have yer own father, don't ye? Why don't ye go talk t' him?"

There was an awkward silence as they stared at each other. Thomas didn't know what to say. Rachel held Thomas gaze with fire in her eyes.

"Well, maybe I should. I guess I'll be on my way then."

At this Thomas left the store. He felt horrible about the whole thing. He hadn't realized how upset Rachel had been. Thomas felt like a heel for visiting MacDonald as often as he did. Maybe visiting once of week was too often. Maybe he ought to cut back to once a month. It felt bad to Thomas to think of only seeing his dear friend once a month, but he felt so guilty about Rachel, he didn't think he could bring himself to visit more than that. Thomas wondered if maybe he was too hungry and wasn't supposed to want to come weekly. He didn't know what to do.

Before he got home he determined to cut his visits to monthly, and that he'd find a way to bear it. Rachel certainly had a right to her own father. Thomas felt he had no right to MacDonald, since he wasn't even a relative. Thomas felt as though something had been taken out of him, leaving a hole behind. He brushed aside tears as he neared home. In spite of his best efforts, his tears continued to flow even as he arrived home. Thomas walked around the property trying to regain control of his emotion. He couldn't stop wondering what he'd do only seeing MacDonald once a month.

Rachel knew Thomas came to her father for a listening ear, and she even felt for him some, but she didn't want to share her father with anyone else. Rachel didn't want to risk losing her special relationship. She had broached the subject with him the last time Thomas had come. Her father had been kind and understanding about her fear. At the same time, Mr. MacDonald had been firm about his desire to continue his friendship with Thomas. He'd said, "How can I not serve one in need when my Father in heaven has so graciously given to me?"

Rachel had not been satisfied by her father's response, but she knew when he set his mind to something, there was no changing it. Part of the problem was that Rachel didn't have many friends. She only had one girlfriend. Her father was her best friend. She chatted with a few of the local girls that came into the store, but they were just acquaintances.

Rachel enjoyed letting Thomas have it. She was relieved when he didn't visit all the next week. She was pleased when he didn't visit the second week either. When Thomas failed to come the third week, she felt a twinge of guilt creep into her mind. When the fourth week was well underway, she began hoping Thomas would visit and was relieved when he finally arrived.

"Rachel, can I talk with your father?"

"Aye, he be in the back."

Thomas nodded and cautiously crept into the back room. He waited by the door until the old man noticed him.

"There ye be, lad. Where hae ye been all this time?"

"Uh..." Thomas wasn't sure what to say. He didn't know if MacDonald knew why he'd waited to come back. Had he and Rachel spoken? Thomas decided to just wait.

"Cat got yer tongue, lad. I say, where hae ye been these four weeks?"

"Uh, well, I just thought maybe I was visitin' a little too much. I, uh, thought maybe I should wait a bit till I came back."

"Whatever for, lad? What gave ye the idea that ye were visitin' too much?"

"Uh, I don' know. I just don't wanna be selfish with ya time or anythin'. I just thought comin' every week might be overdoin' it. I know ya got a busy store an' a daughter an' everything."

"A busy store an' a daughter?" repeated MacDonald.

MacDonald didn't understand what Thomas was trying to say. He knew something had happened since his last visit, but he didn't know what. MacDonald was scratching his head when Rachel came in. Since Thomas had stood near the door, she had heard almost everything said. Partly she couldn't help hearing with Thomas so close, and partly she had been trying to listen. Rachel normally wouldn't consider eavesdropping, but her guilt and curiosity got the best of her. She'd wanted him to come less often, but now that she could see and hear the misery in his voice, she felt sorry for the boy. Rachel knew enough about trees to hear Thomas's misery.

"I think I can shed a bit o' light, Father."

"Ye can, Rachel?"

"It's 'cause o' me the lad hasn't been comin'. I was too hard o' him the last time he was 'ere."

"O' what do ye speak, lass?"

"I was wrong, an' I'm sorry. Last time Thomas came, I was jealous an' angry, an' I told 'im I didn't like 'im comin' to see ye so often. I went so far as t' suggest he speak wi' his own father. I'm sorry, Thomas. I was angry...and jealous, but I went too far wi' ye."

"What have ye done, lass? How could ye let yer anger get the best o' ye like that? Do ye realize what ye hae done to a lad whose only just gettin' t' know 'is tree? Do ye know he hae no other t' go t'? Although they be farmers, 'is own don't know much 'bout what makes lads grow."

"I know, father. I'm sorry t' the both o' ye."

MacDonald sighed and exhaled his anger at his daughter. He was softened by her contrition. He realized he had a part in this too. MacDonald shook his head slowly from side to side.

"Oh, Rachel. I done ye wrong too. I failed t' see what me time wi' the lad was doin' t' ye. O' course ye be jealous. I failed t' talk wi' ye 'nough 'bout me an' Thomas... It be me that needs the forgivin'. Will ye forgive an old man for not seein' the leaves o' his own daughter?" Rachel rushed into her father's arms and wept.

Thomas was greatly relieved at Rachel's interruption. Rachel surprised him with her confession. Thomas figured she'd still be angry with him. He smiled at both daughter and father.

After releasing his daughter, MacDonald looked to Thomas with kindness and firmness. "Lad, ye must 'ave had a long month."

"Yeah," was all Thomas said as he nodded and looked at his boots.

Thomas was reluctant to say too much about his deliberations over the last month, but his eyes filled with water in spite of his efforts to hold back his emotion. He had agonized over how long to wait, and when to go visit again. Many times he'd been to town and almost visited the Feed 'n Seed, only to turn away. It was only his strong dose of self-control that kept him away from MacDonald. He had longed to see the old man, and was lonely without him. Thomas found himself left to the refuge of his chores like an old familiar coat that has holes in it. The coat provides some relief from the cold wind, but not much.

When MacDonald merely waited, Thomas decided to say more. "It was a terrible long four weeks. I often started to come here, only to force myself to wait a bit longer. I guess I felt bad for takin' ya away from Rachel an' thought maybe I should wait a bit longer between visits. I thought I was being too hungry." Thomas looked down at the floor, ashamed to look at his old friend, fearing what he might see.

"Oh lad, nothing could be further fro' the truth. Ye're only beginnin' to let yerself hae an appetite. An' I got plenty t' go 'round fo' ye an' me Rachel both. But I'm afraid ye brung some o' this o' yerself, lad. After ye an' me Rachel had words, what kept ye from talkin' wi' me 'bout it? Oh lad, there was no need fo' ye to spend the better part o' a month frettin' o'er it. Ye could hae talked t' me 'bout it right off."

"But Mr. MacDonald, it don' seem right to take time away from a girl's father."

"Noo lad, that's between me Rachel an' me. That's not fo' ye t' be concerned aboot."

"How can it not be my concern if I'm the one takin' ya time?"

"Lad, what be yer concern has t' do wi' ye an' meself, an' not a thing more. If me Rachel's havin' her leaves ruffled by oor time spent, that's fo the lass an' me to work oot. Ye see?"

Thomas rubbed his damp hands on his pants as he thought over MacDonald's comments. "Well, I still don' see how the thing with Rachel don' concern me, but I get that I'm the one that made myself wait a whole four weeks an' nobody else. Damn, I guess I was a fool t' not jist come an' talk it out with ya. Maybe I din't have t' go through all that."

"Weel lad if ye see that much, maybe some good'll come oot o' this. Ye need t' take better care o' yer own tree. An' Rachel an' I got some tendin' t' do as weel. Ye know lad, maybe all this needed t' happen. Some things jist gotta be gone through for ye t' grow. Reminds me o' somethin' I read in that Poor Richard's Almanack by that Benjamin Franklin lad outta Philadelphia; he writes, 'Experience keeps a dear school, yet Fools will learn in no other'." MacDonald laughed heartily. "Weel lad, I s'pose we all been fools this time."

Thomas's boots seemed a bit lighter and he moved a step quicker. The walk home seemed to take almost no time at all. He felt more hopeful and was grateful to his old friend, and to Rachel. Thomas felt great relief that MacDonald hadn't confirmed his worst fears of telling him to come less often.

Sally's voice caught Thomas's attention, as he could hear her voice coming from her room. Thomas walked into her room to find her. "Hey there, Sally. What 're ya up to?"

"Oh, just playin' with my dolls."

"Is that right. So how's your day been?"

"I don' know, I guess 'bout the same as usual." There was little energy in Sally's voice. Her voice sounded tired, as if it were bearing a heavy load.

"Another borin' day, huh. Din't ya have anyone to play with?"

"Yup. It was mostly just me an' the dolls," confirmed Sally.

"Maybe most o' your days 're lonely?" suggested Thomas.

"Well, I have been alone most o' the day, if that's what ya mean."

"No, that's not what I mean. I'm not askin' who's been 'round; I'm askin' 'bout your tree."

"My tree?" repeated Sally. "Thomas, what on earth are ya talkin' 'bout. What tree?" Thomas laughed heartily. Now he had gotten her attention.

"I'm askin' 'bout your insides; ya know, how you're feelin'. Our trees 're the center o' us, an' our leaves show how the tree's doin'. It probably sounds kinda silly, but I think there's somethin' to it. An' your leaves look lonely to me, maybe they're droopin' a bit, I think for wantin' to talk with other folk."

Sally looked puzzled. She wasn't sure if her brother was crazy or saner than anyone else she knew. "Thomas, I don' know what you're talkin' 'bout. But just the same, there might be somethin' to what ya sayin'; what exactly I can't say."

"Maybe you've been waitin' for someone t' talk to," suggested Thomas. Sally looked doubtful, and felt uncomfortable with the direction of the conversation, yet she didn't want it to stop either.

"Maybe," was all she said.

"Look Sally, I know it probably sounds crazy to talk o' trees an' leaves an' such, especially when I ain't never mentioned it before. But it's somethin' I never woulda known if it weren't for Mr. MacDonald. He helped me see that I needed someone t' talk to, an' that I wadn't doin' so good without it. He taught me to talk 'bout myself, an' my own tree. 'Course I din't know it, but I found out I was waitin' for someone that knew how to draw me out. Ya know Sally, I never felt better in my life since I got to know Mr. MacDonald. Anyhow, maybe none o' this makes any sense, an' maybe ya don' feel lonely or even wanna talk. But if ya do, I wanna be the one to talk with ya. Okay?"

Thomas paused for a moment, and then left the room. He could see the puzzled look remaining on his sister's face, and thought she probably needed time to think it over. He didn't want to push her too much. However, he hoped she'd come around and accept his invitation to talk. He hated to think of her leaving herself lonely, and he knew what that was like.

Sally was indeed puzzled. She didn't know what to make of all this talk of trees and such. And yet she hoped to talk about it with Thomas again. Maybe hope awakened just a little bit and stuck its head above the ground for the first time for Sally. She decided to go ask Mama. Sally found Mama sweeping the floor in the front room.

"Mama, what do ya know 'bout trees an' leaves an' such?"

"What kinda trees are ya wondering 'bout, dear? We have several different kinds on the property."

"No, I don' mean that kind o' tree, I mean ya inside tree. Ya know, like when ya need to talk to somebody." Mama was thinking hard, screwing up her face.

"Sally, what on earth are you talkin' 'bout? I'm sure I have no idea 'bout an inside tree. I've never heard o' such a thing. It would just make a big mess to bring one o' them things inside the house. Now Sally, ya know ya can always talk to me if ya need to. Is that what this is all 'bout?"

Sally was trying to decide whether to pursue the subject more, and finally decided there probably wasn't much point. Sally was disappointed. She had hoped Mama would know all about inside trees. "Yes Mama, I know I can talk to ya," Sally said without much energy in her voice.

Mama seemed satisfied with this response and went back to her sweeping. "Okay now, but don' ya go an' bring such a thing to your father. He won't have nothin' to do with it, an' probably just get him mad."

"Yes, Mama." But Mama needn't have worried, for it wasn't even a thought for Sally to mention trees to Father.

Father and daughter had some tree tending to do. MacDonald sat down next to Rachel and put his arm around her shoulder. At first he merely held her without speaking. "Oh Rachel, my dove. I know we talked a wee bit 'bout me an' the lad, but I gather we din't talk 'nough. Hae ye felt ye weren't gettin' 'nough time wi' me?"

"Part o' me want to say 'aye,' but I don' know if it be true," answered Rachel. "Even though ye spend more time wi' Thomas than I'd like, ye still seem to spend plenty o' time wi' me."

"Maybe it's not so much the time I spend wi' the lad, but maybe it be how yer feelin' aboot that time," suggested MacDonald. Rachel pondered her father's words before responding.

"Aye, maybe yer right, Father. Maybe I've been afraid I'd lose what I hae with ye; that you'd want t' spend more an' more time wi' the lad, an' that ye wouldn't want t' be wi' me much."

"Oh, Rachel, nothin' could be further fro' the truth. I could no more pull away from ye than I could stop meself from breathin'. I'm sorry ye've been afraid. This talk o' yer fear makes me think o' yer mither."

"What aboot 'er?" cautiously asked Rachel.

"Weel, we haven't talked 'bout her much o' late, but I know ye miss 'er something terrible."

"Aye, I miss me mither e'ery day, but what hae that t' do with me feelings 'bout ye an' Thomas?"

"Oh, Rachel, after losin' yer mither at such a tender age, how could ye not be afraid o' losin' me as weel?" responded MacDonald.

Rachel began to cry. MacDonald pulled her close and held her for as long as she needed. He silently thanked God for him and Rachel being able to talk about such matters. At the same time, he couldn't imagine how he'd neglected to see how his time with Thomas impacted his precious daughter. Maybe he hadn't wanted to see.

A couple days later Thomas prepared to head into town to post a letter for Father. By now Father regularly asked Thomas whenever he had need of an errand to town. Sally had been watching for an opportunity to go to town with her brother, and overheard Father's request.

"Hey Thomas, ya goin' to town?"

"Yeah, little sister. Ya wanna come?"

"Ya bet I do."

Thomas enjoyed seeing the look of delight on Sally's face. It was rare to see anything like delight from her. He smiled and went out to hitch up the horse and cart. On the chance that Father would say no to her, Sally carefully avoided Father on her way out to meet

Thomas. She slipped out the back door as quietly as her hampered leg would allow. The old adage proved itself in this case: "where there's a will there's a way." Sally could be as quiet as anyone else when she really wanted to; she just wasn't as quick or nimble.

As they rode on toward town Thomas thought of how to best broach the subject of trees with Sally. He didn't want to press her too much on the new subject. However, as he pondered his options, Sally beat him to it.

"So Thomas, I been thinking 'bout our conversation the other night. I still wonder if you're crazy or somethin', but I wanna hear more 'bout trees an' leaves. I keep thinkin' 'bout what you were saying 'bout havin' someone to talk to. I don' know, maybe it would be nice to have someone to talk to sometimes."

"Ya know little sis, that's what it come down to for me - havin' someone to talk to. Someone to talk to that understands," said Thomas.

"Well, I thought more 'bout that too. Ya do seem happier since ya started talkin' to Mr. MacDonald. I hadn't really noticed the change until ya said something 'bout it the other night."

"I feel much happier, almost like a different person, really. I want that for ya too. I mean, I don' wanna force anything on ya, but I want ya an' Ben to be happy. I've tried talkin' to Ben 'bout trees an' leaves, but he says he don' see no need for that. It's jist nonsense to him."

"But Thomas, I don' get what there is to talk 'bout. I mean, what kind o' things do ya say? It jist seems strange to me."

"I know Sally, at first it seemed strange to me too. But anyways ya talk 'bout whatever's on ya mind like we be doin' now."

Sally thought quietly. It was as if Thomas spoke a whole new language to her, and yet it was as if he put words to something she'd always known. It was strange, and she didn't know what else to say. Anyways, they were just pulling up to the general store to post Father's letter. Of course, Thomas wanted to visit the old Scotsman on the way home.

Sally immediately found Rachel after she and Thomas arrived at the Feed 'n Seed. The two girls sat down and got right to talking. They were beginning to become friends, as Sally often accompanied Thomas on his visits now.

When Thomas sat talking with MacDonald, he spied the prized black box sitting on the table. MacDonald's reluctance to discuss his sword only fanned the flame of Thomas's curiosity and interest. He'd wanted to learn more about the secret blade ever since he first saw it, but MacDonald had successfully put him off each time. When Thomas caught sight of the sword, his excitement doubled. He was dying to find out more.

"Come on, Mr. MacDonald. Ya showed some swordin' to my brother, but ya won't show me. What did ya show 'im"?

MacDonald looked hesitant, yet he saw that he would have to tell Thomas something more or risk hampering the mutual trust he sought to build. "Weel lad, I din't plan to show yer brither anything. I be practicin' the sword when he came."

"Ya did! I din't know ya knew how to use that thing. I thought it was just somethin' your father gave to ya."

MacDonald lowered his head to his chest as memories of his father flooded him. He took a moment to collect himself. His eyes shone when he looked up at Thomas. "Me father learnt me t' use the broadsword. It's somethin' e'ery Highlander from the old country knows."

"What's a Highlander?"

"In the ol' country there's Highlanders from the high country an' there's Lowlanders fro' the low country. Me kin were fro' the high country."

"So where is ya father, is he still alive?" MacDonald looked away and spoke in a lowered voice.

"I don' know where he be, lad." Thomas just waited, figuring there must be more to this story.

"I don' know, he run off," said MacDonald.

At this MacDonald quietly wept. In spite of trying to hold back the emotion, MacDonald's dam was overrun and the emotion swept over him. Thomas was taken aback to see the old man weep, never having seen such strong emotion from him. He felt uncomfortable seeing MacDonald in such pain, and wasn't sure what to do. However, by now Thomas had learned enough about trees to just let the old man be, and let him tell him more when he was ready. After a time, MacDonald's weeping slowed and he sat down and looked at Thomas.

"Mr. MacDonald, I've never seen ya that like before. Are ya all right?"

"Ye see, lad. Me mither died when me brither be born. She died 'n childbirth. Me brither made i' through, me mither din'. Me father took 'er death hard. He was angry wi' God, an' he was angry wi' himself. I think he felt responsible fo' her death, seein' that he made her be wi' child."

MacDonald paused as he recalled the painful memories. After a moment he continued. "Me father locked himself up i' a room fo' weeks an' din' come oot. I thought he' would ne'er come oot. The only thing that come oot o' that room was food trays, an' many o' 'em not touched. Sometimes I tried t' go an' talk wi' him, but he'd hae nothin' t' do wi' me an' sent me away. Finally, after a long time me father came oot an' called me t' him. He had a serious look o' his face an' he sat me down fo' a talkin'.

'Robert, I hae t' go away fo' awhile. I'm leavin' ye 'ere wi' ye grandparents fo' now. I'll be back when I can.'
I began t' beg him t' not leave, but he'd hae none o' it, an' then he left. I still remember starin' oot the window watchin' him walkin' down towards the town. I still remember the worn an' stained dark brown suit he wore, and the black boots on 'is feet. I can still see 'im lookin' down his feet all the while he walked. That was the last I saw o' him. I don't know what came of 'im... He ne'er came back."

"I'm sorry, Mr. MacDonald."

"Aye lad, I'm sorry too," MacDonald said slowly.

While MacDonald talked he'd picked up the broadsword and set it on his lap without thinking. When he finished his story he looked at the sword strangely, as if wondering how it came to be there. The sword brought so many memories, many of them painful. Eyeing the sword as well, Thomas asked about it.

"How did ya come to have ya father's sword?"

At the mention of the sword, the old man looked down again. "I' be the only thing me father left behind. Me grandfather tol' me that me father wanted me t' hae it. Tis the only thing I hae o' me father's. Before me mither's death, father showed me the skills o' the sword almost e'ery day, 'cept for the Sabbath o' course. When he was done wi' 'is work, I'd be waitin' an' he learnt me the use o' the broadsword."

MacDonald paused as if lost in thought for a moment. Then he continued. "After me father left I sat i' his room an' stared oot the window fo' many days, I don't know how many. Grandfather tried t' talk wi' me, but I'd hae nothin' t' do wi' him. I think I was watchin' fo' me father t' come home. Somewhere along the way the waitin' an' hopin' turned t' anger. I finally left the room an' began stealin'. Aye, it shames me so t' tell ye this, lad, but I started stealin' from other folks i' town. I'd get oot o' bed at night after e'ery one be asleep an' go in t' other folks' homes. I'd steal fro' right under their noses while they slept. Finally folk got wise t' me, an' got a dog or waited up fo' me. A couple times they almost caught me. Ye'd think that woulda git me t' stop, but noo. I was determined t' keep up the stealin', but now I started takin' me father's sword wi' me for protection. Then one night it happened."

"One night I took me father's sword an' slipped into a house. I thought e'eryone be asleep, but I be mistaken. I made me way into the kitchen an' there be a young man waitin' fo' me. He jumped up from 'is chair when he heard me, an' started wavin' a knife a' me, an' tellin' me t' leave his house alone. I din't even think, but the next thing I knew me father's sword was out the sheath an' i' me hand an' the lad was hollerin'. At first I din't know what happened, an' then I finally saw. On the ground lay his knife, an' it be still in 'is hand."

MacDonald slammed his hand down onto his leg and shook his head in both disbelief and self punishment. "I stood 'n shock for a bit, an' then when his hollerin' had brought others oot o' bed I went runnin'. The next thing I knew I was cleanin' the sword an' puttin' it away i' the upper garret room where no one might find it. The only thing I could think o' was that someone might take away me father's sword. Once the sword was safely hidden, I thought aboot the lad's hand. The vision o' his hand lyin' o' the floor wouldn't leave me mind. I din't sleep a wink all night cause o' the sight o' it. The next mornin' I heard someone come knockin' a' the door. I could hear me grandfather talkin' wi' someone, but I cu'n't hear what they were sayin'. Then Grandfather walked into the room."

'Lad, what hae ye done?' Grandfather asked."

"I jus' stared a' him. I din't know what t' say. I knew I'd done wrong by the lad, takin' his hand fro' him. I hae little memory o' that day. I think me grandfather took me down t' the constable an' had me confess the wrong doin'. I don' know how he worked it oot, but I went t' work fo' the family o' the man whose hand I took. He no longer could work, as he was a shoe maker. Weel, he worked as much as he could, an' I did the rest. To this day I don't know how the man tolerated me bein' in his shop, wi' what I done to 'im."

MacDonald looked down at the ground again. He shook his head showly. The shame wasn't as fresh and sharp as it had been, but it still stung. After several minutes MacDonald continued. "After the incident, me grandfather no longer tolerated me shuttin' him oot. The truth is I was quite willin' t' talk. The shame I bore would hae killed me if I hadn't talked aboot it."

"What did he talk to ya about?" asked Thomas.

"Oh lad many things, many things. First he talked wi' me aboot what I done t' that poor man, an' what I done t' 'is family. I remember what he said t' me. "Robert, me boy, yer just gonna hae t' make it right as best ye can by doin' the work he would hae done. At least until 'is lad is old enough t' do it himself." An' I did work fo' the man almost e'ery day for three years. But mostly grandfather talked wi' me aboot me mither dyin' and me father leavin'. I din' want t' talk aboot them at first; it jus' hurt too much."

"Then how did he get ya to talk 'bout 'em?"

"Weel lad, he be patient. He gave me time, but let me know in no uncertain terms that I hae t' talk aboot 'em. I kept tryin' t' tell 'im that they were dead an' gone an' there was no point in talkin' aboot 'em. But he wouldn't hear none o' that, sayin' that me mither and me father may be dead in their bodies, an' me father may noo be dead in 'is body, but either way they were still alive in me soul. He kept sayin' we'd get t' them when I was ready. I s'pose I was ready after a time."

A smile broadened across MacDonald's face and he nodded slowly.

"I remember grandfather comin' into me room one day, like he did e'ery day, an' askin' aboot me tree. I din' hae no idea what he spoke o'. I thought he might o' been askin' 'bout me chores. The garden was a part o' me chores. I must hae been aboot as mystified as ye were yerself when I first spoke to ye o' trees. That was the first time I heard aboot the tree o' the soul, lad. Anyways, he must hae realized I had no idea aboot it."

"He tol' me, 'Robert, me boy, yer tree is the inside part o' ye. I mean yer soul, lad. Ye haven't been tendin' yer tree, an' when ye don't tend t' yer tree, the leaves wither. T' put it plain, lad, yer face is tellin' me all 'bout the sufferin' o' yer soul - that be yer tree, lad. I been watchin' yer soul e'er since yer mither died, an' e'er since yer father left. Yer soul took a nasty blow when ye lost yer mither an' yer father; a blow that would knock any man down. Robert, me boy, there be no shame 'n being knocked down, but yer not pickin' yerself up; yer not pickin' yerself up an' yer soul's turnin' black. Yer tree lad, it's dyin' an' no one's been tendin' t' it. It's time we be getin' t' tendin' yer tree, lad. I'm not gonna stand for ye t' keep neglectin' yerself no more, lad'."

"I said, 'I know I'm not fairin' so well, but I hae no idea what t' do aboot it, an' I don't see how ye can help neither'."

"Weel Robert, me boy, we're gonna start tendin' that tree o' yers. What do the trees in the garden require, lad?"

"Weel lad, I was a bit confused by 'is question, but I told 'im that ye hae t' feed 'em an' water 'em an' trim their branches when they're young so they don't go wild."

"That be right, Robert, me boy. An' we're gonna feed ye an' water ye an' trim yer branches so ye don't go wild. We already hae done some trimmin' o' yer stealin', an' we done some trimmin' wi ye workin' fo' the shoemaker. Now it's time t' give ye some feedin' an' some waterin'."

"Grandfather, I'm gettin' plenty t' eat ye know. Grandmither, she feeds me all I need."

"Grandfather laughed as he said, 'Nae lad, I'm not speakin' o' yer stomach; I want t' help ye feed yer soul. We're t' feed yer tree as well as yer stomach, yer stomach is not what's worryin' me. Ye see Robert, yer needin' t' go t' the house o' sadness. Ye lost yer mither an' yer father an' ye need t' grieve their leavin'. Ye turned yer grief t' anger an' t' stealin', and it be time we return yer grief back t' grief.' When grandfather spoke o' grief, I knew he was on t' somethin'. I knew I was needin' help wi' me mither an' me father. I knew I wasn't just angry."

"How did he help ya with that?" asked Thomas.

"Ye know lad, 'tis hard t' put t' words. I think he mostly jus' helped me talk aboot missin' me folks. I think he helped me t' visit the house o' sadness. Ye know lad, there be a season t' jus' be sad.

Grandfather helped me t' hate me mither an' father fo' leavin', an' then t' be sad. I guess I jus' needed t' hate for a bit as weel. I hated 'em for a wee bit, lad."

Thomas felt for his old friend and couldn't imagine what it'd be like to lose either mother or father, not to mention both about the same time. Thomas's eyes turned down to the broadsword. Thomas asked, "Mr. MacDonald, would ya teach me to use the broadsword?"

"Oh lad, I don' know. Why would ye want t' learn t' wield an ole sword like that?"

"I might need to protect myself some day. I don' know the first thing 'bout how to do that," said Thomas.

"I don' know, lad. The broadsword may not be the best way t' protect yerself. I don' know. It's quite a responsibility wieldin' a sword, ye know."

"Oh, please Mr. MacDonald. I really want to learn it. I can be responsible, please!"

"I don' know, lad. What if ye went off an' hurt another lad. I just can't be part o' somethin' like that again," said MacDonald.

"Oh, I wouldn't do somethin' like that. Come on, ya know me."

MacDonald didn't look convinced. He looked at Thomas and studied his face. "Weel, I'll hae t' think aboot it."

"Well, okay, Mr. MacDonald."

Thomas was disappointed. In spite of his disappointment, he knew it would do no good to push the old man too much. He knew when MacDonald was resolute. He decided to just wait and hope for the best, although he didn't feel much hope he'd hear the answer he wanted to hear.

After Thomas left, MacDonald sat down to ponder his young friend's request. On the one hand MacDonald hesitated to train anyone with the broadsword, partly because the sword brought up painful memories. MacDonald knew these memories would be right before him if he agreed to train Thomas.

On the other hand, MacDonald saw the opportunity to further help Thomas. MacDonald noticed how poorly Thomas stood up for himself when his Rachel confronted him. He also reflected on some of the stories Thomas had recounted of his angry father, and Thomas cowering before him. MacDonald saw Thomas shrinking back from his own anger and the cost of doing so. He feared for his young friend in later life. How would he be able to stand up for himself if nothing was done? Perhaps properly crafted sword training just might give birth, or rebirth, to his ability to take care of himself when challenged. Perhaps proper training might help the lad to come to terms with his own anger, and get beyond shrinking from it. MacDonald understood that Thomas didn't want to explode like his father, but shrinking and cowering was a poor substitute.

MacDonald sighed at the personal cost, but he had some hope that training Thomas might also help him come to better terms with his own past. MacDonald decided to sleep on it. He didn't like to make any important decisions without giving himself a night to let it sift around within. The next day he felt the same way. He'd agree to train Thomas, for both their sakes.

Thomas was tempted to go see MacDonald the next day. He quickly finished his chores and had the horse saddled and ready to go. He was just about to jump up into the saddle when he had second thoughts.

"What am I doin'?" he wondered. Thomas remembered MacDonald saying he'd need time to think about it. Frustrated with himself, Thomas unsaddled his horse and led her back to the barn. He realized Mr. MacDonald would probably feel pressured if he asked him again this soon. Thomas decided he'd just have to wait. He didn't want to do anything that would hurt his chances of Mr. MacDonald teaching him the broadsword.

A few days later Thomas decided he couldn't wait any longer. It's hard to tolerate waiting in suspense for long. Thomas arose early and rushed through his daily chores in his hurry to leave. He had thought of inviting Sally to go with him, but decided not to. The cart was the only way to bring Sally with him, short of carrying her on his back, and he didn't want to take the extra time it took for the cart to get him to town. Riding his mare was faster than the slow plodding of the horse-drawn cart.

Thomas had his mare saddled and was just leading her out of the barn as he caught sight of Sally. Sally saw Thomas as well and guessed where he was off to. She hurried over as fast as her leg would allow. "Thomas, are ya goin' to the MacDonalds'?"

Thomas heart sank before the question was out of her mouth. He knew what it would do to her to miss an opportunity to see the MacDonalds. "Yeah Sally, I am," he said sheepishly.

However, she quickly overlooked the slight. "Oh, can I come with? Can I please come with ya?"

"'Course, little sister; let's go hitch up the cart."

On the ride over Thomas checked in with Sally on how her week was going, which was becoming a regular part of their relationship. Sally even asked about Thomas every now and again. Sally was beginning to put words to her inner life. The time Sally spent with Rachel also helped Sally learn to talk about herself, as Rachel was quite skilled in talking about herself as well as hearing another. Today Thomas and Sally were both eager to see the MacDonalds. Sally missed her new friend.

Thomas almost ran into the Feed 'n Seed, then remembered his sister. She could get out of the cart on her own, but it was much easier if someone helped her. Thomas ran back and quickly helped her out of the cart, then checked himself. He didn't want to scare the old man off by being too eager, and slowed his pace before entering the store. Walking alongside his limping sister seemed like a good speed.

Rachel stood behind the counter as brother and sister walked in. She was finishing up with a customer, and Thomas and Sally wandered around the store until she finished. It frustrated Thomas that the customer kept socializing with Rachel once business had been concluded. Finally the customer ran out of things to talk about and left.

"Hello Sally, Thomas. Me father's not 'ere right now. He be makin' a delivery an' should be back soon," said Rachel.

Frustrated at the additional delay, Thomas shuffled into the back room to wait and left the girls to talk. He knew they'd rather be alone, as he would want to be with the old Scotsman the moment he returned. Thomas kept the back door cracked open, so he could watch for the old man coming up the road in his delivery cart. He checked for him every two or three minutes.

Sally and Rachel quickly settled down to their visiting. Sally and Rachel both enjoyed their time together, and Rachel's newfound friend helped her feel less jealous of Thomas's time with her father.

"So Rachel, do ya know much 'bout trees o' the inside?"

"'Course I do," said Rachel.

"Really, how do you know 'bout them?" asked Sally.

"Probably the same way you do. I'm guessin' ye learnt 'bout trees from Thomas, an' he learnt 'bout trees fro' me father." Sally nodded her assent at Rachel's guess.

"Father talked t' me 'bout me tree since before I be old 'nough to talk."

"Wow, you're so lucky! I wish I had a father to do that with. I can't even picture Father or Mama talkin' 'bout such." Rachel chuckled at Sally's idea.

"You mean, neither yer father nor yer mither talk with ye 'bout yer tree?" asked Rachel.

"No, not at all. I asked Mama 'bout trees one time an' she thought I was talking 'bout the trees on the property. She had no idea what I was talkin' 'bout; an' Father, I would never think to ask him 'bout such. He would be mad. An' he might make Thomas stop talkin' to me, an' I couldn't risk that happenin'."

Rachel was silent a moment while she reflected on Sally's family. "I'm sorry for ye, Sally. I guess I never thought others din' get the same kind o' father I got meself. I figured maybe others got more than me, since I don't have a mither."

"I'm sorry ya don't have a mother, Rachel... but I think ya might o' got more from ya father than I got from both my parents put together. Don' get me wrong, I love my mother an' father. I don't know what I'd do without Mama."

Rachel teared up. She could hardly even remember her mother. Rachel walked over to a shelf behind the store counter and pulled out a handkerchief. Sally joined Rachel at her side. Rachel pulled back the last fold and a picture in a small silver frame was unveiled.

"This is me mither," said a tearful Rachel. Sally nodded as she looked closely at the beautiful woman looking back at her from the frame. Rachel's mother appeared young and with a hint of sadness to her countenance. In spite of her sadness, there shone forth a twinkle in her eye that reflected an alive woman. Sally noticed a similarity between mother and daughter.

"Ya have ya mother's eyes."

"Do ye really think so?" asked a hopeful Rachel. "Me father hae often told me so, but I din't know whether to believe 'im 'r nae."

"'Course I think so, but why din't ya believe ya father?"

"Oh, I just thought he might just be tryin' t' make me feel better," said Rachel.

"Do ya miss her all the time?" asked Sally.

"She's always in the back o' me mind, but I miss her most when I dressin' fo' church. I miss having a mither t' help me pick out a dress, an' help me do me hair an' help me t' look pretty. I never know what t' do when I'm tryin' t' fix meself up fancy. I wish I had me mither to teach me all aboot being a lady."

Sally mulled over Rachel's lament. Sally took for granted that she had a mother to help with all those kind of womanly things. It felt risky, but Sally decided to take a chance.

"Ya know, Rachel, I'm pretty good with all that lady stuff. Mama's taught me real good. I'd love to help ya with all that."

"Oh, I don' know, Sally. I couldn't ask ye t' do somethin' like that t' me."

"I wouldn't even pretend to take the place o' ya mother, but I can be a good friend. Rachel, ya helpin' me so much with my tree, an' you're the only true friend I've got; well, besides Thomas o' course. I can't hardly wait to see ya each time I come. Let me give back to ya. I wanna do this for you!"

"No, I uh ... I just can't! Thank ye, but... I just can't," stammered Rachel.

Thomas paced back and forth with his hands clasped behind his back. It felt like he'd been at it for hours. He glanced out the back door, disappointed not to see the familiar delivery cart pulling up. Every couple minutes he wiped the sweat from his forehead. He took deep breaths, trying to calm himself. At first he imagined MacDonald telling him that he's too young to learn the sword. Then he pictured MacDonald saying he wouldn't teach him at any age. At times he thought he could see MacDonald saying "Aye lad" with a smile on his face. But whenever he hoped for the last outcome, the first two would crowd it out. Thomas thought through what he might say in response to each of the imagined responses, and was interrupted by the sound of a cart. He half ran to the ajar door and threw it open.

"Hi, Mr. MacDonald."

"Oh, hello there lad. Ye've been waitin' fo' me?"

"Yeah, but not too long," answered Thomas.

"Oh lad, I know yer waitin' t' hear if I'll learn ye the broadsword."

"Will ya?"

MacDonald took a deep breath, and then let it out slowly. "Come sit down, lad. I want t' get a few things straight." MacDonald waited for Thomas to take a seat across from him.

"I can't hae no part o' the broadsword being used fo' evil. The broadsword has only one legitimate use, and that be protection. Ye can use it t' protect yerself an' yer loved ones. It hae no other use! Do I make meself clear, lad?"

"Oh yeah, Mr. MacDonald. Ya gonna teach me!"

"Now hol' on, lad; I'll learn ye the broadsword, but only o' me own conditions. If I see o' hear o' ye using the broadsword fo' any other use, the learnin' ends. Do I make meself understood?"

"Oh yeah, I get it. I'll do whatever ya say," said Thomas eagerly.

"All right, lad. Now don' ye go an' forget that. If yer t' wield the broadsword, yer to learn the proper use."

"So, when can we start?"

"Weel lad, I sent away fo' a couple o' proper broadswords, an' they oughta be 'ere inside o' the month."

"Sent away for? Why can't we just use your father's?"

"Oh noo, lad. Me father's sword stays where it lies. We begin when the proper learnin' swords arrive," said MacDonald firmly.

"Where did ya send away for 'em?"

"Me brither. Me brither lives i' Boston an' can lay his 'ands on a couple o' proper trainin' broadswords right quick. He's got the proper connections i' the big city. The swords'll be 'ere afore ye know it."

Thomas didn't know whether to be excited or disappointed. He looked over to the shelf where the prized sword lie, and then back at his old friend.

"Well, can ya teach me anything today?"

"Absolutely, lad. I'll learn ye the most important lesson aboot wieldin' the broadsword. Learnin' the sword begins wi' yer tree."

"My tree?" said Thomas. "What that gotta do with it?"

"Aye, lad. Make no mistake, the proper use o' the broadsword begins wi' the proper attitude o' yer tree. A man who's bent on evil will find it. A man who's bent on good will also find it. Ye only wield the sword i' ye hae to. If there be any chance t' avoid sheddin' blood, ye go that way first, lad. With much learnin' comes much responsibility, lad. Yer tree'll need t' grow along wi' yer learnin' o' the broadsword."

He thought about what the old man said. Thomas had been thinking of the sword merely as fun and possibly a way to protect himself should the need arise. "I'm not sure what ya mean 'bout my tree havin' to grow with my sword trainin'," Thomas said.

"I mean t' say that wieldin' a sword hae more t' do wi' yer head an' yer heart than yer hand o' yer arm. A broadsword's properly wielded fro' a noble heart, lad. The more yer tree matures, the more ye can do good wi' the broadsword. An' the more a man's tree turns black, the more evil can be done wi' it. Yer first lesson will be t' learn t' be slow to pull the sword fro' the sheath, lad. A man wi' a sturdy tree finds few occasions t' need to unsheathe his sword. The young sapling finds an occasion 'round ev'ry corner. Ye see lad, the more ye learn to wield the sword o' yer tongue, the less ye'll find need to wield the sword at yer side."

Thomas looked thoughtfully at MacDonald. MacDonald recognized the look of confusion on his young friend's face, and realized he would have to be patient with Thomas's understanding and maturity. "Now one last thing, lad. When the proper time do come fo' ye t' wield the sword, ye must not let fear prevent ye from actin' swiftly. Men get hurt when fear slows 'em from actin' when another man'll hae it no other way. When a stubborn man requires ye t' act, ye must act an' ye act withoot hesitation," admonished MacDonald.

MacDonald saw that his young apprentice wasn't taking in all that he said, but thought there would be plenty of time to talk more about the wielding of a sword. For now MacDonald was content to merely plant a few seeds, and later he would water and harvest them.

"But I thought ya said that I ought to be slow to pull the sword?"

"Aye."

"Then how can I be slow to pull the sword, and yet quick to act without hesitatin'?"

"Aye lad, that be a fine question. I wan' ye to be slow to find occasions to pull yer sword, due to findin' most occasions handled weel 'nough with the sword o' yer tongue. But once ye see plain 'nough that a man will hae it no other way, then ye must act swiftly. When ye hesitate fo' long, ye allow fear to git the better part o' ye. Do I make meself clear, lad?"

"I think so, but I have to think on that one."

On the way home Thomas could tell his sister was upset. She hadn't spoken two words, and they were already halfway home. It wasn't like her to be quiet like that.

"Somethin's on ya mind, sis."

"Yeah, I guess I'm thinkin' 'bout what Rachel said to me."

"Ya wanna talk 'bout it?" Sally went on to tell Thomas about the offer she'd made to Rachel and her response.

"I don' understand why it bother me though."

"Ya were hurt by 'er not takin' ya offer," suggested Thomas.

"Yeah, maybe so."

"Rachel might need time for such a gift."

"But why? I'm only tryin' to help her."

"I know, but your offer might o' stirred up a good bit o' pain for 'er," said Thomas.

"She do seem to miss her mother."

A couple of days later, a knock came at the Chittenden door. A sheepish looking Rachel standing on her doorstep surprised Sally. Rachel held her hands in front of her, and didn't hold Sally's gaze.

"Hello Sally. Can I step in for a wee bit?"

"Oh sure, come on in," invited Sally.

"Is there some place we can talk?" asked Rachel.

"Uh, come on in my room." They walked the few paces to Sally's room underneath the stairwell. Sally wasn't sure what to expect, especially since Rachel had never visited their farm before. Sally sat down on her bed and waved Rachel to the one chair in her room, a rocker.

"Sally, I uh, I be a wee bit sad the other day when we were talkin' aboot me mither. I uh, I be wonderin' if yer offer still stands?"

"Ya mean to let me help ya with lady things?" inquired Sally.

"Aye. I talked it o'er with me father, an' he helped me see that I be aboot t' miss oot on a fine offer, an' maybe a chance for some healin' as weel. If ye'll still..."

"Oh sure it does! I'm so glad ya changed your mind." Rachel nodded and smiled in relief.

"Weel, maybe there be somethin' ye can teach me today?" suggested Rachel.

"Yeah, let's see..." Sally pondered a moment and then caught sight of Rachel's hair. Rachel wore her hair the same every day: pulled back into a single ponytail and tied with string. Her hair style was okay, but it reminded Sally of something a man at work would do. Sally realized that surely more could be done with Rachel's hair.

"I've got it; we'll start with your hair," Sally said.

"What's wrong wi' me hair?"

"Nothin'. It's fine, but it's plain. Maybe it's okay for work, but I'm sure there will be times when somethin' a bit more ladylike would be nice." Rachel looked uncertain.

"Come on, Rachel. It'll be fine. Ya can wear ya hair however ya want, but I'm gonna teach ya a thing or two." Rachel felt a little comforted by Sally's explanation and nodded her readiness to get started.

"Okay, I'm gonna show ya several other ways to do ya hair. First, that string's gotta go. How 'bout wearin' somethin' like these." Sally walked over to her dresser and took out bows of several different colors. She waved Rachel over to look at them.

"Now look at how pretty these 're. Let's see, ya wearing a yellow dress, so let's try this yellow bow on," continued Sally.

Sally pulled Rachel over to the mirror above her dresser so she could see the new bow in her hair. "Now, tell me that don' look nice, huh?" asked Sally.

Rachel turned this way and that to see how the yellow bow looked. A smile slowly crept over her face the more she examined her hair. "Weel, I hae t' admit it do look grand," said Rachel.

"'Course it does. Now, there are bits o' red an' green in your dress. So let's see how a red or a green bow would look."

Sally went on to show her various combinations for her hair. She created many different options of ribbons, bows and combs. "Wow, Sally. Ye've shown me so much, I think I'll stop fo' today an' let me little mind take it all in. I never knew there be so many things a lady might put in 'er hair."

"Yeah, maybe I'm showin' ya too much for one day. Here, take these home with ya an' try 'em out, an' we'll try other things next time," suggested Sally.

"Aye. Ye know... I'm thankful that yer takin' time t' do this fo' me," said Rachel with shining eyes.

"Ya very welcome, Rachel. I'm not sure which one o' us getting' more outta it."

The weeks past slowly as Thomas eagerly awaited the training swords' arrival. Each day waiting felt like a month to him. Several times he tried to convince MacDonald to begin training him with his father's sword, but MacDonald was unmovable on this point. Eventually Thomas gave up trying to change his mind and resigned himself to waiting for the mail coach to arrive.

Thomas imagined how MacDonald might train him and what sort of moves he might learn. Many times he fantasized about a ruffian attacking the family farm, with Thomas fending off the ruffian in a lengthy, dangerous sword fight. They would circle round and round each other, searching for weaknesses. Thomas would allow the ruffian to inflict minor cuts, while Thomas would slowly disable the unwanted intruder. He imagined several different endings, but his favorite one involved Father humbly thanking Thomas for saving the family's lives. Finally, the day arrived; what had seemed many months to the eager boy had actually been three and a half weeks.

May 16, 1753 - Hampshire Grants

Having eaten or lost all of their meat to the wolves, food supplies became a serious issue. The scouts did not believe they were likely to catch the Yorkers any time soon. Thomas looked around the camp until he spotted Scout and Haskins.

"Gentlemen, I understand from Lt. Chambers that we're outta beef." Both men nodded.

"I've wanted to put it off as long as possible, since I don' want anythin' slowin' us down. But we gotta feed ourself. So how we gonna make up huntin' parties?" asked Thomas.

"What do ya mean hunting parties, Cap?" Haskins asked with a sneer. "Ya just leave it to me an' Scout to get ya some meat. All ya have to do is just say the word, an' we'll get ya all ya want."

"No, I don' want both o' ya away at the same time. Pick two other men to pair up with an' get started first thing tomorrow," ordered Thomas.

Haskins and Scout selected Pumroy and Morse to be included in the hunting parties based on having some experience with game. The first hunting team of Haskins and Morse left before first light the next morning. They set off looking for deer, but would kill any edible meat they came across. The hunters went in search of their game's water source, knowing they normally drink around dawn and dusk. Haskins and Morse hoped to locate a water source by dawn, in order to be there for their morning water intake.

The rest of the camp became busy at first light. Breakfast of grits and coffee was served. Hoping to make up for lost time fending off wolves, the regiment hit the trail immediately after eating.

By midafternoon Thomas and John heard galloping horses coming up behind them. They turned around to see Haskins and Morse riding up to the rear guard. "Any luck?" asked John. Both men slowly shook their heads with a look of disappointment.

"No, Lieutenant, no luck. We din't come 'cross any game. We did find a water source a couple hours after first light, but there weren't no game there," answered Morse. "Based on the tracks an' droppings in the area, it looked like we were in the right place but after the right time. The droppings suggest a handful o' deer had been there this morning."

"Well then, I figure that means no meat for supper tonight then," said Thomas.

"I'm sorry, Captain," replied Morse.

"Nothin' to be sorry for, Morse. We'll be all right without meat for one day. But wouldn't the river be the obvious water source for game?" asked Thomas.

"Yeah. But deer often drink from a smaller water source, like a small creek or pond," said Morse.

"They do that to avoid exposure to predators," Haskins said. "We did check the river near last night's camp an' found a few scattered droppings an' tracks there as well. But it was clear that the creek we found was in greater use by game."

"By the way, Haskins, how's that arm?" asked Thomas.

"Oh, it ain't nothin'," said Haskins.

Around dusk the regiment had identified a camping place for the night. Once camp was pitched, the men sat down by a fire to eat. Grumblings could be heard amongst many of the men who rarely went a day without some kind of meat, not to mention a long day on the trail. Supper only included some dried fruit and hastily made bread. Being that Chambers's supply of flour had nearly disappeared, the bread portions were no more than what a young child would receive at home, not nearly enough to satisfy grown men.

Thomas decided to send out a hunting party before the vanishing sun took with it all trace of daylight. The hope was that the hunters might be able to identify a likely water source tonight, and not have to search in the morning. Scout and Pumroy hurried off to search as they chewed the last bit of supper.

An hour after dark, Scout and Pumroy returned. They rode up at a gallop, which seemed strange for a hunting party merely searching out a likely watering spot. Their excitement soon became clear enough. Not bothering to dismount, the hunters rode right up to their captain's tent. Thomas sat out by the fire smoking his pipe.

"Captain, got news!" shouted both hunters at once. "We found us a settlement! A good sized settlement at that, probably with supplies and all!" reported Scout.

"Well now, that is good news," said Thomas with a smile.

The news of the settlement spread quickly throughout the regiment. Whoops and hollers erupted as men began dancing about. Fantasies of an evening in town quickly took shape in most of the men's minds. Thoughts of ale and a home-cooked meal with meat inspired excitement and eagerness to leave for town immediately, sooner if possible. Some of the men hoped for an opportunity to engage with women. Many in the regiment were lonely for some sort of sport with women, whatever form that might take. The goals amongst the men were quite varied and in some cases quite imaginative.

"Captain, requesting permission to go into town for supplies," said a beaming Pumroy.

"Now hold on, Pumroy. I want to think this through before we storm the town," answered Thomas. "Officers, step into my tent immediately for conference."

Chambers, Dickens and John hurried into their captain's tent. Chambers was particularly excited about getting new supplies and could hardly contain himself long enough to talk things through carefully. Thomas opened the conference.

"Gentlemen, we have a great opportunity to resupply. However, I'm concerned 'bout turnin' loose a half-starved regiment on an unsuspectin' town. Suggestions on how we go 'bout this?"

"Suggestions, Captain? We ride into town right away an' git the supplies we need. What's there to think 'bout? We're wasting time while the general store might be closing," said Chambers.

"Now hold on Chambers," began Thomas. "The general store likely has long since closed. It's well after dark. We probably can't git supplies 'til morning. But, the town's tavern might be open, an' I don' want my men causin' a raucous."

"The captain's right, Chambers. We don't want to cause a problem, and with the state some o' the men are in, nothin's more likely," agreed Dr. Dickens.

"What do ya mean with the state the men are in?" wondered Chambers. "They ain't gonna cause no trouble. They're just excited to have a home-cooked meal and maybe a little fun. Let's not take this too seriously."

"Exactly the kinda fun the men might have be what worries me. I don' wanna deny the men a bit o' fun, but I know what we be capable o', 'specially if the fun be lubricated with a pint or two o' ale," said Thomas.

"Captain, what if we limit the amount o' ale the men are permitted to drink? Do ya think that would do it?" asked John.

Thomas pondered John's suggestion. "I don' know, John. I just don' know. Maybe I'm bein' too cautious here. But, we don' even know what kind o' town we're lookin' at. I think I'd feel better 'bout keeping half the regiment here at camp, to guard camp an' to avoid scaring the town's folk," said Thomas.

"Oh, come on, Captain, there's no need for that. Two men can easily guard the camp," interjected Chambers.

"No, I must disagree Chambers, we need to approach this town with some caution an' wisdom," answered John.

"Okay then, John, ya pick ten to twelve men to take with ya into town. Since Chambers is so eager, make him one of 'em. But John, I want ya to keep a close eye on the men. I'll stay at camp with the rest. In the morning, I'll take the the other half into town for breakfast," decided Thomas.

John wasted no time selecting a dozen men to take with him into town. Of course every man in the regiment wanted to be selected. When they came into sight of town, John stopped and called the men over for last minute orders.

"Men, a couple things before we git there," began John. "We don't know anything 'bout the town we about enterin'. I want us to be careful to not say nothin' 'bout our mission. We don't know the politics o' this town. They might be Yorker."

Dawning awareness brought nods to a couple of the men's faces. They hadn't considered the town could be Yorker. Most had not cared and still didn't, as all that interested them now were the amenities the town had to offer. But all the men nodded their assent to John to hurry their release to storm the town. "I want ya all to limit yourselves to two pints o' ale. We don't want no trouble if ya catch my meanin'," continued John.

At this the men spurred their horses forward. It was all they could do to wait out their lieutenant's concerns. After many days on the open trail, defending themselves against wolves and going without meat all day, the men were chomping on their bits for town.

John slowed them down to a trot as they entered the town. He didn't want to arouse unnecessary attention. The town was situated next to one of the creeks running into the river, and was probably a mile or two from the large river. There didn't appear to be much to the town. A combination feed-and-general store and a tavern were all that could be seen. However, the men were relieved to see the lights on in the tavern, as nothing else really mattered at this point.

The tavern sat adjacent to the store, both being made of logs and sharing a common wall. What the tavern lacked in space it made up for in smells. Smells of ale, freshly cooked meat, and baking bread filled the air. It was everything the men had hoped for. Fortunately, there weren't many customers in the pub, and the men had no trouble finding a couple of empty tables to accommodate them. John made sure to sit with his back to the wall with a clear view of the door.

An older man turned to look at them with a lingering glare. John and the man briefly locked eyes. He wore well-worn overalls covered by a coat, with a hat that almost concealed his eyes. His beard was completely grey, yet somewhat well kempt for a farmer. The man threw back the last of his ale, gave John and his men one last look, and stepped out of the door.

In contrast, the pub's proprietor welcomed them warmly, seeing a great opportunity in the dozen men. It wasn't often that he had that many in his establishment at any given time, and relished the chance to pad his wallet. The proprietor wore an apron over rumpled cloths, and he bore a portly girth owing to his habit of testing all food before it left his kitchen. His wife bore a similar build and worked back in the kitchen, poring over her oven and stove. The proprietor came immediately over to the men's tables.

"Gentlemen, you are most welcome in my humble establishment. My name is Worthington, and I am completely at your service. To what do I owe the honor of your visit to the Ox an' Ale?"

"We're after some no good..."

"We're after some good food an' ale, an' lookin' to do a bit of explorin' up this way," interjected John before the fool gave their mission away.

144

John shot the man a warning look, and felt relieved when their host made no issue of it and moved on to business.

"Well, it's all the same to me, I'm sure. May I bring ya some refreshment? I have plenty of ale," invited Worthington.

A chorus of affirmative responses sent the host back to the kitchen to retrieve ale for all. All had accepted his invitation except John, who had preferred a cup of water. The ale appeared in front of the men a moment later, immediately raising the men's spirits.

"Now, I have fresh venison and may have a trout or two left over. I also have fresh baked bread and boiled potatoes. What'll it be?" asked Worthington.

Everyone went with the fresh venison and boiled potatoes, and of course the bread. Worthington bowed slightly and returned to the kitchen with a sly smile making its way onto his lips.

Soon each and every man had eaten to his satisfaction. Even John had relaxed and eaten without reserve, feeling less on guard, as their visit was going well. By the time the meal was over, John felt comfortable enough to join the men as they ordered their second pints of ale. The only other patrons left in the tavern by now were two men sitting quietly in the corner, but they seemed to take no notice of the militiamen.

The half regiment was in the midst of enjoying their pints when about ten of the locals walked through the door. Leading the way was the older man who had eyed them suspiciously. The man now had a smug look about him as he stood there with arms folded across his chest and legs a little more than shoulder width apart. A younger, middle-aged man stepped forward to address John and his men.

"What'r you fellas doing 'ere in town?" Before John could respond one of his men shot back a quick retort.

"I don't see that it's none o' ya ..."

"Now hold on there, Chipman," interrupted John. "Let's show a little respect, seein' as we're the guests." Then John turned to address the local. "We're just some Connecticut boys passin' through town an' enjoyin' a nice meal."

The local eyed Chipman with contempt, then recognizing John as the leader turned to address him. "Well, that's all well enough, but we don't want no trouble. We're peaceful farmers just wantin' t' be left to mind our own business. I'm the town magistrate and would be obliged if you fellas would finish your ale and move right along."

The magistrate said the above politely enough, but without a smile nor a nod. He wanted to make it clear he meant business.

"Well, we don't want no trouble neither, Magistrate, an' we'll be on our way just as soon as we finish our pints," agreed John.

"No, we're not gonna be rushed no place. We'll leave when we're good an' ready to," interjected Chipman.

The glazing of his eyes and the flushing of his face were evident to John. The two pints of ale had left its mark on Chipman. John felt anxiety rise within him. "That's enough, Chipman ..."

Unfortunately, John never got to finish. Another of the men standing behind the magistrate answered Chipman's challenge.

"That right, fella? Well, we'll just see 'bout that. Why don't ya just step outside and we'll settle this right quick. I don't figure t' need much time to teach ya some manners when ya talkin' to the magistrate."

"No, no, that won't be necessary," interrupted John. "Chipman, that's enough! Leave it be! We don't want no trouble here."

John's efforts were well intentioned, but too late to prevent a scuffle. Before John could get the words out of his mouth, Chipman had pushed back his chair and was on his way outside to accept the man's challenge. John attempted to grab Chipman, but he eluded his reach and stepped through the door before John could get to his feet. John headed for the door to make a last attempt to prevent the fight, but was stopped by a couple of the locals.

"Hey fella, this don't concern you. They's gonna settle it man-to-man with no interference like." Before John could respond, a couple of his men stepped forward to fire back.

"Hey, take you're hands off the lieutenant!" At this point things happened so quickly it would be confusing to try to give an accurate accounting. Knives flashed out of sheaths, fists were thrown, shoves found their targets, and blood appeared on many clothes on both sides.

Being skilled in hand-to-hand fighting, John quickly knocked a couple of the locals onto their backsides. Just as the second hit the floor, another of the locals came at John from behind and cut his right arm, knocking his back against the wall. One of his men rushed to his aid and knocked his assailant to the ground before he could inflict further damage. John's head swam with dizziness as he tried to gather his thoughts. A wave a panic mounted, which he attempted with only partial success to suppress.

"Morse, ride for the Captain – now!" John bellowed. Morse quickly mounted his horse and galloped at full speed the two miles back to the camp.

The men left behind in camp were disappointed. Some of them were angry, and some merely resigned to their fate. A few understood the need for caution; most did not. Outwardly the men mostly grumbled, but privately the officers, especially Thomas, were denigrated as incompetent, yellow-bellied cowards, kill joys, and many other names worse than these. A few were brave enough, or angry enough, to talk with John directly, but none were satisfied with his response. However, the men respected John enough not to challenge him face-to-face.

Some of the men, although also disappointed, found themselves in the unenviable position of defending the officers' decision. After John and half the regiment had left for town, a few fights broke out amongst the men. Thomas had foreseen there might be some trouble and had been watching the men with one eye as he'd enjoyed what remained of his evening's pipe tobacco. Perhaps the worst of them was the confrontation between Pumroy and Haskins. Thomas heard the yelling across camp and hurried to the scene. He couldn't hear the specific words, but what he heard was enough. Upon arriving at the scene, Thomas immediately stepped in between the angry men, pushing them apart.

"What's the meaning o' this?" Thomas demanded. Pumroy looked down at the ground, with flushed face and perspiration dripping from temples to chin.

Haskins responded immediately. "What's happenin' is that I'm tryin' to explain to Pumroy here how his duty is to hear his captain's orders an' obey, even if the orders don't make no sense," stated Haskins pedantically.

"Haskins, you will stand down an' I will deal with Pumroy myself," ordered Thomas. Haskins hesitated. "Take a step back Haskins," Thomas said more emphatically.

Haskins rolled his eyes, and then stepped back a few paces. Satisfied, Thomas turned to Pumroy. "An' what do ya say to the charge o' openly challengin' my orders?" demanded Thomas.

Pumroy looked down, his eyes searching amongst the dirt and pebbles. He began to speak several times, but nothing came out. The captain was content to wait. Finally Pumroy found the words he sought. "It just don't seem right, Captain, ya makin' us stay behind an' keepin' us from the fun. I don't git..."

This was all Haskins could tolerate hearing said. "Ya still ain't gettin' it, soldier, even though I been tryin' to explain to ya the chain o' command, even when ya know more than those above ya," said Haskins evenly. Thomas had wisely remained in between the two men.

"That's enough! You will stand down, Haskins!" ordered Thomas again. Haskins glared at Thomas, and then reluctantly took a step back.

"I'm simply explainin' to Pumroy how it works when..."

"Ya see, Captain, this man thinks he can tell me what I can an' can't do. Who's he to tell me anythin'? He's no officer," said Pumroy.

"I'll tell ya who I am, unlike you green horn, I got more experience than..."

This was as far as Haskins got. Thomas had turned to Haskins to back him down again. Fortunately, Thomas had maintained an eye on Pumroy in his peripheral vision and saw Pumroy charge Haskins, fist raised.

Thomas quickly stepped out of the way of the charging Pumroy and drew his sword as he stepped back. Before Pumroy could reach Haskins, Thomas hit Pumroy with the flat of his sword, sending him sprawling onto the ground. Pumroy was trying to figure out what hit him when Thomas quickly put the business end of his sword to his throat. Pumroy looked bewildered. He'd had no idea his captain would deal out discipline physically and had fully expected to get away with a good thrashing of Haskins. Most of the men remaining in camp had gathered around the excitement by now, and Thomas knew he must act swiftly. Thomas looked around for men he felt confident trusting in a situation like this.

"Scout, Dobson!" called Thomas.

" Sir?" they both answered.

"You will take Pumroy to his tent, relieve him o' any an' all weapons ya find there, an' prevent him from leavin' his tent until I meet ya there. Pumroy an' I will have a conversation once he's settled down some," ordered Thomas. Then Thomas turned to Haskins. "An' you will leave the situation alone, without 'nother word to Pumroy!"

Scout and Dobson moved towards Pumroy who immediately took two steps back, raising his hands in front of his chest. The look on his face spoke of warning. Dobson took another step towards Pumroy, but was stopped by a firm hand on his shoulder. An annoyed Dobson turned to see Scout shaking his head and pulling his back.

"We had 'bout enough fighing for one night, don't you think?" said Scout. Most of the men were too afraid of Scout to cross him, but Dobson was too angry to care about Scout's intimidating presence. Dobson could be hot-tempered under the right circumstances, and this was one of them. Dobson started for Pumroy when Scout yanked him back hard enough to land him on his backside. Thomas had seen enough.

"Damn it, Dobson, ya not helpin' the situation! Back away, now!" yelled Thomas. "You stay here while me an' Scout walk Pumroy to 'is tent."

Dobson grabbed a handful of dirt and threw it at a nearby bush, stood up, and kicked the dirt some more for good measure. Thomas watched him walk away before turning his attention to Pumroy. Pumroy walked to his tent without further incident when he saw that Thomas and Scout allowed him the dignity to make his way to his tent unaided. Thomas stood outside the tent while Scout searched the tent for weapons. Pumroy paced back and forth until Scout emerged from the tent with a knife and a pistol.

Thomas thought it wise to allow Pumroy time for his anger to cool and regain clearer thinking. Pumroy was not well-known to Thomas, but he knew him to be a man of some character. Once an hour or so had expired, Thomas made his way back to Pumroy's tent. Thomas excused the men standing guard over Pumroy's tent, not wanting to further embarrass the man anymore than was necessary. Pulling back the tent flap, Thomas called Pumroy out.

"Pumroy, walk with me."

A sheepish looking man emerged from his tent, appearing somewhat embarrassed. Thomas felt pleased by what the man's face suggested, thinking it better that a man come to his own repentance than at the hands of another. Wanting to finish his business with Pumroy in private, Thomas walked him down to the river and away from earshot of the others.

"Ya know Pumroy, I'm surprised at what ya did with Haskins today. It ain't like what I seen o' ya. But anyways, tell me how ya think 'bout tonight's events," said Thomas.

Pumroy walked with head down and hands in pocket, and responded almost immediately. "Oh, Captain, I messed up. I don' do stuff like that. I don' know what got into me. I shouldn't o' said nothin' to Haskins. Sometimes I can't take no more o' his hot air."

"An' why shouldn't ya said nothin' to Haskins?" Thomas asked.

Pumroy was surprised by the question and looked to see if Thomas was serious. Seeing nothing to suggest otherwise, he responded. "'Cause it's not right to question the captain's orders."

Thomas was pleased with his response, but wanted a deeper understanding. "Yeah, it's not right to question my orders with 'nother man in the regiment," answered Thomas. "However, if ya have a problem with one o' my orders, an' we're not engaged in military action, I welcome ya to come to me directly."

"Really?" asked a surprised Pumroy.

"Really. I welcome ya to come to me an' discuss the matter in private an' with respect, but I will not tolerate my orders being debated amongst the regiment. Do I make myself clear?" asked Thomas.

"Yes, sir."

"Good. Now for the matter o' your discipline, what do ya think would be fittin' for ya crime?" Thomas asked.

"Well, Captain, you already punished me with your sword. Ain't that enough?" hoped Pumroy.

"No. That was discipline for attackin' a fellow soldier. I will not tolerate a soldier under my command attacking another. However, we still have yet to deal with ya insubordination; that be another matter. So, what discipline would ya think fittin' of your crime?"

"Well, I don't know, Captain. I guess that's up to you."

"Yes, it will be up to me if you won't suggest somethin'. But Pumroy, I hope ya won't require me to do that. I would much prefer ya t' come up with a proper discipline yourself; it would be o' more personal profit," said Thomas.

Pumroy thought this over and couldn't see how it would be better, but he thought he might get off lighter if he suggested something himself. "Well, maybe I should stay behind when you an' the others go into town in the mornin'," suggested Pumroy.

"Accepted," said Thomas. "That seems quite fittin' to me as well. Done." Thomas slapped Pumroy on the back as he offered his respect. He then headed back to the camp.

"Here are ya weapons, Pumroy. You're free to move 'bout as ya wish," said Thomas.

As Thomas turned to walk away, Pumroy stopped him. "Wait a minute, Captain. I want ya to know that I feel bad 'bout challenging ya orders; it'll never happen again."

"Ya know, Pumroy, a wiser man than me once said, 'Experience keeps a dear school, yet Fools will learn in no other.' Ya see, some things ya just gotta learn by goin' through 'em. This time the fool was you, next time it might be me."

"Who said that?"

"A young writer named Benjamin Franklin."

Thomas wearily walked back to his tent, only to find Haskins waiting for him. Haskins looked up as Thomas approached. Haskins grinned confidently. "Look Haskins, it's been a long day. Can this wait till mornin'," said Thomas.

"Ya know, all along I figured you're young an' without much experience, an' it might take ya awhile to appreciate the full value o' my skills. So I've tried to be patient with ya an' give ya time to see how bad ya need my experience on this here mission. But ya ain't gettin' it! I can't work with nobody that don't know what he's about. Likely you'll get most o' these boys killed. So I had my fill."

"Haskins, it's clear to me that you an' Scout got skills we need on this mission, but maybe the problem is that you appreciate ya own skills too much," countered Thomas.

"No. It's too late for talk. Just gimme my pay an' I'll be on my way," interrupted Haskins.

"Ya leavin'?"

"That's right," said a resolute Haskins.

Thomas thought about trying to talk out their differences, but decided against it. He figured that Haskins was unlikely to hear much, and truthfully, Thomas would be relieved to get rid of Haskins. Without another word he stepped into his tent, and came back with money in his hand.

"There ya go, Haskins. By my figurin' that's what ya got comin' for ya services up til now." Haskins stuffed money into his pocket without counting it and turned immediately to leave. His gear was already packed and tied onto his horse. He put his foot in the stirrup and rode off at a gallop.

Thomas watched Haskins ride off and was still pondering the conversation when a rider rode up at a gallop. Thomas heard the commotion and looked behind him to see Morse pulling up on his reigns, appearing flushed and worried.

When Thomas saw Morse and his state, he immediately feared for the men who had gone to town. "What is it? Has there been trouble?" asked Thomas.

"Captain, trouble in town; men hurt," blurted out Morse between gasps for breath.

Thomas quickly scanned the men within sight. "Scout, saddle up ya horse. Bring no firearms, but do bring ya knife. We won't further any fight, but we might well end one! Let's go!"

"Lemme come too, Captain!" yelled several of the nearby men.

"No! The rest o' ya stay put and keep a close watch on camp."

Minutes later the two men galloped to town. Thomas didn't want to take the time to gather all the relevant data, sensing that speed outranked thoroughness in this situation. As they approached town, Thomas could see the scuffle, which by now had poured outside the pub. Thomas jumped off his horse, barely taking time to securely tie her up, and fired his pistol into the air.

The shock of the loud noise temporarily halted the fighting. By this time, most all of the men on both sides were bloodied and bruised. Thomas groaned inwardly, as he saw the very thing he'd feared, and maybe worse.

"What is the meaning o' this?" demanded Thomas. The local magistrate stepped forward.

"The meaning o' this is these men have caused a riot in our peaceful town! Are they under your command?"

"Yes, these men are under my command. And this will stop immediately. Every member o' the regiment will fall in behind me," ordered Thomas.

The men momentarily hesitated, as if reluctant to let go of doling out their punishment of the unwelcoming locals.

"I said, fall in behind me! Now!" yelled the captain.

The sternness in their captain's voice seemed to wake them from a trance. At this point the men slowly picked themselves up, dusted themselves off, and walked over behind their commanding officer. Thomas replaced the pistol into its holster and addressed the magistrate. "I apologize for whatever part my men have played in this here brawl. Their behavior is unacceptable as ya guests."

"You damn right they behavior's unacceptable. Your men owe us all an apology," responded an angry local.

This was too much for the militia to take, and several men behind Thomas fired back angry comments. The fight began to erupt anew, and would have but for the captain's actions. Thomas and Scout turned and quickly backed his men away from the locals by pushing them with hands on chests.

"You will cease these outbursts! I an' I alone will now speak! Is that clear?"

No one said anything, but their angry looks said enough. Satisfied the outburst ceased, Thomas turned to address the locals.

"Ya may well be deservin' of an apology, an' when all is known, that will be decided. For now, there will be no more fightin' that any o' my men will be a party to."

"Guess you Connecticut boys got a yellow-belly for a captain. Figure he can't stomach fightin'," fired back one of the locals.

Two of the militiamen stepped forward intent on throwing punches, yet Thomas quickly gave each the flat of his sword against their backs, knocking them to hands and knees.

"You will fall in behind me an' stay there!" ordered Thomas.

"Now, if one o' you local boys is in need of further fightin', he may step forward an' I will make myself at his service. I would hope ya'll see there's been 'nough fightin', but if you require it, I will accept any man's challenge one at a time," answered Thomas.

By this time everyone had gathered around, including the proprietor and his wife. Thomas did not want any more fighting and was trying to quell any further inclinations towards conflict, but preferred to fight himself than allow any of his men to further the brawl. The outspoken local drew his sword and stepped forward. Thomas took a deep sigh and pulled off his coat as he stepped away from his men. He turned to Scout. "Scout, you will keep the men from interferin', no matter the outcome." Scout stepped forward in between the locals and the regiment. Thomas tossed his coat aside.

"We will fight to the first cut, agreed?" asked Thomas.

"Agreed," replied the local swordsman.

The swordsman lunged at Thomas, who easily stepped out of the way. The local had one strategy and kept coming. This went on for some time with the local making repeated attempts to lunge and thrust. Thomas hoped the man would tire and give up in frustration, as he hadn't come close to cutting Thomas. Thomas would be disappointed in this, as the man neither tired nor became easily discouraged. The local redoubled his efforts and made more and more aggressive lunges. Thomas had even less difficulty stepping aside as the local's intensity increased. Thomas did not want to unnecessarily hurt the man, as MacDonald had drilled that lesson into Thomas.

As time went on and the local kept coming at him, Thomas had exhausted his ideas. He couldn't think of how else he might bloodlessly end the fencing match. The men misunderstood their captain's actions, thinking him unskilled with the sword and overly passive. They could see he was making no effort to go on the offensive. Several of his men shouted encouragement to attack.

While Thomas searched for the elusive solution, the local man was becoming careless, taking more chances. Then the local slashed wildly, missing Thomas completely and cutting the proprietor's wife across her thigh. She immediately collapsed into the dirt, with blood flowing freely from the wound. The local felt remorse, yet his remorse brought no healing to her wound.

The woman's brother rushed to her side and knelt briefly and looked at her wound. Then he looked at Thomas with anger and pulled his pistol from its holster. Thomas stepped sideways out of harm's way and slashed his sword across the man's arm. The pistol fell to the ground without being discharged. Thomas kicked it to Scout, while turning back to face his original adversary in time to parry his thrust and cut the back of the man's sword hand. The local's sword dropped to the ground. The man yelled out in pain yet reached for his sword with his left hand, refusing to accept defeat. Thomas placed his boot on the sword.

"To the first cut," reminded Thomas.

Still unwilling to accept defeat, the man swung at Thomas with his left arm, only to have it broken with the flat of Thomas' blade. Being a heavy sword, it didn't take much force to break a man's arm. At this the man fell to his knees, both arms disabled. Thomas scanned the rest of the locals.

"Be that enough for tonight?" Thomas asked rhetorically.

The locals turned and slowly walked away. John ordered every man to mount up and head back to camp. Thomas took a last look at the man at his feet, and turned to his own horse without another word. The militia returned to camp and many sought the ministrations of Dr. Dickens.

Thomas approached as Dr. Dickens finished wrapping up John's arm. With a wry smile Thomas inquired as to the patient.

"Is he gonna live, Doc?"

"Oh he'll live, all right. I don't know if he'll be throwin' any more punches for awhile. It's gonna be sore for a spell," predicted Dr. Dickens.

Thomas playfully punched John in his good arm. John smiled and pushed back, which Thomas took for a good sign. He couldn't afford to have his most reliable soldier get too down in his spirit.

"Hey Doc, is it safe for me to talk with the patient, or does he have to be in bed?" asked Thomas.

"Very funny, Captain." Dr. Dickens got the hint and left the two officers to consult.

"Thomas, look I'm really sorry 'bout tonight. I know I let ya ..."

"It's okay, John. I'm sure ya did your best to keep the men 'n order," Thomas answered.

"I don't know, maybe if I'd been a little quicker to act, or maybe if I'd ..."

"Stop it, John. Don' do that to yourself. Maybe ya could o' done somethin' an' maybe ya couldn't o', but it won't help to let your guilt run away with ya. Anyways, I need ya thinkin' clearly to help me decide what we're gonna do 'bout the townsfolk, but first tell me what happened."

John gave Thomas a detailed recounting of the evening, and Thomas sat in silence taking it in, sighing at several points. Both men sat in silence for several minutes once John was done. No easy answers coming to either of them as they thought through what might be done now.

"Look, John. I wanna find some way to at least try to make amends to them. It's our fault that poor woman was badly injured. Dear God, let her be okay. Damn it, John! It's my fault that poor woman was injured! I failed to act quickly when I had the chance! MacDonald tried to teach me there's a time and place to stand up for yourself with strength, or for those under your care. MacDonald told me that I allow my fear to keep me from being as strong as I need to be. I know he's right. Sometimes I let people walk all over me. Damn it all, John. I failed to act!"

"Wait a minute Thomas, how did ya fail to act?" asked John.

"I let that cursed swordfight go on too long. I should've cut 'im quickly an' ended it. I allowed it to go on an' on 'til that poor woman got cut, an' her injury is on me!"

"Now hold on, din't ya just tell me not to let my guilt run away with me? Ya talk like it was your sword that cut that woman."

"It may as well o' been my sword, John. My own fear o' hurtin' someone in anger held me back from actin' with determination an' speed. I let my fear get the best o' me, damn it!" Thomas stopped to think a moment.

"Ya might be right 'bout my guilt some, but damn it, I could have ended that swordfight quickly," said Thomas.

At this John was silent, realizing that his friend probably had to face something in himself. He knew Thomas well enough to know that Thomas struggled with making use of his strength. John too knew what it was to face hard things about his own tree. Few experiences are more humbling than staring at one's own character in the mirror. John knew there were times when there was nothing to do but sit with his friend and just be there. After painful reflection Thomas spoke again.

"Well, I must do what I can to make things right for the townsfolk."

"Are ya thinking o' going back into town?" asked John.

"Yeah. Somethin' must be said to the people o' that town. I'm just not sure what yet." After another silence of reflection Thomas continued. "There's another thing. What are we gonna do with Johnson? Did ya see his face on the trail today?"

"Yeah I saw," John replied. "He was in quite a bit of pain. I don't know how he's gonna keep doin' that."

"I hate to say this, but I'm considerin' leavin' him in town; if they'd take him o' course," said Thomas.

"Really? I don't like the idea o' leaving Johnson behind with men we jist fought with. Who knows what they might do with 'im."

"We couldn't leave Johnson with 'em unless we can find a way to mend fences with 'em. I'm just not sure how we can do that," said Thomas.

"I wonder if there's anything we could do for them," suggested John.

"I wish there was something, but what?"

"What if we offered to fix whatever was broke inside the pub?" suggested John.

"Was there much damage?"

"I'm not sure, but I think maybe a couple o' chairs and possibly a table were broke," John guessed.

"That's an idea. I don' know if they'd accept, but we could sure offer. I have to try," said a determined Thomas.

John got up and walked back to his tent. Thomas sat and pondered his options. He wished his old friend Robert MacDonald was here. Thomas knew MacDonald would be able to shed some wisdom on the situation. He tried to imagine what MacDonald might say in a situation like this. At first nothing came to him.

"Oh, Mr. MacDonald. I wish ya were here to help me with this whole mess. I'm jist not quite sure what's t' be done," Thomas said under his breath.

Thomas could almost hear his old friend saying the words: "As much as ye can be at peace with all, but not at any cost. Be ye strong and o' firm conviction in it all, no matter the outcome," MacDonald had often said.

A sense of calm confidence came over him. He felt as though he'd talked with MacDonald himself. Thomas felt grateful that his old friend was with him, always within. MacDonald had become a permanent part of his tree by now, as though a part of his old friend lived inside him. At first Thomas needed MacDonald's physical presence, but over the years he'd been learning to make use of his memories with MacDonald. Thomas still wasn't sure what he'd do tomorrow, but he now figured that he'd be able to handle the situation, even if it became difficult. That settled it. Thomas would start by trying to make peace with the town, and if successful, he would try to leave his injured man with them.

The next morning Thomas went into town with only Scout and Pumroy. Next to John Jackson, he trusted Scout and Pumroy the most amongst the militia, even after last night's events. John had wanted to go, but Thomas insisted he stay behind to oversee the camp. They decided the night before that John would organize new hunting parties, as their meat supply remained depleted. If they were to spend another day off the trail, then to replenish their supplies had to be part of the plan.

On the way into town, Thomas made it clear to Pumroy and Scout that they were to leave the talking to him, and that he wouldn't tolerate any unprovoked hostilities. Thomas also let the two men in on his plan for the trip into town. Prior to leaving the camp, Thomas ordered the men to bring tools for repairing broken furniture. Although puzzled at the strange request, the men brought the simple tools required.

The three militiamen walked their horses as they entered town. They didn't want to give any impression they intended to resume fighting. Thomas and the two men only brought concealed pistols and their blades. He couldn't risk the townsfolk seeing muskets in their hands. The few people out and about looked at them suspiciously as they passed by. The militiamen headed directly to the tavern to inquire after the injured woman.

The men walked into the tavern with their hats in hand, wanting to portray a conciliatory attitude. As they entered the pub, the proprietor looked up from his work with a mixture of suspicion and fear.

"Let me assure you that I have no intentions o' startin' another fight, my good man," began Thomas. "I'm here to offer my apologies for the injury to ya wife an' the damage to ya establishment."

Worthington simply nodded and continued to maintain his look of suspicion and fear. As he didn't speak, Thomas continued.

"How does ya wife fare, sir?"

At this question Worthington seemed to soften a bit, at least enough to answer Thomas's genuine inquiry. "The doctor says her cut is deep an' that she lost much blood, an' that her recovery will be slow. At least he expects that she will recover."

"An' thank God for that!" said Thomas with relief.

"Well gentlemen, if you'll excuse me, I have much work to be done an' one less wife to help me with it."

"I understand sir, but if I may trouble ya a moment longer," requested Thomas. Worthington turned back around to look at Thomas, although his wariness had not disappeared.

"Sir, I would like to repair the furniture damaged in the fight," offered Thomas.

At this offer Worthington's wariness turned to a look of surprise. He hadn't expected Thomas to want to make genuine amends. Worthington's face softened further.

"Alright then. Two chairs an' a table were damaged. If your offer to fix them is real, I'd be obliged," responded Worthington.

"It's settled then," Thomas said with content. "Scout, Pumroy, I trust ya know your work."

The men required no further prodding and immediately fell to the work. Both men had some experience with woodwork; Pumroy's father was an amateur carpenter and had taught his son more than enough to make such simple repairs. Reattaching legs and reinforcing the table was all that the furniture needed to be almost as good as new.

As the men began repairs Thomas learned from Worthington where he might find the town magistrate. Worthington directed Thomas to the town church, which also served as the meeting site for the town council.

Thomas left the men to their woodwork and walked into the church. Three men sat at a small table in a small office adjoining the sanctuary. They looked up in surprise at the visitor. None of the councilmen recognized Thomas at first, yet would have been surprised to have any visitor today, as they rarely had visitors to their council meetings.

"Good morning, gentlemen," said Thomas. The men nodded slightly, but perceptibly.

"My name's Captain Chittenden. Ya might remember me from last night's fight." Dawning awareness came over the men's faces one by one.

"Let me begin by assurin' ya that I do not come for another sword fight, or another fight o' any kind. Instead I come to offer my apology for the fight. My men have no excuse for brawlin', even if they might have been provoked. Also, I deeply regret that poor woman being injured durin' the sword fight. I take full responsibility for her injury an' would be willing to offer any medical supplies an' medical attention that she might require."

The man to the left of the magistrate became visibly red with anger as Thomas spoke, and almost cut Thomas off in his eagerness to respond.

"Ya damn right you ought to be apologizin'. That brawl was completely your men's fault, and I believe you and ya men should stand trial for the crimes committed!"

Thomas turned to address the angry councilman. "Sir, I make no excuse for my men's behavior. I intend to do all I can to make amends to the people sufferin' harm, as well as anyone with damaged property. However, I will not place myself or my men in your hands for criminal charges. I will answer to the Colony o' Connecticut, an' the Colony o' Connecticut alone."

"You damn sure will answer to us if we arrest ya and..."

At this point the third man on the council interrupted the angry man. "Now hold on there, George! We don't want no further trouble with these men. Isn't it enough that he's apologizin' and offering to make amends? I'm not even sure it was his men's fault in the first place."

"Wait a damned minute, Franklin! I don't know who you're talkin' to, but I heard many reports that his men provoked the fight. Are you meanin' to let them off with no responsibility?"

"I'm just saying that if we'd been more hospitable to our guests, maybe no fightin' would have happened," answered Franklin.

"More hospitable! How can you say that? Are we to interrupt our business to cater to any and every traveler that comes into...?"

At this point the magistrate interrupted the growing conflict within his own council. "Now hold on, both of you! Are we to fight amongst ourselves? We must reach an agreement about this man and his offer of apology and amends."

Thomas decided to intervene at this point. "Gentlemen, I won't have my men an' I relieved o' all responsibility for last night's fight. My men were clearly wrong to fight an' absolutely part o' the problem. I too will not accept all responsibility for the fight. It nearly always takes two to fight. However, more to the point, I offer my sincere apology to the town an' the council as its representative. Furthermore, my men are repairin' the damaged furniture in the pub right now. I have inquired as to the wounded woman an' would be glad to provide her what she might require. Please accept my sincere attempt to make amends. If there's something I've overlooked that could be done to repair damage to the persons or property o' this town, by all means make me aware of it."

At this the councilmen paused to allow Thomas's offer to sink in. After a moment the magistrate spoke. "I accept your offer of apology and your acts of repair. There is one further act that would help."

"If it be in my power, I will gladly oblige," answered Thomas.

"We have a surplus of flour that will spoil before the town is able to make use of it. We will sell it to you at a fair price."

"Done," said Thomas. "I will have my supply officer work out the details with the town's representative."

"Good enough," said a grateful magistrate. "You will find our representative in the general store."

"Now, there is one favor I have to ask," said Thomas.

George, the angry councilman, took a breath as he prepared to reply. The magistrate quickly put his hand on George's arm to suppress any ill-advised retort.

"We will hear your request but make no promises," answered the magistrate.

"I have an injured man, a badly injured man. He is not well enough for travel. I would pay a fair price for his room an' board if I might leave him in good care."

"How was he injured, and what is the nature of his injury?" asked the magistrate.

"He was mauled by a wolf. Both of Johnson's arms are deeply torn. The wolf got 'em pretty good an' will require many weeks to heal enough to travel. He can barely use his arms."

A couple of the councilmen visibly winced at Thomas's recounting of the injury. None of them had encountered hand-to-hand (or rather hand-to-claw and teeth) combat with a wolf, yet their imagination served them well as they unwillingly pictured the horror of such an encounter.

"I see. We as a council will consider your request and let you know o' our decision," answered the magistrate.

"Good enough, sir. I expect we will be leaving the area tomorrow. When do ya expect to have reached a decision?"

"We will inform you later today," said the magistrate.

"Good. Then I will await your answer. We will be at the pub repairin' the damaged furniture."

At this Thomas bowed slightly and took his leave. He went back to the pub to see how Pumroy and Scout were making out with the furniture. The soldiers were gluing a leg onto a chair as Thomas entered the pub. They still had another chair and a table to repair yet. Thomas left them to their work and went back to camp to get Chambers to negotiate the purchase of the surplus flour.

Predictably, Chambers was thrilled to hear of the offer to purchase flour. Although wolves don't eat flour, they had spilled some in their efforts to get to the meat, leaving Chambers short on flour. It's bad enough for men to go without meat a few days, but to go without meat or bread would be almost unendurable.

Thomas brought both Chambers and Johnson with him back to town. He hoped the council would accept his request to leave Johnson with them.

"Johnson, there's somethin' I haven't told ya yet," said Thomas. "I asked the town if they'd take ya in."

"What! Ya can't leave me here!"

"Think 'bout it, Johnson; ya can't travel at more than a walk, an' I can't afford to travel that slow. I just can't allow the Yorkers more time on us," explained Thomas.

"Oh, Captain. Don' leave me here! Our men jist fought these folk. What if they turn on me?" complained Johnson.

"Well, I want ya to make a visit with me, an' then we'll see," said Thomas.

The three men entered the tavern as Scout and Pumroy were cleaning up their work. Thomas inspected their work and, as he expected, he couldn't tell where the damage had been except for the wet glue in a spot or two.

"As I expected, the furniture looks as good as new," complimented Thomas. "Have you heard from the town council yet?"

"No sir. Nobody been here 'cept for the owner o' the place," answered Pumroy. "Guess he was checkin' up on us. Maybe he though we was fixin' to make off with his furniture."

"The man has reason not to trust us," responded Thomas. "Come on, Johnson. I want ya to meet somebody."

Johnson looked up warily, but followed Thomas to the back of the tavern just the same. Not seeing the proprietor from the door to the kitchen, Thomas knocked on the door post. Worthington quickly appeared, as he'd been listening to the happenings in the front of his establishment and had heard the men reenter.

"Yes?"

"Mr. Worthington, may I present Johnson," said Thomas. "As you can see from his bandaging, he's badly injured... mauled by wolves."

Worthington looked impassively at the bandaging across both arms and his face. He nodded his understanding. Then Thomas addressed Johnson.

"Johnson, this poor man's wife was badly cut due to my own failure last night. I feel responsible for her injury. Mr. Worthington, would it be too much an intrusion if me an' Johnson here were to look in on ya wife?" Thomas inquired.

Worthington started to shake his head "no," but checked himself as he again looked at Johnson's bandages. He paused as he reconsidered.

"Well, maybe just for a minute; but mind you, just for a minute."

"'Course. I certainly don't wanna tire her as she's recovering," responded Thomas.

Worthington looked again at Johnson's injury, as if he were still unsure if it were safe to admit the visitors. Then he turned slowly and bade the men to follow. Johnson looked at his captain with uncertainty as if he wasn't sure if he wanted to see the poor woman. He also wondered what the captain had in mind. However, Thomas waved him to follow and that decided it.

Worthington led them up a wooden stair that led to a loft behind and above the tavern. The loft was simply furnished with a wooden dresser, a lamp, and a plain yet sturdy chair. Up against the back wall of the loft was a small window, and under it was the bed Mrs. Worthington laid upon. The woman's leg was thickly bandaged and resting upon a rolled-up blanket, but the men could see nothing of it as she had a blanket pulled up to her neck that completely covered her legs. Only her tips of her stocking feet stuck out from the end of the blanket, as the blanket was a few inches too short.

Mrs. Worthington lay with her head turned away from the men, yet turned to see her visitors when she heard them step into the room. Mr. Worthington walked over to whisper to her.

"My dear, the captain from last night and his man have asked to see you. Do you feel up to visitors?"

"What do they want?" she asked.

Thomas overheard her response and inserted himself into the conversation as he stepped forward. "Mrs. Worthington, I'm sorry for the intrusion. I'm Captain Chittenden and ..."

"You were the man in the sword fight last night," Mrs. Worthington interupted.

"Yes ma'am, the same. I've come to apologize for your injury," continued Thomas.

Mrs. Worthington looked confused. "How are you to blame? It wasn't your sword that cut me."

"No ma'am, it wasn't my sword. However, I'm afraid I allowed the sword fight to carry on much longer than necessary. Please accept my deepest apology."

Still confused, she didn't know quite what to say. It didn't make sense to her that the captain was responsible for her injury. She wasn't even angry at the local man whose blade actually cut her. Mrs. Worthington thought of her injury as merely an accident, nothing more nor less. She had little experience with someone taking responsibility, not to mention having genuine concern for how their actions hurt her. As she attempted to understand his apology, she looked up at Thomas quizzically.

"I'm not sure I understand exactly how you allowed the injury to happen, Captain, but if you want me to accept your apology, I s'pose I can do that."

"Thank you for your grace, ma'am. Now, how are ya fairin'?"

"Oh, well my leg hurts quite a bit, especially when I move it. The doctor did give me something for the pain, which helps some."

"I'm sorry for ya suffering," Thomas said. "Is there anything I can do for ya that might make ya more comfortable?"

At this the woman looked at her husband, who shrugged his shoulders. "I don't know, Captain. I can't think of anything."

At this point Thomas remembered Johnson. Johnson still stood at the top of the stairs, either uncertain or unwilling to enter the recovery chamber completely.

"Ah, please forgive my bad manners. Ma'am, this is Johnson, one o' my men. Ya might notice his bandages. He was attacked by wolves."

Johnson bowed slightly as he was introduced. Mrs. Worthington just looked at him, appearing to examine his bandaging and perhaps feeling a sense of shared fate with the injured man. She smiled at Johnson. He averted his gaze, feeling awkward. Johnson still was unsure what he was doing in the injured woman's bedchamber. After all, he wasn't even present at the previous evening's fight.

"Mr. and Mrs. Worthington, we are on a mission o' the utmost urgency," began Thomas. "Speed is essential for us to be successful. We had two men attacked by wolves; fortunately, the other man is able to travel well 'nough. However, Johnson here suffered such injuries that he is unable to travel but at the slowest pace, an' even in great pain at that. I've asked your town council to consider allowin' me to leave Johnson with the town that he might recover without hindrance. With Johnson's consent, I would be most grateful if ya would consider providin' him lodgin' to recover in. Of course, I would expect to pay for his care."

The Worthingtons were clearly surprised at this strange request, and each searched the other's face for an answer. In the meantime Johnson shifted nervously in the background.

"Please feel free to think it over; I'm not expecting an answer right off. Johnson an' me will go back down to wait for the council's answer, as I wouldn't think o' leavin' Johnson without their permission. Mrs. Worthington, I leave ya with my wishes for a speedy recovery."

At this Thomas and the startled Johnson made their way downstairs to where Scout and Pumroy awaited their return. The surprised Worthingtons watched them go, both speechless.

The two amateur carpenters were reclining at one of the pub's tables when Thomas and Johnson reappeared downstairs. They appeared bored, having finished their work and with nothing else to occupy their time. Thomas and Johnson sat down at their table to await word from the town council.

"So tell me, Johnson. What ya think 'bout staying here with the Worthingtons as ya heal?" asked Thomas.

"I don' know, Cap. I don' like the idea o' stayin' with complete strangers; especially with me being all banged up an' all. I think I rather have ya just leave me along the trail to fend for myself."

Thomas laughed heartily. "Come now, Johnson; it's not so bad to be in need o' tendin'."

"I don' know, I can fend for myself. I know that I can't travel fast enough to stay with the regiment, so just leave me with some supplies an' my tent an' I'll tend to myself."

"I'll have no part o' such a fool's errand, Johnson. I'll leave ya in good hands that can watch over ya or I won't leave ya at all," said Thomas firmly.

"But Captain, I can..."

Johnson was interrupted by the town's magistrate coming through the door. The magistrate studied the men at the table from the doorway before slowly walking over to them.

"Captain, gentlemen," the magistrate said with a nod of his head. "I will grant your request with a condition."

"We're listening," said Thomas.

"We will allow your injured man to be tended by us for as many days as his injuries require; however, once healthy he will repay us for our care by working one day for each day he received our care and lodging."

Thomas smiled with satisfaction. "Well Johnson, I suppose it's up to you whether to accept the town's conditions," said Thomas.

Johnson looked from Thomas to the magistrate with uncertainty. He seemed at a loss to decide his own fate. Not finding the answer he searched for, he whispered in Thomas's ear.

"Captain, a word in private, sir?"

"'Course. Gentlemen, you'll excuse us a moment," said Thomas.

Johnson and Thomas stepped outside to converse. Johnson seemed agitated and paced back and forth.

"It's just, I don' know, Cap. I'd still rather ya just left me to make my own way."

"I won't hear of it! Johnson, ya'll either stay with the town or ride hard with us to overtake the Yorkers. I won't order ya to stay here, but I think ya'd be a whole lot more comfortable. Think o' your injuries, man! I'd hate to see you ride hard with those arms. Drop your pride an' allow the kind townsfolk to tend ya."

Johnson resumed pacing and looking off into the forest. Then he shrugged his shoulders and relented.

"All right, Cap. Ya don' leave a man much choice. I don' see that I can ride hard, no matter how much I tried. At least I'll get to repay the folks for their help," concluded Johnson.

"It's settled then! It takes more o' a man to accept help than to stubbornly insist on bein' self sufficient. Well done, Johnson!"

Thomas put his hand on Johnson's shoulder as they walked back in to where the others awaited them.

"All right then, Magistrate. We'll accept your hospitality an' your terms," said a smiling Thomas.

"Good enough," said the magistrate. "And Mr. Worthington has agreed to accept you into his home."

"Yes. I can make a room for you out of the old nursery. You see, our kids are too old for it," said Worthington as he sighed. "Truth is, we could use all the help we can get. Ever since we left Boston, we've never had enough hands for all the work."

"What did ya leave behind in Boston?" asked Thomas.

"Oh, we was living with Jane's folks. It was tight quarters, but we had a roof over our heads and never went hungry. I helped out with the family tavern, an' learned the trade along the way. Soon after I started working the tavern, I began dreaming of having my own. As time went on, I thought about it more an' more. At first Jane just rolled her eyes an' wouldn't entertain it for a moment. She said I was just being a daydreamin' fool. But once the little ones came along an' she started feeling cramped, then she started taking my dream seriously. Anyways, we finally scraped together enough to make a start out here in the Grants about five years ago. I tell you, there's something about having your own thing that's hard to put a price on."

"Do ya regret the move?" asked Thomas.

Worthington paused before responding. "No, I don't regret the move. I sure wouldn't want to go back to Boston. There have been times when I've given serious thought to moving back though. Now with Jane hurt an' all, I don't know how I'm gonna keep up the tavern. Maybe I can get Johnson to take on some of her duties."

"Johnson, ya do whatever ya can for these folks now," instructed Thomas.

At this, Thomas and the men said their goodbyes to Johnson, found Chambers at the general store, and headed back to camp. Thomas couldn't bear to wait another minute before resuming the trail, so camp was broken immediately and the trail remounted.

The men were in lighter spirits to be leaving the place of the fight. It also helped that the hunters brought back enough deer meat that morning to feed the men for a couple of days. The expectation of meat for supper improved the attitude of most of the men.

Fall 1747- Salisbury, Connecticutt

After Rachel's first visit to the Chittenden home, Sally wondered how she might further help her with womanly things. She hoped Rachel would experiment with the bows and ribbons in her hair, but she wanted to do something further for her. Sally thought about addressing Rachel's clothing. Rachel wore women's clothing, but her dresses were well out-of-date and well-worn. An idea came to Sally that Mama might be able to help.

"Mama, do ya have any dresses that are too small for you?"

"Why yes, of course dear, with the weight I put on, I got several dresses that I jist can't git into any longer. But I don' think ya're big enough to wear 'em yet, dear. I been savin' 'em for ya."

"Oh I'm not thinkin' o' me, Mama. I'm happy with the dresses I have. Do ya remember Rachel MacDonald?"

"Sure, ain't that the young lady that visited a couple days ago?"

"Yeah that's the one," confirmed Sally. "I wanna give her a couple dresses, Mama."

Mama had been looking out the front door, but suddenly turned her head to Sally. Her eyes were wide and mouth open. "Oh Sally, I don' know 'bout that. I've been savin' those dresses for you. Why would ya wanna give them to that MacDonald girl?"

"Mama, please try to understand. Rachel don't have a mother. She died when Rachel was a little girl. She don't have nobody to show her how to dress like a lady, an' I really wanna help her. Rachel's been so good to me, Mama. Please let me do this for 'er."

"Oh Sally, that's nice ya wanna help her out, but do ya understand those dresses cost money, a lotta money?"

"I know, Mama, but some things matter more than money. Ya don' know what it would mean to her."

"Oh Sally, I don' know... Let me talk to Father 'bout it.

169

"No, don't talk to Father! If ya have to talk to Father 'bout it, then just forget it."

"Oh dear, I just don' know if I can give away perfectly good dresses without talkin' with Father 'bout it. He might be upset if he finds out I just gave 'em away."

"Why does Father have to know, Mama? Can't ya just leave him outta it just this once?"

"I don' think so. I always ask Father 'bout things that cost money. He would be hot as a hornet if he knew I din't ask him."

"So what if he's hot, Mama. Maybe he'll just have to get over it." At this Mama looked incredulously at her daughter. How could Sally suggest such a thing? Maybe Sally would have to wait until she had a husband to understand such adult matters.

"Sally dear, I'm sorry ya don' understand. Maybe when you're older ya'll understand the seriousness o' me makin' sure Father don' get angry. I just can't take the chance," said Mama.

"Okay Mama," said Sally with little energy in her voice.

At this point Sally could see that Mama wasn't strong enough to give away those dresses on her own. The irony being that not only did Sally understand better than Mama thought, Sally actually understood better than Mama. With a deep sigh of resignation, Sally turned to leave the room. At this comment, Mama's face brightened.

"Oh Sally, I'm so pleased ya could come to understand. That's so very mature o' you to get it. I'm so proud!"

Sally slowly returned to her room. She sat heavily in her rocker and slowly rocked back and forth while she pondered the road block she just came across. After enough rocking to put most babies to sleep, Sally had another idea. Ever since Thomas and Rachel had taught her about her tree, she found more use for thinking. The back and forth movement seemed to both soothe and promote thought, a rare combination to be treasured wherever it might be found.

Sally sprang up from her chair, not giving a thought to her injured leg, nor feeling any pain at this moment. She quickly made her way
to her dresses, neatly folded in her dresser. Rifling through them, she finally found the one she wanted. Sally's blue dress had always been too large for her, and because of the poor fit, she never wore

it. Holding it up to remind herself of its size, she wondered if it would fit Rachel. She hoped it would. Being two years older, Rachel wore a size larger than Sally.

"Dear God, let this dress fit my friend," Sally asked aloud. Sally wrapped up her blue dress in some brown paper and tied it up with string. Adding a blue bow to give it the appearance of a gift, Sally was satisfied and set it aside until she could next get to town. It wasn't long before Sally had her opportunity, as Thomas went into town often to inquire about the swords.

Having been disappointed countless times by now, Thomas wasn't getting his hopes up. His face lit up with excitement as MacDonald wordlessly produced a large package from behind the counter. MacDonald set the box on the counter and allowed his young friend to open it. The first thing Thomas saw was two sticks. Not knowing what to make of the sticks, he set them aside to dig deeper. Thomas figured the sticks must be part of the packing. Further digging yielded two swords in the bottom of the box. The blades were completely protected by black leather scabbards, revealing only the metal handles. The hilts were dull grey in color, and not much bigger than a large man's hand.

Thomas pulled one of them out of the box, quickly slipping his hand onto the hilt. Black leather covered the hilt, providing a comfortable berth for his hand. Beneath the leather covering the hilt was hard wood, and beneath that was the foundational iron. To hold the leather covering in place, a thin wire wound around the black leather.

Thomas pulled the blade from its protective scabbard to get a look at the business end of the sword. Emerging from its covering slid a straight, double-edged, iron blade. The blade alone measured 34 inches, while the sword as a whole stretched 41 inches. Except for an opening through which to place one's hand, an iron grating surrounded the hilt. Thomas examined the grating, wondering what it might be for.

"Mr. MacDonald, what're these bars 'round the handle for?"

"T' begin wi' lad, the handle be called a 'hilt,' an' the bars 'round the hilt be called a 'basket hilt.' The basket protects yer hand, lad. What ye hold in yer hand be a basket-hilted Scottish claymore, protector o' the Highlander."

"What do the basket thing protect me from?" Thomas asked.

"From 'nother man's sword, or fro' yerself. Ye see lad, ye don' want yer hand t' slip down onto the blade," MacDonald laughed.

"Oh, I see now. It's like little armor for your hand."

"That's it, lad. The hand be one o' the most vulnerable places fo' a swordsman."

"Okay, so can we start? Will ya teach me something today?" Thomas asked eagerly.

"Aye lad, straight away. I be all ready for ye. Come on oot back behind the store."

MacDonald picked up a shovel and a wooden post on the way out the back door. Thomas brought the swords with him.

"Nae lad, ye won't be needin' the swords quite yet. I'll take those. Here, take the shovel an' the post."

"What do these have to do with learnin' the sword?" asked Thomas.

"Plenty, lad. Be patient an' ye'll see. Okay now, I want ye to dig a hole fo' the post 'bout here, and makin' sure it be a good two feet in depth now. Let me know when ye're done. I got some work t' attend t', an' I'll be inside when yer through."

"But Mr. MacDonald..."

"I'll hae no buts 'bout it; dig the hole an' then we'll see 'bout learnin' ye somethin' o' the sword today."

Thomas couldn't imagine what digging a hole had to do with learning to use a sword, and was frustrated at what seemed to be a further delay in his lessons. However, he shrugged off his frustration and began to dig the hole. The ground behind the store didn't easily yield to the spade, and it was a good forty-five minutes later that he wiped sweat from his brow and went to look for MacDonald.

"Okay, Mr. MacDonald. I dug the hole. Now can we start the lessons?"

"Oh aye, lad. I jist be 'nother minute 'ere."

MacDonald finished his work, picked up the "sticks" that had come with the swords and a burlap sack and led Thomas out back. MacDonald first inspected the hole and was satisfied with its depth. He picked up the post and placed it in the hole and began to kick the shoveled dirt back into the hole. He finished replacing the dirt and packed it down firmly. MacDonald tested the post to see if it would easily move. Satisfied that it wouldn't, he picked up the burlap sack and wrapped it around the post. He lashed the burlap in place with rope at the top and the bottom of it. Then he picked up one of the "sticks."

These "sticks" were actually training swords, made of wood with dulled edges to prevent injury. They measured the same length and shape as the real swords. The Scotsman wanted Thomas to start with the wooden training sword until his skill progressed enough to safely use the iron sword. MacDonald handed Thomas one of them.

"What's the post an' the sticks for?" asked Thomas.

"Aye lad," laughed MacDonald. "These 'ere sticks be proper trainin' swords. They be what ye'll start wi'. As fo' the post, we've made a proper pells, lad. The burlap stretches roughly fro' a man's knees t' his head. These be the proper places t' land yer blow. Ye'll start yer learnin' upon the pells. Once I find ye've advanced weel enough, then ye'll spare wi' me."

Thomas only nodded in response. He still didn't really understand why they didn't just pick up the iron swords and start swinging away.

"Okay lad, we begin wi' balance. Here be how I want ye t' stand. Ye'll notice my weight lies weel o'er both me feet. This make a fine base. Ye're feet 're t' be shoulder width apart, an' maybe a touch more. Ye're t' point yer left shoulder t' yer adversary. Hold yer sword shoulder level wi' the blade up," instructed the Scotsman.

Having given Thomas instructions for the basic stance, MacDonald walked over and gave him a shove. Thomas stumbled and almost fell.

"Nae, lad. That'll ne'er do. Ye hae t' hold a stronger position than that, lad. Come now, make me a strong base so I can't move ye wi' me wee finger," MacDonald said with a smile.

Thomas tried again, this time assuming what he thought would be a stronger base position. Once again, MacDonald easily knocked him off balance.

"Aye lad, that young lass o' yer sister be knockin' ye off yer balance like that. Come now, pay careful attention to how I form me strong base."

This went on for some time until Thomas got the proper feel of it. Thomas began to learn to move his feet quickly to maintain balance when MacDonald "attacked."

"Now there ye go, lad. Withoot a firm base an' footwork, no amount o' sword skill will do. A skilled man will knock ye o' yer back straight away. Okay, now we can look t' the sword. Come o'er t' the pells, lad. Now assume yer strong base. There ye go. Now we work the pells. First ye need t' get a feel for the sword in yer hand. Ye need t' get a feel for her weight an' her motion, lad. Ye first learn her feel wi' the pells. A fine swordsman knows 'is sword as well as 'is own arm, lad."

"I still don' git why I'm usin' a stick? Why can't I use the real sword?" Thomas asked.

"Make no mistake lad; this be a sword. It be a real trainin' sword t' be exact, an' the proper length an' weight. Once yer skill wi' the trainin' sword progresses weel enough, then we'll talk aboot the iron sword."

MacDonald taught Thomas the basic striking blows with the sword. Thomas practiced the blows on both sides of the post until he tired himself. MacDonald watched awhile to make sure Thomas directed his blows correctly, as he didn't want him learning any bad habits he'd later have to break. After correcting Thomas many times, the boy seemed to get a feel for the proper motions. Once he was satisfied, MacDonald returned to his work inside.

It's unclear if exhaustion or lack of light got the best of Thomas first. He reappeared inside the store at dusk. He appeared weary, yet his excitement was readily apparent.

"So lad, be ye finished trainin' fo' the day?"

"Yeah. I think I'll stop for now. Anyways, I'm not sure I can lift my arm o'er my head anymore," said Thomas.

"Aye lad, ye're in fine farmin' shape I'm sure, but it be 'nother thing t' be in fine swordin' shape. Ye'll need to work on yer condition."

Rachel was making a delivery and wasn't back to the store yet. Sally's excitement kept her from wanting to sit still, so she continued to pace the aisles of the store while she waited. As she rounded the back aisle, she looked again at the door and saw Rachel tiredly walking in.

"Hi, Rachel."

"Oh, hello Sally."

"Makin' deliveries?" inquired Sally.

"Aye, more than the usual today." Sally's face formed a wry smile.

"Hey Rachel, there's a package for ya over on the counter."

"Really? I don' remember orderin' anything." Rachel picked up the package and turned it over in her hands.

"There's no address. How did it get here?"

"It's from me silly," laughed Sally.

Rachel looked nervous and excited, wondering what her friend had brought. Opening the package, a blue dress fell onto the counter. She quickly took in her breath in surprise. Rachel had seen dresses like it in the general store, but she'd never thought she'd have one of her own.

"This be for me, lass?"

"That's right," returned Sally.

"Oh, shall I try it on now, do ye think?"

"Well it ain't just for lookin' at." Rachel stepped behind the counter to gain some privacy and quickly took off her simple, faded working dress and put on the blue one. The friends shared a smile and a laugh as she finished buttoning it up. As if a secret signal were exchanged, they simultaneously ran over to the mirror in the corner.

At first Rachel was delighted with the refection looking back at her. Rachel caught her breath as the full impact of her feminine image sunk in. Sally too was enjoying every moment of her friend's emerging femininity. Then Rachel turned the other way and her face suddenly turned to ice. After a moment of frozen animation, Rachel half-screamed and half-cried.

"Oh my, get this horrid dress off o' me. I don' want it. Take it away," cried Rachel. Rachel quickly freed herself from the torture of its image, threw it on the counter, and ran to the back room. MacDonald was outside with Thomas. Rachel found herself alone to cry, and cry she did.

Sally sat stunned for several minutes. She couldn't understand what had just happened. One minute she and her friend were enjoying a new dress and a sacred moment between young women, and the next the previously prized dress was thrown on the counter and abandoned. Once Sally recovered herself sufficiently, she went in search of her friend.

Sally quickly found Rachel huddled and sobbing in the corner of the back room. Sally threw her arms around her friend in comfort.

"Rachel, what happened? What's upsettin' ya?" Sally asked.

For several minutes sobbing was the only response. After Rachel's sobbing subsided a bit, she handed Sally the picture. Sally looked at the picture of Rachel's mother that she'd seen before, and at first didn't understand.

"I know Rachel, it's ya mother. But what's that gotta do with..." Rachel responded by pointing to the dress her mother wore in the picture. Things quickly fell into place for Sally. The dress her mother wore in the picture looked just like the one Rachel had just tried on. Sadness for her friend flooded Sally.

"Oh Rachel, I'm so sorry! I had no idea!" After her tears lessened, Rachel was ready to speak.

"When I, when I turned the other way... it be like, it be like I saw my mither lookin' back at me."

Rachel's tears returned in another flood of feeling. Sally didn't know what to do, and decided to just sit with her friend and wait. Sally was still fairly new to dealing with emotion, and sat wringing her hands.

"Oh Rachel, ya must miss your mama somethin' terrible. I'm so sorry my dress reminded ya." Rachel nodded in reply. Tears continued to stream down her face.

"I wish the dress ye picked hae not been the same, but it be not yer fault."

"Yeah, I guess so, but I feel bad that my dress made ya hurt so bad," said Sally.

"It be true that yer dress brought up memories fo' me, but don't feel bad. Ye got nothin' t' do wi' me losin' me mither. I jus' miss her so bad." The girls sat in silence.

"I s'pose nobody can take ya mama's place, but maybe we can learn to be ladies together. With you knowin' lots 'bout trees an' me knowin' lots 'bout dressin' up and such, maybe we can help each other out."

"Maybe," said Rachel doubtfully.

"An' I'll take my blue dress home so that..."

"No! Leave me dress where it be. I hae t' face missin' me mither. I ain't gonna hide from it. So leave me the dress. As much as it gave me a fright, it be a chance for me t' face me grief."

"Are ya sure, Rachel? I won't take it personal if ya rather have me look for another one."

"Nae lass, ye just leave me this one. Anyways, this blue dress matches the color o' me tree right now." Both girls laughed as they embraced.

Thomas wasn't able to get away from the farm until a few days later. Although he was eager to resume his training, his sore and fatigued muscles were grateful for the time to recover. He still felt a faint stiffness in his muscles as he and MacDonald walked out back to train, but a little discomfort wasn't going to dampen Thomas's excitement to resume his training.

"Okay lad, show what's come o' yer trainin' a few days past. Let me see ye make each o' the proper blows 'pon the pells."

Thomas took up his strong base position and began to deliver the blows.

"Nae, lad. That won't do. Yer form o' the blows is fine, but the problem is yer stoppin' between the blows. As soon as ye hesitate fo' even a moment, a skilled adversary will finish 'is work on ye. Yer t' keep yer sword in constant motion for now. I don't want ye t' even hesitate for a moment," MacDonald instructed.

Thomas took a deep breath and applied his blows again, this time attempting a continuous motion.

"There ye go, lad. That be fine work."

"But Mr. MacDonald, I couldn't keep up that kinda speed for long."

"Yer unlikely t' have to lad. Encounters o' the sword normally last but a few moments. The sort o' thing ye see on the stage wi' men swingin' at one 'nother for twenty minutes an' dancin' aboot the stage makes for a nice fairy tale, but oot on the battlefield it be quite a different story. Most men'll be wounded o' worse afore a minute hae passed. Yer quickness an' yer skill must be in strong supply if ye hope t' walk away fro' the encounter."

"Okay, but can we spare together now?"

"Oh noo lad. Ye'll need t' work a bit more a' the pells afore ye're ready for 'nother man. Ye must be patient lad; there's no replacin' proper trainin'. If we hurry things along afore ye're ready, we may train ye just weel enough t' be a danger t' yerself an' others. It be the same as yer tree, lad. There's no short cuts t' raisin' a proper tree that'll be strong an' healthy with a proper base."

"Well, can I at least take home one of the trainin' swords to practice with at home? I can only git away from the farm a couple times a week, and I don' wanna have to wait forever to learn," asked Thomas.

"Weel, okay lad. But I'll only agree t' ye takin' a sword if ye promise t' make a proper pells at home an' only practice alone. No practicing on other folk now."

"Sure okay," Thomas quickly agreed.

Thomas was so excited to be allowed to take home one of the training swords that he would have agreed to almost any conditions the Scotsman may have placed upon him. Thomas quickly packed up a training sword, a burlap sack, and his sister. He wanted to get away before Mr. MacDonald changed his mind.

The next day Thomas found time between chores to find a suitable tree to make a proper pells. He felled the tree, cut off the branches, dug a two-foot deep hole, and affixed the burlap MacDonald had given him. When he thought no one was watching, he pulled out his training sword and went through his routine. Midway through his second round of blows, Ben came into view. Ben eagerly came over to make a closer inspection of the strange looking behavior of his younger brother. After watching from behind for a few minutes, he decided Thomas must be practicing some kind of fencing.

"Hey Thomas, what are ya about with that thing?"

"Oh, Ben. I din't know anyone was watchin'."

"Are ya tryin' to keep this a secret or somethin'?" questioned Ben.

"Well, I s'pose so. I guess I'm kinda embarrassed to have anybody see me when I'm just a beginner."

Ben's face suddenly brightened. "Hey Thomas, teach me how to use that thing!"

"Okay you bet," Thomas responded without thinking. Then Thomas had a second thought. "Wait a minute. I can't teach ya without permission."

Thomas had two concerns about teaching Ben; the one he expressed, and the other came as he imagined what Ben might do with a sword. He thought of Ben's temper and stubbornness, and figured it wouldn't take much provocation for Ben to hurt somebody.

"Permission? Who do ya need permission from to teach ya brother to swing a wooden sword about?"

"I'm sorry, Ben. Mr. MacDonald is teachin' me to do this, an' I'm sure he'd want me to ask 'im."

"Ah come on, Thomas. Old man MacDonald doesn't have to know nothin'. I won't tell him, an' you don' have to tell him. He's not gonna find out."

"No, Ben. Ya don't understand. He'd consider that a betrayal of his trust, an' I would too."

"Ah, come off it. Who gives a hoot 'bout trust? Now don' go talkin' like a preacher. When did ya start caring 'bout trust? Ya makin' too big a thing outta nothin'." Then Ben stopped himself and had another thought.

"Did ya go and get religious on me, Thomas Chittenden? That's it, isn't it? That crazy old man is puttin' some crazy religion ideas in your brain. I'm right, ain't I?"

"No, Ben. It's not like that at all. Mr. MacDonald has been nothin' but good to me. He's less crazy than anyone else I know."

"Come on, Thomas. Do ya hear yourself talk? Ya talkin' crazy. Ya worshippin' some old man that's fillin' ya mind with some foolishness. Ya best stay away from him. I don' know Thomas, maybe I oughta talk with Father 'bout this. I'm worried 'bout ya. I know somethin' 'bout that old man. I remember he used us to do some work 'bouts his yard once. He's probably just usin' ya again."

Thomas didn't know what to say at this point. He just looked at his brother sadly. It was the first time he'd considered how little his brother understood of his relationship with MacDonald. Then Thomas began to wonder if Ben might even be jealous of his relationship with his old friend.

"Look here, Ben. I'm sorry if it don' make sense to ya, but take it or leave it. I'm gonna ask Mr. MacDonald before I teach anybody with his sword."

"Well, I'll just go talk to Father 'bout this," muttered Ben.

Thomas thought better of responding to Ben's threat. Thomas figured it was an empty threat. Thomas and Ben both knew neither of them would likely be doing anymore training if Father had anything to say about it. It seemed like a good idea to Thomas to end his training for the day. He packed up his training sword, burlap and rope so as to not attract much attention to his training site. He was careful to see that Ben was not watching when he selected a hiding place for his gear.

Ben got over his initial anger at not being able to talk his younger brother into training him, and his clearer thinking prevailed. He too realized it would be foolish to mention anything about the sword to Father. By the time supper was finished, Ben privately approached Thomas. Having had a few hours to cool off his temper, Ben was prepared to be a bit more humble.

"Hey, little brother. Look, I don' get why ya have to ask the old man 'bout trainin' me. But if ya have to, then do it. I really wanna learn to use it; just think how impressive we'll be if we really know how to use one o' those things. I can't wait to show off to my friends. An' the girls won't be able to stay away from us."

"All right, Ben. I'll ask him," agreed Thomas unenthusiastically.

"Okay, an' make sure ya tell him I'm at least as responsible as you, maybe more," added Ben. Thomas laughed.

Several days later Thomas was out behind the Feed 'n Seed working away at the pells. MacDonald corrected his technique a bit here and there, although Thomas seemed to have the basic motions down fairly well.

"Weel done, lad. I think yer beginning t' get it. Ye've been workin' the pells at home, I see."

"Yeah, I have. Oh, that reminds me. My brother Ben wants me to train 'im with your trainin' sword."

MacDonald looked astonished. "Oh aye, lad. Ye can't be serious. Ye're just beginning to learn yerself. Yer in no condition t' be learnin' another."

"But Mr. MacDonald, what harm would it do to teach Ben what you've already taught me?"

"What harm? Lad, hae ye learnt nothin' aboot the first lesson o' the broadsword? It be noo enough t' teach a man the motions o' the sword. Ye might do that weel enough. But are ye ready t' be teachin' and discernin' the tree o' yer brother? If not, ye might be preparing him t' take another man's life o' limb withoot need. Did ye think aboot that, lad?"

Thomas thought some about the condition of his brother's tree, and remembered his own concerns. He'd seen the temper his brother had, and had been afraid many times. Thomas also remembered Ben's words about impressing his friends and shuddered.

"Ya're right, Mr. MacDonald. I did think some 'bout what Ben might do."

"Weel okay, lad. Maybe this be a good time t' be reminded o' the seriousness o' the first lesson. I'll hae no man wield one o' me swords unless I know weel 'nough the condition of his tree. If yer brither wants t' learn the sword, he'll hae t' come t' me."

Thomas dreaded Ben's reaction to Mr. MacDonald's decision. He hoped Ben would forget about the sword, yet without much thought he quickly realized that was unlikely. Thomas spent the ride home thinking through how he'd respond to his brother's disappointment. He decided he'd just have to let Ben be disappointed and angry; there was no avoiding that. As expected, Ben cornered Thomas within an hour of his returning home.

"Hey little brother, come here," ordered Ben. Thomas reluctantly approached his brother.

"So, did ya get permission to teach me the sword?" Ben eagerly asked.

"Uh, no I din't. He said 'no,' Ben."

"What? No he din't. Well, it don't matter what he says. Ya'll teach me anyways."

"No, Ben. I'm not gonna teach ya."

"What! Ya kiddin' me, right, little brother? Ya can't be serious 'bout carin' what that old man says," said Ben incredulously.

Thomas looked his older brother straight in the eye. "No, Ben. I'm gonna respect his wishes. If he don' want me to train ya, then I won't."

"How can his wishes make a hill o' beans worth o' difference? This is between you an' me, little brother, an' we're family."

"Look Ben, I get that ya're disappointed. I'm sorry 'bout that, I really am. But I'm not gonna teach ya. I'm not ready to teach ya. I'm not ready to teach anyone the sword."

"I don' care if ya're not an expert teacher or somethin', just teach me what ya know. I'll learn as you learn, little brother."

"I'm sorry, Ben. I just can't take on the responsibility to teach somebody else yet. It'd be a fool's errand. I don' even know what I'm doin' yet."

"A fool's errand? Where did ya learn to talk like that?"

"I just don' know enough to teach anybody else yet."

"What can there be to know? It can't be that complicated. Ya're just learnin' to swing a sword about. How much responsibility can there be in that?" asked Ben.

"Ben, I don' know if I can make ya understand. For me it's not just 'bout swingin' around a sword; it's 'bout learnin' to responsibly wield a lethal weapon. Ben, ya take a man's life in ya hands when you unsheathe a sword!"

"A man's life? When did ya go an' get all serious on me? I'm not plannin' to go out an' kill anybody I please. I just wanna impress my friends an' girls, an' maybe be able to take it to somebody if it comes to that."

Thomas repeated himself, "I'm sorry, Ben."

"I'm sorry, little brother, because 'I'm sorry' ain't gonna cut it! I don' give a rat's ass what that old man said! We're brothers! Isn't that more important than some ole man in town? I guess you're tellin' me the ole man is more important to ya than I am. Is that it?"

"No, Ben. That's not it. It's much more complicated than that, but I can see that I'm not gonna be able to make ya understand," said Thomas. Thomas paused briefly. "I don' know what else to say, Ben. I don' wanna end it like this, but I don' know what else to say."

"There is nothin' else to say, little brother. Ya care more for that good-for-nothing ole man than ya do your own family! I figure there's nothin' else to say after that. Good day to you!"

"Ben, wait a minute. Go an' ask Mr. MacDonald to train ya. An' maybe even take time to talk with 'im..."

"Oh come on, little brother; ya think I'm gonna waste my time on that old fool just because you do? I got better things to do with my time than that."

"Wait a minute, Ben! Hear me out. Ya might be surprised at what ya get outta talkin' to Mr. MacDonald. Just give 'im a try. An' lemme warn you, ya gotta have a good attitude or he ain't gonna train ya."

Ben turned on his heels and stormed out of the barn with a dismissive wave. Thomas started to go after him, but thought better of it and slowly walked to the house instead. It saddened Thomas to see what was becoming of his relationship with Ben. Ben had been his best friend in the world, and now it seemed they were becoming enemies. Well, at least unfriendly. Thomas wondered what he could do to repair his relationship with Ben. He certainly didn't want to leave things the way they were now. He could understand how it might appear to Ben that MacDonald was more important to him; it might even be true. However, he still loved his brother and wanted to be on good terms with him. Thomas determined to try to talk this over with Ben, but to wait for Ben to cool off first.

Not to add further salt to Ben's wound, Thomas vowed not to practice the broadsword when Ben was around. Thomas decided to move his practice pells to a more remote location, one that Ben didn't know about. He wasn't sure where that would be, but he'd find a place.

Finally the day arrived when MacDonald judged that Thomas's skill had developed enough for hand-to-hand sparing. Thomas felt he'd been ready for weeks now, but had tried to remain patient and wait for his teacher to decide the time was right.

MacDonald watched his protégé practice his complete routine several times without flaw before announcing his readiness. MacDonald went back to retrieve the second training sword.

"Okay lad, now yer ready fo' hand-to-hand. I'm gonna come at ye an' I want ye t' stop all blows. Ye ready, lad?"

"Am I ready? I been waitin' for this ever since the swords got here. Let's get to it!"

MacDonald laughed mirthfully. "Okay lad, here I come at ye."

And with that MacDonald slowly applied blows to Thomas from every direction, testing his apprentice's ability to protect each part of his body. Thomas successfully parried the initial, slow coming blows. MacDonald then slowly increased his speed, to give Thomas a chance to adjust to a faster rate of combat.

As soon as the skilled master increased the speed of his blows, every second or third blow struck home. Thomas's initial confidence in his skill suffered as many blows as his body and sword arm. After a few minutes, MacDonald backed off.

"Okay lad, ye done weel enough fo' yer first time goin' hand-to-hand."

"Well enough? I only blocked half o' your blows. How can that be well enough?" responded Thomas.

"Come now, lad. This be yer first time practicing wi 'nother man. Did ye expect t' block each blow? Ye done weel enough t' start."

"I don' feel like I did good at all. I thought I'd be able to block most o' your blows at least. Come on, I've been practicin' almost every day for over a month now."

"It be one thing t' practice well with a fence post; it be somethin' else to do weel wi' 'nother man, especially 'nother man with quite a bit more time spent wi' a Claymore in his hand. Don't go forgettin' that now, lad."

"Huh."

"Come now lad, ye may weel exceed my skill some day, but ye can't have expected it t' be yer first time goin' hand-to-hand wi' me," soothed the master.

Thomas just grunted in reply. Perhaps he had expected to hold his own with the older man his first time, or perhaps he'd just expected to make a better showing for himself. Not only was he disappointed in his performance, but he hadn't expected it to matter to him as much as it did.

Thomas's bruised pride turned from disappointment to determination on his way home. Although the tired sun was beginning to set in the west, Thomas had his mind set on getting in another practice session today. He hurried out to his secret practice area and went at the pells with renewed fury. Of course the pells merely accepted the blows, but Thomas felt better after a satisfying practice session. Exhausted, he put away his training equipment and headed off to the house for supper.

The perfunctory supper prayer having just been said by Father, Ben looked Thomas in the eye before reaching for the food plates. Thomas didn't know what was coming, but he didn't like the mischievous grin on his brother's face.

"Say, little brother. What were ya up to before ya came in for supper?" inquired Ben.

Thomas was taken off guard and asked Mama to pass the potatoes to buy a little time. He'd hoped Ben would never bring up the sword training around Father, but his developing intuition about people had told him Ben likely would. Thomas quickly decided to meet the issue head on. He took a deep breath and responded in honesty.

"Been out practicing with my trainin' sword," Thomas simply said.

"With what?" asked Father in surprise.

"A trainin' sword, Father. I'm learnin' to use a broadsword." Thomas looked over at Ben to see a smug look of satisfaction. He was grinning from ear to ear, although trying not to seem too interested in the conversation.

"Where'd ya get a broadsword, son?"

"Mr. MacDonald loaned me his."

"An' is Mr. MacDonald teachin' ya the proper skills o' the sword?" Father further inquired.

"Yes, Father."

"An' does Mr. MacDonald have sufficient trainin' an' skill to teach ya the sword?"

"Oh yeah, Father. Mr. MacDonald learned the broadsword as a young boy in Scotland. He's known how to use it all his life," answered Thomas.

"I see. Ya know, Thomas, I don' recall givin' permission for ya to be learnin' the sword," Father continued.

Thomas looked at Father and felt relieved to see a lock of satisfaction mixed with the usual sternness on his face. Thomas relaxed a bit. "Ya right, Father. I shoulda asked your permission before I started trainin'. I s'pose I forgot in my excitement to get started with it all. I'm sorry."

Father smiled almost imperceptibly. He continued to hold onto a sternness he didn't feel, but thought it necessary to portray as the head of the family. "Okay son, I'll overlook this disrespect o' my authority this time. But I do expect ya to show me what ya been learnin' tomorrow. Understood?"

"Understood sir," Thomas replied.

Thomas looked at Ben and enjoyed the startled look of disappointment on his older brother's face. Clearly the conversation had not gone as Ben had intended. Perhaps Ben had underestimated the pride Father would feel in having his son learn a respectable form of weaponry.

The next day after morning chores had been tended to, the family sat down to the midday meal. Father quickly brought the conversation back to the sword. He'd grown more and more curious about Thomas's sword training.

"Okay, Thomas. After dinner I wanna see what ya up to with that sword o' yours," Father announced.

Thomas merely nodded his assent. Ben's face almost looked a light shade of green with the envy. The plan had not only failed to evoke the ire of Father as he'd hoped, but now Thomas was getting Father's pride and attention. His malicious plan had backfired.

After the men had finished eating, Thomas led Ben and Father out to his original sword training site, as he still didn't want it known where he worked out with the sword. He took care to retrieve his practice sword when neither Ben nor Father was watching. Thomas picked up his pells and set it in the hole in the ground. Father merely grinned as he watched his son prepare for training. Thomas looked at Ben and Father to see that they were far enough away to be out of danger, then he quickly went through his routine of each attack and defense three times.

"Well, now look at that," said Father. "Ya look like ya almost know what you're 'bout there, son."

Thomas nodded in reply. Thomas noticed Ben standing with his arms folded and a scowl on his face. Father was beaming with pride. He thoroughly enjoyed his son's skill with the sword, almost as much as if Father had demonstrated the skills himself. It was unusual for Thomas to see his Father pleased like this.

"Huh, it don' look like much to me. It's easy 'nough to hit a defenseless post, but another thing to defend yourself 'gainst a real man," said Ben.

"Nonsense, boy. Thomas did a fine job with that sword. Any fool can see that he knows what he's 'bout with that thing," retorted Father.

"Huh," was all Ben offered in response.

Thomas didn't like the direction in which things were going. "Well, 'nough with the sword. We've all got plenty o' work to attend to. Let's get to it," redirected Thomas.

Ben thought over the events of the preceding day all morning. Thoughts of Father's beaming smile at Thomas kept in his mind's eye. Ben went about his chores mindlessly, doing them by rote. Without really deliberately deciding to, Ben found himself riding his horse into town and wondered what he was doing. Ben was not a particularly self-aware person, but quickly realized he was headed to the Feed 'n Seed to find old man MacDonald. Ben figured that if

MacDonald would teach Thomas, then the old man would teach him as well. Ben stepped into the Feed 'n Seed and quickly found Mr. MacDonald.

"Hello, Mr. MacDonald. How're ya doin'?"

A surprised MacDonald turned around to find Ben standing in his store. MacDonald couldn't recall Ben visiting him since he'd done some work for him, and was curious about the sudden visit. "Hello, Ben. What can I do ye for?"

"I was thinkin' that if ya'll train my brother on the sword, then ya'll train me."

MacDonald chuckled to himself, amused at Ben's line of thinking. "I see. An' why do ye want t' learn the sword, lad?"

"Oh, I just want to... seem like it'd be a fun thing to do."

MacDonald looked at Ben with a grin on his face, not believing he was getting the truth, or at least not the whole truth. "Weel Ben, the broadsword be not a toy t' hae fun with, it be quite a serious weapon."

Ben laughed, as though a grade school teacher were underestimating her student. "I know that a sword is a weapon, sir, but I still think it'd be fun to learn."

MacDonald shook his head sadly, for the teacher had not underestimated his prospective student. In fact MacDonald carefully assessed his student with all that he said in words and without words. With good cause, the savvy old soul was concerned with Ben's motives. "I don't teach the broadsword for fun, lad."

"What's wrong with learnin' the sword for fun? Can't it be fun?"

"Nae lad, it can't be. The broadsword be no hobby. It be a dangerous weapon that be made more dangerous i' the wrong hands. I refuse t' teach ye 'cause o' yer reasons. I'll hae no part of puttin' a sword in the hands o' a lad that lacks respect for her an' what she might do t' a man," decided MacDonald.

"Oh, come on, ole man. I'm ain't gonna hurt nobody. I just wanna have a little fun, like Thomas," retorted Ben.

"Come now, lad. Thomas be up t' more than fun. He might be havin' some fun, but the lad hae respect. I'll learn no man the broadsword who lacks respect. Now me offer still stands; if ye want t' start makin' visits, we might git ye t' be ready for the sword, lad."

"Now I see where my little brother gets his weird ideas. Ya take yaself too seriously, ole man. Ya messin' my brother up with your weird, cockamamy ideas. I've tried to warn Thomas t' stay away from ya, that you're a bad influence, but ya've got him so brainwashed he won't no longer listen to reason. Ya stay away from my little brother, ole man. Ya hear me?"

"I Hope ye'll think more o' me offer,"pressed MacDonald.

"'Course not; why would I wanna visit to just talk? I got better things to do than just be idle. If ya want someone to talk to, ya'll jist have to find someone else. If ya ain't willin' to teach me the sword, then I don' want nothin' to do with ya."

MacDonald wisely remained quiet. It saddened him that Ben wouldn't allow him to help. He had sensed Ben's distress the day he attempted to steal from him, and he still sensed it now. MacDonald felt for the boy, and could hear the hurt behind his anger. He also didn't want to further provoke Ben, especially when Ben seemed to be fairly lathered up already. MacDonald could see how quickly Ben lost his temper with little provocation, which gave MacDonald more appreciation for why Thomas might fear angering his brother.

When MacDonald didn't respond Ben tried a couple more times to prod the older man into a mud slinging episode, but the Scotsman would not be provoked. Far from provoked, MacDonald's sadness for Ben increased the more he heard. Ben finally gave up, stormed out of the store, and raced home.

May 18, 1753 - Hampshire Grants

Scout had come to expect to find the Yorker tracks leading from river to creek, and creek to river. However, today the markings seemed to turn suddenly northwest, away from the northeast direction they had followed for many days. Scout took more time to examine the tracks. After an hour or more of inspection, Scout was satisfied the trail did turn northwest and committed the regiment to the new direction.

"Scout, we givin' them Yorkers too much time. Sun's already been up awhile, we gotta go!" prompted Thomas.

"If you hadn't sent Haskins off, this wouldn't take so long," barked back Scout.

"That ain' fair! Ya know Haskins run off."

"He wouldn't have left if you'd just given him his due respect," Scout retorted.

"It's somethin' other than respect he's lookin' for," countered Thomas.

"Maybe you're just threatened by a man like that," said Scout. Thomas pondered Scout's comment a moment, and then decided against responding. He mounted his horse and ordered the regiment back on the trail.

The next day the regiment awoke to a gentle spring rain. No one wanted to leave their relatively dry tents. The camp slowly came to life with a cold breakfast being served. Chambers didn't bother even trying to light a cooking fire in the rain. Breakfast wasn't satisfying, but it provided enough to get the men going on the trail. Many of the men reacted testily with one another, especially with no coffee this morning. Some people just can't have a good day without their coffee.

As usual, the scouts went ahead to get a reading on the Yorker trail. With Haskins gone, Morse took over his duties helping Scout.

The scouts took more time finding the trail in the rain. The trail continued to lead northwest, and by now Thomas had developed some theories about their destination.

A wide clearing near the top of a hill provided a place to stop for a brief rest and a bit to eat around midday. Thomas consulted with his officers over the meager meal.

"Gentlemen," began Thomas, "I've been chewing on somethin' ever since we left Litchfield. Why the Yorkers takin' these folk to the Grants? Why not take the shorter route to New York? New York couldn't be more 'an forty or fifty miles from Litchfield."

"I've wondered the same thing," said John. "It just don't make sense to take the prisoners this far north. For what? An' the turn to the northwest don't make no more sense than the northeast."

Lt. Chambers spoke up. "An' how are they feedin' them folk?" Lt. Chambers's mind often went to thoughts of food.

"I hope to God they are feedin' 'em," Thomas said. After a brief pause, Thomas continued. "The only thing out this way is the Grants. I can't think o' no other reason to bring 'em this way. But what'd they want with 'em out in the Grants?"

Just as Thomas finished his thought, the scouts rode up at a gallop. "Captain, it's almost certain we're being shadowed," said Morse.

"Shadowed?" asked John

"That's right," said Scout.

"How'd ya know?" asked Thomas.

"The last hour Morse and I have seen a brief movement here and there," said Scout.

"Who is it?" asked John.

"Don't know. We haven't had a clear look at 'em yet, just a bit here and a bit there," answered Scout.

John looked worried. "Captain, I think we should set a front an' a rear guard an' have the rest carry muskets at the ready."

"Now hold on, Lieutenant. We don' want to alert 'em, whoever they be. Set the front an' rear guard an' tell the others, but I don' want us to tip our hand just yet. Leave the muskets where they be. An' be quiet 'bout it. Scout, find out who it be."

With a nod the scouts remounted their horses. John made himself walk slowly off to set up the guards and quietly inform the rest of the regiment. The regiment remounted and returned to the trail. In spite of Thomas's precautions, the men appeared worried and were looking about more and talking less. So much for not tipping our hands, Thomas thought. We look like we're walking into battle, and the only thing missing is bayonets mounted on our muskets.

Thomas and John rode near the back of the regiment, as they usually did. The only difference was the rear guard behind them. They couldn't keep themselves from looking about a bit more themselves, as much as they tried to appear unconcerned.

Morse and Scout were feeling anything but unconcerned. They had doubled their efforts to look over anything and everything. The scouts paid particular attention to the lay of the land they led the regiment through. Leading the regiment into an ambush would be the last thing they wanted to let happen.

With dusk approaching, the officers decided to pitch camp. They hadn't seen any further signs of being shadowed, which left them even more nervous. The only thing more frightening to men on the trail than an enemy was an invisible enemy.

"So Thomas, what are we gonna do?" John asked. "We don' even know what we're up against!"

"Don' know that we can do much."

"I don' like that answer," said John.

Thomas nodded. "Well old friend, let's not let our fears get the best of us. I won't deny that I'm a bit jittery o' what might be out there, but I can't think o' what else we can do 'bout it."

John hated the helplessness of just waiting for whomever (or whatever) was out there. Maybe there wasn't anything out there. Maybe Scout and Morse imagined they saw something. Not knowing just gave his fears more rope with which to work.

Scout slept with a loaded musket across his chest. He awoke the next morning, sat up, and rubbed the sleep from his eyes. He waited, listening and smelling. Sensing nothing unsual, he stepped out of his tent in a crouch. He surveyed the land as far as his eyes could see: again, nothing of concern. But he knew that they were being shadowed. Scout had tracked and been tracked enough to know. And whoever they were, they knew what they were about. It was rare for Scout to be eluded for an entire day.

Scout slowly circled the perimeter of the campsite. Then he checked with the front and rear guard of the camp, wondering if anything had happened since his watch - nothing. Nothing until he saw Chambers talking with the captain over by the mess tent.

"I just can't figure it, Cap. It just don't look the same," said Chambers.

"Ya sure there's no sign o' teeth or claw marks?" pressed Thomas.

"What happened to the stores?" asked Scout.
With a nod of his head, Chambers invited Scout to take a look for himself. Scout bent down next to the meat and examined it closely.

"That meat's been cut by a man," said Scout.

"How did any man get into this camp without bein' seen by two stations o' guards?" asked Thomas. Scout just shook his head and walked away.

Scout walked down to the creek to splash his face with water. Just as he reached down for a second dipping of water, he suddenly felt the hair on the back of his neck stand straight up. He knew that familiar, uncomfortable feeling. Scout slowly looked upstream and downstream. Seeing nothing, he slipped casually and naturally back into cover amongst the underbrush and waited. After several moments of neither seeing nor hearing anything, his instincts urged him to move to denser cover and wait longer. He circled around to higher ground a hundred yards upstream and waited.

Wearying of waiting, Scout was just about to leave his cover when something caught his eye. A couple hundred yards downstream he detected minute movement amongst the brush near the river's edge. It appeared to be a man, but he couldn't be sure. Scout checked the loadings of both his pistols, kept one in his hand and replaced the other in his belt. Keeping an eye on the spot he saw something, he noiselessly made his way down to the site. Scout stopped every eight or ten paces to listen, moving on when he heard nothing.

About halfway down to the river, Scout heard leaves rustle. He quickly hid himself behind a cluster of trees. Scout deliberately slowed his breathing down, which long years of practice had refined. He then cautiously peered out from behind the trees. The brush was dense and he didn't see anything out of place, so he waited. Finally he heard almost indiscernible footsteps. They sounded so close that he didn't even hazard to look. He soundlessly replaced his pistol and unsheathed his knife. Scout squeezed himself further into the trees, yet only found them to yield another inch of cover. Then he saw the front half of a boot plant itself just within his view of the ground to his left. Requiring himself to remain patient, he waited until he saw the other boot land in front of the first. Scout sprang from his lair and landed on his prey's back with his knife at the man's neck. The man fell hard to the ground. Although it was dim light conditions amongst the brush, something about the man seemed familiar.

"Damn it, Scout. Git your knee out the middle o' my back, an' I'll kill ya if you draw blood from my neck!" cursed Haskins.

"Haskins? What are you doing creeping about the place like a horse thief?" demanded Scout.

Scout released Haskins and offered his arm to help him up. Haskins refused the offer and stood under his own power. Scout observed the irritated looked on Haskins's face. A moment later Haskins saw Scout's curious look, and instantly Haskins's face took on a smirk with a mischievous bearing.

"Now don't go an' get cocky on me. I knew where ya be all along, an' thought I'd be generous an' give ya confidence a shot in the arm," Haskins explained.

Scout crinkled up his face momentarily before responding. "Be that as it may, are you back to help out or just to harass me?"

"Oh, I'm back to help. I figured the young captain just don't know help if it bit 'im in the arse. I can't expect 'im to 'preciate the kind o' services a man like me has to offer. So, I'm prepared to overlook his ignorance an' return to the mission before he gets everybody kilt," offered Haskins.

Scout cast Haskins a curious glance, and then turned and led the way back to camp. On the way Scout found himself thinking over Haskins's reasons for returning. Something just didn't quite add up for him, but he couldn't put his finger on it. Scout walked directly to Thomas with Haskins in tow.

"Hey Cap, look what I found down by the river." Thomas eyed Haskins with surprise and uncertainty.

"Haskins, a word in private," said Thomas. Once they were out of earshot, Thomas stopped and faced Haskins. "Haskins, I need men I can count on for the mission. Are ya back to stay, or do ya intend to come an' go as ya please?" asked Thomas.

"Now don't go an' be like that, Cap. I figure I was too hard on ya back there. Now don't ya fret. I'm back, an' I'll guarantee ya that I'll lead ya an' all the rest straight to them prisoners," Haskins replied with a sneer.

"Look, Haskins. I can use your experience as a tracker, but if ya leave again, ya won't be welcome back. Do we have an understandin'?"

Haskins's face turned dark only for the slightest moment, and then he threw back his head and laughed with the appearance of amusement on his face. "Yeah, we understand each other perfectly, Cap. Maybe by the end o' all this you'll understand too; we have to see." With that Haskins slowly shook his head and turned and walked back to find Scout.

As Thomas watched Haskins walk away he was rememebered something MacDonald had told him, "Many a tree pride themself on bein' larger and greater 'an others. They like to provide shade for others, while grabbing most o' the sun's light for themself. Whether it be true or no, they tend to boast o' havin' the strongest wood of all, bein' quite impenetrable to both axe an' elements. The irony be that while they may appear to be the grandest in all the forest, they actually fear they be the smallest trees, unable to defend themself against the most feeble o' foes. Now some o' these can be most pleasant, often findin' many willing to sing their praises. It be well-known that some people look for large-appearing trees to attach their limbs to. The tragedy be that the trees stretching to be the largest tend to fall with the greatest crash an' carnage. Often too late and to their horror, these tend to find that their trunks be hollow."

The regiment stopped briefly to eat something after an uneventful morning. The scouts went ahead to survey the tracks while they ate on horseback. This time they hurried back to where Thomas and John stretched their legs while eating.

"We found something," said a breathless Scout. John nodded for them to proceed.

"We've come across a campsite," continued Scout.

"We come across many campsites," remarked John.

"But this one's different," began Haskins. "This one's still warm, while all the other sites been completely cold. O' course ya realize what this means?"

Thomas and John looked at each other. This was the best news they'd heard since beginning their mission. "How far ahead do ya figure they are?" asked Thomas.

"They can't be far. If we're right in guessin' some of 'em are on foot, they could be just over the next hill, an' they can't be much farther than that," answered Haskins.

"Do ya think they know we're here yet?" asked John.

"I know they ain't seen nothing o' me an' Scout, but I don' know 'bout the rest o' you boys with all the racket ya make," said Haskins.

"Okay, recommendations for how we proceed? I don' want them to know nothin' 'bout us. We will keep the element o' surprise!" said Thomas.

The scouts looked at each other as they thought over the options.

"I think we oughta go ahead and check it out, just me an' Scout," said Haskins. "Once we can find them an' see what the situation is, then we can best make a plan." Scout nodded.

"Okay, get on it right away. I want 'em found today," ordered Thomas. Then turning to John, he spoke. "And I want all the men to stay in camp, goin' no further than the river."

At this the scouts hurried to remount their horses and were off to find the Yorkers. They moved out at a moderate pace, not wanting to stumble across the Yorkers and blow their cover. As they mounted each hill, they dismounted their horses and walked slowly to the crest. They carefully circled around each opening amongst the trees. The scouts had the experience to know when the terrain might give away their presence. They took all precautions to ensure the secrecy of their approach.

Several hours later, Haskins and Scout approached yet another hilltop. It seemed like the twentieth they'd mounted that day, but in reality it was only the fourth. They dismounted as they had the previous hills, but this time they felt a need for added caution. The scouts tied their horses to a tree and walked to the crest of the hill slowly and in a crouched position. As they peered over the crest, Haskins quickly dropped to the ground. Scout hadn't seen anything, but trusted Haskins enough to drop to the ground instantly. Scout looked inquiringly at Haskins without uttering a word. Haskins used his hands to signal - found prisoners. Haskins waved Scout to move forward to get another look, crawling on their bellies.

As they peered over the edge of the hill there was nothing to see. Haskins pointed to where he'd seen people walking. Scout nodded. At this point they withdrew back from the crest of the hill and consulted.

"Figure we oughta leave our mounts an' travel on by foot. They can't be far," said Haskins.

"What did you see?"

"Jist the back o' a man on horseback disappearin' behind that rock there," answered Haskins.

"You sure it was a man?"

"'Course I'm sure! I ain't no idiot! I know what I saw. Ya think I'm one o' them greenbacks back in camp?" Haskins asked.

Sticking to the tree line, the scouts scampered toward the position where Haskins had seen somebody. They discovered distinct tracks as they approached the position. The trackings evidenced both horse and human markings, although it was difficult to tell exactly how many there were. Many of the tracks were found on top of one another. The scouts continued their pursuit of the tracks as quickly as they dared proceed. Neither Haskins nor Scout felt worried about their own physical safety, as they were confident that they could find plenty of cover in the form of rocks, trees, bushes, ravines and hillsides in which to hide themselves. Maintaining secrecy was in the forefront of their minds.

The tracks led into a ravine through which a creek quietly bubbled. The scouts decided to take the high ground that ran alongside the ravine in the hope of getting a better view of their prey. They hurried along the back of the hillside until they made their way to the end of the ravine. Having found a good spot along the hilltop to take up their position, they went down onto their bellies and crawled up to the crest. They carefully stayed amongst the low bushes as they crawled. As they crested the hill they found a particularly dense patch of brush from which to look.

The scouts paused before taking up their final position. They looked over their gear and quickly buried anything metal; they didn't want to have anything on them that might create a sun reflection and give away their position. Satisfied that they were ready, they slowly eased their way up to the edge of the low brush and looked back down the ravine. Nothing moved. Haskins and Scout could see fifty yards back down the ravine from where they lie. The scouts figured they probably had reached their position before the others and must be ahead of them. They could see no sign of tracks. They decided to be patient and wait to see what might come.

Ten minutes passed and nobody appeared. Scout and Haskins grew impatient, but decided to wait a bit longer. Fifteen or twenty more minutes passed, and nothing happened. They withdrew from the edge of the hill.

"You think they're ahead of us? I can't believe they'd be taking this long to get here," asked Scout.

"No way they're ahead o' us, the way we move. The man I seen was walkin' 'is horse. An' there's no other way for 'im to go. You head down to the ravine an' have a look. I'll signal ya if somebody comes," said Haskins.

Scout retrieved his buried knife and pistol, scampered back behind the hill for cover, and then started toward the north end of the ravine. He prepared to enter the ravine a hundred yards north of Haskins's position. He stopped behind a large tree and listened for any sound. Scout looked south back down the creek bed. He saw a gentle, slow moving creek that gurgled softly. The foliage was denser near the water, making it impossible for Scout to see much. He couldn't see nor hear evidence of anyone moving.

Scout looked north and saw that a small gentle-sloped valley opened up before him. As he surveyed the beauty of the view, he noticed a glint of sun-reflected water off in the distance. He climbed higher to get a better view and saw a wonder before him. The water appeared larger than any of the rivers they'd seen along the way. Scout figured that the water must be either a very large river or a lake. Scout knew time was of the essence and dismissed the water for now. He needed to find out if any tracks led out of the ravine.

Looking back down the ravine again, Scout could still see no one. Satisfied that it was safe to inspect the ravine, he quickly made his way down to the creek at the bottom. Once again he looked south to see if there was any sign of movement coming his way. Not seeing anyone, he made a hurried inspection of the opening of the ravine and the creek that flowed out of it. Where Scout first looked, the ground was hard and unlikely to display any tracks. He walked a little south to find softer ground. Forty yards up creek, he found what he wanted: soft ground and even some mud on both sides of the creek. With another quick look up creek, Scout knelt to inspect the soft ground. Scout figured if anyone had recently walked through here, this muddy ground would show some signs of it, especially of a company of a dozen or more. The only signs the ground offered were a couple of animal tracks, probably game seeking water. Scout didn't see anything that could be human or horse.

Scout straightened up for one last look around as he prepared to head back. Suddenly, a low bird call caught his attention. Scout quickly looked up the hill where he'd left Haskins. He heard the bird call a second time, and now he was sure: that was the warning sound on which he and Haskins had agreed. Although he felt momentary panic, Scout deliberately made himself move quickly but without running scared. Scout had enough experience to know that running in a panic was about the best way to give away his position to anyone nearby. It wasn't so much the sound of the running itself, but the inevitable dislodging of rocks or loose dirt that made the telltale noise.

Scout didn't risk another look up creek until he was back behind the trees from which he'd just surveyed the north end of the creek. Lying flat on the ground, Scout peered around the thick tree trunk, not risking any quick movement. At first he didn't see anything unusual. A few moments later he saw two men coming around a bend in the ravine. The riders walked their horses and appeared to be talking. Scout didn't like the look of the one on the far side. A moment later came another rider and then a number of people on foot.

The group on foot looked haggard and dirty, with tears in their clothing. They were thin and boney. Their hands were bound in front with a rope connecting all of their necks together. There were two women and two men, one man first in line and the other last. The prisoners mostly looked down. They looked beaten, and probably figured any attempt at escape would likely result in a hanging or a broken neck. Scout counted nine prisoners: four adults and five children. Two of the children appeared to be crying. All nine were still alive!

It was hard to tell from this distance, but they seemed to be in okay health, but maybe that's just what he wanted to believe. "Okay health" might be a generous description, but they were able to walk. Following the prisoners came several more men, all on horseback. After the whole company had come into view, Scout counted twelve men with horses. Each of the guards was armed with a musket stuck into his saddle. None of the captors held his musket nor looked around much. They appeared at ease. As the prisoners passed, Scout could see their faces better. They looked worse than at first glance. Scout wondered what story their faces told, but whatever story it was, it wasn't good. But that would have to wait for later.

Scout waited until the company marched well past his position. He wanted to take note of which way they went once they cleared the end of the ravine. They headed further northwest. It was not lost on Scout that they headed in the general direction of the large body of water in the distance.

Now that the company was clearly out of sight and sound, Scout made his way back to Haskins. Haskins breathed a sigh of relief to see his friend unharmed. He hadn't been sure Scout had heard his warning call. Haskins had been tempted to go in search of his friend, but reason had held him back. He knew he might not only be unable to help, but might hurt his friend by alerting the Yorkers.

They briefly conferred on what they'd seen; Haskins had also counted nine prisoners and twelve armed men. The scouts took the time to note the land markings of their position and then hurried back to the rest of the regiment.

The captain and lieutenant rode ahead of the group scouting for water and a good place to camp for the night, as they had throughout the journey. The captain pulled his hat off his head and wearily wiped the sweat off his brow. Captain Bull Deeters and his brother, Lieutenant Bill Deeters, looked down from a rise at a small creek that had enough open space adjacent to it to set up a decent camp.

Bull was born Jacob Deeters. He had been called Jacob as a boy, but had earned his nickname during the militia's campaigns to clear northeastern New York of Indians. Bull and Bill had joined the militia when settlers were having trouble with the Indians stealing their animals and leaving some of the settlers for dead. During one of the raids on an Indian village, Jacob had charged his horse into a group of fleeing women and children, overrunning and killing all of them. He made several passes to make sure than none got away. The other men had said he looked like a bull charging the Indians, and the name stuck. Bill had been more reserved in his approach to the raids and had earned no nickname. He wanted to protect his family and the others in the region, but he had no thirst for blood. Bill killed only when his hide was on the line.

Bull and Bill bought adjoining parcels in the Grants, sight unseen, from the New York governor last year. They decided to take a look at the land before moving their families there. Bill had a wife and a daughter, with another child on the way. Bull didn't exactly have a family of his own, although he lay claim to Bill's. It was the closest thing to family he had since both their parents had passed on when the men were in their teens.

When the Deeter brothers first arrived at their land grants, they thought they were in the wrong place. There were already two men and a woman building temporary shelters on the land. After scratching their heads for awhile, the Deeters went back into town to confirm the exact location of their grants with the magistrate. Turns out they had been in the right place. The Deeters went back to find out what the others were doing on their land, and that's when all the trouble started.

"Figure that's as good a place as any. We camp here," decided Bull. Bill nodded and informed the others where to set up.

Bull unsaddled his horse and threw down his saddle blanket and bedroll. He took the bit out of his mare's mouth and let her find her own supper. Bull knew she wouldn't go far. Nobody left Bull, unless he wanted them to. He looked up and saw the prisoners being tied to a nearby tree. Bull particularly enjoyed this time of day.

"Any o' you ladies in need o' relievin' yourself?" asked Bull with a mischievous grin.

Alice nodded, while May just looked off blankly. By now they were used to the rules; if they wanted to relieve themselves, they had to go with Captain Bull. Bull only allowed them to attend to nature's call right before and right after the day's march. The only other option was to wet themselves, which made the rest of the day almost unbearable.

The other men in the militia were responsible for taking the men and children to relieve themselves. Bull kept that grin on his face while he untied the women and led them away to a clump of trees. Hugh glared at him. Bull either didn't notice or didn't care. When they got behind the clump of trees Bull merely stopped. Alice and May no longer bothered asking him to give them some privacy. By now they'd learned that Bull insisted on watching. It was clear to them that he took pleasure, not only in watching them partially undress, but in their discomfort at being observed in such a private endeavor.

Bull leaned up against a tree and enjoyed the show. The best part for him was the women's discomfort. Alice looked away to lessen her embarrassment as much as possible, but really there was no getting around it. May acted as though she didn't even know Bull was there. When they finished, Bull slapped each of them on the behind and led them back to camp.

"Now if you ladies ain't gettin' satisfaction from you men, you just let ole Bull know," Bull offered with a laugh.

The first time Alice had given him an earful when he'd made a similar comment, Bull slapped her hard enough across the face to leave a red mark that lasted two days. That was the first and last time either of them had protested.

If the ladies hadn't already had enough reason to fear Bull, he'd given them another just the other day. Hugh had been relieving himself under guard of two of the militiamen. Actually, Hugh had only been pretending to make water and carefully watched until both men guarding him were looking the other way. Then he knocked one out cold with a fist to the head and wrestled the other one to the ground when Bull intervened.

"I might stop right there, Connecticut boy," said Bull without emotion. Hugh looked up to see his son with Bull's knife to his throat. His young face showed his father a look of terror mixed with supplication.

"Ya know, Connecticut boy, I kinda hope ya don't stop, seein' as that would give me the chance to send this boy to the devil. But I leave it up to you. I s'pose I could go either way on it," said Bull.

"Let 'im go, Hugh! Let 'im go, for God's sake!" screamed May.

Hugh thought about it for a second or two longer and then got off the Yorker. Hugh paid for that with five lashes from the horse whip that Bull carried. Captain Bull set it up so he got his blood either way. Bull probably would have gone further, but after the fifth lash, Hugh dropped to his knees. At that point Bill intervened.

"That's 'bout enough, Bull. We want the man able to march," reasoned Bill. Bull reared back for another lash before Bill grabbed his arm.

"I said, that's 'bout enough," Bill repeated.

Bull rolled his eyes, yet relented. "You Connecticut boys 're lucky my brother here's a man o' mercy," said Bull.

Once Bull was out of earshot, May nearly bit Hugh's head off for trying a stunt like that and risking their son's life. May tended to be more obedient to the Yorkers, hoping her compliant behavior would reduce the chances of them getting hurt. Rarely did she yell at anyone, but when it came to her children, she became a mother bear.

Throughout the ordeal, Bull had made numerous suggestive comments to May and Alice, and each time May just looked away. It was harder for her to do so on the occasions when Bull went so far as to touch her. Not only had he slapped her behind numerous times, but on a few occasions had touched her in more intrusive ways. Both May and Alice had often lamented not having more clothes to put on. Anything that gave them more protection from Bull would be welcomed. Unfortunately, they'd been taken with only the clothes on their backs. And by now those clothes were showing tears and other signs of wear. Before the women were retied to their families, Alice decided to risk a request.

"Captain, would ya finally allow us to wash our clothes? They gettin' awful dirty."

"Oh, you betcha. I'd be obliged to walk you ladies down to the creek for a good washin'," said an enthusiastic Bull.

"Never mind," mumbled Alice. She understood the implications of his offer. The price was too high to pay. She'd continue to endure the smell.

"Everything okay May?" asked Hugh. When he got no response he asked her again.

"Huh? What'd ya mean?" responded May. May stared at her husband as though from a hundred miles away. He couldn't quite tell if she was looking at him or not. Her eyes didn't seem to focus fully. He worried that his wife might lose her mind before this nightmare ended. Hugh tried another approach.

"May, how are ya weatherin' this whole mess?"

"What? Oh, it ain't so bad I s'pose," she said without emotion as she turned away to straighten her dress.

Captain Chittenden wasted no time in getting the regiment back on the trail. Thomas and John decided they wanted to see where the Yorkers camped for the night before it was too dark to see. Although the Yorkers showed no signs they suspected being tracked, Thomas didn't want to count on the Yorkers making a noticeable campfire. Without a campfire, their chances of finding the Yorkers in the dark were slim to none, especially once they were asleep.

The scouts initially led the regiment at a fast pace, riding hard up to the south end of the ravine. Haskins went ahead to ensure the trail through the ravine was safe from ambush. They didn't want to take the time to move the entire regiment around and above the ravine as the scouts had done earlier. Soon thereafter Scout heard the "all safe" call from Haskins, and led the regiment through the ravine. Scout realized they might come across the Yorker party quite quickly and decided it would be wise to slow the regiment down to not much faster than a walk, having now reached the north end of the ravine. They'd be more exposed once out of the ravine.

In the meantime Haskins went ahead to follow the Yorkers' tracks and see if he could catch a glimpse of them. Haskins examined the tracks leading out of the northern end of the ravine, and then headed west and slightly to the north. Haskins followed the tracks, being careful to spend most of his time amongst the cover provided by the land. He had no trouble finding rocks and brush large enough to hide behind. Haskins avoided open spaces completely.

The ravine in which they had first seen the Yorkers had led through a pass in a mountain range. The land below the pass was all downhill into a small valley. Most of the trees were pine and of many varieties. These trees tended to be large, which was a blessing and a curse. The large trees provided Haskins and the regiment with excellent cover, but provided the Yorkers with excellent cover as well.

Haskins had yet to catch another glimpse of the Yorkers. Looking up at the sun, Haskins figured sunset was still a good two hours away. He was relieved he still had time to find them, yet felt the urge to track quickly. It really was a risk-reward situation; he could risk speed and detection and more likely be rewarded by finding his prey, or he could choose safety and maintain a cautious pace and risk not finding them before dark. Haskins decided he'd be patient for now and see what happened.

As time went on, Haskins began to wonder more and more why he hadn't overtaken them yet. He figured he had to be traveling more quickly than bound prisoners. Beginning to lose his patience and not wanting to lose them in the dark, he decided to risk a look from higher ground. To his left arose an outcropping of large rocks on a low hill. Haskins cautiously climbed the hill, staying low to the ground, as he didn't want to make a silhouette against the skyline. He peered through an opening between two of the smaller boulders. At first he didn't see anything of note. He decided to wait a bit longer, as the boulders gave him a view of many miles of ground slopping down into the valley.

Haskins continued to scan the ground below him, paying particular attention to the clearances between groupings of trees. Then something white caught his attention out of the corner of his eye. Haskins quickly looked to the left to discover the source of the white flash that he saw. At first he couldn't find anything, but then the white flash appeared again. The sun reflected off something moving amongst the trees. Fortunately, a minute later the Yorker company appeared plainly in a clearing. They still walked two abreast with guards in front and behind the prisoners. Haskins was thankful for the muskets the Yorkers carried, which reflected sunlight well. The scout watched carefully, making a mental note of the landmarks the Yorkers passed.

From his vantage point, Haskins could now see that the huge body of water was a lake, and a beautiful lake of a size he'd never seen before. As he made his way back down the hill, he stepped on a rock that gave way. He regained his balance without falling, but the rock made noise rolling down the hill. Haskins quickly crouched down behind a tree, cursing himself for his carelessness. He peered out toward the Yorker camp, hoping they hadn't been alerted. From this distance it was hard to tell. Haskins thought he saw a couple of them looking his way, but he wasn't sure if he was just imagining it. They had to be a mile away.

Having accomplished his goal, Haskins made his way back to the rest of the regiment. He found them resting just beyond the northern end of the ravine, with many of the men filling their water bottles in the stream. Their horses drank from the creek and grazed in the grass nearby. Thomas, John, and Scout had been watching impatiently for Haskins's return. None of them wanted to be sitting idle with the Yorkers so close now. The others huddled around Haskins as he dismounted and caught his breath.

"Okay, they made camp 'bout five miles from here, down by a creek. We gonna have to take it slow, seein' as we gonna be comin' from the high ground," suggested Haskins. "We gonna be easy to spot if theys any light."

"Ain't much light now," commented Morse. "At five miles, we oughta be okay to move in."

"How many prisoner situations ya been in Morse?" asked Haskins with a haughty laugh.

"We sit tight till dark, then we move in for a closer look," decided Thomas. "No fire after dark. Chambers, any cookin' ya wanna do best be done now."

Chambers cooked a hasty meal, and the men choked down a quick bite. Then Haskins led the full regiment to a position a couple miles southeast of the last place he'd seen the Yorker company. He wanted to get them to lower ground. Thomas and John wanted to see the Yorkers and the captives for themselves, so Haskins took them ahead to relocate the company. Scout remained behind to set up sentries to guard the regiment's position in the meantime. Thomas insisted on leaving Scout behind, although Scout protested strongly. Thomas wouldn't hear of leaving the regiment without either himself, John, or Scout. Besides John, Scout was the only other man in the regiment that Thomas truly trusted.

The landmarks were about as Haskins had remembered them, and he had little trouble finding the place he'd been when he'd last seen the Yorker party. He bent down and examined the tracks to be sure of their direction, and waved the rest to follow. Then Haskins suddenly stopped.

"I switchin' to hand signals only from here on," whispered Haskins.

The three men walked slowly along, alert for any sign of the Yorker camp. Then a faint cry arose. The three dropped into a crouch and looked at each other with shrugged shoulders, not knowing what to make of the sound. They listened for the cry to repeat. For a few minutes they could hear nothing. Just as they resumed their march, the cry rang out again. They came to a halt again, straining to listen. It didn't sound like animal or man. The strange cry ceased. They continued forward with muskets at the ready, when suddenly Haskins held up his hand to stop. He pointed off about two o' clock to a dull light. Thomas could barely see the trees in that direction, being dimly lit up. It was now past dusk. Just ahead was a low rise and Haskins waved them forward.

Haskins signaled to go down to a crouch as they approached the top of the low hill. The three men inched forward until they reached several low bushes at the crest of the hill. Haskins peered through the brush for a minute, and then waved Thomas and John to come forward to join him. Thanks to a well-fueled fire, they looked down at the surprisingly well lit Yorker camp.

A number of men sat around the fire on saddles and blankets. They ate and talked rather loudly. One of the men made water onto a nearby tree, while two of the others growled at him for not taking his personal business farther away. Behind the fire and to the left were their horses tied to nearby trees, yet with enough rope to comfortably graze. To the right were two other men who talked quietly and sat apart from the others. Thomas couldn't hear what they were saying, but he didn't like the look of them. Farther to the right were two other men sitting on a log, eating with muskets across their laps. But where were the prisoners?

Thomas nervously scanned the scene back and forth, searching for any sign of the prisoners. Had they been taken somewhere else? Had they been killed? Then Thomas caught some movement over by the two men with muskets. There seemed to be movement on the ground beyond the men on the log. Thomas could barely make them out, as they were a good distance from the fire. As his eyes adjusted to the light he discerned two women and several children huddled together. There may have been others, but Thomas couldn't tell. They sat against a couple trees.

Then the strange cry rang out again. It seemed to come from one or two of the children on the ground. One of the women pulled a child closer. Thomas strained his eyes in attempting to discover the condition of the prisoners, but they were just too dimly lit. One of the children seemed to put something into his mouth with both hands, and at this movement, Thomas could see that the child's hands were tied together. He couldn't be sure, but the prisoners all seemed to be there. Thomas would have liked an exact counting, but decided not to risk a closer look. Thomas looked back at the Yorkers and counted twelve, including the man watering the tree.

Once they got back, Thomas signaled Scout to join them. He'd been waiting up for them.

"I tell ya I don' like it. It just looks too easy," said Thomas.

"Believe you me, it is that easy. Them damn fools have no idear we gotta surprise comin'. They must o' thought nobody'd come lookin' for 'em. Well, we gotta little somethin' for 'em," said Haskins.

"Guess I din't know what to expect, but I din't figure they'd be that easy to spot with a big fire an' all. An' with no sentries," said John.

"That cause they fools that don't know no better," explained Haskins.

"That may be, but I wanna plan for better 'an fools," began Thomas. "I want us to make a plan that'll be good 'nough for prepared soldiers."

"It'll be easy Cap," said Haskins. "Just leave all that to me."

"Look Haskins, I don' want ya underestimatin' them Yorkers. The lives o' them prisoners depend on it. We make a plan like they know we comin'," ordered Thomas.

"All right Cap, take it easy. I got it all under control. Just relax and leave it to me," said Haskins with a condescending smile.

"What do ya have in mind?" asked Thomas.

Haskins bent down and picked up a nearby stick and cleared a smooth spot of dirt. He made a drawing of the Yorker camp as he explained. Between the four of them, a plan was agreed upon.

"Okay Lieutenant, wake up the whole regiment beginnin' o' the fifth watch," ordered Thomas. "For now let 'em get whatever sleep they can. Speakin' o' which, I'm headin' off to get whatever I can. I'll see everybody at the fifth."

When John woke Thomas, he felt like he'd been asleep about ten minutes. He wondered if he would have felt better just staying up all night. Since his eyes weren't working yet, his nose helped his hands find their way to the coffee John offered him. Thomas rubbed his eyes, trying to brush aside the cobwebs in his head.

Once everyone was assembled, Thomas addressed the regiment. "Men, ya probably all know that tonight's the night we all been waitin' for. 'Bout three miles from where ya now sit be the Yorker camp," began Thomas. "Our plan is to leave as soon as possible in the hope o' surprisin' the Yorkers in they sleep. I hope most o' ya got some sleep, cause I'm gonna need clear thinkin' soldiers tonight, or make that this mornin' if ya like. We will leave two o' ya to guard camp. One will be Dr. Dickens. We will ride till we get 'bout two miles from 'em, an' the rest on foot. All right, Haskins will explain the plan o' attack."

Haskins ceremoniously stood up and assumed center stage. He allowed a pregnant pause to add dramatic effect. Then he explained in minute detail every man's task and position, including a map illustrating where each man should be. Haskins presented his instructions as though the men were simpletons learning elementary mathematics. Once he was done, Thomas stood up.

"Gentlemen, let me be clear: our mission be not to kill them Yorkers. Our mission be to free Litchfield folk taken prisoner. Everybody clear on that? I will have no unnecessary killin'! Anyone killin' except to protect himself or the prisoners will answer to me personally. It be not our place to decide when another man's time's up. But if the Yorkers call for it, fight with courage an' do not hesitate. Any questions?"

No one asked any questions. Most of the men were relieved to hear their captain declare his bloodless intentions, but a few were disappointed and still hoped for a chance to kill a Yorker or two. Thomas gave final instructions.

"Good. Now, go pack up with nothin' but water, horses an' weapons. We leave in ten minutes, sooner if possible."

"An' Chambers got coffee an' biscuits ready for the ride," interjected John. "An' no lighting o' any kind o' fires from here on out; that means no pipes. We must be invisible and with no sound. An' once we leave the horses there will be no talkin'. That means hand signals only. Got it?"

Scout and Haskins were already packed and left immediately. They rode at a gentle trot as they sipped coffee and gnawed at dry biscuits. Neither felt much awake yet. The coffee would help some, at least the little that found its way into their mouths. It would be impossible to say whether the scouts or the horses wore more coffee. However, they did feel a bit more alert by the time the coffee cups were empty. They tied up their horses far enough away to prevent the Yorker horses from smelling them, and set out on foot. They were careful to approach from downwind.

Both men checked their pistols to see that they were properly loaded, and that their knives were in their sheaths.

"Alright, Scout. Ya ready for a little fun?" asked Haskins as he gave Scout a little shove.

"Fun? I don't know about that," answered Scout. "I'm here to turn the tables on a bunch of bullies trying to have their way with smaller kids."

"'Course we'll do that along the way, but I'm fixin' for a fight; been too long, know what I mean?" said Haskins.

Scout gave Haskins a sideways look, and then set off for the Yorker camp. Both knew any further talking would have to wait. Scout looked up and noticed a half moon. That was ideal; not too light and not too dark. Both men picked it up to a trot, as they wanted to arrive well before the regiment to assess the situation.

By now the fire had died down to smoldering embers, with faint outlines of the Yorkers lying around it. Seven Yorkers slept around the fire, with two guards sitting on the log near the prisoners. One of the guard's heads bobbed back and forth as he fought to stay awake. The other guard whittled on a stick, the knife in his hand moving slowly. The scouts looked left and right, up and down. Where were the other three Yorkers? Scout compared notes with Haskins; he only saw nine as well.

Haskins signaled to move in for a closer look. They had to know where the others were. The scouts retraced their steps and circled around to the west. The trees were so dense Haskins considered circling farther around, but he saw the thick stand went on as far as he could see in the moonlight. Instead, the scouts went down on all fours and slowly made their way through the thick brush. Once they had gone a few yards into the thicket, it became pitch dark. Haskins and Scout suffered numerous scrapes across the face from branches, which finally convinced them to find an alternate route.

They turned back and circled around to the east. Although they'd have to go farther, it looked more passable. Finally the scouts inched their way up to the far side of the camp, coming from below. Scout picked out a fallen tree from which to approach. They crawled up to the tree, about thirty yards from the fire. They peered over the tree and enjoyed a clearer view of the sleeping Yorkers. Scout checked the line of sight with the two guards, making sure they didn't have an unimpeded look at them. He looked back at the fire and craned his neck for any other Yorkers that had escaped their notice earlier. But no additional Yorkers could be seen. Scout shifted his position and looked left at the prisoners. One of the children slept on top of each mother, while the others were lying next to the two women. Scout shivered as he noticed they had no blankets. Then he noticed the end of a rope on the far side of one of the women. He looked across the other woman and saw loose rope lying next to her as well. Where were the men? Scout twisted further around to see if the men slept away from the others - nothing.

Scout slid back and slowly pulled himself up into a crouching position. While Haskins drew himself up, he momentarily lost his balance and stepped back onto a twig, snapping it in half. Both men froze. They looked back at the guards. The one guard fighting off sleep continued to bob, yet the other looked in their direction. He picked up his musket and walked toward the scouts. Scout looked back and spotted a stand of bushes ten yards away. He signaled Haskins to follow, but Haskins had already started moving toward nearby trees.

The guard walked up to the fallen tree and squinted in the darkness. He scanned left and right, and then walked over to the trees that hid Haskins. Haskins saw him coming and eased himself farther around the back of them. The guard stopped right next to Haskins's tree and listened. Haskins held his breath and pulled out his knife. If the guard walked any further around the tree, Haskins knew he'd be seen. The guard continued to stand and listen, and then looked toward Haskins. Haskins held his breath. He could smell the Yorker's foul breath. He cursed his own sloppiness. Haskins could only see the musket and the tip of the guard's hat.

He didn't know how much longer he could hold his breath. Haskins would have to hazard a breath soon if the guard lingered much longer, and with the foul air, he might gag.

Scout unsheathed his knife. He debated in his mind what to do. Should he just leave Haskins to fend for himself? Certainly Haskins was plenty skilled. Should he take the man out with a knife throw? The last thing he wanted was the man to cry out and alert the rest of the camp. However, leaving a dead guard for the Yorkers to find would alert them plenty. Scout held his knife and watched while he thought through his options. He knew if he moved, he likely would be heard. Finally, the guard shrugged and walked back to his perch. Haskins slowly exhaled and breathed in greedily.

Thomas and John walked their horses toward the prearranged meeting place. They knew they were close, but they weren't sure how much farther in the dark. Just as Thomas turned to ask John, their horses whinnied. They should have known to rely on their horses more than their own senses. Thomas and John gave the reigns to their mares and were soon dismounting alongside the scouts' horses.

"Figure we here first," said John.

"'Spect so," answered Thomas. "Pick out a man to leave with the horses." John moved off to arrange the guard. Thomas heard something and felt for his sword. He slowly knelt and waited. A moment later the scouts gave the call sign. Haskins trotted down the hill followed by Scout.

"Captain, there's been a change," Haskins reported.

"A change? What change?" asked Thomas.

"Three o' the Yorkers is missin'," said Haskins.

"An' the prisoners?" asked an alarmed Thomas.

"Two missin'," informed Haskins.

"Damn it! Damn it, we din't act fast enough!" Thomas cursed.

"Now keep ya voice down, Cap," whispered Haskins.

Thomas stood up and paced. John saw the scouts and hurried over. "Everything the same?" inquired John. Thomas shook his head.

"Two prisoners missin' an' three Yorkers gone," said Haskins.

"Gone! Where in the hell they go to?" asked John.

Haskins shrugged his shoulders. Scout shook his head. "Likely stretched 'em or plugged 'em. It's the men that's missin'," said Haskins.

"Well, we don't wanna jump to conclusions just yet," John said.

"Damn it all!" said Thomas. "We just took too damn much time! Maybe Haskins's right an' they kilt 'em."

"Hold on, Cap. We don' know that yet. Let's not get ahead o' ourselves," soothed John.

"Okay, Scout, recommendations," Thomas asked.

The scouts looked at each other. "I'd like to get a look at the tracks an' go after 'em myself," suggested Haskins. "They's a chance they still alive."

"Scout?"

"Yeah, I think we should look at the tracks and then decide," said Scout.

"Okay," said Thomas, "let's go. I wanna see this for myself. Lieutenant, you stay an' watch o'er the camp. Let's go, scouts!"

Thomas pulled his pistol out of his belt, loaded it, and returned it to its place. He reached down and felt reassured at the cold steel of his Scottish Claymore. Haskins took the lead as the three men set out on foot. An hour later the men peered down from the same clump of trees from which they'd observed about twelve hours before. They settled into their position just before first light. Thomas surveyed the camp and saw that it was as the scouts reported: three Yorkers and the two Litchfield men unaccounted for.

"Okay, scouts. Go see what ya can make o' them markings," ordered Thomas. "An' Haskins, if it look like the other prisoners been led away, go an' follow 'em. An' don't engage the Yorkers, unless it's to defend yourself or the prisoners. Scout, you come back."

Spring 1748 - Salisbury, Connecticut Colony

By the age of nineteen, Thomas regularly volunteered to go into town for any and all occasions. He'd been going on supply runs for Father for some time now, but had only in the last few weeks begun offering to go to the general store for Mama. After wondering about this change in Thomas for awhile, she eventually caught on to the reason behind the mystery. Mama was thankful that Thomas had met a young woman that interested him, even if it had taken till Thomas was nineteen. She was relieved he'd found anything that interested him.

Mama was glad to see Thomas happier, and it eased her guilt. She figured the cause of his happiness must be the new girl, and she tried to find extra opportunities for Thomas to go into town. Sometimes she'd send him to town on errands she really didn't need done. She was eager to be able to do anything to help Thomas, especially since she'd felt so helpless. What Mama didn't know was that her son's emerging happiness had more to do with his relationship with MacDonald than a new romantic interest. Since his relationship with MacDonald had begun, he was a changed person. In some ways he was the same young man, but in another sense he was a new man; which was confusing. It also helped that Thomas now valued his relationship with his sister, which had blossomed over the past few years since they'd begun talking. Sally now visited the MacDonalds regularly with Thomas.

Thomas had first met Liz when he'd gone to town to pick up supplies for Mama at the general store. He'd only been in the store a few minutes when he noticed Mrs. Lewis. Seeing Mrs. Lewis in the store was nothing unusual, yet seeing a pretty young woman at her side was different. Thomas was immediately struck by her beauty. She wore long, wavy brown hair. Her green eyes sparkled and contrasted with her pale, milk-white skin. Thomas took note of her trim, yet nicely rounded figure. She appeared to be about Thomas's age, yet dressed like a mature woman. Her clothes looked nicer than what most Salisbury women wore. Thomas couldn't imagine her working in such clothing.

He was so struck by her beauty that he hadn't been looking where he was walking. Thomas walked directly into a bag of flour, successfully tripping himself onto the floor and knocking another bag onto his back. Red-faced and deeply embarrassed, he quickly picked himself up off the floor, carefully replacing the fallen flour. He hoped the girl hadn't seen his performance. Unfortunately, a quick look around told him that everyone in the store had witnessed it.

Being humiliated, Thomas quickly turned to get out of the store as fast as possible. In his haste, he almost knocked Mrs. Lewis and the girl over on his way out.

"Oh, sorry," apologized Thomas.

"Oh, hello Thomas. No harm done," replied Mrs. Lewis.

"Uh, okay, uh, hello Mrs. Lewis," Thomas said.

Thomas quickly walked out the door of the general store. He finally slowed after getting across the street. A few moments later he realized he hadn't picked up Mama's supplies. The last thing Thomas wanted to do was walk back into that store while the pretty girl was still in there. Looking around, he noticed a tree farther down the road and hid behind it. He peaked out from the tree every minute until he saw Mrs. Lewis and the girl leave the general store and head off down the street. For the first time, Thomas noticed a third woman with them. Thomas would later learn that this was Liz's mother. Once he was sure they were well out of sight, he went back into the store and obtained the items for which Mama had sent him.

Thomas thought about the new girl all the way home. He wondered where she came from. He was pretty sure he'd never seen her before. Thomas knew everybody in town, and there weren't that many to know in a small town like Salisbury. Everyone knew everyone. Thomas certainly would have noticed a pretty girl of about his age if she'd been in town long. Was she just visiting the Lewis's? Had she recently come to live with the Lewis's? Many possibilities came to mind, and he intended to find out.

Thomas got right to work on his intelligence gathering upon arriving home. Mama regularly kept up with the Salisbury gossip.

"Hey Mama, here's ya supplies. Be there somebody visitin' the Lewis's?"

"No, I ain't heard o' nobody," Mama said. "Why do ya ask, dear?"

"Oh, no reason really; just wonderin'."

Mama may not have been the brightest star in the sky, but she certainly knew when her son's interest was stirred. She wondered what could have raised his curiosity about the Lewis's and any guests they might have. Now Mama's curiosity was piqued. "Perhaps I'll ask around," she said to herself.

Mama decided to walk over to the Oldhams' and see if Janine knew anything helpful. The Oldhams' farm butted up against the western slope of the Chittenden farm, making Janine Oldham the nearest neighbor. Mama found Janine washing laundry on her back porch. "Hello, Janine."

"Oh, hello, Mary. What brings ya down this way? I'm guessin' it's not to help with my laundry."

"No, it's not ya laundry," Mary said with a laugh. "Thomas asked me 'bout a visitor at the Lewis farm. I thought ya might know something 'bout that."

"Oh, yes. Mabel an' Elizabeth Cranfield have been stayin' with 'em."

"Really," said Mary, "an' who are Mabel an' Elizabeth Cranfield?"

Janine was excited to let Mary in on the latest town news. She hung up the last sheet and pointed to a chair on the porch as she took a seat herself. "Elizabeth is Hannah Lewis's niece," continued Janine, "and the daughter of Hannah's sister, Mabel. Mabel an' her family live in Guilford, by the sea. Well, at least Mabel an' Elizabeth used to live in Guilford. 'Bout two weeks ago they moved to Salisbury. The word is that Mabel lost her husband somehow. I don' know what happened to 'im though. Anyways, after sortin' through their finances an' what they'd been left, they figured they couldn't make it on their own. Even though they had a farmhand, he's an older man an' couldn't do all the work himself, even if Elizabeth helped some. Though she wouldn't of been much help anyways, seein' as she only worked in the house. They ended up figurin' that they'd have to go live with someone. Fortunately, Hannah took 'em both in."

"I see. That explains Thomas's interest. He must o' seen young Elizabeth in town today," Mama figured.

"Oh that certainly explains any interest Thomas might o' had. I understand she's a beauty."

Liz was a bright girl. It hadn't taken long for her to notice this shy-looking boy paying her special attention. She'd felt sorry for him when he'd tripped and fallen, and purposely looked the other way to not add to his embarrassment, yet she hadn't been able to prevent a giggle from escaping. She couldn't help smiling to herself, as it had been rather funny seeing Thomas sprawled out on the floor like that. Liz enjoyed this young man's interest in her. She found herself curious as to who he was.

Having just come to Salisbury in the last two weeks, bewilderment well characterized Liz's state of mind. Mostly she felt confused and overwhelmed with all the change in her life. Liz missed her father terribly. She struggled to accept that he was really gone. She kept expecting him to come around the corner any moment. In her head, she knew he was gone, but she kept looking for him just the same. It was like her heart hadn't caught up to what her mind knew.

Living in Salisbury seemed strange to Liz. She'd only known life in Guilford, where she'd been born and raised. Salisbury had a small-town feel that seemed odd to her. Compared to sprawling Guilford, Salisbury was tiny. She guessed she'd just have to get used to it. The people were warm and inviting, especially when they heard the circumstances under which she and her mother had arrived. Liz hadn't met many other teens yet, except for Aunt Hannah's son and daughter. Sarah had been friendly with her from the start, for which Liz was thankful. However, a thirteen-year-old cousin seemed a bit young for company to the eighteen-year-old Liz. James, Sarah's sixteen-year-old brother was closer in age to Liz, but he hadn't been friendly. Cold would probably more accurately describe James's reception of Liz. So it was a treat having anybody about her age show interest in her.

"Aunt Hannah, who is that boy from the store?"

"Which boy, dear?"

"Oh, come now, everyone noticed that poor boy that tripped and fell on his face," laughed Liz.

"Oh, you mean Thomas Chittenden," said Aunt Hannah with a chuckle. "Yes, I felt sorry for the poor boy."

"Where do the Chittendens live?"

"They live out on the north side of town. Why do you ask?" inquired Aunt Hannah with a grin on her face. She had a pretty good idea why Liz asked.

"Oh, no reason, Auntie. Just curious, I suppose."

Thinking about Thomas had given Liz a brief and welcomed distraction from her grief. However, her feelings returned all too quickly as thoughts of Papa reemerged into her mind. She longed for something else to think about besides Papa. She hoped to meet anyone about her age that could offer her a distraction from the unending sense of loss.

Thomas hurried to MacDonald's. He could hardly wait to talk with Mr. MacDonald about Liz. Thomas had learned her name from Mama. He was excited to finally see the Feed 'n Seed up ahead. He'd been carrying around his excitement and nervous feelings for a couple of days now.

"Mr. MacDonald, I have to talk with ya!"

"Really, lad. It be rare t'see ye be soo energized."

"I met this new girl in town. Well, I din't 'xactly meet, but I seen her. Her name's Liz. She's just as pretty as a picture o' them girls in catalogues."

"Oh I see, lad. Ye've discovered the fair world o' lasses," chuckled MacDonald.

"Yeah, an' I don' know what to do."

"Weel then, we'll just hae t' figure something out ther, lad."

"I saw her at the general store a few days past. She was there with Mrs. Lewis. I was so distracted by 'er that I fell o'er somethin' an' landed all over the floor. I was so embarrassed that I almost knocked both them ladies over on the way out."

MacDonald laughed heartily. "Oh, that's just precious, lad. I'm almost fallin' o'er myself just hearing 'bout it. I'm sure ye made a lastin' impression." Thomas's face became redder.

"Oh, don't take noo offense, lad. Ye hae to admit, 'tis quite a sight t' imagine."

"I'm tryin' to not imagine it anymore," said Thomas. MacDonald continued laughing.

"So, what do I do?" asked Thomas.

"What do ye mean, lad?"

"I mean, I don' know what to do 'bout her."

"It seems quite clear that ye hae t' meet 'er," said MacDonald.

"But, how?"

"Weel lad, we'll just have t' come up wi' somethin'. Do ye know anything 'bout her?"

"Uh, let's see, I know she an' her mother are livin' with the Lewis's," answered Thomas.

"Weel, there ye hae it. Ye'll just have t' head o'er t' the Lewis farm an' introduce yerself."

"Are ya kiddin' me? Ya want me to jist walk up to 'er and say 'hello'? There's no way I'm doin' that!"

"Come now, lad. We'll just have t' come up wi' a way t' do so natural like," explained MacDonald.

"How could it ever be natural like to just show up where she's livin'?"

"Okay now, let's just use oor heads a wee bit. Now, who else be livin' at the Lewis farm? They hae lads 'n lasses, don' they?"

"Yeah, there's Sarah an' there's James," answered Thomas.

"Okay, then. Now do ye know either one o' 'em?"

"Well, a little. I used to be in school with James. I s'pose James an' I used to be mates a little."

"There ye go. Isn't it 'bout time t' catch up wi' yer mate James?"

Thomas laughed nervously. "Okay, okay, I get it. I go over to the Lewis's to hang out with James an' hope for a chance to meet Liz. Is that it?" asked Thomas.

"Now yer catchin' on, lad."

"But ain't I sneakin' 'bout like one o' those people sellin' potions?"

"Oh, be that what's botherin' ye, lad. I don't mean ye need t' deceive nobody. 'Course ye're there t' meet Liz. I'm certainly noo suggestin' that ye lie 'bout that. Mean what ye say, just don't say all that ye mean," counseled MacDonald.

"What? Mean what I say, but what?"

"What I mean, lad, be don' say anythin' that don' be true, but I also mean don' go bein' a fool an' answerin' questions that nobody's askin'."

Thomas thought about MacDonald's suggestion. After a time of chewing on it, he understood MacDonald's wisdom. It helped some, but it didn't take away his nervous stomach.

"Okay, Mr. MacDonald. I guess that's what to do. I can't think o' any other way to meet Liz, an' I don't wanna just wait."

"I want ye t' know lad, I understand perfectly weel that it will take ye an extra helpin' o' courage t' go through wi' it. For it always do when ye be afraid."

Somehow his nervous stomach didn't seem as bad now. That settled it; he would go to the Lewis farm tomorrow. Now that he'd decided, why wait. "Okay, Mr. MacDonald. I'll let ya know how it goes."

"Ye do that, lad. I'll be thinkin' o' ye tomorrow now."

Thomas awoke the next morning earlier than usual, with sunrise still a ways off. He wondered why he'd awakened so early. Then he quickly remembered what he had planned for the day. Thomas tried to roll over and return to his sleep, but gave up after an hour of tossing and turning. Remembering that Father didn't know of his plans, he quickly dressed and went out to attend to his daily chores. Two hours later Ben and Father joined Thomas in their day's work.

"Thomas, how long ya been out here?" Father asked.

"Just gettin' an early start on my chores. I thought I might pay a visit to James later today."

"To James? I din't know he was much of a friend to ya."

"I s'pose he ain't," Thomas admitted, "but I think I'll pay him a visit just the same."

"Okay, long as ya chores 're done."

"Yes, Father."

Although it seemed strange to him that his son wanted to see James, Father wasn't the type to think much about mysteries. Being practical, as long as the farm work was done, he didn't much care what Thomas's motives might be.

The work seemed to pass quickly, even though Thomas worked through the morning without a break. Finally, by noon he'd finished the chores for the day. He stepped inside the house for a bite to eat, realizing for the first time that he was famished. Having restored his energy, Thomas washed up and changed into fresh clothes. Walking out to the barn he found the horse seemed equally eager for an outing. He patted her head gently, and she nuzzled her nose against him. Thomas saddled her up and off they went.

The Chittenden farm stood on the northwestern side of Salisbury, while the Lewis farm sat on the southwestern portion of town. This made the ride a good five or six miles long. Thomas was glad for the time to think through what he'd say when he arrived. He hadn't wanted to think on it too much prior. MacDonald had cautioned him about over rehearsing the day, and that sometimes just showing up and letting events unfold as they may was best.

The Lewis farm started out on a level plateau, with the remaining land falling away to a shallow valley with a creek running through it. The farmhouse sat on the plateau near the front of the property and was the first thing visible on approach. The farmhouse appeared quiet with no activity as Thomas neared. He feared that the farm might be deserted at the moment. Slowing his horse down to a halt, he climbed down and cautiously unlatched the front gate. He walked her up the path to the house and tied her loosely to a sturdy tree. Now what? Thomas thought through his options. He hadn't expected to find no activity. Perhaps they were around back. He walked around to the back porch and was relieved and alarmed to hear activity as he rounded the corner of the house. Nerves shot through his stomach and sweat emerged on his palms and forehead. Thomas spotted James.

James brushed down a horse in front of the barn. No one else appeared to be about. Thomas took a deep breath, trying to calm himself as he approached. "Hello, James. What are ya up to?"

"Who's there? Is that you, Thomas?" Thomas nodded with a flushed face.

"What brings ya out this way?" answered James. "I ain't seen ya since we stop goin' to school."

"Well, I heard there were some city folk abouts, an' I thought I'd pay a visit an' see what they look like."

"Oh, ya must mean Aunt Mabel an' Liz. Yeah, they're stayin' with us for now. I s'pose the whole town knows by now."

"It's too bad what brought 'em here," said Thomas.

"Yeah. Anyways, ya want to grab that extra brush an' help me? After I'm done we can go off an' get something cold to drink, an' you can meet Aunt Mabel an' Liz."

Thomas exhaled deeply. He felt relieved beyond words that James had been welcoming. The first potential barrier had been crossed. Thomas had feared feeling much more awkward when he first arrived. Sure, he'd be glad to help give the horse a rubdown as the price to meet Liz. Shoot, James was almost done anyways.

Thirty minutes later, Thomas and James were walking back up a gentle slope to the house. The conversation with James progressed naturally. They both seemed to have plenty to say, having not seen each other for awhile. As the boys walked up the steps to the house Thomas noticed butterflies flying in formation about his stomach, and as he entered the kitchen and saw Liz sitting at the table, the butterflies seemed to be flying out of formation and bumping into each other. He hoped Liz and the others couldn't hear the butterflies. They seemed loud to him.

Liz sat at the table with her mother and Mrs. Lewis. They were sipping cold lemonade and nibbling on a midafternoon snack.

"Well, hello, Thomas! This is a surprise seeing you here. I hadn't known you were coming," said Mrs. Lewis.

"Hello, Mrs. Lewis. Yeah, my visit sorta came at the last minute."

Thomas privately wished she had left out the not knowing he was coming part. He didn't want to draw attention to the reasons for his visit, and hoped she wouldn't ask any more questions.

"Well, either way, it's nice to have ya visit. Please sit down an' I'll get you an' James some lemonade," welcomed Mrs. Lewis.

"Thank ya," was all Thomas said. Thomas exhaled deeply and sat down in a nearby chair.

"Oh, and let me introduce you to my sister and my niece. Thomas, this is Mabel Cranfield and her daughter, Liz."

"How do ya do, Ma'am. Ma'am," he repeated as he looked from one to the other.

"Pleased to meet you, Thomas," said Aunt Mabel.

"Hello," was all Liz said, although her smile was encouraging. An uncomfortable silence ensued for what seemed like minutes, but probably lasted a few seconds until Mrs. Lewis returned with the drinks.

"Here ya go, boys."

Thomas couldn't think of anything to say, although he searched his mind for anything to begin a conversation. Mrs. Lewis sensed his awkwardness and mercifully ended the strained silence. She had guessed the reason for his visit, being a sensitive and thoughtful person, as well as having put two and two together with Thomas's general store performance last week.

"James, why don't you take Thomas an' Liz an' show them around the property? I don't think either of them has seen everything, especially with the new parcel. We old women have some private talking to do anyways."

"Yeah, okay."

Thomas quickly turned his head away as he couldn't suppress a smile, and his heart rate increased to a gallop. Liz simply nodded her assent. The three teenagers strolled out to the back porch for their tour. James took them to the northern corner of the land, which, being the highest point on the property, afforded the best view. Liz stepped into place next to Thomas. She wasn't as shy or feeling as nervous as him.

"So, Thomas. Have you lived here all your life?"

"Yeah, Salisbury be the only home I know."

"Do you like it all right?" Liz inquired.

"Yeah, I s'pose so. I don' have much to compare it to, but I like it okay.... So ya come from a city?"

"Yes, Guilford. It's a pretty good-sized city, I suppose. Salisbury sure seems small when Guilford is the only home I've known," answered Liz.

"Yeah, I s'pose it must be quite a shock for ya, 'specially under the circumstances. I'm sorry 'bout ya father," offered Thomas.

"Yes, thank you."

Liz lowered her eyes to the ground at the mention of Papa, and then quickly changed the subject. "It's been a difficult adjustment for us here," she continued.

"Do ya think you'll settle here?"

"I, uh, well, we don't know yet. I think we're just trying to get on our feet for now, and decisions like that will come later."

The tour reached the high point on the property. James pointed out the various landmarks on the property. Thomas offered polite interest, but his mind was elsewhere. Liz didn't even bother showing any interest, although she looked in the direction James pointed. James pointed out the new parcel his family had bought from the neighbors, and led the others off to see it up close.

Having made the complete tour, the threesome headed back to the house. Thomas wanted to ask if he could see Liz again, but was unsure how to go about it. As he pondered what he might say, MacDonald came to mind. He remembered MacDonald advising him to not rehearse too much, and that sometimes it's best to just show up and be you.

"Well, here goes," thought Thomas. "I enjoyed visitin' with ya today, Liz." Thomas paused, but Liz just smiled. He fidgeted with his hands, wordlessly imploring her to say more, but she simply waited.

"Could I come back an' visit ya again?"

"I'd like that," she simply said.

Thomas exhaled audibly and his face brightened. "Alright, then. Well, I figure I best be goin' then," he said. And with that Thomas straddled his mare and was off.

Liz went out on the front porch to be alone. She didn't have a private room since she bunked with Sarah. Liz enjoyed meeting Thomas. It excited her that he'd asked to visit again. The distraction Thomas provided from her grief was welcomed; but not just that, she found him an interesting boy. Liz had just begun to take an interest in boys back in Guilford before they left. There had been one or two boys who had called on her, one of them she'd liked. The other one eventually caught on and stopped calling. They left Guilford so quickly that she hadn't even said goodbye to the one she'd liked. She hoped Thomas would keep his word and call again.

Thomas contained his excitement until he was out of sight, then he whooped and hollered. He felt that the visit with Liz couldn't have gone much better. He couldn't wait to tell MacDonald soon enough and headed for the Feed 'n Seed. Thomas almost turned to head toward home when he realized how low in the sky the sun had dropped, but decided that Mama and Father would just have to wait.

Thomas pushed his horse to a brisk trot, and the Feed 'n Seed came into view in no time. He quickly tied up his horse and raced in the front door. A moment later he found MacDonald in the back going over some paperwork.

"I did it! I did it! I can't believe I actually did it, Mr. MacDonald!"

"Oh aye, lad. That's great! Ye met yer lass then?"

"Yep. I just came from there."

"Weel then, tell me the whole tale withoot leaving nothin' oot."

"Okay, well, I went over to visit the Lewis's just like we talked 'bout. Thank God, James was friendly when I got there. That could o' ruined everything!"

Thomas went on to recount the whole visit including asking if he could visit her again; of course, not failing to include her affirmative response.

"Great God in heaven, lad. That's the best news I've heard all week! An' t' think ye almost didn't go through wi' it, lad."

Both of them had a good hearty laugh over Thomas's timidity before the visit. A brief pause followed, and then MacDonald said, "Ye know, lad. This being one o' those moments for us t' mark with a milestone. Ye were fearful, an' for good reason, yet ye found yer courage an' went through wi' it just the same. Many would hae turned away an' missed oot. I'm mighty proud of ye lad, an' ye should be mighty proud o' yerself."

Thomas sat with MacDonald's words for several minutes, trying to take them in. At first he wanted to brush them aside and call the whole thing no big deal. Yet after more reflection he realized he'd faced his fear in a way he never had before. A widening smile emerged on his face. "I couldn't have done it without ya help, Mr. MacDonald." Thomas jumped up and surprised MacDonald with a warm embrace.

"Oh, ye're very welcome, lad. It brings tears o' joy t' my face t' see yer tree growing so. Ye're startin' t' become a man, lad."

Thomas let go of MacDonald and saw water in the old man's eyes. MacDonald wasn't ashamed to show his tender feelings to Thomas, as he wanted the boy to know that he truly shared in his success. "So, now what do I do?" asked Thomas.

"I think ye know, lad."

"After a brief pause," Thomas responded, "Yeah, I s'pose I just need to take her invitation an' visit again."

Mr. MacDonald just nodded with a knowing grin on his face, wanting Thomas to think for himself when he could.

"Well, how soon should I visit again?" asked Thomas.

"Weel lad, how soon do ye want t' pay the lass a visit?"

"I don' know. Ya mean, I should just go back when I want to - that's it?"

"An' why not, lad?"

"Ain't there a number o' days ya s'posed to wait or somethin'?"

MacDonald gave another of his hearty laughs. "Noo lad, that's just somethin' folk made up. Ye go back when ye want."

"Well, let's see. I got a bunch o' work for tomorrow, but maybe the day after."

"Good enough, lad; the day after it be then."

"It seem so simple the way ya explain it," said Thomas.

"An' it oughta be hard, lad?"

"I don' know, it just seems like it oughta be."

MacDonald laughed. "Aye lad, that just be what ye been taught."

"Seems like it'd be easier if there would be some kind of pattern to follow," said Thomas.

"Aye lad, in some ways soo, but in other ways maybe nae."

"Well, I best be gettin' home. Sun's already almost down."

Thomas mounted his horse and hurried off home. Father didn't like Thomas getting home after the sun, and it usually meant extra chores when he didn't make it home before dark. Many times Thomas had argued with Father over the exact point of dusk. Tonight Thomas would probably not even bother to argue, as he didn't care about extra chores right now.

As Father scolded Thomas for his late arrival, he couldn't suppress a smile. Father interpreted his smile as disrespect, so Thomas bit his lip to hide it. Thomas accepted being told to do one of Father's chores with a nod and a "yes, sir".

May 20, 1753 - Hampshire Grants

The grey of dawn slowly brought more light on an awakening camp. The prisoners were the first to stir, due to the uncomfortable nature of sleeping while tied up. The younger children awoke with stifled sobs. They'd awakened that way each day of the miserable march. They'd learned to keep their sobs low, as they'd been slapped across the face a couple times by the Yorkers for awakening them. The two mothers did their best to comfort their children. Even from a distance Thomas could see the worn faces of the mothers. One mother placed the smaller child on her lap and rubbed another's head with her hands. Thomas couldn't imagine what else she could due with her hands tied, and shook his head at her plight.

Slowly the rest of the camp came to life. Thomas observed a fire being rebuilt, a coffee pot set into the embers, and a simple breakfast cooked. Several of the men still slept. One of the guards got up and walked over to one of the sleeping men, kicking him a couple of times. The sleeper batted the foot away as he sat up, rubbing sleep from his eyes. The kicker laughed and then said something to the man awakening. The Yorker slowly stood, rolled up his bedding and woke up another Yorker. Both men poured cups of coffee and walked over to the prisoners. The two guards stood, stretched, and left their post.

Thomas watched as the Yorkers ate and talked, laughing on occasion. He couldn't hear anything that was said. Once everyone had eaten, a Yorker walked over to the prisoners and threw some jerky and a canteen on the ground in front of them, laughed, and walked away. Thomas heard a sound behind him and turned to see Scout waving him to come.

"We found five tracks leading further northwest," began Scout. "We followed them for a mile or more, two on foot and three on horseback. Haskins continued on after them. He said he'll rejoin us once he finds out where they lead."

"Where the hell they takin' 'em?" said Thomas.

"Don't know, but I figure if they were going to kill them, there'd be no reason to go that far."

"All right, let's get back to the others," said Thomas.

The prisoners awoke to muskets prodding them. It seemed like the middle of the night as it was pitch black. It took a few minutes for the two men to be awake enough to understand that their captors were taking them somewhere else. Hugh and Daniel were untied from the rest of their families and then retied together, neck to neck. Their hands were left tied together in front of them.

As the three guards led the men away from their families, the women begged the Yorkers not to kill their husbands, the young children cried, and the older children just looked panicked yet made no sound. However, the women's pleas were ignored and the two men were led away to the north. They had no idea where they were going. The Yorkers hadn't really told them anything of substance since taking them captive. The only things said to them were vague comments about breaking the law of the New York Colony.

Hugh and Daniel had known each other about seven years. The two men and their wives grew up in Litchfield together, and the men got to know one another once Hugh began courting May. The men had been acquaintances, as everyone knew almost everyone in a small town like Litchfield. Daniel and Alice had already been married a year when Hugh started calling on May. Alice and May were not only sisters, but best friends. They kept no secrets from one another, and neither would have agreed to marry without the other's approval of the match.

Five years ago Alice and May's folks, Mr. and Mrs. Polter, left Litchfield and returned to New Haven. They'd grown up in New Haven, moving to Litchfield to try their hand at farming. After many years of hard toil, they decided to return to a less physically demanding life in New Haven. They'd been able to raise crops adequately, but every year something kept them from gaining a comfortable margin. The Polters never lived far from poverty. The first few years, the Polters lost much of their harvest due to beginners' mistakes. In later years, they'd had trouble from crops freezing and being eaten by wild animals. When Mr. Polter's father died and left him a small but profitable printing business in New Haven, they decided it was time to give up.

The Polters left their farm and home to their daughters. Once Hugh and May married, the two couples lived together on the Polter property. For a few years, they were satisfied to share the small farm. By now they had enough experience to make good use of the land. Life seemed good while it was just the four of them, but once they started having children, the farm began to feel small and crowded. They made plans to build a larger house to accommodate their growing families. Once they thought more about it, they realized the small plot of land would never yield more than a meager living. They just couldn't afford to buy more land in Litchfield. With land prices the way they were all over the Colony of Connecticut, the thought of moving to the Grants became attractive. The two familes began setting aside money two years ago. The men worked long hours to help save extra. The women had grown and pickled their own fruit to help in the cause. Finally, two months ago, they purchased adjoining plots in Middlebury town out in the Grants.

The Yorkers marched Hugh and Daniel northwest out of the camp. At first Daniel's thoughts remained clouded, as he had been awakened from a deep sleep, or at least as deep as he slept in captivity. He never woke rested. Sleep only came from exhaustion.

As his thoughts cleared, Daniel began to think about where the Yorkers may be leading them. Daniel's first thought was that they were leading the men away to kill their wives and children. Then he feared that he and Hugh were being led far enough from camp to be murdered without their families' knowledge. Daniel's stomach churned as he pondered the possibilities. For the hundredth time he thought through escape possibilities, and for the hundredth time none of them seemed to have a snowflake's chance in hell. Even though the Yorkers had consistently refused to answer any specific questions, out of desperation Daniel decided to try again.

"Hey, where you takin' us?"

Daniel's question was answered by a musket butt to the back that threw him to his hands and knees, knocking Hugh down in the process.

"Ya find out soon 'nough, Connecticut boy," chortled Bull with a laugh.

While they marched on, Daniel prayed silently that their families would still be alive whenever, if ever, they saw them again. At this point, the dream of creating new lives in the Grants had faded, and surviving the nightmare they'd awakened to had replaced their dream.

In the dark, it was next to impossible to tell where they were going. Hugh and Daniel often stumbled over the rugged terrain. The men had been aware for a couple of days that they were near the area of their grants. Although the adults were not permitted to speak amongst themselves, they had stolen brief conversations here and there, wondering if they were being taken to their grant land. And if the Yorkers were taking them to Middlebury, why? Why go all that way just to kill them? By now Daniel was convinced that they would be killed.

As the night wore on and the march continued hour after hour, Daniel's prayers for survival turned to requests to be allowed to rest. He became so desperate for rest, that he would welcome a stop even if it meant he would be hurt. Both prisoners began to fall asleep on the march. Each time they dosed, they fell. The fall woke them immediately, and if it hadn't, the choking rope around their necks would have.

Just after first light, the prisoners saw that they were being led into a town. They recognized Middlebury at once. They gave each other a knowing look. Each noticed a vague uneasiness within, fearing what may await them in town.

Before reaching town, the captors led the prisoners over behind a clump of trees. Bull and Bill walked away from them and conferred briefly in hushed tones while Gilroy stood guard over the prisoners. After several anxious minutes, Bull and Bill returned to address their captors.

"Well boys, now we find out if ya got much more 'n shit for brains. Ya likely figured we brung ya here on account o' your false land grants, issued illegally by the fool that claims to be gov'nor o' New Hampshire. Ya both oughta be thankful for my more than generous brother; more generous than his own good, I say. If it was up to me, ya both would be stretched by now," said Bull.

Here Bill produced a document and stepped forward as he explained.

"As you can see, the offer is all legal an' everything. I also hope you can see that it be a damn fair offer, better offer than ya deserve."

At this Bull gave his brother a glare. Bill merely held his gaze, nonplussed. Bill handed the document to Daniel.

"Now, once ya agree to the offer, an' ya damn well better if ya know what's good for ya, then we march down to town, continued Bill. An' ya know what's there?"

The two captors looked at each other and shrugged. The fact that Middlebury was the location of their grants seemed too obvious an answer.

"Since I can see ya both idiots, I'll tell ya what's there. That be Middlebury an' the building ya see through them trees be the town magistrate's farm. Once ya agreed, we head down to the magistrate's so he can make legal ya turnin' over ya rights, illegal though they be, to me an' Bill here," Bull concluded.

The two prisoners examined the document and exchanged surprised looks at the number on the offer.

"That's only 'bout half of what we paid for the grant!" Daniel blurted out.

"Well, we can fix that right quick," began Bull as he unsheathed his knife.

Bill quickly placed a firm hand on his brother's shoulder. "Now hold on, Bull. They's no need for that. Gentlemen, ya'll certainly understand that by New York law, ya grants ain't worth the paper they written on," Bill explained. "We believe the offer generous given the fact that ya grant is in direct violation of a legal New York grant o' the same land. You'll understand that the colony of New York don't recognize ya grant as meaning nothing! Do not let emotions cloud ya thinkin'. I figure that clear thinkin' will see the generous offer being made you. Look, I'd like us to do this as pleasant as we can. I take no pleasure in hurtin' ya. An' we will give ya time to think it over."

"Wait a damn minute! retorted Hugh. Why have ya brought us way out here? Ya could o' made the proposal to us in Connecticut?"

"Guess ya wasn't payin' no mind, Connecticut boy. We said the town magistrate has to make it legal like. Ya think ya miserable company's enough for us to march ya all the way out here? You jist think over that offer. Believe you me, it's the best offer ya gonna git," fumed Bull.

"An' what if we say 'no'?" asked Daniel.

"Well, Connecticut boy. If ya foolish enough to refuse, then ya be makin' my day. That will give me plenty reason to shrug off my brother's warnings an' have some fun with ya families," answered Bull with an unnerving smile.

"What do ya mean?" inquired Daniel.

"I mean bad things happen out in the wild. Wolves been known to tear apart folk, bears been known to flat out eat people, Indians been known to scalp folk, wild men been known to have they way with women folk. Anything might happen out here in the wild, ya git my meaning, Connecticut boy? Ya jist think real hard 'bout ya situation here."

At this final statement Bull walked away laughing. Bill slowly followed his brother, as though he had thought of saying more. They withdrew far enough to give the prisoners some privacy to talk over the offer, yet kept them in sight in case they tried something foolish. Gilroy sat on a nearby rock with his musket across his lap. Although they were tied up, if left alone long enough the prisoners would be able to extract themselves from their bonds.

Hugh and Daniel shifted nervously in their bonds, not at all liking the implications made by their captors. Once they were alone, Daniel started the difficult conversation. "So, what are we gonna do?"

"You're not considering the offer, are ya?" asked an incredulous Hugh. "No way in hell are we takin' that! An' that ain't no offer; that's just plain ole blackmail, that's what that is. That's jist plain insultin'!"

"Now keep ya voice down! It may be blackmail, but what choice do we have? What 'bout his threats?"

"They wouldn't dare hurt innocent women an' children!" answered Hugh.

Daniel shook his head. "Who ya foolin', Hugh? Ain't ya got the feelin' that it don't take much for Bull to snuff a life out? I git the feelin' he would even enjoy it. What if they did somethin' to one o' ya little ones? Can you live with that?"

"I tell ya, if those sons o' bitches do somethin' to any of my kin, I'll hunt 'em down till they all dead!" growled Hugh.

"I said keep ya voice down! That Gilroy ain't far away," said Daniel with a look over his shoulder. "Avengin' the dead would be fine, but that won't bring back my little ones or my wife. I can't take that kinda chance. Hell, I wonder if we gonna make it out o' this alive no matter if we accept o' not," said Daniel.

Hugh looked up at the Yorker brothers, as if trying to assess their intentions. "Those sons o' bitches, if they think..."

Daniel could see Hugh becoming more and more worked up and decided it was time to settle his friend down. He didn't want them making life and death decisions while they were all lathered up in anger, or at least while Hugh was.

"Now hold on there, Hugh. I don't know what we're gonna do, but we ain't decidin' nothin' while we're so mad we can't see straight. Ya git my meaning? We're talkin' 'bout the lives of our kin! Let's just settle down a bit an' clear our thinkin'."

Daniel's level-headedness slowed down Hugh's train that was headed for disaster. Hugh took several deep breaths and calmed himself a bit before responding. Hugh had his moments of temper, but most of the time he was not impulsive or explosive. The whole ordeal the two families had been through had pushed him beyond his normal sensible self, and who could blame him. It takes a huge toll on a person to live in constant suspense for weeks.

Daniel was angry and scared too, and he would have shown it more except that he had to be calm for the two of them. Daniel had always been the more sensible of the two, but if Hugh had been calm, Daniel might have lost his temper.

Hugh continued to be angry, but felt remorse for the peril he had almost put them in. "Damn it, I'm sorry. I guess I'm too upset to decide anything right now. I would never forgive myself if I got my kin kilt!"

"I understand that. I'm upset too. I wish I could drive my knife right through all three of 'em damn Yorkers' hearts right now! But we can't lose our heads! Our families 're dependin' on us. Now, let's think through what we gonna do," Hugh said.

Both men were silent while they thought over their dilemma. Neither man wanted to accept the unfair offer, but what else could they do? After many minutes of pondering, Hugh spoke.

"Do ya really think them Yorker boys would hurt our kin?"

"I think Bull's capable o' just 'bout anything. Come on, don't you? I was just tryin' not to picture what he might do. Don't ya remember how he woulda kilt one o' his own men if Bill hadn't stopped 'im? And I heard some o' them other boys jokin' 'bout the things Bull done in the Indian wars. Didn't ya catch none o' that?"

Hugh slowly nodded. Daniel looked over at the Yorkers, who were talking while they enjoyed a smoke. "I just can't take that chance."

"Maybe there's a way we might call their bluff an' see," countered Hugh.

Daniel eyed Hugh suspiciously. He didn't like the comparison to gambling. "Like how?"

"No, I got it!" answered Hugh. "We make 'em an offer back. We ask for more money an' see what they do. Maybe they want the land bad enough to take it."

"I don' know. I was thinkin' they workin' for somebody. I don' even know if the land's theirs."

"Maybe. They might be hired guns," acknowledged Hugh, "but maybe we can buy some time."

"An' then what?" asked an unconvinced Daniel.

"Here's the thing; I figure if we can somehow git 'em damn Yorkers to take us back to our kin, then at least we gotta fightin' chance to protect 'em if somethin' goes wrong."

Daniel pondered Hugh's idea some. He liked the idea of trying to get back at the side of their wives and children. If anyone tried to hurt them, he sure wanted to be there to do whatever he could. The utter helplessness of being miles away from the families was the worst part.

"Okay, Hugh. I like the idear of tryin' to git back to our kin. I'm not so sure 'bout the idea of callin' out their bluff, but maybe we can make 'em an offer back. After all we've been through, I'm not sure I wanna move my family to the grant anyways."

"Okay, now we gettin' somewhere! So how much we gonna ask for?" asked Hugh.

"Well, they offerin' us 'bout half o' what we paid, how 'bout we ask for three quarters o' what we paid?" suggested Daniel.

"Damn it all! I sure hate the idea of sellin' out to those sons o' bitches, 'specially sellin' out with a gun to our heads an' all."

"I know! I hate the idea too, but what other choice do we have?" said Daniel.

Hugh merely shook his head, and then looked away at the Yorkers. Daniel gave his friend time to think through the counter offer a bit more. After a few more minutes, Hugh was ready.

"Alright, damn it. I'll go along with it. Maybe it best we sell out. I s'pose I'd feel some better 'bout it if we can get a little more."

"Then it's settled. An' one more thing, Hugh. Leave the talkin' to me. I don' want ya gettin' all hot under the collar with the Yorkers, got it?"

Hugh reluctantly nodded his agreement. Daniel stood and waved the Yorkers over. The Yorkers stubbed out their smokes and sauntered back to where they'd left the prisoners. The captain spoke.

"You Connecticut boys come to a sensible decision?"

Daniel responded quickly to not give Hugh a chance. "Yes sir, I believe so."

"Well, maybe ya ain't as dumb as I thought then."

"Well, not exactly," continued Daniel. "We hoped ya'd consider a counteroffer."

"Counteroffer! Hey, you Connecticut boys don' git it. This ain't a negotiation! We're makin' ya the only offer ya gonna git."

"Okay, just hear us out. Give us that much," Daniel pressed.

Bull was silent, which Daniel took as assent and continued. "We'd be willin' to accept three quarters o' what we paid for the land, an' we'd sign over all rights to ya, right now."

The Yorker brothers burst out laughing and shook their heads. They hadn't expected the prisoners to have the nerve to do anything but accept their terms as stated. Shaking his head haughtily, the captain answered.

"You Connecticut boys definitely don' git it. Maybe you Connecticut folk ain't as sharp as us Yorker folk. This ain't no bargainin' table an' never will be."

"Come on, now. Let's see if we can't work somethin' out we can both live with," reasoned Daniel. "Look, we paid good money for our grants, legal or not, an' we don' wanna just walk away from 'em."

Bull seemed to think about Daniel's comment briefly, and then his mouth returned to its familiar sneer. "I don' know, Connecticut boy. I think that first offer might be all ya gonna git. Well, we ain't gettin' nowhere here. Alright, Gilroy. March the prisoners back to camp."

Hugh and Daniel felt great relief to hear they were being taken back to the camp, although they tried not to appear too relieved. They risked a brief glance at each other when the Yorkers were looking the other way, but didn't try to say anything.

Haskins had to track slowly at night, but enjoyed every moment of the challenge. He came across the Yorkers just after dawn. He heard the sounds of low conversation through the trees. He crept forward until he achieved a view of the two Yorkers smoking and talking. A moment later he found the third Yorker sitting on a rock with his musket. Haskins heard a couple of snippets.

"Ya think them boys'll take the offer, Bull?"

"Don't know if they git it. Might take somebody dyin' first."

"Damn, I just want this whole mess to be over!"

"Don' worry, it'll be over one way or another soon 'enough."

"Look, Bull. We can do this without killin' nobody."

"We'll see 'bout that."

Then Haskins saw the prisoners wave to them, and the Yorkers walked over. Haskins couldn't hear any of what was said from then on. One of the Yorkers stayed at a distance, holding his musket across his chest. The other two conversed with the two prisoners. The talking came to an end, and the Yorkers mounted their horses and started back toward Haskins.

Haskins quickly moved thirty or forty yards to the west to give them more of a berth in which to pass. The third Yorker rode behind the prisoners and nudged them forward with the barrel of his musket, although the prisoners appeared to willingly move out.

The march back to camp seemed much shorter than the midnight hike. Although thoroughly exhausted from little sleep and much walking, Hugh and Daniel felt plenty of energy about getting back to camp. Some fearful thoughts reentered their minds about their families being hurt while they were away, but they did their best to brush them away. It did them no good to allow such fantasies to linger. They took comfort in the thought that the Yorkers probably wouldn't hurt their families yet, not knowing the outcome of today's "negotiations."

After a couple of hours, Daniel and Hugh began to walk slower. Gilroy jabbed them in the back to encourage a quicker pace. The prisoners briefly resumed a quicker pace, only to slacken back to the pace of an old man's shuffle. Bull and Bill turned around to see them well behind.

"Damn it, Gilroy. Get them damn Connecticut boys moving," shouted Bull. "I ain't got all day."

Having found his musket jabs minimally successful, Gilroy gave each of the prisoners a stiff kick in the backside. Hugh turned to give Gilroy the evil eye, while Daniel crumpled into a heap, bringing Hugh down on top of him. Bull rode back.

"What's the problem, Gilroy? Why can't ya keep the damn prisoners movin'!" cursed Bull.

"They jist won't do much more than a crawl; don' know what more I can do, Bull."

"Well, maybe a little..." Bull pulled out his knife, but was interrupted as Bill rode up.

"Hold on, Bull - a word in private." Bull shrugged his shoulders and walked over.

"When was the last time them prisoners ate?" asked Bill. "Don't know 'bout you but I'm mighty hungry myself, an' maybe them prisoners can't go nowhere till they had somethin'."

"I figure I can put a little fire in 'em with my..."

"Hey Bull, we want 'em able to march, right?" remonstrated Bill.

"Ya know, ya take all the fun outta this," said Bull sulkily. "Go ahead an' feed 'em if ya must, but I won't have no part o' ya babyin' 'em."

Haskins watched the Yorkers dismount and pull something out of their saddle bags. All five men sat down and refreshed themselves with some kind of food and water. The Yorkers each had their own canteen, while the prisoners shared one.

Gilroy stood up and wiped his mouth with the back of his hand. He walked over to the one who seemed to be in charge and said something. Then he walked off towards the east, and was soon out of sight. Haskins decided to go see what he was up to.

Haskins found Gilroy making water behind some trees. He was surprised at the unusual distance the man went to relieve himself. Haskins looked over his shoulder and saw that the others were well out of sight and sound. Haskins had been watching for a chance like this, and he rubbed his hands together in anticipation. Haskins slipped around behind the trees, careful to make a soundless approach. Gilroy was buttoning himself back up as Haskins put a hand over his mouth and in one motion slit Gilroy's throat. Gilroy immediately collapsed to the ground.

"Well it's 'bout time. I ain't felt this good in a damn long time," Haskins said under his breath.

Haskins looked around and saw a steep hillside not far away. He picked up Gilroy's limp body and carried him to the edge of the rocks. Haskins looked over the edge and was pleased to see a drop of a hundred feet or more. He swung the body back and forth before pitching it over the edge. The body bounced and tumbled all the way to the bottom. Haskins went back to the sight of the slaying and carefully removed all signs of his presence, including burying the spilled blood. He picked up Gilroy's musket and laid it on top of the rock from which he'd thrown Gilroy.

Spying higher ground with good cover, Haskins found a good place to lay in wait and watch. Not long passed before Bull appeared. He quickly found the place Gilroy had made water and knelt down to examine the ground. Bull stood up and trotted over to where he saw Gilroy's musket. He stood on the rock and stared down momentarily. Then he suddenly dropped into a crouch, put Gilroy's musket at the ready and methodically searched his entire field of view.

"So, I got ya attention, ya sons o' bitches. Now the fun's begun," Haskins quietly chuckled to himself. "Ya thought ya be all alone out here. Well, hate to pop ya balloon, but ya best know I'm here."

Bill emptied out his pipe as Bull came back into view. At first he didn't note anything out of place. Then it dawned on himself that something was missing. "Hey Bull, din't ya find Gilroy? Where'd he run off to?"

Bull looked around absent-mindedly for a moment before responding. "Yeah, I found 'em; found 'em at the bottom of a cliff. Figure the damn fool got careless an' fell."

"Ya mean he's dead?" asked an incredulous Bill.

"If he ain't, then he's grabbin' a bit o' sleep down in a creek," returned Bull unemotionally.

"Ya sure he slipped? That don't sound like Gilroy to me," returned Bill.

"Well, just in case, we best be on the lookout," said Bull as he put one foot in the stirrup and stepped onto his horse.

They reached camp and the rest of their families an hour before dusk set in. Embraces, tears of relief, and thankfulness abounded. The young children were clingier and held onto their fathers the rest of the evening. Daniel's little daughter even insisted on sleeping next to Daddy that night. It was difficult to manage with the ropes, but Daniel found a way to make it happen. He understood she felt scared he would abandon her again.

Spring, 1748 - Salisbury, Connecticut Colony

Thomas climbed into bed and stared at Ben's bunk above him. His thoughts ran to Liz. He planned to visit her tomorrow. When Thomas imagined how it might go, he pictured Liz appearing at the door with a look of surprise on her face that seemed to ask - whatever are you doing here? Darts of nerves shot through his stomach. He tried to shoo away that image, willing himself to picture an eager Liz, glad to see him. Thomas could see this Liz for a moment, but she kept changing back into the unpleasantly surprised Liz. He succeeded in pushing all thought of Liz out of his mind, and told himself he'd just show up and make the best of it. At first this worked, and he drifted off to sleep.

He woke a short time later in a cold sweat. Thoughts of standing awkwardly at the Lewis farm's front door plagued him. He reaffirmed his plan to just show up, and turned over to go back to sleep. This time the strategy didn't work as well. He proceeded to toss and turn for what seemed like hours. Eventually he got up and paced the downstairs back and forth, in his stocking feet in order to not wake anyone. He didn't want anyone asking him why he was up. Finally, out of sheer exhaustion, he drifted into a troubled sleep for a few hours.

The work seemed to go by quickly today, and before he knew it he was done. Thomas was grateful for the distraction of his chores and worked through the midday meal. He then cleaned up inside, changed clothes, and grabbed a quick bite to eat from the leftovers. As he was saddling up his horse, Ben walked up.

"Where ya off to, Thomas?"

"Oh, I'm off to visit the Lewis's."

"The Lewis's? Ya goin' over to visit with James?" asked a surprised Ben.

"Well, sorta."

"Sorta? What's the big secret?"

"I guess I shoulda told ya. I figure I'm kinda embarrassed to say, but I met a new girl who's staying with the Lewis's," explained Thomas.

"Oh, I see. Now that explains a lot. I've been wonderin' why ya been workin' so hard. An' ain't like ya to get up early."

"Yeah, I've been tryin' to clear up time to visit with Liz," said Thomas.

"Ya din't have to keep this from me, little brother. I've got a girl myself. I get it."

"I know, Ben. I'm sorry."

"So tell me 'bout her."

"Well, she real pretty. She's got beautiful, long brown hair, big green eyes, an' a smile that'll melt ya. She an' her mama are stayin' with the Lewis's since her father jist died. They just got into town a few weeks back, an' I just met her this week. The best thing's that I like the feel o' her tree."

"Her what?"

"Oh, I mean the kinda person she's like," said Thomas.

Ben laughed mockingly. "So what kinda tree she got, little brother - a fir tree?

"No Ben," Thomas laughed as well, "that ain't the kind I mean."

"What other kind is there?"

"The kind that live inside," said Thomas.

"What kinda nonsense ya talkin' 'bout? Where ya gettin' these fool idears?"

"Never mind, it won't make no sense to ya."

"That's right, little brother. It don't make no sense to me, an' it won't make no sense to nobody. Wait a minute, ya gettin' this fool talk from ole man MacDonald, ain't ya? Now it's all comin' together. Damn, Thomas. I thought I warned ya to stay away from that crazy ole man."

"Mr. MacDonald make more sense that anybody I ever met," countered Thomas. "An' ya had a chance to visit 'im too."

"So, I'm right then! I knew it. That ole fool's got ya believin' 'im. Difference atween you an' me is that I was smart enough to stay away from that ole man, an' you wadn't."

"Look Ben, think whatever ya want 'bout Mr. MacDonald, but don't tell Mama or Father or nobody else 'bout me an' Liz. I wanna keep this private, for now. Okay?"

"Okay, little brother. I'll keep it under my hat, at least for now," Ben added with a mischievous grin.

"Come on, Ben. I'm serious."

"Okay, okay," said Ben laughing. "I won't say nothin'."

"Well, I best be off. I wanna have a good bit o' time with Liz. I'll see ya when I get back." Thomas jumped on his horse and headed off for the Lewis farm.

Thomas dismounted and went straight up to the front door. On the ride over, he'd decided to ask for Liz right away. Although he felt more nervous asking for her directly, it seemed like the right thing to do. He was there to see her, nobody else. Sarah opened the front door after Thomas knocked. He asked for Liz, and Sarah went off to find her, not seeming too surprised. Thomas paced about the porch with his hands in his pockets while waiting for Liz to appear. He worried about how she'd receive him. She'd certainly been welcoming of another visit two days ago, but how would Liz feel about him showing up today? His nervousness increased as the wait lengthened. Thomas looked back at the partially opened door, but it hadn't budged. She seemed to be taking forever!

"Maybe she's thinkin' over whether she wants to see me," Thomas wondered privately.

After what seemed like an hour, Liz finally appeared. Thomas quickly searched her face and saw nothing but a welcoming smile; he immediately sighed with relief. Unbeknownst to Thomas, Liz had taken the needed time to freshen up herself before she let him see her. She'd been helping clean up after the midday meal and wanted to look a bit nicer. She had no ambivalence about receiving him.

"Hello, Thomas. What a nice surprise."

"Uh, hello, Liz. This be a good time to visit?"

"Sure. I just finished in the kitchen."

"Oh, okay."

Thomas wasn't sure what to do next. He hadn't planned beyond asking for her at the door. "Uh, uh, would ya like to take a walk?" suggested Thomas.

"Sure, let me just fetch a coat."

Liz turned around, went back into the house, came back with her coat over her arm a moment later, and off they went. It's not certain how they decided on their direction, but they ended up heading toward town. Once they navigated the initial awkwardness and nervousness, their conversation became more lively and natural.

Liz spoke of her life in Guilford, the friends she'd had there, her schooling, her family farm. The one topic she avoided discussing was her father. It still pained her deeply to talk of him, with the wound being fresh and deep. Instead, she appreciated the opportunity to speak of other things. Liz still lived through days in which she struggled to think of anything other than Papa.

Thomas spoke mostly about his family life on the farm. He mentioned MacDonald briefly, but didn't feel ready to say too much about him. MacDonald held a place of immense importance in Thomas's life, yet he wasn't sure Liz would understand. Thomas thought it strange that MacDonald wasn't his father or even in his family. Uncomfortable questions might be asked. While not knowing of the other, both Thomas and Liz had their somewhat hidden relationship.

A couple of hours later found them walking back up the road to the Lewis farm. Neither had spoken it, but both sensed it was time to end their visit. With a little less apprehension, Thomas once again asked if he might return for another visit. Liz nodded and smiled as before. After today's visit, he could see her interest in him.

Thomas instinctively headed off to see MacDonald after the visit with Liz. This time he didn't concern himself with the sun or how late in the day it might be. He knew he needed to speak with MacDonald. Thomas had grown comfortable with his need for MacDonald, no longer feeling guilty. Needing to talk with MacDonald now seemed as natural as needing to eat supper after a long day on the farm.

"Mr. MacDonald, my tree's doin' pretty good, but I'm not sure what to do 'bout Liz."

"I see. Ye visited the young lass again."

"Yeah, I just came from my second visit," explained Thomas.

"Weel, how did it go, lad?"

"Good, I think.... I mean, we got on well enough, an' she said I could call again. I mean, I jist don' know how to go 'bouts this. I've never visited a girl before. I don' know, how do ya go 'bouts havin' a girl?"

"Oh, now the water's comin' clear," MacDonald said with a chuckle. "Ye don't know how t' court a lass. I s'pose it's time for that conversation, lad. "

"Yeah, it's definitely time. I feel like a schoolboy going to the schoolhouse for the first time an' not knowin' what to do there."

"Aye, lad. Hae a seat an' let's see if we can clear up the muddy water a bit."

MacDonald waited for Thomas to gather his thoughts. MacDonald didn't want to do his thinking for him. After a pause, Thomas continued. "I guess I just don't know how much to visit."

"Lad, ye visit as often as ye an' the lass like."

Thomas looked out the window and thought. "Yeah, but... I mean, how do I..."

"I think ye may also be wrestling wi' how t' be when ye are wi' yer lass."

"I s'pose I don't know what else to talk 'bout with her. I mean I already told her 'bout my life on the farm. What else be there for me to tell 'er?"

MacDonald chuckled, "Oh, come now, lad. Hae ye learnt nothin' from oor talks? Do the lass know anything o' yer tree yet?"

"My tree? Well, no, I figure not much," answered Thomas.

"An' why not, lad?"

"Don' that be kinda personal?"

"Aye, lad. But how else can ye find oot if ye an' the lass be a good fit?"

"Uh, I don' think I'm followin' ya, Mr. MacDonald. Ain't I just tryin' to make a favorable impression?"

MacDonald responded with a grin. "Sure, ye want t' make a fine impression, but do ye think yer wantin' to lure a fish, lad? Ye see, it be fine t' put yer best foot forward an' all, but if that's all ye do, what will ye end up with?"

"I guess Liz won't know much o' my tree."

"That's right, lad. Is that the way ye want it t' be with ye an' the lass? Is that the way ye want it wi' me, lad?"

"Oh, no, Mr. MacDonald. I've come to count on ya knowin' 'bout me. I wouldn't want it any other way atween us."

"Then why would ye want it any other way with yer lass? Do ye think ye'd be happy any other way, lad?"

"But what if she doesn't wanna know 'bout my tree? What if she don' want me to know 'bout her tree?" asked Thomas.

"Aye lad, an' what if?"

Thomas had to think about that one. He realized that's how it had been for him before he'd met MacDonald. He remembered he hadn't even known about an inner life. He remembered how boring and dreary his life had felt. He remembered telling MacDonald that boredom was the only feeling he knew. No, he didn't want that again. Thomas had long relied on going to MacDonald to talk, but he hadn't thought that he might have that kind of relationship with anyone else.

"I guess I would only wanna marry 'er if we could talk 'bout our trees. I don' wanna boring life with her."

"Noo, lad. I'd hate for ye to hae that. I too know what 'tis t' be alone. An' I don't mean to hae no one aboot. I mean to hae no one know 'bout me. There be few things worse than that, lad."

"Okay, Mr. MacDonald. So how do I do that with Liz?"

"Just like wi' me, lad."

"But I don' think she's gonna ask me in for tea."

MacDonald laughed so hard, he couldn't talk at first. "Aye lad, ye can't count on that then."

"So what do I do?"

"Ye show her some o' yer leaves an' see what she does with 'em. An' ye show some interest in the condition o' her leaves as weel," MacDonald explained.

Liz watched as Thomas rode off toward town. After he was well out of sight, she rushed into the house to find Mother. She quickly found her upstairs in her room. Lying down is about all Mother did in her room. Sometimes she'd stay there all day. On better days, she might only be in there till noon.

"Mother, what are you doing in bed?"

"Oh, hi dear. I just wanted to lie down for awhile. I'm tired you know," she said with a leaden voice.

Liz immediately noticed the heaviness of her mother's face. She'd seen that look many times now, and it scared her. Her face appeared drained of all life, and her features hung on her face, as if gravity were twice as strong in her room. Mother was lying on her side when Liz came into the room, and sat up when she saw her daughter. Liz saw deep creases on Mother's arms and face, and a dark red mark on her jaw bone. Liz put her hand over her mouth when she saw the markings. Then Liz's shoulders sank, along with her chin. Perhaps being in Mother's room sapped the energy of anyone who darkened its doors, as though a vacuum pulled all life down through the floorboards.

"How long have you been in here? And you have the drapes drawn. It looks like a dungeon in here," Liz said. Liz walked over to the window and opened the drapes.

"Oh, no, dear. That's too bright! Close them, at least part way. Come now, you're always making things hard on me. Don't you know I need my rest? I work harder than anyone else around here, and nobody seems to appreciate it. Can't a hard worker get a few minutes' rest without being bothered about it?"

"Mother, I don't want you to lie in bed all day, like you were when we first got here."

"Oh, just give me a few more minutes to gather my energy, dear. I'm just so tired. It's the least you can do for me, with all I do for you every day."

She'd lain in bed for several days after Papa's funeral and for two weeks after they arrived at Aunt Hannah's. Liz shrugged her shoulders and closed the door on her way out. She slowly walked down the stairs, and then remembered she had wanted to talk with Mother about Thomas. Not knowing what else to do, she went downstairs and sat down. A few minutes later Aunt Hannah passed by. She recognized the forlorn gaze of her niece.

"Liz, what troubles you?"

"What? Oh, I just saw Mother in bed. I, uh, I just hate seeing her like that."

"Yes, I feel concerned for her too. She's been in bed all afternoon," noted Aunt Hannah.

"What's wrong with her, Aunt Hannah? She's just not herself... I'm scared. I'm scared Mother is never going to get out of bed again. If I thought she just needed to rest for awhile, I could live with that. But I fear she's gonna stay there. I don't think I could bear it if she never got up, if she was never her old self again. She hasn't been the same since Papa died. Will she ever be?"

Liz began to cry softly. Aunt Hannah sat down next to Liz and put her arm around her. Liz's soft crying turned to deep sobs. Aunt Hannah sensed that Liz just needed to be, and didn't interrupt by saying anything at first. She had been well aware of Liz's sadness.

"I know, Liz. I know. It must be terribly frightening to see your mother like that. And you need her. And when she's in bed, she can't help you."

Liz sobbed more deeply. "When she's in bed, I feel like I don't even have a mother."

"Oh, Liz. That's an awful thing to feel. I'm so sorry."

She'd been storing up grief, waiting to be able to tell someone. Liz had tried to talk with Mother about her grief many times, but Mother quickly changed the subject or would tell her it's going be alright. Although she was hurting, it felt good to Liz to have someone to tell. Liz surprised herself by how long she cried. Aunt Hannah also surprised Liz by sitting with her for so long.

Liz's sobs eventually turned to gentle crying, and later she lay still in her aunt's arms. After several moments she looked up smiling. "I met a boy."

"Oh, you mean Thomas?"

"Yes. Did you know that he called on me today?"

"He came again today? Oh, I didn't see him. Well, tell me all about your visit."

"Okay," Liz said with enthusiasm, and recounted her visit.

Later that day Liz walked into the kitchen to see if Aunt Hannah needed help with supper, and was surprised to see Mother already there helping. Liz felt relieved to see Mother out of bed. Mother smiled broadly as she turned and saw Liz.

"Oh, hi, honey. How was your day?" inquired Mother.

"Oh, hello, Mother. You're out of bed."

"Oh yes, I just needed to rest a minute. So how was your day?"

"I had a nice visit with a boy today."

"That's nice, honey," Mother said with extra energy.

Mother immediately turned back to her work of preparing boiled potatoes for supper. Liz noticed the ear-to-ear smile remained on Mother's face, as if plastered there permanently. Liz gazed at her mother, examining her face. Mother's smile seemed so big. Liz wondered if she could really feel that much better. And how could she be so happy after appearing like one almost dead an hour before? Liz had previously observed these puzzling changes in Mother.

"Mother, are you feeling better?"

"Oh, honey, I feel great!" replied Mother. "When folk leave me be to get my ration of rest, I'm just fine."

"But, an hour ago you looked awful."

"Oh, honey, you worry too much. I wasn't feeling awful; I was just a little tired. That's all. You're always making a mountain out of a molehill. Come now, don't exaggerate."

Liz gaped with her mouth wide open, and then she quickly covered her mouth with her hand as Mother turned to look at her. It was as if Mother had put on a mask she kept on a table by the door in her room - a happy mask. The mask seemed to be on when Mother was out of her room, and off when in her room.

"Okay, Mother," was all Liz said. Liz's mouth slowly closed, and she turned and asked Aunt Hannah if she could help with something.

Liz had talked to Thomas briefly about her mother, which had caught his interest. Thomas asked MacDonald about Liz' mother and the loss of her husband. MacDonald said, "Aye lad, many a tree struggle to withstand the loss of a great branch. The ability to both acknowledge the loss an' mourn it be a rare combination. Many a tree in this situation deny the branch be gone, while others don' allow themself to know the branch bein' gone be o' any great consequence. Sadly, a few fall into incessant droopin' an' droppin' o' leaves, an' may appear as a weepin' willow, even though they don' be. Only a few can allow themself to droop an' drop for a season, only to return to vigor an' flourish in a later season. No tree passes through a season o' loss withoot the help o' other trees."

Thomas arrived home and had just finished rubbing down his horse when Ben approached. Ben had that grin on his face again.

"So, Thomas. Tell me 'bout ya new girl ya been hidin'."

Thomas laughed. "I guess it must seem like that." Thomas went on to tell Ben about his visit with Liz and how they'd met and all the particulars.

"So, Ben. Ya gonna marry Anna?"

"Shoot, don' rush me, little brother. I don' know."

"Rush ya! Ya been visitin' that girl for a good while now. What has it been, two years?"

"Yeah, I know. She's startin' to say things."

"Things?"

"Well, she says things like, 'a feller ought to know after a season o' visits if a girl's to be his wife' and 'some boys just can't make up their minds 'bout a girl.' Well shoot, Thomas, I knows she's talkin' 'bout me."

"I figure she is," said Thomas laughing. "So, what are ya gonna do?"

"I don' know. I just wanna make sure she's the one. Ya know what I mean?"

"'Course I do."

"I figure I need to think on it some."

"Maybe ya don' know yet. An' maybe ya scared," said Thomas.

"No, I ain't scared. I just wanna make sure. I don't wanna make the wrong decision. Some fellas end up pickin' the wrong girl an' then they miserable the rest o' their days. I don' want that. I just gotta make sure."

"How are ya gonna make sure?"

"I don' know. I just gotta wait an' see. I always figured a man just knew when he met the right girl. I figured it'd be easy to tell the right one. Well, I don' know if it's Anna or not."

"Ya might always be a bit unsure," suggested Thomas.

"Naw, it'll come to me. But I don' like not knowin' yet; it don't seem natural. I figure the important things oughta be sure. Like take wheat. You can always tell the right time to harvest the wheat by lookin' at it. Either it's ready or it's not. Why can't pickin' a girl be like that? I figure I oughta know."

"I don' think it works like that," Thomas chuckled.

"Well, it should!"

Several days went by before Thomas could find the opportunity to call on Liz again. Sunday after church, Thomas excused himself from the family and walked to the Lewis farm. He planned to talk with Liz about his tree some, but he wasn't sure exactly what he'd say.

Liz was busy cleaning the house when he arrived, so Thomas agreed to wait out on the porch while she finished up. This provided him a few minutes to think. He realized he felt nervous, and was apprehensive about how Liz would respond. Thomas wavered on whether he ought to bring up more personal matters. At this point, his thoughts were interrupted by Liz.

"Okay, Thomas. I'm ready."

"Oh, okay. Let's go. Ya wanna go for a walk, or is there somewheres ya'd like to sit?"

"A walk would be nice."

They headed off in the general direction of the river, walking to the south along the road. They first caught up on the past few days since they'd seen each other. Eventually, they ended up sitting down on a rock overlooking the river. Thomas decided he could no longer put off his plan to bring up more personal matters. His palms felt damp, and he wiped them off on his pants. His throat was dry, and he needed water. Thomas hopped off the rock and took a few steps down to the river. He bent down and drank. In a moment, Liz was at his side, drinking out of her cupped hands. The silence was becoming awkward, so Thomas decided to plunge in. He briefly pondered how he might begin.

"So, how are ya doin' 'bout your father?"

"My father? What do you mean?" asked Liz.

"Uh, I mean, do it still hurt?"

"You mean his death? Why do you bring that up? I don't think I want to talk about my father."

"Oh. Uh, okay. I uh..." Thomas's head began to spin, and he felt dizzy. He sat down to avoid falling. Thomas stole a glance at Liz, who sat staring off toward the river. Thoughts failed to form, although he willed them to. His thoughts scattered in many directions, like a bird caught inside a house and desperate to get out.

"Should I ask 'er another question? Maybe Liz don' wanna talk 'bout her tree. Maybe she don' talk 'bout personal things. Maybe I oughta say something 'bout my own self. Maybe this whole tree thing ain't going to work with Liz. Maybe I oughta just try an' think o' anything to talk 'bout."

Finally Thomas sorted through the fog sufficiently to form a coherent thought. "Uh, well, do ya wanna walk back?"

"Yes, let's go back. I should be getting back to help with supper."

At that the two stood up and headed back to the Lewis farm. Liz was angry with Thomas's question. Many questions came to her mind. "Does he think it's too soon for me to be courted? Does he wonder if I'm somebody he shouldn't court? Is he worried about me being from a family with no father? Or is he just trying to make conversation?"

She considered asking him, but wasn't sure what to ask, and she was still angry. Instead, Liz just walked without speaking. As they walked along in silence, Thomas continued to mull over whether to try and talk further. Perhaps he could explain himself better. Or maybe Liz was angry and wouldn't want to hear any explanation. On several occasions, he began to comment on the beautiful surroundings, but such comments seemed awkward even without being spoken. Fearing he'd make things worse, Thomas decided to let the silence be. The walk back to the Lewis farm seemed twice as long as the walk over.

Much to both their relief, they finally arrived back at the farm. To avoid further prolonging the awkward silence, Thomas simply said goodbye and left. Liz was also thankful for the walk to be over and slowly walked inside. She immediately looked for Mother. Liz found her in the kitchen with Aunt Hannah preparing supper.

"Oh, hi, Liz. Get an apron on and lend a hand," Mother said.

"Okay," Liz said glumly. She picked up a knife and began slicing tomatoes for supper. It was unusual for her to be quiet, and Aunt Hannah took notice.

"Liz, why the long face?"

"Oh, the visit with Thomas didn't go well this time."

"Oh, really? Do you want to talk about it?" offered Aunt Hannah.

"The visit was going okay, and then he all of the sudden asked me about Papa, and I didn't know why he was asking about him."

Aunt Hannah pondered a moment. "What exactly did he ask?"

"It was something like...oh, he asked how I was doing about my father, and did it still hurt."

"Oh, dear. I can see how that kind of question may have caught you off guard, with you two just getting to know each other," said her aunt.

"Why would that boy want to know about Papa anyways?" interjected Mother. "Does he think you're not good enough for him?"

"I wondered the same thing," said Liz.

"Let's not get ahead of what we know now. We don't know anything for sure about Thomas's reasons for asking. It won't help to put motives in his mind we're merely guessing are there," Aunt Hannah cautioned.

"Humph," said Mother.

"Maybe Thomas was merely trying to express concern about you, although he may have done it in an awkward manner," continued Aunt Hannah.

Mother quickly interjected, "I think you're giving that boy too much credit. Who does he think he is, asking such personal questions? I don't care what his motives are. I think he's just trying to force his way into your life, paying no never mind to whether it's wanted or not."

"Now, Mabel. I know you're upset about his death. You're still grieving. But this isn't helpful to Liz, who is also grieving and trying to get to know a young man as well. She needs our support to give this courting every opportunity to succeed, as long as Liz wants it to succeed."

"Oh, maybe you're right. But I don't like anybody nosing around in our business like that. Doesn't he understand what Liz and I have already been through? How dare he put me through that again! He must be an insensitive boy!"

"Asking an inappropriate question does not necessarily mean he's nosing into your business," said Hannah.

"Well," said Mother in a huff. "I don't know whose side you're on. Nobody around here seems to understand what I've been through, and how I put on a brave face and carry on as best a person can. Who would think I could be doing most of the housework right after my husband abandoned me!"

"Mabel, I'm not on anyone's side. I'm trying to help Liz. Don't let your grief blind you to Liz's needs. She needs our support. She needs your support."

"Well, I think I'll go lie down until supper. I'm feeling tired now," Mother announced as she walked out of the kitchen.

Once Mother was out of the room, Liz began to cry silently. Aunt Hannah went over and put her arm around her shoulders.

"I hate it when she goes to bed! She's never going to stop doing that," she added.

"Oh, Liz. Your mother struggles with her grief. Right now it is more than she can bear. But I also know that you need your mother now, as much as ever."

Liz continued to cry softly as she crumbled into her aunt's arms. Hannah just waited and held her as she cried. Knowing her sister couldn't be the mother Liz needed right now, Hannah was glad to do what she could for Liz. Liz gratefully accepted, although she wished her mother could be the one to offer her comfort and support.

Liz sighed deeply, thankful for Aunt Hannah's support and relieved at her wisdom concerning Thomas. Liz realized her aunt was right: she really didn't know Thomas's reasons. She hoped to find out.

Thomas rode to MacDonald's as quickly as he could. He felt embarrassed to tell MacDonald about his visit with Liz, but he felt even more desperate for MacDonald's help. As usual, Thomas found MacDonald in his store. He was just finishing up with a customer when he walked in. Thomas walked nervously about the store, waiting until the customer left. The woman chatted about the weather, her farm's crops, and asked if MacDonald had noticed her new dress. Finally, the customer was satisfied and left.

"Oh, Mr. MacDonald. I really need ya help," said Thomas.

"Aye lad, what be on yer mind?"

"The visit with Liz was a disaster! I messed up real bad!"

MacDonald interrupted, "Hold on there, lad. Slow down an' tell me what happened."

"The visit was going just fine till I started talkin' 'bout trees, then everything got all messed up."

"How did ye bring up trees?"

"I asked her 'bout her father, and she din't want to talk 'bout him. Then we walked back in silence. I din't know what to say. I guess I did it all wrong. I don' know if she'll want to talk to me again."

"Oh, lad. I'm so sorry it went badly," said MacDonald.

"Yeah, I ruined everything!" Thomas stood up and began pacing about the store. He felt so agitated, he couldn't sit still.

"Now hold on, lad. I know yer upset, but let's not go an' get ahead o' oorselves. Let's see if we can't sort out what come t' pass. Come 'ere an' set yerself down so we can talk. It can't be as bad as yer makin' it sound."

Thomas put his head down and looked at the floor. He sighed deeply and slowly walked over to MacDonald and sat down on a bag of flour.

"So, what do I do? It's all over. I don' see how it can be fixed."

"Okay, lad. Now tell an ol' man what came t' be."

"Well," said Thomas slowing down a bit, "everything was goin' okay till I asked her 'bout her father."

"What exactly did ye say, lad."

"I don' rightly remember, but it was something like, 'how are ya doing 'bout your father'?"

"That was your first comment 'bout trees, lad?"

"Yeah."

"Oh aye, lad. I can see how things went badly then."

"Did I say the wrong thing," Mr. MacDonald?

"Nae lad. Ye didn't say the wrong thing, but ye asked 'bout a sensitive subject right oot o' ye gate. Ye probably scared the poor lass right off. Ye see lad, when ye approach any living thing, ye want t' be gentle, show 'em ye mean no harm. Yer intentions were right, but I think ye scared her off, yer lass not knowing if ye meant good o' harm. Talking 'bout people's trees be a sensitive matter, an' the lass needs t' know ye hae yer arm 'round her shoulders, lad."

"Ya mean I messed up by goin' too fast?" asked Thomas.

"Aye, lad. I think yer lass will best know yer intentions if ye start oot a bit slower."

"Like what?"

"Weel, maybe ye could ask 'bout her outer leaves before the inner ones. Ye see, lad, the inner ones be closer t' the trunk an' roots an' tend t' be a bit more sensitive t' touch. One can touch many o' the outer leaves withoot hurtin' a tree a bit, but messin' wi' the roots o' the trunk can hurt right off. Can ye think of a question that might go after the outer leaves a bit more?"

Thomas thought for a moment. "Maybe I could ask 'bout her stay at the Lewis's."

"There ye go, lad. Do ye see how that question stays a bit more respectful o' the trunk an' roots?"

"I guess so," said Thomas hesitantly.

MacDonald understood Thomas still had much to learn. "Ye see, lad, the right t' talk 'bout someone's roots an' trunk needs t' be earned. Ye earn that right when they feel yer respectful touch upon the outer leaves, an' only move further in when yer invited. The lass will let ye know when she be ready. Ye might also start by talkin' 'bout yer own outer leaves."

Thomas paused as he thought a few moments. "I think I understand what you're sayin', but I don' know if I can visit Liz again, not after today."

"An' why not, lad?"

"I just don' know if I can face 'er again," said Thomas.

"Lad, that be exactly the right occasion for an old fashioned apology."

"An apology? What would I ..."

"Ye don't need to say much, lad. Just tell 'er after thinkin' it o'er, ye know ye weren't being sensitive by askin' 'bout her father right off, an' could you try again."

"That's all?"

"That's all, lad. She just needs to know ye realize yer misstep."

"But what if she's still mad an' won't talk to me?"

"Weel lad, there's a chance she won't. But how will ye feel if ye don't even try?"

"I s'pose I would always wonder what if."

"Aye, lad, that ye would."

"So ya think I should go talk to her again?"

"It don' be my place to decide for ye. But I would hate t' see ye miss oot just based on one misstep. Listen t' what the trunk o' yer tree tells ye an' ye can't go wrong, lad."

Thomas took the opportunity to think over the day's events on his walk home. The more he thought, the more the dust settled in his mind. Thomas washed up for bed and was sitting, thinking in his room, when Ben came in.

"Hey, Ben. What do you an' Anna talk 'bout?"

"What do we talk 'bout? Why would ya ask a thing like that?" asked Ben.

"Oh, just wonderin'. I'm not sure what to talk 'bout with Liz."

"Oh, I see. We mostly talk 'bout what we did that day, or what we're gonna do the next day. Sometimes we don' talk much at all. On occasion we talk 'bout the future."

"Is that all?"

"I think so. What else would there be to talk 'bout?" asked Ben.

"I don' know, maybe nothin'.'"

After a short pause Thomas continued. "Some folk like to talk 'bout the inside stuff."

"The inside stuff? What would there be to say 'bout that. I'm not interested in that religion stuff. I don' go to church no more."

"No, Ben. I don' mean religion. I mean talking 'bout feelin's, dreams an' fears - ya know, the important stuff."

"Now don' go off on that again, little brother. Forget 'bout whatever that old fool told ya. It ain't that complicated. Ya just talk to Liz 'bout your day, an' pretend to be interested when she talks 'bout her day. It really ain't that hard."

"Well, this whole courtin' thing is new to me. I guess I'm still tryin' to figure it out."

"Just take after me, little brother, an' ya can't go wrong. She'll be butter in your hands. Them women just want a man to listen, and pretendin' is just as good."

"But don't Anna know when ya not really listenin'?"

"Naw, ya jist gotta know when to nod, say 'uh huh,' an' ask the right question."

"Ya make is sound so simple, Ben."

"It is that simple, little brother."

"I don' know, Ben."

"Oh, ya just new at it. You'll see I'm right afore long. Well, I'm goin' to bed; see ya in the mornin'."

Thomas turned into his own bed. As he lay awake in bed, he thought about the very different sounding advice of Ben and MacDonald. Ben made it sound so effortless, which made his advice appealing. Yet Ben's advice seemed too simple, and Thomas wondered if Ben and Anna knew their trees at all. He didn't think they did. Thomas wondered if Ben ever felt lonely only talking like that. Thomas knew he would be lonely if he only talked with Liz the way Ben suggested. MacDonald's advice seemed better, but Thomas had an idea of how hard it would be to apply. He didn't know if he could pull it off. Thomas wished MacDonald's way didn't require such a large dose of courage. At this point, Thomas fluffed his pillow, turned over, and drifted off to sleep.

The next several days on the farm were long. There was no way Thomas could get away for a visit to Liz. If he'd been asked, he probably would have admitted to not being in a hurry to visit anyways. Ben's visits with Anna didn't seem to be affected by the demands of the farm. He visited her every Saturday rain or shine, harvest or seeding. Ben liked a regular schedule.

Thomas finally found an opportunity to visit. In addition to finding the time, Thomas had needed to find the courage to face Liz. His stomach felt nervous whenever he thought of visiting her again. On his way to the Lewis farm, he slowed his horse to a walk. He wanted the extra time to think over what he might say when he arrived. Thomas had avoided planning anything beyond just getting himself there.

Mrs. Lewis answered the door when Thomas knocked at the Lewis farmhouse. "Oh, hello, Thomas."

"Hello, Mrs. Lewis."

"I'm so glad you came to visit."

"Ya are?"

"Yes, Liz would like to talk with you."

"She would?"

"Why, yes. Wait just a moment while I go and find her."

A couple minutes later Liz appeared on the front porch where Thomas had been waiting. She appeared pleased to see Thomas, and smiled apprehensively. Thomas had felt encouraged by Mrs. Lewis's reception, but seeing Liz brought his rapid firing nerves back on line.

"Hello, Thomas."

"Hi, Liz. I hope its okay that I visited."

"Yes, I'm glad you did."

"Look, Liz. Lemme get right to it. I wanna apologize for bein' insensitive with my question 'bout your father last week. After thinkin' 'bout it later, I realized it was probably too soon for me to ask 'bout somethin' like that."

"Well, you did take me by surprise. I didn't understand what you were after."

"Liz, please accept my apology, an' can we start over?"

"Of course. Yes, I would like to start over, but I want you to know that I'm not sure I'm ready to talk about my father yet. After all, we are just getting to know each other."

"Yeah, I understand that," agreed Thomas.

"Yes, well, I'm glad we have an understanding about that. I'd have to get to know you a whole lot better before I'd want to tell you about Papa."

"Okay. Well, would ya like to ride into town?"

"Yes, let me just change into riding clothes."

Thomas couldn't help grinning as wide as his face would allow; he didn't even try to hide his grin when Liz returned. Liz also felt her spirits lifted. She hadn't known if Thomas would ever visit again, nor what would happen if he did. After talking things over with Aunt Hannah, Liz wanted another chance with Thomas. She wasn't ready to give up on the relationship yet. She ran over and gave her aunt a hug on her way out the door, as if to say "thank you."

At first they simply caught up on each other's weeks. Thomas knew that one of them would need to make a transition in the conversation eventually. This time he was prepared to touch her outer leaves gingerly, not wanting to startle her like last time.

"So Liz, how do ya like living on the Lewis farm?"

"Oh, I like it okay, I suppose." After a brief pause Liz continued, "I'd like it better if I had my own room. It's a little hard to get used to having a roommate after having my own room my whole life."

"Yeah, I'll bet that be quite a change. Do ya expect to be sharing Sarah's room for long?" Thomas inquired.

"I don't rightly know. We haven't really discussed it yet. I hope not."

"I share a room, too. Ben an' me share a loft. We done that as long as I can remember."

"Oh, is that right. Does it work okay?"

"I s'pose so. I don' know any different though."

"I miss the privacy of having a place to go to be alone. Time alone is hard to come by at the Lewis farmhouse. I mostly have to go outdoors to find it," said Liz.

"Is that right?" After a pause, Thomas asked, Are ya gettin' used to Salisbury yet?"

"Not really. I still miss Guilford. But people have been kind to me here."

Thomas just nodded. He was thankful things were going well, but he wasn't sure what to do now. He had gotten as far as he had foreseen. Thomas wondered if he ought to begin talking about his own leaves some. The lengthening silence was beginning to feel awkward. But he didn't want to make another mistake and ruin the nice conversation they were having.

Much to Thomas's relief, Liz interrupted his thoughts with a question of her own. "How do you like your work on the farm? I have an idea of how hard you work, but that's about all I know about it."

"Oh, I like it okay. I do wish there wasn't so much work. Well, sometimes I wish Father would hire more help so Ben an' me might git some time off. Sometimes it helps when I think that some day the farm might be part mine, an' maybe I won't mind it so much then."

After another brief silence, Thomas decided to risk asking further about Liz. "Do you mind your work at the farmhouse much?"

"I don't mind. I do want to help out, and especially after Aunt Hannah took us in and all."

At this point Thomas thought he'd asked about as much of her leaves as he dared. He felt like a newborn colt taking its first steps: he wanted to keep walking on his shaky legs, but might fall at any moment. Liz also seemed content to just allow the conversation to return to more comfortable, light conversation. They were now walking around town.

Thomas could have left his horse at the Lewis farm and ran all the way to MacDonald's. He jumped up on his horse and let her run all the way to the Feed 'n Seed instead. In no time, Thomas was tying his horse up in front of the store and running in to find the old man.

"Mr. MacDonald, I think I did it! I really think I did it!"

"Hello, lad. So what's all the excitement 'bout? Did ye visit the lass again?"

"Yeah, I just came from there."

"Weel good, lad. Tell me 'bout it."

"This time I asked 'bout how she's likin' stayin' with the Lewis's, an' I apologized for the last time. An' she accepted!"

"Oh that be terrific, lad."

"She din't get mad this time, an' she even asked 'bout my leaves some too. I think it might be okay. I think my messin' things up's gonna be okay."

"Oh lad, I'm so proud o' ye. It took a mighty bit o' courage what ye done. Many would have shrunk away. Ye ought to be proud o' yourself, lad."

"I din't know if I could go through with it. But somethin' inside told me I had to try."

"That be right, lad. Many hae left themselves t' wonder what would o' been."

Thomas was quiet. "So, uh, what do I do now, Mr. MacDonald?"

"Hmm," MacDonald chuckled. "Ye don't give yerself long to enjoy what ye already done, do ye lad?"

"But I need to know what to do when I visit Liz next."

"Aye, lad. I know ye're uneasy. What do yer trunk tell ye would be right?"

Thomas was used to such questions, and knew MacDonald wanted him to listen to his innards. Thomas paused to reflect. "I don' know for sure, but I think what seems right to me be to take it slow - talk more 'bout the outer leaves for a bit longer, an' then we'll see."

"Aye, lad. Ye're listenin' to yer own soul there. An' I think yer trunk's givin' ye a good headin'. It'll do no good t' force the time wi' Liz beyond what ye're both ready for. Take it slow; there really be no hurry, lad."

"But how will I know when to take it further?"

"Aye, lad. Ye need to be invited to go beyond that. Ye'll know when ye're invited."

"I will? How?"

"Just listen t' yer trunk, an' the lassie's, lad."

Liz ran in to find Aunt Hannah. She now went directly to her aunt, not even looking for her mother. She found her aunt washing potatoes in a basin, preparing for supper. Liz instinctively washed her hands and started helping with the food.

"Aunt Hannah, my visit with Thomas went so much better!"

"Oh, really? Tell me about it."

"Thomas apologized for asking about Papa, which really helped. And then we started out more slowly. He asked about my stay here, and I asked about how he liked working his family farm. It was a much more comfortable visit."

"Oh, that sounds much better, dear."

"Now I'm excited about him again. After the last visit, I was ready to give up on him. But I'm really glad I gave him another chance. Thank you for helping me to, Aunt Hannah."

"Oh, you're very welcome, dear. I'm so happy things went well today. I was so hoping it would when I watched you and Thomas start out on your ride. Maybe you and Thomas are beginning a wonderful courtship."

"Well, we'll see," said Liz blushing.

Liz picked up another potato and started to wash it. She realized she didn't know her aunt's opinion of Thomas. "Aunt Hannah, what do you think of him?"

"What do I think of him? Oh, Liz, I barely know the boy. He comes from a respectable family, but I don't know how much that means. Most of what I know of him is from you. Although I can say that I feel hopeful for you and Thomas after today. I guess I'll just have to get to know him as you do."

"Oh come on, tell me what you really think," pleaded Liz.

Aunt Hannah gave Liz a sideways glance, as if deciding whether to say more. She paused and smiled briefly before responding. "Liz, I don't like to say much about someone before I know them directly. I don't know if this will make much sense to you yet, but whatever else I say about Thomas would have more to do with me than him."

"Huh?"

"Basically everything I know about Thomas is through your eyes. I have almost no firsthand knowledge of Thomas, except saying hello to him in the store on occasion. So anything else I'd say would have more to do with my own imagination than Thomas himself."

Liz turned her aunt's words over in her mind, working hard to make sense of them. Something about what her aunt said felt right to Liz, but she couldn't quite get her mind around it. Aunt

Hannah's comment felt reassuring, yet Liz was also frustrated that her aunt wouldn't just say more. Aunt Hannah watched Liz for a moment.

"Well, maybe that isn't helpful just yet. We'll talk more about Thomas as we get to know him together."

Liz continued to feel frustrated and disappointed in her aunt's response. It was only months later that she came to appreciate Aunt Hannah's wisdom in reserving judgment. Liz learned from her aunt to have an open mind and to wait and see what kind of person others would prove themselves to be.

Thomas and Ben had just finished their midday meal and were walking back out to the fields. It was a warm day, and the sun was almost directly overhead. Thomas put his hat back on.

"Thomas, I've been thinkin' more 'bout gettin' married," said Ben.

"Really? I thought ya weren't feelin' ready."

"Well, I don' really feel ready. But I been talkin' to Mama an' Father, an' they tell me Anna's right, that it been long enough, an' I should know by now whether she's the one for me. Father says it shouldn't take more 'an one full season to figure it out. Mama says that's 'bout right, although she thinks it can take a little longer if you're unsure. Well shoot, Thomas, I been calling on Anna for more 'an two seasons now. Maybe they're right 'bout that being long enough - maybe too long."

"Well, do it seem right to ya, proposin' marriage now?" Thomas asked.

"I don' know, little brother. If it was up to me, I might wait a bit."

"Why do ya think you'd wanna wait?"

"I still just don' know if she's the one for me. I can't put my finger on any particular concern, but I'm not sure how you're s'posed to know."

"What sort o' wife do ya think you'd want?" queried Thomas.

"Well, I wanna wife that's purdy, an' proper, an' don' talk too much. An' I wanna a wife that takes good care o' the house, an' the little ones. An' I wanna wife that'll keep herself up, an' not get fat or ugly. An' I wanna wife that's sensible with money, an' don' spend too much. I guess that's 'bout it."

"An' do that describe Anna pretty good?"

"Uh, well... I figure Anna fits the bill pretty good, 'cept that sometimes she gets up a head o' steam an' talks my ear off. But I got pretty good at just lookin' like I'm listenin', so that one's okay. So I guess Anna fits the bill pretty good."

"Okay, Ben. She fits the bill pretty good, but what's the hesitation in ya?"

"What'd ya mean?"

"I got nothin' against Anna, but there's somethin' inside ya that's holdin' ya back."

"I know, Thomas, but I figure I can't pay that no mind. I just wanna do what's right. An' if it's the right time to make a proposal, an' there's no good reason not to, then maybe I should."

"Well, Ben, I guess you gotta do what you think is right, but I hate to see ya go ahead with it until it seems right on the inside."

"What's all this talk 'bout the insides? I don' care a hill o' beans for that; I just wanna do what's proper. What difference do it make if it feels right? That ain't got nothin' to do with it. Anna meets all my requirements, an' that should be all I need to know. Ya know what I mean?"

Thomas thought a few moments before responding. He debated whether to push Ben anymore. "Well Ben, I'm a bit confused 'bout all that myself. But I do think you gotta decide what's right for ya, an' if you're ready to make a proposal, well, okay then."

"Like I said, I wanna do what's proper. I figure it won't look right if I wait much longer. An' I don' wanna miss out with Anna. She might go off an' marry a quicker movin' fella. So I figure I best get a move on."

Ben and Thomas put their shoulders back to their work. Thomas found himself continuing to think about his conversation with Ben. At first he felt deep concern for Ben pressuring himself to decide and act before he was ready, and yet he also wondered if maybe Ben was right. Maybe he should decide based on what's proper and the usual way to court a lady. A part of Thomas agreed with Ben's way of thinking, and had often made decisions based on what seemed proper. Another part of Thomas, perhaps a newer part, strongly disagreed. This newer part of Thomas placed more importance on what his tree told him. Thomas didn't know how to reconcile these competing ways of thinking.

Thomas also noticed the difference in what he and Ben wanted in a wife. Thomas wanted some of the same things, but the most important thing to him was a wife that would know his tree, and he hers. Without that, the rest didn't seem to matter much. Thomas hoped Ben would be happy with his marriage, but he had his doubts.

Several days later Thomas found an opportunity to go into town and see Mr. MacDonald. Thomas continued to be confused after talking with his brother, and hoped MacDonald could help him sort it all out. Thomas first stopped off at the general store to pick up the things Mama wanted, and then headed over to the Feed 'n Seed.

When Thomas arrived, he found MacDonald in the back teaching Rachel something. Thomas said hello and then waited in the front for MacDonald to finish with Rachel.

"Hello there, lad. I'm sorry to keep ye waitin'. I'm learnin' my Rachel how t' write up supply orders."

"Mr. MacDonald, I'm confused 'bout something."

MacDonald put his hand on Thomas's shoulders and directed him to the back room. MacDonald then waited for Thomas to gather his thoughts.

"Ben says he figure's it be the right time to make a proposal o' marriage to Anna. But he figures that 'cause other folk tell him he oughta know by now, on account o' it already bein' more 'an a season he's been callin' on her, not 'cause the time seems right to him. I don' know, Mr. MacDonald. In a way Ben seems to be doin' right by Anna. But in a way Ben seems to not be doin' right by Ben. When I asked Ben if he be ready to make a proposal, he said he wadn't so sure. He said that folk were tellin' him that if he's been courtin' her for more than a season, he oughta know by now. Am I makin' any sense?"

"Aye, lad. Ye're worry for Ben be well founded if he's lettin' other folk do the thinkin' fo' him. I be worried fo' him too, lad."

"But how else do ya decide on the right time? Ain't there a proper way to court a lady?"

"Proper according t' who, lad?"

"Uh, well, I don' know; but ain't there a proper way most folk go 'bouts courtin'?"

"I s'pose there might be, lad."

"If everyone does it that way, then maybe it is right. Maybe folk do it that way for good reason."

"Aye, lad," said MacDonald chuckling. "How long have ye been callin' on Liz?"

"Uh, 'bout a month."

"Okay then, lad. How would it be for ye t' decide right now t' call on yer lass till the end o' the season an' then make a proposal, as long as the visits continue?"

"Well, I don' think I'd like that."

"An' why not, lad?"

"'Cause I don't know how long it might take for me or for Liz to know if we're right for the other."

"Aye, lad. Ye can force a courtin' into any time frame ye like, if ye don't mind the fit. For some, a full season may be a bit long, an' for others not long enough t' rightly know. Let me ask ye this, lad. How long does it take for the spring sun to melt the winter snow?"

"I can't really say, on account of it sometimes bein' in March and sometimes bein' well into April afore the snow's all melted."

"That's right, lad. Ye just can't know for sure until ye get there. Don't it be the same with lads an' lasses? How can ye know where ye an' yer lass will be 'til ye get there? 'Tis a terrible thing t' put up those kind o' restrictions afore ye get there."

Thomas paused, rubbing his temples with both hands. "I don' know, Mr. MacDonald. Ain't there no accountin' for time in a courtin'?"

"'Course there be, lad. It's just not an accountin' that can be read on yer pocket watch."

Thomas wrinkled his forehead and he stared back at his old friend. "Then what sort o' time are ya talkin' 'bout?"

"The kind that be measured by yer trunk. Yer inner clock will let ye know. What other kind o' time matters? Lad, how do ye decide it's time t' harvest yer crops?"

"We just know by lookin' at the fruit if it's ready."

"That be exactly right, lad. No clock in yer pocket o' on yer wall can rightly tell ye that."

He wasn't exactly dizzy, but Thomas felt his head spinning a bit. It seemed strange to not think of a courting as having any time boundaries. It just seemed too wide open. He'd always thought that everything had its own time and place.

"Ye see, lad, when tending t' a tree, ye pay attention t' what the tree says. Ye listen t' the color an' feel o' the leaves, ye watch t' see how quickly it grows, ye look t' the fruit produced. Any farmer worth 'is salt listens this way. How can a clock tell ye anything o' the sort?"

"It can't," laughed Thomas. "What ya say makes sense, at least I think it do."

"Aye lad, ye may need a wee bit o' time then."

Thomas stood up to leave and walked slowly to the door. MacDonald put his hand on the back of Thomas's neck and walked him out to his cart. "Okay, lad, ye come back an' see me soon now." Thomas turned and smiled weakly.

Thomas was the last of the family to sit down at the table. He glanced around the table and saw everyone looking at each other. Ben was grinning and red in the face. Mama appeared pleased. Father beamed with pride.

"Well, Ben, are ya gonna tell your brother?" asked Mama.

Ben had a grin from ear to ear and seemed ready to burst. "Okay, little brother, I did it!"

"Uh, ya did what?"

"I made a proposal to Anna!"

"Ya did? I thought..."

"Well, I decided I was ready. Don' tell me no more 'bout them stupid insides an' what not. I'm ready to get married!"

Thomas still felt worried for his brother, yet he could see the excitement and pride on Ben's face and decided to set aside his concerns for now. Thomas offered the most he could honestly say. "Well, Ben, I can see ya quite proud o' yourself," Thomas said with a hint of a smile.

"Ya damn right I'm proud o' myself!"

"On account o' this bein' a special occasion, I'm openin' a bottle o' wine. I been savin' this one for a special occasion, an' my son doing right by his girl seems to be just that," announced Father.

Father opened the wine and poured out a little for everyone, including Sally. He then raised the glass up and proposed a toast.

"To Ben - who grown to be a man, doin' right by his girl. I'm proud of ya, son. It takes a man to know the right thing an' do the right thing. It takes a man to take on a proper wife. It takes a man to realize his girl has done her part an' waited the proper time for his proposal. Ya did good, son."

Everyone raised the glass to their lips and drank. Sally puckered her mouth afterwards, and shuddered involuntarily. Thomas caught Sally's eye and laughed with her. Ben continued to grin, but now with a look of greater pride, having eaten up his father's praise. Mama began to weep. She gently wiped her tears on the sleeve of her dress. After setting down his wine glass, Thomas had a couple of questions.

"So, when the celebration gonna be?"

"We don' know for sure yet. Mama an' Anna's mother are gonna work out the details, but were thinkin' maybe in a month. We gonna have it down at the Covenant Church; Anna's family attends there on occasion too," said Ben.

"Only proper place for a weddin' be a church," said Father. "Ain't a true weddin' if it ain't done in God's sight."

"I can't wait to git married myself!" said an excited Sally. "All this talk o' Ben's weddin' gets me dreamin' 'bout my own."

Father and Mama exchanged a worried gaze. Nobody spoke for several uncomfortable moments. "Well, don' know if that gonna happen, Sally," said a dour Father. "Ya see, it be a big responsibility takin' care o' a girl like you. Don' know if ya gonna find a young man up to it."

Tears streamed down Sally's face. "What'd ya mean, 'a girl like me'?"

Father looked to Mama. Mama kept her eyes on her food, even though her plate was empty. Not finding any help, Father continued. "Don' make this any harder than it is to say, Sally. Ya know what I mean."

"Yeah. Ya mean since I'm a cripple, no one will want me!" Sally cried.

"No. I don' mean.... Sally, it take a certain folk to understand ya situation. I don' like the word 'cripple,' but ya leg ain't right; an' ya leg ain't never gonna be right. Ya ain't likely to find a boy that would see things right. Ya see, Sal, only Mama an' me have the patience an' true 'preciation o' the situation to give ya all that ya need. Ya deserve to be treated the right way."

"Ya think I'm still some kinda helpless baby! I'm not a baby an' I'm not a cripple. Won't ya ever git that?"

"Sally! How can ya talk to ya father like that?" interjected Mama. "Don' ya know he's only sayin' this 'cause he loves ya? Ya need someone special..."

Mama didn't get to finish her thought, as Sally burst into renewed tears and fled the room. Thomas slowly stood, excused himself, and followed her.

The wedding plans came together quickly. Ben and Anna left most of the details to the mothers to work out, although Anna did pick out her own dress to wear. Ben didn't really care about any of the details; he just wanted to know what day to bathe, shave, and show up. He joked with Anna that he might even cut his hair the week of the wedding. Anna told him he better cut is hair that week if he knew what was best for him.

As the week of the wedding arrived, almost all family discussions surrounded the ceremony and reception. Father and Mama gave Ben a steady stream of instructions on proper etiquette for the wedding day. They made sure he knew what to wear, how to stand, where to stand, and the proper moments for standing. Mama had Ben practice standing with his hands at his side at just the right angle. She explained that it'd be a shame to have creases in his jacket on account of not knowing how to stand. Mama instructed Ben on how to hold a cup, a fork, a knife, and how to use each of the above. Things like table manners didn't normally rate much attention at the Chittenden household.

Father made sure Ben knew how to be a proper man before, during, and after the ceremony. Advice ranged from how to tie a tie, proper shaving technique, handling of the dowry, to heading up a family. By the end of the week, Ben felt like he'd been through exams at school all over again. However, he took it all in stride and tried his best to understand all the proper etiquette. He wanted to do it right, and would be deeply embarrassed if he found out he hadn't.

Thomas wasn't sure what to make of all the fuss over the particulars. He had no idea there were so many things to be done properly. He didn't think he'd want to fuss over proper etiquette at his wedding, but he kept his opinion to himself for now. Thomas usually just excused himself when the conversation turned to wedding plans.

Thomas and Ben pulled the family cart up to the steps of the church. The rest of the family piled in, and Father took the reigns. Halfway home Mama turned to Thomas.

"Ya seem awful quiet today, Thomas. Is somethin' wrong?"

"What? Oh, no, nothin' like that. I was just thinkin' 'bout what the preacher had to say."

The reverend had spoken on the first Beatitude: "Blessed are the poor in spirit, for theirs is the kingdom of heaven." The point the reverend returned to again and again was that "the kingdom of God has to do with an attitude of the heart more than correct behavior."

"What did ya think o' the sermon today?" Thomas asked.

"Oh, I thought it was just fine. I'm always inspired by what the reverend has to say," answered Mama with a smile.

"He's preachin' the Word o' God, as he should," interjected Father. Thomas turned away and frowned. He returned to his pensive demeanor the rest of the ride home. After putting the cart and horse away, Thomas caught up with Sally.

"Hey, Sal, ya gotta minute?"

"Sure, what's on ya mind?" asked Sally.

"Ya know, I never had much interest in church, but today somethin' happened that got me thinkin'," Thomas began. "When he talked 'bout how we all be poor in spirit, it reminded me o' things MacDonald says. Like how we all got broken places inside us that need tendin'. Ya know, Sal, I feel 'poor in spirit' like that. I know I got lots o' places that be broken an' need help. I don' know, maybe there is somethin' to this whole thing 'bout God."

"Huh, I din't get much outta the sermon myself."

"I ain't never got anything outta the sermon 'til today. Maybe the preacher be talkin' 'bout the inside of trees some, just like MacDonald."

"If it be what ya sayin', maybe there be somethin' to it," said Sally. "I never really gave church much thought. It always just seemed to me like somethin' ya gotta do to keep God from gettin' mad at ya."

May 21, 1753 - Hampshire Grants

Hugh and Daniel quietly filled in their wives on their midnight march and the Yorkers leading them to the outskirts of Middlebury. They went on to explain the offer the Yorkers had made them for the rights to the land, including the insulting price. Alice wasn't surprised at this news, as it was clear to her by now that the Yorkers wanted their land. May listened without commenting, and seemed only mildly interested. Hugh figured she hadn't been concerned about him and was hurt; he was mistaken.

Hugh just finished informing the women about their counteroffer when Bull and Bill approached. The smug look on Bull's face was intact; in fact, he rarely showed any other faces except perhaps one of irritation. Bill had his arms folded across his chest, looking at the ground. The captain spoke.

"We been discussin' the offer you Connecticut boys made. We guess you boys ain't gettin' the seriousness o' ya situation. We figure we best better explain the situation t' you boys. We makin' you a take it or leave it offer. There ain't no room for bargainin'. Ya know, I thought I made it real clear like this mornin', but I figure I din't. Maybe I wasn't clear enough, an' maybe you Connecticut boys 're just plain idiots. It don't make no never mind anyways. We figure if you Connecticut boys can't understand, then maybe your women folk can explain to ya how serious your situation is. We figure we might git through t' the women folk a might bit easier."

At this point Bull laughed maliciously, enjoying his own humor as well as the fearful expressions it generated. Bill shuffled his feet, eyeing Bull with discomfort.

"How do ya mean our women folk might explain it?" asked Daniel.

"Well, it's like this. The lieutenant an' me thought we might have a private conversation with the women, seein' as they can't be no dumber than you boys."

Bull let out a sadistic laugh, which increased as he noted dawning awareness on the prisoners' faces. Hugh was first to respond.

"Damn you, Yorkers, if you mean t' violate the women then I'll..."

This is all the further Hugh got before Bull's fist smashed into his mouth, knocking him to the ground. Blood oozed from one side of his mouth.

"Okay, we get it! You ain't gonna consider our offer, but don't violate our women. We can work this out man-to-man!" pleaded Daniel.

"Oh, it's too late to save ya women folk a good, shall we say 'talking', Connecticut boy. You shoulda thought o' that this mornin' when you had the chance. We tried to remind you boys that folk git hurt out here in the wild. Maybe ya be more reasonable tomorrow mornin' after the women folk explain the situation to you boys."

Daniel had been watching Hugh out of the corner of his eye and immediately caught sight of his movement. Hugh stood up and glared at the Yorker captain. Daniel watched Hugh carefully, alarmed by what he saw. Hugh stood stock still, boring his eyes into Bull without a hint of a blink. Bull caught his meaning.

"Let's go, Connecticut boy. Gimme ya best shot," challenged Bull as he took a step toward Hugh.

Daniel stepped between Hugh and Bull, pushing Hugh back.

"Now is not the time for this! Ya just gonna get killed. Stop it!" Hugh looked away, almost imperceptibly nodding.

"Ya disappoint me, Connecticut boy; got my hopes up for a little fun. I woulda enjoyed sendin' ya to meet the Devil," lamented Bull. "'Course you gonna meet 'im anyways, but I'd like to arrange a sooner meetin'."

At this point the Yorker captain issued instructions to his men. "You men keep muskets pointed at them Connecticut boys, case they try somethin' stupid. And you go set up a tent."

"But I thought ya din't like to sleep inside no..."

"Shut ya mouth an' do what I say!" Yelled Bull.

And then he turned to the last two men standing nearby. "And you two untie the women folk an' bring 'em to the tent."

"Please, Captain, Daniel pleaded, don't do this! Leave 'em out o' this! This be between us men! Don't dishonor yourself an' our women folk by doin' this!"

"You sons o' bitches," mumbled Hugh under his breath. Bull stopped short and turned.

"Offer still stands, Connecticut boy. You just make a move. I promised my gentle brother here to not kill nobody. But if you start somethin', I damn sure will finish it."

Daniel held Hugh back; he could feel the blood pulsing through his veins with intensity. They watched in horror as the women were led away to the captain's tent. Alice looked back at her family before she stepped into the tent. She had tears in her wide eyes. May didn't turn. The younger children cried while the older ones made threats of their own.

Once the women were out of sight, Daniel let go of Hugh. Not being able to restrain himself any longer, Daniel fell to his knees and hit the ground in frustration.

"Damn it, damn it, damn it all! Why? Why God? Why are ya doing this to us? Why won't ya stop it? Make 'em stop! I just can't take it no more! Make it all stop!"

Daniel slumped to the ground, and the pent up flood of emotion poured out of him. His three children reached out to comfort him with wide eyes. The children had never seen their father like this.

Hugh tore off a piece of his already tattered shirt to blot his mouth. He pressed the shirt with pressure to stop the bleeding. As he felt around in his mouth, he noticed a loose tooth. He cursed the Yorkers under his breath and vowed revenge; he vowed revenge for the whole nightmare they'd been put through. Hugh looked at his children and saw them both crying, and put his arms around them. Hugh would not be described as a nurturing father, as he did better with firmness and teaching the little ones to look after themselves. But Hugh did the best he could for his children.

The women found themselves pushed into an unoccupied tent. It was lit by a lantern hanging from the top of the tent, which shed a faint light throughout. Having just been set up, the tent was utterly vacant, with merely a canvas cloth adorning the floor. The women were left to imagine what horrors might await them. Alice debated in her mind whether or not she would fight her would be violator. Her first impulse was to fight and exact as much price as she could for what she would suffer. She imagined gouging out an eye or two. Alice smiled as she noted her untrimmed, long fingernails. It sickened her to think of passively allowing the men to do whatever they wanted with her. She felt a stab of pain as she realized that she may not survive the encounter if she did resist, and shuddered at the thought of abandoning her children. She began to slump to her knees, then had a change of heart and quickly steeled herself.

Alice felt a sudden urge to collaborate with her sister and turned to May. Just as her mouth began to form the words, she stopped. May had taken off her boots, loosened her collar, and lain down upon the canvas floor.

"May, honey, what're ya doin'?"

"Time to go to bed," was May's simple answer.

"Bed? May, them Yorkers are 'bout to come in. What're we gonna do? cried Alice.

"Maybe we'll talk 'bout it in the mornin'," May responded.

"But..." Alice stopped herself, hearing muffled Yorker voices approaching. Then the voices became more distinct.

"Damn it, Bull, don't do this! Ya gonna ruin any chances o' negotiatin' with them folk," urged Bill. "I don't give a damn if I do. I won't be deprived o' my enjoyin' them women folk. If ya decide not to participate, well then, I guess more fun for me."

"Wait a damn minute! Have your fun with 'em, but don't violate 'em! We just have to kill 'em if ya go that far. Stop a damn minute an' think!"

"Why do I care if we have t' kill 'em? retorted Bull. "I'll personally see to it myself with pleasure. Truth is, I been 'spectin' to kill 'em all along."

"Wait! I gotta idea," said Bill. "What if ya just..." At this, Bill's words drifted off into a whisper, and Alice heard nothing more for a minute.

"Oh, alright. I don't know why I let ya talk me outta things. I swear, if there's a bigger killjoy 'round these parts, I don' know who it is," growled Bull.

Bull pulled back the tent flaps and entered. Alice took two steps back, putting her hands to her mouth. He stood there leering at them, first Alice and then May. He gave May a quizzical glance, then shrugged his shoulders and turned back to Alice.

"So, what do ya wanna talk 'bout first," said Bull as a dark smile slowly emerged at the corners of his mouth.

By now Alice had decided not to put up a fight. She couldn't bear to think of returning to her children all beat up, or worse. May made no conscious decision, and appeared to be asleep. Alice made no reply to Bull's rhetorical question. She looked behind him, wondering about the lieutenant. No one else entered the tent, but she thought she saw a faint silhouette just outside the tent.

"Guess ya ain't too talkative then," said Bull. "Well then, figure I'll do the talkin' for the three o' us. By the way, sorry to break the news to ya, but the lieutenant ain't gonna be joinin' this party. Left all the fun to me, ya might say."

Bull took a step to Alice, reaching up to put his hand on her shoulder. She flinched when she felt his first touch. He looked at her a moment before walking around her, trailing his hand across her backside and up to the other shoulder. Then he stood in front of her again. He put his hand on her mouth. Alice tightened. She tried to hold her breath, as Bull's reminded her of sour onions and dead animals being skinned. Bull noted her discomfort and lingered.

He rubbed his hand across her face and then down across her breast. He smiled as she stiffened again. His hand stopped at her stomach, pausing to see what effect it would have. Alice turned her head and gulped air, no longer able to hold her breath. Bull took this as encouragement and massaged her belly. Alice put her hands across her mouth, preferring their smell to his.

"So, ya like my hands best on your belly then," mocked Bull. "Well then, we'll just have to oblige ya with more o' that."

Alice's voice sounded muted, coming through her hands. "Just get it over with," she pleaded in a whisper.

"Now that wouldn't be no fun. I'm gonna take my time an' enjoy every bit o' it."

The guards pulled back the tent flap and ordered the women to follow them. They looked surprised to see May asleep on the bedding. Alice didn't want May to see her family yet and stalled for time by begging the guards to allow her to relieve herself in the woods. The guards reluctantly agreed, and the women found themselves with a little more time to compose themselves. Alice tried to help May, and spoke to her in a whisper. Alice feared the impact on May's children if they saw her not only vacant, but unable to respond to them.

"May, you're gonna scare your little ones lookin' that way. I know ya just tryin' to manage this whole nightmare, but ya gotta come back for the children."

May looked surprised, as if she couldn't imagine what Alice was talking about. Alice tried again. "May, look at me. I want ya to come back to me. I know ya went away, maybe ya had to; but I need ya to come back now. I don't want ya Sammy an' Tammy to see ya like this."

May suddenly caught her breath at the mention of her children's names. The names seemed to jar her back to herself. Alice breathed a sigh of relief and hugged May.

"Oh, May, thank God ya finally back! "

May slowly began to cry softly as she thought of her children. She now felt the need to be with them. May quickly got up and walked back to her family with a relieved Alice following.

Little Tammy quickly got up and embraced her mother. Tammy would have run if she weren't restrained by the ropes. She had been afraid her mother might not come back to her. She held onto her mother as if she'd never let her go. Sammy remained a bit aloof and looked uncertain. He just stood with arms folded across his chest and watched his mother.

Alice collapsed into her husband's arms. She sobbed uncontrollably. At first Daniel just held her and let her be. He began to form words several times, but no sounds came out. He pondered what he might say, but everything that came to mind seemed wrong. May sat with Tammy on her lap, staring off into the trees. Hugh looked at May, unsure of what to do.

"What did them damn Yorkers do to ya?" Hugh demanded. May turned her face to Hugh and looked him in the eyes for a moment, and then frowned and turned her eyes back to the trees. Hugh started to repeat his question, then awkwardly put his hand on her shoulder. She looked at his hand as if wondering what it was doing there. Hugh noticed her strange stare and removed his hand.

"May, how far did they go? What did they do to ya?" demanded Hugh more emphatically.

"Stop it, Hugh! May needs some time, an' they din't touch her," interjected Alice.

"Didn't touch her?" repeated Hugh.

"No. They left her be."

"What'd they do to you?" asked Daniel softly.

Alice began to sob again, the anger leaving her. She put her head down on Daniel's chest. Daniel stroked her hair, putting his cheek against her head.

"He, uh... he touched me. He touched me with his hands." Alice paused as the emotion flooded her anew. After a few minutes, she looked up at Daniel, who held her gaze. "He molested me, but he din't violate me," explained Alice as her chest heaved with the emotion.

"He din't, uh, touch you down there?" asked Daniel cautiously. Alice met his eyes. "With his hand. He put his hands here an' here," as Alice pointed to her body.

"Ya mean, he din't...."

Alice shook her head. Daniel sighed deeply. She laid back into him and rested. Then Alice picked her head up to search May's face. Alice grimaced at what she saw, and then whispered in her husband's ear. Then Alice crawled the few feet to Hugh.

"Take the children a bit; I have to help May," Alice instructed.

"We're tied up, where do ya want me to take 'em?"

"Just hold 'em for a bit; I'm worried 'bout May," answered Alice. Hugh nodded and pulled the children to him. He had to pry Tammy off May, but Sammy came willingly. Alice pulled May as far away from the children as the ropes would allow, then turned and held both her shoulders.

"May, look at me. I don't know if ya can tell that ya went away again." May held her gaze, but didn't change expression.

"I know ya managing as best ya can. But I'm worried 'bout ya; I'm worried that ya might go so far away that you'll never come back. I can't lose ya, May. Your children can't lose ya."

May's eyes focused a bit more clearly. Alice felt encouraged by the change. "Go away some when ya need to, but I need ya to come back some too. I know ya gotta be scared."

"I ain't scared," said May.

"That's what worries me; ya oughta be scared! We all scared."

"Ya are?" said a surprised May.

"Yes!"

"What'd ya do when ya scared?" asked May.

Alice averted her eyes as she thought. "I don't know; I think I just let myself be scared. But I also tell Daniel, an' that helps some," Alice explained. "It helps more when he don't try to stop me feeling."

A lone tear formed in May's eye. She put her head down, straightened her dress, and then wiped away her tear. "Hugh don't get scared," said May.

"Then tell me," offered Alice. "But don't try an' manage all on ya own. Nobody can do that too well." May looked up at her sister, her eyes welling with tears now. She threw her arms around Alice and wept softly.

Minutes felt like hours sitting idle while waiting to hear from Haskins. Thomas kept hoping the Yorkers would bring the two male prisoners back to camp. He was haunted by thoughts that they might have been a single day late and the men were now dead; this would be especially difficult to accept after spending two days at that town.

John wrestled with his own demons. Mostly he struggled with guilt over allowing the fight to occur that delayed the regiment. He feared for the prisoners as much as the possibility of having to live with his guilt. A couple of times during the day, Thomas and John had talked, trying to help each other with their struggles. Thomas spent much of the day pacing back and forth from one end of camp to the other. He knew the exact number of paces to the top of the hill from which he looked for Haskins. Thomas had smoked most of his remaining stock of tobacco, trying to calm himself.

Haskins trotted into the regiment's camp. He looked up and saw that Thomas and John noted his return, and then turned and made his way to Scout. Haskins began filling in Scout on his findings as he dismounted, slowly unfastened his saddle, and pulled the saddle blanket off his mare. He untied his tent and bedroll, and then knelt down to set up his tent. A smile of satisfaction slowly dawned on him as he saw the captain and lieutenant standing nearby.

"So, Haskins, what did ya find?" asked Thomas.

"Well, I found 'em alright."

"And?"

"They tracks was easy 'nough to follow. They stopped 'bout ten or twelve miles north o' here, an' then had some kinda talkin'. Couldn't hear much o' what they said," said Haskins slowly and with apparent indifference. Haskins paused.

"An' then what?" urged John.

"Well, then they came back," answered Haskins.

"The men prisoners are back, an' alive?" asked Thomas.

"Yeah. The prisoners 're alive, but one o' the Yorkers ain't."

John and Thomas exchanged puzzled looks. "Damn it, Haskins, speak plainly!" demanded Thomas. What happened to the Yorkers?"

"Relax, Cap. Two of 'em are okay. But one of 'em had an accident; he fell off a cliff," said Haskins with a widening grin.

"Haskins, get to the point! What happened to the other Yorker?" pressed Thomas.

"I took 'im out. To get to the point, I cut his throat with the point o' my knife," explained Haskins.

Thomas's and John's eyes grew wide as they searched one another for reactions. "Ya mean you kilt one o' the Yorkers yourself?" asked an incredulous Thomas.

"That's right. Now ya only got eleven o' them damn Yorkers to worry 'bout," boasted Haskins.

"Damn, how'd that happen?" asked John.

"Overly confident Yorker went off out o' sight to make water, an' I made 'em pay for his mistake."

"Who was in danger?" asked Thomas with growing anger.

"Just the Yorker, I s'pose."

"Damn it, Haskins. Ya jeopardized the mission by alertin' the Yorkers to our presence, an' without cause!" confronted Thomas.

"Relax, Cap. They don't even know what hit 'em. I made it look like 'n accident."

Thomas smoldered. He paused to regain control of himself before speaking. "This time ya arrogance put the prisoners an' the regiment at risk. How can they not be on the watch after one of 'em got kilt? We can't assume they be that stupid."

"Come on, Cap. I know what I'm doin'. With my experience an' skill, it won't be any problem for me to free them prisoners," Haskins laughed. "It don't matter much if they expectin' me or not."

"Ya won't be goin'," said Thomas calmly. "Your experience ain't the issue; I know ya got plenty o' that. The problem is ya head's too big for ya shoulders, an' the weight's too much for the regiment to carry any longer. I'm relievin' you o' ya duties, effective right now."

Haskins threw back his head and laughed. Then he shook his head and looked at Thomas as though he were a naïve child.

"Come now, Cap. Don't do somethin' stupid; we both know this mission can't succeed without me."

Thomas held eye contact with Haskins and remained unmoved. "Whatever ya may think, Haskins, the mission's goin' on without ya. You will not engage the Yorkers, nor be within sight nor sound o' their camp."

"Damn, Cap, you really are the fool I thought ya was. Guess ya figure you can pull this off on your own. Well, I'd like to see ya try without me an' Scout," Haskins retorted.

"This ain't got nothin' to do with Scout; he's still part o' this mission," said Thomas evenly.

"Ya think Scout's gonna let ya send 'em to his death on ya fool's errand? Ya send me away, ya send Scout away. We came together an' we leave together."

Thomas turned away from Haskins and went in search of Scout. Enough time had been wasted; it was time for action. Thomas, John, and Scout retreated to the edge of camp. Thomas rubbed his growing beard.

"Just so ya know, Scout, Haskins's been relieved o' his duty...." Scout nodded solemnly. He'd overheard the proceedings. "I need to know if ya still with me," said Thomas.

"'Coure I am - why wouldn't I be?"

"Haskins said if he leaves, you leave."

"Naw. I don't care what Haskins said. I'll see the mission through."

"Thank God. Okay men, recommendations for a plan o' attack," ordered Thomas.

"I think we oughta go check out the Yorker camp before we decide anything," suggested John.

"Naw, I think we know enough. I say we move on it straight away," countered Scout.

"Agreed," said Thomas. "The time for caution is past - time to get them folk outta there. Last time we waited, we almost lost two of 'em. John, order two men to stay with the camp; make one of 'em Chambers, an' I want Dr. Dickens with us. Then prepare the rest to march on foot. Scout, I want you to help me come up with a plan o' attack that don' include Haskins. Let's move!"

Scout was just finishing preparing for the attack when he noticed Haskins standing over him.

"I don't have time for this now, Haskins," said Scout.

"Exactly what I was thinkin'," said Haskins. "We don't got no time for the fool's plans. He's more 'an likely gonna get them prisoners kilt. Them Litchfield folk need men with our experience; it's their only chance."

Scout looked up at Haskins suspiciously, but didn't say a word.

"Look, Scout, ya know we can free them folk just the two o' us. Come with me an' let's get this done without no fool farm boys in the way," urged Haskins.

Scout shook his head sadly. "No. I'm not going around the captain. I'm finishing the mission with him," said Scout firmly.

"Ya can't be serious! You'd rather go into a fight with him than me?" Haskins asked.

"It's not about you versus him. You had your chance to be part of this mission, and you blew it! You didn't play by the rules, Haskins. I'm starting to think the captain might be right about your head being too big for your own good, or the mission's good."

"Damn, Scout. You as much a fool as that boy pretendin' to be a captain. I've a mind to finish the mission by myself."

"You'll do no such thing," said a voice behind Haskins.

Haskins turned to see Thomas with sword in hand, point towards the ground. Haskins laughed mockingly. "Ya challengin' me to a duel, boy captain?"

"There's no need for that," Thomas responded, "but I will take your pistol for safe keepin'. I heard enough to know I can't leave ya armed till after the attack."

Haskins smirk widened. Then suddenly he pulled his pistol from his belt, only to find it lying on the ground a moment later. Haskins grabbed the back of his right hand in pain, surprised at the blood on it. He had no thought of Thomas being quicker than him.

Haskins looked up at Thomas and glared, staring daggers into him. Then he turned and walked away.

"Lieutenant," Thomas said turning to John, "place Haskins under guard until after the attack. I hate to give up two more men, but it must be done. I want his wound tended, an' then he's to be bound hand an' foot. Have 'im searched for weapons."

Summer 1749 - Salisbury, Connecticut

Ben and Anna's wedding day finally arrived. Anna's mother, Mrs. Morven, and Mama had been busy planning the special day for the past two months. Anna involved herself in the planning some, but it was assumed by all that the mothers were in charge. Ben kept himself completely out of the planning and was glad of it.

The one bit of planning Ben took on pertained to the newlyweds' living arrangements. Ben and Anna decided to live with Ben's family in the new house. Just last year, Father and his sons built a newer and larger farmhouse in anticipation of Ben marrying and needing space for him and his new bride.

Father, Mama and Ben immediately moved into the new farmhouse upon its completion. Thomas and Sally decided to remain in the older, smaller farmhouse. The other three Chittendens didn't understand Thomas's and Sally's reasons for staying in the old house and vigorously argued to convince them to come to the new house. Mama felt hurt and thought her two children didn't want to live with her. Father and Ben just thought Thomas and Sally stubborn and pig-headed, and often told them so. However, the others relented, and Thomas and Sally settled into having the old house to themselves.

Ben woke early on his big day. The truth is he didn't sleep much that night, turning over in his mind the list of things he was to do again and again. When Thomas awoke, he dressed and went up to the new house, and was surprised not to find Ben there. Thomas went back outside and found Ben tending to chores.

"What are ya doing, big brother?"

"Oh, I thought I'd get a few things done around the place," said Ben. "After all, I won't be around the rest of the day to tend to the farm."

"Tend to the farm?" said a bewildered Thomas. "Today is your weddin' day! For heaven's sake, you're allowed a day off on ya weddin' day." Ben just shrugged. Thomas looked his brother over and knew his brother well enough to know when he's nervous.

"Ya couldn't sleep much, could ya?"

"Naw, not really," Ben admitted. "But hey, it's no big deal, an' I really did need to get a few things done 'round here anyways."

"Alright, big brother, then at least let me help ya. What can I do ya for?"

"No, no, I'm alright. Ya just go on in."

"Come on, Ben, I insist. I'm gonna stand here anyways, so ya might as well lemme help out."

"Suit yourself, little brother."

The brothers worked side by side in silence, grooming the horses. Ben worked faster than his normal pace. Thomas deliberately worked more slowly than usual. "Ya thinkin' much 'bout later today, Ben?"

"Oh, ya mean the weddin'?"

"Come off it, Ben. Ya know what I mean. What else's goin' on today?"

"Yeah, I s'pose I'm thinkin' 'bout it some."

"Ya wanna talk 'bout it?"

"Oh, I'm thinkin' like will I remember how to do everythin' right. Ya know, where to stand an' what to say an' how to eat proper an' all that stuff."

"I'm sure ya'll do fine, Ben. Ya always been good at stuff like that."

"Yeah, I know."

The brothers worked silently for awhile. Thomas waited to see what else Ben may want to discuss. "I figure I keep wonderin' what it'll be like to be married to Anna," Ben admitted.

"Are ya havin' some doubts 'bout Anna bein' a good fit?"

"Oh no, nothin' like that, marryin' her's the right thing to do."

"Ben, it's okay to have second thoughts. I think it's only natural. Maybe ya jist nervous 'bout gettin' married."

"No, it ain't nothin' like that. I'm jist tryin' to remember ev'rything I gotta do today."

Thomas turned his head away, not wanting Ben to see his look of frustration. He wished there was more he could do for his brother, but he didn't know what it would be. At this point Thomas decided to let it be. Maybe the best he could do for his brother today might be helping with the tasks that needed attending to. The brothers finished with the horses and then went inside for breakfast.

Mama and Sally were carrying food to the table as the boys walked in. The food smelled inviting and delicious. There's nothing like the smell of coffee, eggs, bacon and fresh bread in the morning. Everyone eagerly fell to the eating. The conversation at the table surrounded what needed to be done and who would do what and when.

After breakfast Thomas volunteered to help Sally clean up the kitchen, as Mama wanted to supervise Ben cleaning up and dressing for the wedding. Once the others were safely out of earshot, Sally wanted to talk. "So, Thomas, what do ya think 'bout Ben an' Anna gettin' married today?"

Thomas shot a quick glance over his shoulder before responding. "I don' know, Sally. Anna's a nice enough girl an' all, but somethin' just don' sit right with me 'bout it."

"I know, me too! Everybody keeps talkin' 'bout all the stuff that's gotta be done like it's just another day o' chores. It seems like there's somethin' else we oughta be talkin' 'bout."

Thomas sighed in response. "I tried to talk with Ben 'bout maybe bein' nervous today or somethin', but he'd have nothin' to do with it. I mean, today's a big day for Ben, an' it's a big day for the family, but nobody's talkin' like it is. I don' know why, Sally, but I just feel kind o' sad. I feel like somethin's missin'."

"Well, somethin' is missin' Thomas; nobody's talkin' 'bout what today means, as though it just be another regular day."

"Maybe that's it." Thomas sighed again, this time more deeply.

Father came into the kitchen dressed in his Sunday best, which included black boots, black tie, white shirt, and black pants and coat. He'd even shined his shoes and brushed his coat and pants, which he rarely did. The last time he'd dressed up this nice was the day he married Mama.

"Wow, Father, ya look nice!"

"Thanks, Sally."

Father blushed and looked away, and then quickly moved onto the reason for his appearance. "Thomas, come help me hitch up the cart. We need to leave inside o' thirty minutes."

Thomas nodded and followed Father out to the barn. They readied the cart in silence and began walking back to the farmhouse.

"So, Father, what'd ya think 'bout the big day?"

"I think it's good. They courted the proper time an' they both the proper age. An' I think Ben learnt all the stuff he s'posed to do today."

"So ya feel good 'bout the match?" Thomas inquired further. Father shot Thomas a sideways glance, screwing up his eyes into narrow slits.

"The match? Why wouldn't I?"

"Oh, I don' know. It jist seem like an important question to wonder 'bout."

"Ya know, Thomas, sometimes ya come up with awful strange things to say. Sometimes I jist worry 'bout ya, son."

"It's strange to wonder 'bout how good a match be?"

Father shook his head and rolled his eyes. "Bring the cart over to the house an' we'll load everybody up. We need to git on over to the church."

As usual Father drove the cart. Ben rode in the front in between Father and Mama. Thomas and Sally rode in the back of the cart. Mama insisted on Ben riding next to her. She didn't want him to mess up his clothes or hair, which she'd just spent the last hour preparing. Mama fussed with Ben's appearance throughout the ride to town. Ben repeatedly brushed her hands aside, but she was not to be dissuaded.

Father hurried everyone into the church as soon as they arrived. Thomas took the cart over to the Lewis farm to pick up Liz, with Sally accompanying him. Liz climbed into the cart next to Sally, since she was ready when they arrived.

"So, Liz, what do ya think of Ben an' Anna gettin' hitched?" asked Sally.

"Oh, I don't really know what to think. I really don't know Anna very well. They seem to get along well when I've been around them, but I don't think I have a good feel for their relationship." Sally nodded.

"Do you have concerns, Sally?"

"Yeah, I s'pose I do. Thomas an' me were just talkin' 'bout it. I just hope it works out for 'em."

"What makes you think it won't?"

"Since Ben says he's marryin' Anna 'cause it's the right thing to do. I'm not so sure I like that reason."

Liz looked at Sally with concern. "Do you mean that's the only reason he gives?"

"That's the only reason I've heard him give. Have ya heard any other, Thomas?"

Thomas shook his head slowly. "No, nothin' else 'cept sayin' she's perdy."

"Oh my!" exclaimed Liz. "That doesn't sound too good."

"I tried talkin' to Ben 'bout it this mornin', but he'd have nothin' to do with it," said Thomas. "I figure it was too late for that."

"Oh my," Liz repeated. "I suppose there isn't much we can do at this point. Maybe we should have said more before."

"I tried, Liz. I tried to talk with Ben many times, but he just kept talkin' 'bout doin' things proper. I don' know what more we coulda done. But it don't make me feel no better 'bout it," said Thomas. The other two nodded.

"I sure don' wanna let myself get pushed into marryin' the way Ben did," said Thomas.

"What?" asked Liz. Just then they arrived at the church, and it was time to hurry in and take their places. Thomas put one arm around Liz and the other around Sally.

The wedding ceremony went well with Ben getting almost everything right, as he'd hoped. Anna looked radiant. Father was proud of Ben's behavior, and Mama felt pleased Ben looked his best throughout the ceremony. The bride and groom retreated to the Chittenden farm immediately after the ceremony, and the rest of the families quickly followed.

After supper Thomas and Liz slipped away for a walk and an opportunity to talk. The couple meandered off onto the more remote portions of the Chittenden property, and soon was all alone. They walked hand in hand talking about the day's events. Once their debriefing of the day wound down, Liz pulled her hand out of Thomas's and took on a solemn demeanor.

"Thomas, there's something I have to ask you about."

Thomas gave Liz a brief, penetrating stare before responding. "Alright, shoot."

"I want to know what you meant by what you said before we walked into the church this morning."

"What'd I say?" asked Thomas.

"You said you didn't want to get pushed into marrying like Ben. What did you mean?"

"Oh, that. Well, I guess I meant I don' wanna feel pressured like my brother did," explained Thomas.

"You mean you don't want to feel pressured to get married?"

"Well, that too, but I don'..."

"Well, if you're feeling pressured by me to get married, then I'm sorry! Maybe you want to take things slower for awhile."

Thomas was dumbfounded. His eyes grew wide. He felt like a runaway cart had hit him that he'd never heard coming. At first he didn't know what to say. "Uh, Liz, I don' understand. What do ya mean take things slower? Are ya sayin' ya want to take a step back?"

"I don't know! Maybe I do. If you're not sure about me and you don't want to feel pressured, then maybe I'm not the right girl for you!"

"Not sure 'bout you? When did I say that?"

"You didn't have to, Thomas, but if you're feeling pressured and want to have your freedom, then you go right ahead and just take it. I'll be fine! But don't expect me to be waiting around for you! At some point a boy has to become a man and commit to a woman!"

"Is that what this is about? You tellin' me that I gotta commit to ya? This is just what I mean; I don' want nobody tellin' me when to commit an' how to do it! That's what everybody 'round tells me; what to do an' how to do it right! Maybe I'm not the right man for ya if you tellin' me I gotta commit! I'll commit when I'm good an' ready!"

"Well, I think its right time for you to take me home, Thomas Chittenden!"

"Well fine!"

"Fine!"

With these final words, they walked back to the barn in silence. They walked several feet apart, Thomas with clinched fists and Liz with arms folded across her chest. Neither one looked at the other. Thomas quickly hitched the cart and took Liz home. The entire ride to the Lewis farm persisted in silence, as both Liz and Thomas were either too angry or too proud to break the silence. When they finally arrived at Liz's home, she simply got out of the cart and walked into the house without a word. Thomas had the cart moving before she got into the house.

Without even thinking, Thomas headed directly to the Feed 'n Seed. MacDonald was not at the store. Then Thomas remembered that Sunday was MacDonald's day off. Thomas jumped back into the cart and headed for the MacDonald home. MacDonald sat on his porch reading and smoking his pipe, while Rachel sat next to him with her own book. Even from a distance, MacDonald could see the stunned look on Thomas's face. As soon as they were face-to-face, Thomas started tearing. He'd held back his feelings until he saw his old friend. Rachel excused herself and went into the house.

"Oh, lad, what happened? Isn't yer brother gettin' married today?" Thomas nodded.

"It ain't that. It's Liz. She an' I, I mean we uh... we fought."

"Oh, lad, I'm sorry. Weel, come sit yerself an' tell me all 'bout it."

Thomas sat next to MacDonald on the porch, and took several deep breaths.

"So tell me 'bout this fight ye had wi' the lass."

"I don' rightly know what happened... We were goin' for a walk an' then all o' a sudden we were fightin'...It seemed like it came outta nowhere. I guess it all started when she asked me 'bout not wantin' to feel pressure to marry. It seemed like she just got crazy on me. I've never seen her like that afore. She just all the sudden went off on somethin'. I don' rightly know what."

"Now hold on, lad. Hae ye known yer lass t' be crazy?"

Thomas thought for a minute. "I guess not."

"Nae, lad, that don' be her way. Somethin' must o' upset 'er. Now take yerself a minute an' think back on what happened."

Thomas was silent. His mind reeled, and he struggled to put his thoughts together. He still wasn't quite sure what had happened. Slowly his thoughts began to form.

"Well, maybe she thought I felt pressured by her to commit; but that's not what I was sayin'."

"Aye, lad, but let's start by understandin' what happened. Ye be gettin' ahead o' yerself. So ye said somethin' 'bout pressure to marry?"

"Yeah, I said somethin' 'bout not wantin' to feel pressured to marry like Ben. Ben's all concerned 'bout doin' it proper. I don' wanna do it proper; I wanna get married when I'm good an' ready, not when someone else tells me I oughta be."

"Okay, lad, an' ye thought yer lass was pressurin' ye t' marry proper?"

"I don' think so, at least I din't feel that way until today. Now maybe I do feel that way."

"Aye, lad, so what did yer lass say t' make ye feel pressured?"

"I don' know, something 'bout how a boy has to become a man some day an' commit to his girl."

"Oh, aye. An' do ye agree wi' 'er?"

"No, I don' wanna feel pressured by her."

"'Course ye don't want t' feel pressured, but that don' be what I asked, lad."

Thomas paused to think for a moment. "Then what did ya ask me?"

"Do ye think a boy hae t' become a man someday an' commit t' his girl?"

"Well, yeah, I s'pose so."

"A' right then, so what do ye think yer lass was tryin' t' tell ye?"

Thomas looked down at his feet while he thought about that one. He swung his feet back and forth nervously. He wasn't sure what his old friend was getting after. Thomas glanced at MacDonald's face, trying to get some clue as to what he was driving at.

"I think Liz wants me to commit to her already."

"That be what ye hear, lad? That nae be what I be hearin'."

"Well, so tell me what ya think she wants."

"I hear yer lass tellin' ye she be scared, an' that yer comment 'bout not wantin' t' feel pressure worried 'er."

"Well, if that's all it is, then why din't she just tell me that?"

MacDonald enjoyed a hearty laugh. "Come now, lad, don' that be askin' quite a bit o' yer lass now? Oh sure, in her best moments, yer lass quite probably could tell ye so, but ye hae t' make allowances for 'er t' be upset an' not say things quite so weel packaged. Do ye think ye say everything yerself quite the way ye'd like?"

"Yeah... well, I guess not."

"'Course not, lad. Thar nae be a soul quite so mature they always say things perfect now. When folk be upset they're likely t' say a great many things they might later regret. Ye hae t' make allowances for such."

Thomas got up and paced the porch back and forth and rubbed his arm. "I don' know, I think you're givin' Liz too much credit."

"Maybe, lad. An' what be the harm in that?"

"Maybe that she gets off it bein' her fault what happened."

"Aye, lad. So ye be thinkin' it all be yer lassie's fault then?"

"Well, maybe."

"Come now, lad. Which o' us dances withoot a partner?"

Thomas smiled, in spite of himself. "Maybe she ain't dancin' alone, but she might be leadin' the dance."

MacDonald threw back his head and gave a twinkle-eyed laugh. "Oh, I see, lad. Yer lass hae most o' the fault, an' ye be merely in the wrong place a' the wrong time."

Thomas tried to suppress a laugh at his own expense, but failed. Once the cat was out of the bag, he laughed vigorously. "I s'pose that do sound silly."

"Aye, lad, thar ye go. Ye both be havin' yer own feelin's 'bout the conversation today. An likely ye both need t' be heard."

"Well, ya've given me a lot to think 'bout Mr. MacDonald; I have to chew on it a bit."

"Ye do that, lad. I'll be here if ye want t' talk some more."

Once the door closed behind her, Liz ran to find Aunt Hannah. Liz found her in the kitchen preparing supper. Liz ran into her arms as she broke into tears. "Aunt Hannah, Thomas doesn't want me! He wants to slow down, and he isn't sure if I'm the one for him."

"Oh, honey. Let me dry my hands and we'll go sit down and talk." Hannah sat down at the table with Liz and finished drying her hands on a towel. Okay, honey, tell me what happened."

Liz took a deep breath and tried to calm her tears so she could talk. "Thomas doesn't want to feel pressured to marry, and he feels pressured by me to marry and doesn't want to. Then he said something about not wanting to commit until he was good and ready. He doesn't want to commit to me, Aunt Hannah. I think he has his doubts about me. He might be getting ready to break it off."

At this Liz began softly crying again. Aunt Hannah offered her hand. "I can understand how you'd be upset, Liz. I'm sorry that you and Thomas had a fight." Liz nodded and held onto her aunt's hand.

"So what made you think Thomas feels pressured by you?"

"Because he said he didn't want to feel pressured like Ben did."

"I don't know what that means," Aunt Hannah said.

"Of course it means Thomas feels pressured by me and wants to go more slowly and maybe isn't even sure about me!"

"Now let's not get ahead of ourselves. You might be reading into things that Thomas may or may not have meant. Now try to remember what Thomas actually said."

Liz nodded and wiped her eyes with her hands while she tried to think back on the fight. "It all started when Thomas and Sally were talking about their concerns over Ben and Anna's marrying today. Thomas said something about not wanting to feel pressured to marry like Ben."

"Okay, now that's something important. What exactly did Thomas say about Ben?" asked Aunt Hannah.

"He said, well, I don't rightly remember, but I think he said something about not wanting to feel pressured to do it properly like Ben."

"And do you know what he means by doing it 'properly'?"

At this question, Liz paused to think back. "Well, I guess he means... well, I suppose I should start before that. Thomas has talked several times about not liking how Ben talks about doing things the 'right way.' I guess he probably thought, well actually Thomas and Sally expressed their concerns this morning about Ben's reasons for marrying Anna. They both were worried Ben married because he thought it was the right timing and the right thing to do."

"And for good reason Thomas would be concerned about that being Ben's reason for marrying. What does he mean by the right timing?" asked Hannah.

"I think he means that Ben felt pressure to marry because he's been courting Anna more than a full season."

"Oh my, it scares me for Ben and Anna to think that might be the basis for their marrying."

"Yes, I suppose," said Liz doubtfully.

"You suppose? Come on, Liz. How would you like it if Thomas knocked on our door tonight and said he wanted to get married to you because you'd been courting the right number of months now?"

Liz allowed herself a muffled laugh at this idea. She didn't want to wholeheartedly laugh and concede that to her aunt. "Well, I don't imagine I'd be too excited to marry with that kind of proposal."

"Of course not. We'd sit down for a serious conversation if I thought you were even considering that kind of proposal."

Liz smiled as she looked down at the table. She liked it when Aunt Hannah showed maternal inclinations toward her, especially since nobody else was.

At this point Hannah continued with her point. "In light of what we've just discussed, what do you think Thomas was trying to say about not wanting to feel pressured?"

"Well, I guess he doesn't want to feel pressured by anybody to get married just because it's the right thing to do. But I think Thomas also isn't sure about me, and wants to slow down and rethink the relationship."

Aunt Hannah looked at Liz with a mixture of compassion and doubt. "Liz, you're afraid. You're afraid of losing Thomas."

"No, I'm not! I'm just not sure if Thomas is mature enough for me!" Aunt Hannah smiled.

"Really?"

"Yes, really!" said Liz.

"Now, Liz, Thomas is probably feeling some pressure, but I'm not sure he's feeling that from you. I understand it scares you to hear him say something like that; however, I think you may be putting words into his mouth that he's not saying. Isn't it better to find out what Thomas means before you go off and decide for him?"

"I don't know, maybe. I guess I need to think more about the whole thing. You might be taking words out of his mouth." Aunt Hannah merely nodded.

"Thank you for listening. Let me help you with supper now," said Liz.

On the way home from MacDonald's, Thomas mulled over his conflict with Liz. He still wondered if his old friend might be giving

Liz more benefit of the doubt than she deserved. However, he had to admit, although reluctantly, that MacDonald might have a point about Liz trying to say she's afraid. That did seem to fit what Thomas knew of Liz. Thomas still felt angry with Liz and wasn't sure he was ready to try to make amends with her. He winced as he remembered a couple of her comments.

The next couple of days, Thomas threw himself into his chores about the farm. He spoke with Sally some, and even briefly mentioned his conflict with Liz. Sally also thought Liz must be afraid, and encouraged Thomas to ask her about that. Sally made an astute observation that it was unlike Liz to say things in anger, and that something must have upset her.

It wasn't until several days later that Thomas felt ready to talk with Liz. He didn't want much more time to go by without attempting to repair the rupture between them. Thomas knew he needed to talk through the whole incident and suspected that Liz did as well.

As soon as he finished eating dinner the next day, he headed out to the barn to saddle his horse. Just as he readied to lift the saddle off the ground, he remembered Sally asking him how he was doing with Liz. Thomas had quickly brushed her off with a vague comment. He realized that he could really use her support.

Thomas left the saddle where it lay and headed back to the new house to look for Sally. Thomas and Sally ate with the family at the new house even though they still lived in the old one. Sally was drying recently washed dishes as Thomas walked into the kitchen.

"Hey, Sally."

"Oh, hi, big brother."

Thomas smiled at her term of affection. "Hey, Sally, can I have a word with ya when you're done here?"

"Sure. I should be done in a few minutes."

"Okay, I'll be out in the barn," said Thomas.

Ten minutes later Sally found Thomas grooming his horse in the barn. She hopped up on a bail of hay and crossed her legs. "What's up, big brother?"

"Hey, I think I, uh, I think I missed out on something with you earlier."

Sally looked puzzled. "What'd ya mean?"

Thomas looked down at the ground and folded his arms across his chest. "Ya asked me how I'm doin' with Liz, and I brushed ya off. I, uh, I think I missed out on a chance to talk with ya 'bout my tree, an' my tree needs some tendin' today." Sally nodded for him to go on.

"Well, the truth is I'm headin' on over to see Liz, an' I'm nervous 'bout how it's gonna go. I wanna try an' talk things out with her, but I'm not so sure how well we gonna do. I think I'm still mad at her, an' I might go an' say somethin' stupid. I'm also worried 'bout what Liz's gonna be like."

"I can see why ya'd be worried, Thomas. I don't have much experience with such things, but I hope Liz will be able to see that ya tryin' to work it out with her."

Thomas sighed. "Oh, that is so true. I really want us to work things out, an' I'm not sure we can."

"What if ya said somethin' like that to Liz?"

"Somethin' like what?"

"Somethin' like ya really wanna work things out with her an' you're worried you two won't be able to," suggested Sally.

Thomas laughed nervously. "Oh, I don' know, Sally. That sounds pretty weak."

"Well, I s'pose ya would be showin' Liz the softer parts o' ya tree. Is that so bad?"

"I guess it's not bad, but I don' know if I can bring myself to say somethin' like that." Sally nodded and decided not to push Thomas too much. "So what are ya gonna say?"

Thomas pondered her question for a bit. "I have to admit, Sally, I really don' know. I know I don' wanna wait much longer afore talkin', but I really don' know what to say to her. I love Liz an' I wanna work it out with her, but I'm not sure how to do that."

"I think ya know what to say, but are afraid to show much o' the soft part o' your tree."

Thomas laughed nervously again and looked up at Sally. "Maybe ya right. I guess I'm tryin' to find a way to work it out without havin' to show much o' my softer bark an' bein' humble."

"Yep. Ya wish Liz'd do all the vulnerable stuff."

Thomas and Sally laughed from their bellies, with Sally almost falling off her seat. Thomas appreciated feeling understood and helped by Sally, although he wasn't sure he liked the implications of their conversation. "I hate to admit it, but I think ya probably on to somethin' here. Ya know, ya pretty smart for a little sister."

"Showin' some humbleness won't kill ya, Thomas. How many times have ya told me to talk 'bout my softer bark?"

"Yeah, I know. Thanks, little sis."

"Well, Thomas, ya just promise to name your first child after me: Sally for a girl and Sal for a boy. Okay?"

Thomas just laughed in response. "Well, I can't put it off any longer. I guess I'll head on over an' see what we can do. Thanks for helpin' me with this."

"You just get goin' before ya change your mind."

Liz felt relieved the first couple of days that Thomas didn't come by. The third day she would have welcomed his visit but would not have minded another day to think things over. By the fourth day, she'd become worried; what if he never came? She found herself glancing up the road leading to the house every hour or so, hoping to see Thomas approaching on his familiar black horse with the white nose. She felt a tinge of disappointment mixed with anxiety each time she saw the empty road.

Thomas normally came right after the midday meal, and Liz had checked the road every fifteen minutes or so once she'd finished dinner. Now that it had been over an hour since she'd eaten, she'd given up on Thomas coming today. The knock on the door took her by surprise. A pang of nerves shot through her stomach when she heard Thomas's faint voice at the door. She quickly checked herself in the mirror before appearing at the door.

On her way to the door, Aunt Hannah gave Liz a wordless hug of support. Liz took a moment to gather herself and opened the door. Thomas paced back and forth on the porch and was just turning to go the other way when Liz opened the door. He'd been trying to muster his courage to show Liz a bit of his softer bark while he waited.

"Hi, Liz," he said shyly.

"Hello." Liz tried to sound more upbeat than she felt.

Thomas felt encouraged by her friendly reception. "Look Liz, I thought we might, uh, I thought we probably need to talk."

"Yes, I'm glad you came."

"You are?"

"Yes, of course," said Liz.

"Oh. I wadn't sure if you'd want to see me after the other day."

"I can imagine," said Liz, "I wasn't sure if you'd come back."

"Really?" Liz nodded affirmatively.

"Oh, I was comin' back; I just needed time to think things over some."

"Yes, I wasn't ready to talk until yesterday."

There was an awkward pause and neither knew what to say at this point. Each glanced with darting eyes at the other. Liz hoped Thomas would say something. Thomas kept forming words in his mouth, only to discard each one. None of them seemed waterproof. Thomas noticed a face looking out the window. A moment later it appeared again. This time he recognized Liz's mother and waved. The face disappeared.

"So, why don' we go for a walk?" suggested Thomas.

"Sure." Both let out a deep breath of relief to have the initial awkwardness negotiated without further damage.

The walk began in silence. They each stole glances at the other, as if trying to read something in the other's face. Liz kept hoping Thomas would begin. Thomas continued to debate within himself how vulnerable he wanted to be, and what would be the best place to begin. He decided to begin on safer ground.

"Well, I guess things din't go so well last time we talked."

Liz laughed nervously at his understatement. "No, they certainly didn't." With a smile on her face she added a playful jab. "No, you were being a horse's ass!"

Now it was Thomas's turn to laugh, but with relief. "Is that right?"

"Yes, that's right, Thomas Chittenden."

"An' I s'pose you were bein' a saint?"

"Well, perhaps not, but close," she added playfully.

Their walking pace slowed to a more leisurely rate. Thomas realized they'd been walking fast. "Look, Liz. I been thinkin', maybe I scared ya with my comment 'bout not wantin' to feel pressured to do it like Ben."

Liz quickly looked at Thomas's face, wondering if he was trying to blame the fight on her. She couldn't tell.

"Maybe. And maybe you were angry at what I said to you?"

"What's that s'posed to mean?" Thomas shot back.

"Nothing. Just don't blame the fight on me, Thomas. You were there too, it wasn't my entire fault."

"I'm not saying it was. So are you sayin' that I shouldn't be angry? 'Cause I think it be alright for me to be angry!"

"Well, maybe you do need to be more careful about what you say when you're angry," Liz retorted.

"So now you're tellin' me what to do with my anger, is that it? I don' need nobody tellin' me the right way t' be angry. I'll be angry any way I please!"

"Well, maybe you don't want me telling you anything then!"

"What's that s'posed to mean?" asked Thomas.

"That means maybe this isn't going to work out between us, and maybe you need to find someone else more to your liking."

"Is that right? Well maybe I'll do just that." They paused. By now they had stopped walking and stood facing each other.

"Oh, Thomas, this is going badly again. I don't want us to do this again."

"Yeah, I know, we're fightin' again, said a softened Thomas. So how can we do this right?"

"I don't know, but I don't want us to fight. "

They resumed walking, now in silence. Liz wrung her hands as she wondered how she and Thomas could address this issue without fighting. Thomas kicked at the dirt with his boots with his arms folded while he pondered what to do.

"Maybe I was angry the other day," Thomas admitted.

"Yes."

"But I don't want nobody tellin' me how to do anger right!"

"Wow, okay!

"Ya know, Liz, I don't like ya tellin' me 'wow', like you're tellin' me not to be angry or somethin'."

"Okay, Thomas, but I don't like you talking about how maybe you're going to find someone else, and maybe we need to slow down. I don't like it that you feel pressured by me. What am I supposed to do?"

"I don' know, Liz. Just don' tell me how to do things right!"

"Well, maybe I won't if you stop talking about slowing down or maybe finding another girl!"

"Damn it, Liz! We're not gettin' nowhere! Maybe we should just take ya back to the farm for now."

"Well, that's just fine with me! Maybe you should take me back to the farm for good and just say your goodbyes now and get it over with! I don't want some long, drawn out goodbye," countered Liz.

"Sounds good enough for me!"

"Well good then!"

At this they promptly turned on their heels and turned back towards the Lewis farmhouse. The march proceeded in stubborn silence, neither wanting to give in to the other, nor risk anymore. Thomas walked with his arms firmly folded across his chest, perhaps guarding his heart. Liz pursed her lips, as if to hold the words inside her mouth. Thomas walked Liz to the door and immediately left once she was inside. Liz slammed the door behind her.

Thomas hung his head as he walked his horse off the Lewis property. He felt like a failure. He couldn't figure out why he couldn't talk with Liz without saying stupid things. Thomas slapped his thigh several times with his hand. Should he go see MacDonald? He felt so ashamed of his failure that he didn't know if he could face his old friend just yet. Unsure of what he wanted to do, he wandered around town on his horse for awhile, how long he had little idea. Without consciously deciding, Thomas looked up to see the Feed 'n Seed arising up before him; perhaps something in him knew to take himself to MacDonald. No one else would do at a time like this.

Thomas moved in slow motion, his head hung and his arms hanging limp at his sides. He shuffled into the store and automatically walked into the back supply room. One look at his young friend told MacDonald what had occurred.

"Oh, lad, things went that badly?"

Thomas merely nodded without looking up. He sat heavily like a sack of potatoes. MacDonald pulled up a chair and sat down. Eventually Thomas looked up at his dear friend. Tears began forming in his eyes, yet the rest of his face remained unmoved. MacDonald wisely waited. A few moments later Thomas slowly began to talk. "I can't do this."

MacDonald held his gaze without speaking. Thomas merely looked up. After another pause, he continued.

"We fought again, an' I think it be mostly my fault."

"So what happened, lad?"

Thomas shifted his position and drew in a deep breath, exhaling slowly. "Well, I don' really know. Before I knew what was happenin', we were fightin' again. I s'pose I got angry."

"'Bout what?"

"Oh, I don' know."

"Come now, lad, don't give up on me. Try an' search ye mind."

"Well, I just felt like she was tryin' to tell me what to do, an' the right way to be mad. That made me mad. I don' want nobody tellin' me what t' do!"

"Aye, lad, I know. What did yer lass say that felt so?"

"Uh, well, she said somethin' 'bout maybe I oughta be careful 'bout what I do with my anger."

"Oh, aye, lad. I'm sure that did poke yer tree a bit."

Thomas nodded and took in several deep breaths, each time exhaling more slowly. He shifted to a more comfortable position and resumed his recounting. "I don' know, maybe I just can't keep my temper with her. Both times I got mad real quick. I say the stupidest things! I wish I'd stop that."

"So, lad, what be poking yer anger so fresh then?"

Thomas had to think about that one. He hadn't considered that something might be helping him lose his temper. Thomas simply thought he ought to better control himself, period. "I guess it just seems like every time Liz tells me what to do, I get mad."

"Aye, then yer reactin' t' feelin' like somebody be controlin' ye," suggested MacDonald.

"Yeah, that's it. I hate it when somebody control me."

"An' it's no wonder ye react so t' bein' controlled, lad."

"Why's that?"

"Tell me now, yer certainly no stranger t' being controlled, lad."

"Ya mean my father?"

"'Course I do, lad."

"Yeah, but what's that got t' do with me gettin' mad at Liz?"

"Everything t' do wi it. Lad, the branch o' yer tree that's 'bout controllin' yer own life's been severely bruised. Yer father saw t' that. An' now yer left wi' a branch that's a good bit sore t' the touch. Ye feel it pretty good whenever somebody says anything that even feels a bit like control. 'Course yer gonna feel the bruise any time 'nother bumps against it."

"So what do I do 'bout it?"

"Weel, lad, ye hae t' tend t' yer bruised branch."

"How?"

"Ye might begin by talkin' wi yer lass 'bout yer bruised tree, an' let her in o' it. But, lad, ye hae t' take responsibility for yer own bruise; it don't be up t' yer lass t' see that ye never get poked. Now, she may very weel be sayin' things that help ye t' feel yer bruise; but make no mistake, the bruised branch be attached t' yer own tree an' not the lassie's."

"But she keeps sayin' pressurin' things that..."

"Now hold on, lad. Yer lass may hae her own bruised branches, but this bruise be o' yer own tree."

At this Thomas jumped up and began pacing the room back and forth with his arms folded across his chest and his jaw firmly set. MacDonald let his young friend have time to absorb what he'd just been told, as he knew it smarted to hear what he'd just said. Having a friend point to your reflection in the mirror is priceless, but the sting of the reflection hurts just the same. Thomas knew there was something to what MacDonald said, but he didn't want to let Liz off the hook just yet and struggled to accept what the reflection showed him.

"So you're sayin' that I'm a damaged tree, an' that I've got somethin' wrong with me."

"Oh lad, ye say it like a sentence pronounced o'er yer head. We all got damage t' oor trees, myself included. An' yer lass be no different. 'Tis no crime t' hae damaged branches, lad, jist so long as ye tend t' 'em. The tragedy be when we behave as though all oor branches be sound an' all the damage be in other trees. There's ne'er been a man t' walk this earth wi' no bruised branches, lad. So don't get no notions that ye oughta hae no damage t' yer tree; tis a human condition t' be one o' the damaged ones. Lad, I want t' help ye tend t' yer bruised an' damaged branches. An' yer lass will need help tendin't' hers as well, an' I hope she has help t' do so."

"So you're not sayin' it's only me that needs to change?"

"Goodness, no, lad! We all require tendin', an' I be one o' the most in need o' it."

"Really? How do ya tend to your bruises?"

"Oh, I hae cherished friends that help me look in t' the mirror an' tend t' what we see."

"Really, you have to git help too?"

"'Course lad; I be no different than ye. I need help tendin' me tree just the same. None o' us can tend t' oor own trees by oor lonesome; we all need somebody t' help us."

It surprised Thomas to think of his old friend as needing much from anyone else, yet in a way the thought comforted Thomas to think of MacDonald having similar needs to his own.

"Well, Mr. MacDonald, maybe Liz and I both be afraid; probably o' different things, but I think we both be afraid."

"There ye go, lad. Ye both need a bit o' understandin' from the other. Ye both hae damaged branches an' need help tendin' t' 'em."

"Thanks, Mr. MacDonald; I think I'm ready to go now."

"So long, lad. I be seein' ye soon then."

No sooner had Liz shut the front door as she began a search for Aunt Hannah. Liz found her aunt reading in the sitting room. Liz began sobbing before she even sat next to Hannah.

"Oh, honey, it must have gone badly."

"Uh huh."

"Oh, honey, I'm so sorry. I had so hoped things would go well this time." Liz continued sobbing, her chest and shoulders heaving as she leaned against her aunt. Aunt Hannah just waited for now. After some time Liz looked up at her aunt, as if to signal that she felt ready to talk.

"Tell me what happened, honey."

Liz wiped away her tears as she tried to gather her thoughts. "Oh, Auntie, Thomas just seemed so angry, I didn't know what to say."

"What did you say?"

"I, uh, well, I guess I told him that maybe he ought to be more careful about his anger."

"And what does that mean?" asked Aunt Hannah.

"That means he says things that make it sound like he wants to slow things down with me and that maybe he's not sure about me."

"Okay, so Thomas says some things that upset you."

"Of course he upsets me; wouldn't comments like that upset you?"

"I'm not sure, Liz, but that really isn't the point. The point is you're having a reaction to something that he's saying, and we need to understand what that's about."

"So I shouldn't be upset by what he said?"

"Oh no, honey, I didn't say that. I mean that something inside you is reacting to Thomas - some others would be upset and some would not."

"So you're saying that not every girl would be upset by the things Thomas is saying?"

"That's right," Aunt Hannah agreed.

"So are you saying that I'm just being too sensitive and that I shouldn't let it bother me?"

"Oh no, Liz, I'm not saying that at all. There's nothing wrong with you having a reaction; we just need to get to the bottom of it."

"So how do we do that?"

"Well, when Thomas talks about not wanting to feel pressured, what impact does that have on you?"

"Like I said, it makes me think he wants to slow down and..."

"Wait a minute, Liz. I'm not asking what you think he's saying; I'm asking how that impacts you."

"I don't like it."

"Okay, can you elaborate?"

"I don't know what else to say; I just don't like it and think he wants to end things."

"No, Liz, that's your interpretation. I think it scares you when Thomas talks about not wanting to feel pressured. I think you're scared that he wants to break off the relationship."

"You don't think he wants to?"

"No, I don't hear him saying that," answered Aunt Hannah. "I hear him having his own reaction to his brother getting married. I hear him wanting to be different from his brother."

"I don't know, Auntie; you make Thomas sound so good!"

"I'm not interested in making Thomas sound good or bad; I'm interested in helping you understand him, and more importantly, in helping you understand yourself. I think you're jumping to some conclusions because you're afraid; and it's okay to be afraid, Liz. As a matter of fact, I think it's pretty understandable that you'd be afraid of Thomas leaving you."

Liz looked at her aunt in surprise. "Why is that?"

"Liz, haven't you traumatically lost someone important to you?"

"Oh, dear God!"

Tears streamed down Liz' face; thoughts of Papa flooded her mind. She hadn't even considered that losing her father could be related. Maybe she had been protecting herself from revisiting those painful feelings of loss.

Throughout the next day, Thomas thought of Liz and what he might say to her. He had much to say and hoped to get away soon to try and talk things through again. He headed for the new house for the midday meal. He walked through the door and took his place at the family table. He reached for the potatoes and then was surprised to see the normally unoccupied chair across from him occupied. Because it was so unexpected, it took Thomas a moment longer to recognize that it was Liz who sat across from him.

"Oh my goodness, what are ya doin' here?"

"Surprise!" Liz smiled, as she enjoyed surprising him. Liz rarely visited the Chittenden farm, and never before without being invited by Thomas. Thomas was still recovering himself as Ben asked to have the potatoes passed to him.

"Huh? What? Oh sure; here ya go."

Thomas continued to stare at Liz. He couldn't help but wonder why she was here. Thomas had a momentary thought that she came to teach him about how to be angry; he quickly dismissed this thought and decided to just wait and hear what she had on her mind. He didn't want to put thoughts in her mind that may not be there. He quickly realized he'd have to wait until after dinner to find out. As the dinner went on, Thomas was relieved to note that Liz seemed to be in good spirits. Whatever it was, it couldn't be all bad. Finally dinner was over, the dishes cleared and cleaned, and Thomas and Liz were able to slip away for a private talk.

Thomas led Liz up toward the back portion of the Chittenden property. The back portion rarely got much traffic, and they'd likely be alone there. Neither of them wanted an audience for this conversation. Thomas looked over his shoulder to make sure no one followed them. Satisfied that they were alone, he let out a sigh, partly of relief and partly of apprehension. Thomas put his hands in his pockets and glanced nervously at Liz, wondering if she would speak first. Liz wrung her hands, trying to form the right words to say. Both feared another ugly fight.

Liz didn't speak right away as Thomas had hoped, and he went searching his mind for a way to begin. He searched for just the right words that would steer them toward a peaceful harbor instead of rocks. Even though Liz had thought about what she might say the whole ride over, she still couldn't find the words she wanted; or maybe she was just afraid to say them. Sometimes fear rules out any and all words as wrong.

Finally Liz spoke. "Oh, Thomas, I guess neither of us knows what to say."

Thomas laughed nervously. "Yeah, I guess so."

Liz decided to plunge ahead, not knowing if she was going off a waterfall or into a gently flowing river. "Thomas, I'm sorry for how I was last time. I think I jumped to some conclusions that you may not have meant."

"I'm sorry too. I can't seem to keep control o' my temper, and I said some stupid things."

"I guess we both said some silly things last time; well, the last two times really. I want us to get off on the right foot this time."

"Well, the last two times was definitely the left foot," said Thomas with a smile. Liz laughed and punched Thomas playfully in the arm. Thomas pretended to be mortally wounded, falling to the ground.

"Get up you big pretender!"

Liz reached down to help Thomas up, who deftly pulled Liz down on top of him, bracing her fall with his own body. As Liz screamed, they went rolling down the gentle slope until they came to rest under a tree with Thomas on top of Liz. He gently kissed her lips; she pulled him closer for a lingering moment of intimacy. They hadn't enjoyed one another like this for a long time, and neither hurried to end the moment even though both knew there was much more to be said.

As they sat against the tree, both gathered their thoughts. Thomas held Liz's hand in his own, and felt affectionate toward her. "Liz, I want ya to know somethin' 'bout me." Liz looked up at Thomas and nodded for him to go on.

"Liz, I have a thing 'bout control. I hate feelin' controlled by anybody. I think I reacted to ya the other times 'cause I felt like you were tryin' to tell me what to do. I'm not sayin' that ya were, but that's just how it felt to me. I think that's why I got angry, an' I think that's why I said some things I wish I could take back. Please, Liz, please be patient with me 'bout this whole control thing."

Liz squeezed Thomas's hand and smiled sympathetically. "Oh, Thomas, of course. I want to help you with anything."

Thomas breathed a sigh of relief. He felt vulnerable showing Liz the tender, underneath side of his tree, unsure of how she'd respond. Thomas had feared Liz would be impatient, or even critical of his problem. "Thanks, Liz."

"For what?"

"Just, just for bein' understandin'."

"You're welcome."

Liz and Thomas sat back and enjoyed a few moments of wordless peace for what they'd accomplished so far.

"Thomas, there's something I want to confess to you."

"Okay."

"I, uh, I think I've been afraid. When you talked about not wanting to feel pressured, I felt afraid you were going to leave me."

At this Liz began to cry. Thomas put his arm around her and held her. After a few minutes, Liz continued. "Thomas, I want to tell you about my father."

Thomas glanced at Liz in surprise, and then smiled reassuringly. "Okay," he simply replied.

"I had been in my room attending to my studies, which Mother and Papa both insisted upon, when my mother came into the room. She said, 'Liz, honey, have you seen your father? He's probably just tinkering out in the barn, like usual. I think he purposefully keeps me waiting when he knows good and well supper is prepared. Anyhow, supper's ready; wash up and come to the table.' Then I said, 'Okay, Mother, I'll be right there. I just have to write one more thing.' Then Mother went out to look for Papa. I had just finished closing my books when I heard Mother cry out, 'Oh, it can't be so! Somebody help! Help! Somebody come quick!' I ran out to the barn as fast as I could. I'd never heard my mother sound so terrified. Mother was kneeling beside Papa when I got there."

Then Liz paused and reached for a handkerchief in her bag. She wiped her tears and then continued. "Mother cried out to me, 'Liz, hurry and get me some clean rags! And some hot water!' I felt panicked, but I ran to get what she asked for. As I ran out to the barn, I could hear her saying, 'Please God, let Papa be okay! Please

God, let Papa be okay!' I found the rags and hot water, which was already on the stove for supper, and ran back to the barn. When I got back to the barn, Mother was crumpled on the ground sobbing, 'No, it can't be so. Don't let it be so. Nooooo!' I yelled out, 'What is it, Mother? Papa's gonna be alright, isn't he? Please tell me he's gonna be alright.' Then Mother looked at me as if I were someone she didn't know. I begged her to tell me that Papa was okay, but she didn't seem to hear me."

Liz stopped and turned her face away. She dabbed her eyes again. In a lower voice she continued. "Finally I got her to answer me, 'No, honey, Papa's gone. I can't believe he went and left me like that.' Her voice sounded so strange, like someone I didn't know."

"Oh, Liz! Shoot, I don' know what to say to somethin' like that," offered Thomas.

"I still remember the stunned feeling I felt all that day. It was like a tornado had picked me up and turned me around a thousand times before setting me down in a different time and a different place," said Liz in a whisper.

Thomas pulled her close to sit and lean against his chest and held her. Her tears were nearly dry, and she stared off into space unseen. Thomas brushed her hair slowly with his hand. "Since my father died, I'm more afraid of somebody leaving me. Oh, Thomas, I miss him so."

Thomas continued to just hold her while she cried. "I'm so sorry 'bout ya father." Liz nodded and continued to look off.

After a pause, Thomas added another thought. "Liz, I want ya to know that I had no thought o' leavin' you. It was never 'bout that for me."

Liz nodded as she continued to cry on his shoulder. "I can see that now. That's what Aunt Hannah said."

"I'm glad ya have her." Liz nodded.

"Ya know, Liz, I don' know what I'd do without Mr. MacDonald. He's the one that told me ya probably weren't tryin' to control me."

"You definitely need him," said Liz.

"What?"

"Don't you ever give him up, you hear me?"

"Is that right?"

"I'm just playing with you. I guess we both need somebody to help us sort out stuff in our trees."

"Yeah, no foolin'." After a pause Thomas continued.

"Ya know, Liz, I know I need Mr. MacDonald a little, but I think you really need Aunt Hannah even more."

"What?"

Liz looked at Thomas and saw that he was playing with her.

"I don't know, Thomas. It scares me to think where you'd be if you hadn't met Mr. MacDonald. I probably wouldn't have allowed you to court me."

Thomas enjoyed the wry smile on Liz's face when she played. She was so fun to play with! "Ya know, Liz, if it wasn't for Mr. MacDonald, I probably wouldn't have even wanted to court ya."

At this Liz punched Thomas in the shoulder again, this time a bit harder. Both of them laughed heartily, enjoying being able to play and enjoy each other again. They rolled around in the grass again, and were in no hurry to stop. It had been a rough week for them. They felt great relief at having navigated a difficult stretch of road in their relationship. Thomas and Liz had endured other conflicts, but none as difficult as this one.

Their necking session on the grass was passionate, fueled by the energy from the emotional conversation they'd just had. Neither wanted to end their physical time together, yet after lingering for quite awhile Thomas had an idea.

"Hey Liz, I want to show ya somethin'." Thomas took Liz's hand and led her up the hill they had just rolled down and beyond into parts of the property Liz had never before seen.

"Where are you taking me?" Liz asked.

"You'll see."

"But, Thomas, how far away is this place?"

"Not far, we almost there."

Thomas found the familiar stream and followed it up to the opening in the rock outcroppings. He let go of Liz's hand to duck under the overhanging tree branches and disappeared from sight. At first Liz thought he'd fallen into a pit or down a hidden ravine.

"Thomas, where are you? Are you okay?" Liz had an anxious moment as she received no immediate response. She began wringing her hands as she cautiously walked closer to where he'd disappeared.

Suddenly, Thomas popped his head back out of the cave opening. "Yeah, I'm right here. Come on in."

Liz ducked her head and entered the cave. A candle already illuminated the rock cave. Liz caught her breath, as the rock's natural beauty surprised her; streaks of grey and black lined a cream background. In spots, flecks of red and peach gave the room a hint of color. The candle danced about creating an illusion of ever changing rock, as if under a moving current of water. A gentle breeze kept the candle flame in perpetual motion.

"Wow, Thomas, this place is beautiful! What is it?"

"It's my favorite place - my place away from everythin'." Thomas said these words with a touch of sadness in his voice. "Ben an' me been comin' here for years. I'm not even sure how long. I guess it be where we come to get away from the farm."

Thomas absently ran his hand across the shelf and familiar markings of his home away from home. Liz interrupted his trance with a question. "What do you come to get away from?"

Thomas pondered her question, as no answer immediately came to mind. "I never really thought 'bout what I was gettin' away from; I s'pose to get away from all the farm things. I don' know, it just seems like Father always wants me to do something else 'bout the farm. When we came here, nobody asked us to do nothin'. I guess it's kinda peaceful here."

"Did you always come here with Ben?"

"No. Sometimes I come by myself. Sometimes I'd come by myself an' just sit for hours. I'm not even sure what I do. "

"Maybe the point is not what you were doing here, but what you're away from?" suggested Liz.

"Yeah," said Thomas sadly.

Liz walked over to the shelf and looked through the books on it. She noticed both books seemed to be about military adventures. Liz was surprised to note that the books were written at an elementary level; something a child would read. Thomas noticed what she was looking at and quickly took the books out of her hands and put them back on the shelf.

"Oh, don' look at those."

"How come?" asked a curious Liz.

"Oh, I, uh, well, I'm embarrassed that I read books like that. I guess I'm embarrassed that I can't read so good."

"You mean, you can't read?"

"No, I can read. I mean, I can read but jist simple books. I can't read stuff that's wrote for adults."

Surprise and curiosity got the better of Liz. In East Guilford where she grew up, almost everyone she knew could read at an adult level. She couldn't think of anyone of about her age that couldn't read well. Liz grew up in an affluent area in which all the kids were well educated; however, there certainly were many less affluent families whose kids had little or no education, but Liz didn't know those kids.

"Didn't you get to go to school?"

"Well, yeah, but I had to stop after a bit. Ya see, I got to go to school a few years, but then Father needed me on the farm; so I had to quit school an' work on the farm all the time. I'm kinda embarrassed, with you being all educated and proper. I mean, Liz, it's obvious that we don' talk the same; you talk all proper an' I talk like a country boy." The sadness continued to lace Thomas's voice.

"Oh, Thomas, I'm sorry; I didn't mean to embarrass you. I was just, well, I guess I was just surprised when I saw the books."

"Ya mean, ya not embarrassed 'bout me not readin' good?"

"No, of course not. Why would I be embarrassed of your reading?"

"I don't know, I just thought ya might be embarrassed to be my girl with me not readin' or talkin' too good."

"Thomas, you must not know why I like you. It has nothing to do with the way you talk. I don't care if you know the King's English. What I like is the kind of person you are. That's why I, well, that's why I..."

"Why ya what?"

"Well, I guess I'm the one embarrassed now," said Liz. "Gosh, I wasn't really planning on saying this; I guess I'd hoped you'd say it first."

"Say what?"

"I guess what I'm trying to say is that I love you," admitted Liz.

"Ya do?" said a surprised Thomas.

Thomas looked stunned, as though he'd just taken a blow to the head. His eyes grew large; he took a few steps back and felt his head spinning. Liz wanted to quickly hear that Thomas loved her too, as she was uncertain how her proclamation of love was received. Thomas's shock did nothing to reassure Liz; she wasn't sure if it was a good stunned or a bad stunned. Thomas slowly sat down on one of the large rocks adorning the cave. He looked up at Liz, uncertain what to say.

Finally, Liz broke the awkward silence. "Thomas, for heaven's sake, say something!" urged Liz.

"Uh, I don' know what to say. Nobody's ever said that to me before. Partly I'm really glad ya love me, but partly I'm not sure I know what that means. I guess it's a good thing."

"Of course it's a good thing! It means I really like you, you silly country boy!"

"Well, that is good then," said Thomas.

Thomas slowly regained his mind, and walked over to cautiously embrace Liz. "I'm not really sure what all that means, but I know I really like you too," said Thomas.

A greatly relieved Liz threw her arms around Thomas's neck. "Oh, thank God! I was so worried what you'd say when I saw that look on your face."

"I sorry, Liz, I didn't mean t' scare ya. Ya just took me by surprise there. I jist ain't used to hearin' nothin' like that."

"You mean your mother and father never said they loved you?"

Thomas thought for a moment. "I don' think so."

"That's so sad!" exclaimed Liz.

Thomas thought about that a minute. "Yeah, I s'pose it is," said Thomas. "Ya know, he never said nothin' like that, but I'm pretty sure MacDonald cares 'bout me that way. At least it feels like it to me."

"How can you tell?"

"Well, it's not really anything he exactly says, but I just feel liked by him. Well, it's more 'an that, I feel enjoyed by MacDonald. Do ya know what I mean?"

"I think so," said Liz. "I get that feeling with my Aunt Hannah, although Aunt Hannah comes right out and tells me she loves me."

"She must be a pretty great lady, that aunt o' yours," said Thomas.

"I'm so thankful to have her. You and Aunt Hannah are really the only people I can talk to."

"What 'bout your mother?" asked Thomas.

"Oh no, I can't really talk with her." It was Liz's turn to carry a hint of sadness in her voice.

Thomas picked up on the emotion in her voice. "How come ya can't really talk with ya mother?"

"Oh gosh, let's save that one for another time," said Liz. "I don't really want to get into that right now."

"Okay. Well, it's probably 'bout time for us to get back. I want ya to have plenty o' daylight to ride back in. Do you want me to ride back to the Lewis farm with ya?" Thomas asked.

"Oh, that's okay; I'll be alright as long as it's still light."

On that note the couple left the cave and hiked back down to the farm hand in hand. Nobody seemed to notice them being gone for several hours, nobody except for Sally. Thomas helped Liz saddle up and saw her off.

Thomas found Sally sitting in her room reading a book. Sally looked up when Thomas poked his head in her door. "Hey, big brother."

"Hey, little sister," Thomas countered. "Hey, ya got a couple minutes to talk?"

"You bet, come on in," invited Sally.

Thomas came in and sat comfortably on the floor with his back against the wall. Sally reclined on her bed. Thomas sat a moment in silence as he gathered his thoughts. "So Sally, what do ya think o' Liz?"

"I like her... Why do ya ask?"

"What do ya like 'bout her?" Thomas inquired.

"Wait a minute, you din't answer my question. Why are ya askin'?"

Thomas looked away. He picked up a toy on the floor and fidgeted with it nervously. "Oh, just wonderin'," said Thomas.

"Come on, Thomas, I know ya better than that. Level with me, what's rumbling in your tree?" asked Sally. "An' don't treat me like I'm stupid!"

Thomas laughed, realizing she'd caught him. "Ya know, little sis, sometimes it's great that ya can see my tree pretty good, an' sometimes it's not so great."

Sally laughed. Sally so appreciated having a brother she could talk with and feel understood by. She didn't know how she'd gotten by before she and Thomas learned to talk.

"Well, to answer your question, I'm actually considerin' askin' Liz to be my wife," admitted Thomas.

"Really, that's great, big brother!"

Thomas laughed nervously and looked down. He switched the toy from one hand to the other. "Yeah, I think Liz's a great gal. I figure I want your take on Liz 'cause I don' wanna do it the way Ben did. I wanna be sure o' the reasons why I wanna marry Liz. I don' wanna marry her just 'cause I been seein' her the right amount o' time, or 'cause I'm the right age or somethin'."

"So, why are ya thinkin' o' marryin' Liz?" asked Sally.

Thomas had to think about that question before answering. "Ya know what; the truth is, I don' know. I don' know why I wanna marry her."

Sally looked at Thomas with wide eyes. "Well, maybe it's 'bout time ya figured that out," said Sally, "or ya are gonna end up doin' it like Ben."

"Yeah, I s'pose so. That's a downright frightenin' thought," said Thomas.

Both Sally and Thomas sat with their thoughts a moment. "Ya know, maybe it's more important what I like 'bout Liz than what you think 'bout her," said Thomas.

"There ya go, big brother, now you're onto somethin'."

"Well, ya given me somethin' t' think on. Thanks," said Thomas.

"Afore ya go, I wanna tell ya something," began Sally. "I met a boy!" Sally smiled from ear to ear, and with a hint of sheepishness.

"Really?"

"Yeah. His name is Noah, an' I actually met him at Ben an' Anna's wedding. They just moved to town earlier this year. He's already called on me twice!"

"Hey, how come I haven't even seen 'im?" asked Thomas.

"I s'pose I din't really want anyone to know yet," admitted Sally.

"So what do ya like 'bout him?"

"Well, he's the first gentleman caller I had," began Sally. "I ain't had a boy like me afore; least not that I knew o'. But the best thing 'bout him is that he don't treat me like I'm gonna break. I hate it that Mama an' Father treat me like a baby that ya have t' always watch out for. I wanna be treated like I can look out for myself some. Noah's like that; he don't baby me like I might fall any minute. Matter o' fact, he don't seem to treat me no different than himself. I like that."

"That's great news, Sal! I'd like to meet 'im sometime," said Thomas.

May 22, 1753 - Hampshire Grants

It was around midnight when the regiment arrived at the Yorker camp. John, Thomas, and Scout cautiously approached the spot. They were surprised to find no lit campfire. It was dark enough that they couldn't make out much of anything.

"Hey Scout, I can't see a damn thing," said Thomas.

"Me neither. Let me move in for a closer look," said Scout as he soundlessly moved forward.

Thomas looked over at John, who shrugged his shoulders. "Ya think anybody down there?" Thomas wondered aloud. John shook his head.

John and Thomas sat in the dark and fidgeted nervously. It seemed like an hour before Scout crept up next to them.

"They've moved. I found 'em a few hundred yards to the north," said Scout.

"Why do ya think they moved?" asked John.

"The only thing I can figure is that they suspect they're not alone," suggested Scout.

"Damn! Now we gotta rethink our plan!" cursed Thomas.

"Maybe not," said Scout.

"Alright then; Scout move the men into position at the new site," ordered Thomas.

Once in position, Thomas and John surveyed the new campsite. The prisoners were the first direction Thomas looked. He was satisfied to see the two men were back amongst them. He counted the prisoners.

"Hey, I'm only gettin' eight. How many you got, John?"

"I got eight too; one's gone," answered John.

"Damn! Thomas swore in a loud whisper. So who's missin'...? Wait, I got it; one o' the lady folk is gone. Where is she?"

"Damn if I know," said John.

"I damn sure hope they din't take her away from camp!" said Thomas.

"Wait a minute; ain't that a lady lyin' next to that Yorker?" asked John.

"Maybe, but I can't quite make 'er out from her. Well, this complicates things. I don't wanna wait no longer; we gotta take action afore anybody else goes missin'. An' I don' like the new position they took up. With the outcrop o' rocks in front an' the creek behind, it gonna be tougher to approach 'em," said Thomas.

"Yep. They picked out a more defensible position, an' we can thank Haskins for that," said John.

"They expectin' somebody, alright; no other reason to move," said Thomas. "Well, Scout, we gonna have to rethink our plan then."

"Maybe not. I still think we can stick to our strategy. I figure those rocks give us an excellent place to set up, as long as we can get there without being seen. We best stay out of the creek though," said Scout.

"We gots two more guards o'er by the Yorker fire, plus the two with the prisoners," noted John.

"Yeah, and all of them are more alert than before," added Scout.

"Okay, Scout, I'm gonna trust ya. We stick with the plan - let's move. John, take ya eight men an' cover the east side. Scout, take yours an' cover the west side. Wait till we got 'em surrounded, then take out the guards. Dr. Dickens will stay out o' it; we need him healthy. Ya got the prisoner guards, John; an' Scout, you take out the guards by the fire. Everybody clear?" asked Thomas.

Scout and John both nodded affirmatively. "Then move on out," ordered Thomas.

Thomas appeared calm and confident, hiding his fear well as he instructed his men. He shifted nervously as he watched them take up positions. His cold and clammy hands reminded him that he felt anything but calm and confident.

"I wish I'd done this before," thought Thomas. "Then maybe I'd feel like I knew what I was doin'. I don' remember trainin' fer anything like this. Well, I guess there's nothin' to do now but make the best o' it. We do outnumber 'em almost two to one. Don' know if we have the benefit o' surprise though. Sure wish that Litchfield lady was with the other Connecticutt folk."

In position behind the trees adjacent to the prisoner guards, John peered out to detect any movement from the far side of the Yorker camp - nothing. John found himself starved for air and realized he'd been holding his breath. He slowly exhaled and soundlessly inhaled deeply. He looked again and saw Scout flanked by Peterson, approaching the guards on the west side.

John signaled Morse to follow. He set down his musket and unsheathed his knife. John stepped out from behind the trees and went down into a crouch, feeling naked with no cover but darkness. The guards sat with muskets across their laps, without talking. Fortunately, both guards faced north toward the prisoners, and away from John and Morse. John walked as though barefoot with sore feet. He looked over his shoulder to find out where Morse was. Waving him forward, John waited till they stood shoulder to shoulder. They were only ten feet from the guards.

John crouched down and turned to the left to catch a glimpse of Scout. Just then Scout and Peterson grabbed the two fireside guards. They made muffled cries, causing the prisoner guards to stand up and look their way. John felt panic rise within and jumped on the left guard, knocking him to the ground. Being powerfully built, John quickly overpowered the man and bound him hand and foot.

The other guard saw Morse coming out of the corner of his eye and whipped his musket around and fired. Morse went down, hit in the leg. The guard reached for the pistol in his belt, but was knocked to the ground by Hugh before he could fire. Hugh fell on the guard and began choking him. John ran to the fallen Morse, retrieved the rope from him and bound the other guard. Hugh eyed John suspiciously.

"Name's Lt. Jackson; I'm with the Salisbury Militia an' we're here to rescue you folk."

Scout and Peterson successfully bound the fireside guards, having caught them off guard. However, the musket shot awakened the rest of the camp. Mass chaos ensued as children cried out, men cursed, and all able-bodied men lunged for weapons.

Thomas leapt from his perch and ran for Alice. Bull had awakened at the musket shot and pulled Alice up by the hair as he grabbed his musket with the other hand. Seeing himself surrounded, Bull dropped his musket and put his knife against

Alice's neck while holding her firmly with his left arm. Thomas stopped five feet before them with his sword drawn.

"Drop it or I plant 'er," growled Bull.

Thomas's mind flew into high gear as he considered his options. Bull sensed his adversary evaluating his chances, and pressed his knife into Alice far enough to draw blood. Her eyes widened even further, as if they might pop out at any moment. Thomas was close enough to see her face muscles clench when Bull's knife drew blood. Out of the corner of his eye, Thomas detected movement. He swiftly pivoted to his left and slashed across the charging Yorker's chest, sending him to the ground screaming in pain. In one motion Thomas swung all the way around and opened Bull's knife hand. Bull didn't hesitate, pulling his pistol from his belt with his left hand and brought it up. Thomas knocked the pistol to the ground with the flat of the blade, and then put the point of his blade to the Yorker captain's chest.

Bull had released Alice when he reached for his pistol. She had run screaming into the woods. Thomas turned to follow her retreat, which is all the time Bull required to retrieve his pistol and level it at his prey. Thomas turned back to see the pistol coming up to knee level and dove to his left. The shot drove into his leg. Thomas rolled and came up on his feet, slashing Bull's left arm.

A volley of musket fire rang out in the night. In the chaos, it was impossible to determine who'd fired upon whom. Thomas looked around, trying to get a sense of the situation. Three Yorkers fled into the woods. Thomas turned the other way to see a Yorker about to swing his musket at a fallen militiaman. Thomas took two steps and threw himself into the side of the man, taking the partial blow in his left arm. He rolled over and rose to his knees, slashing the Yorker across the back of his legs. The Yorker stayed down, clutching his legs as he rolled on the ground.

Thomas ran off in the general direction that Alice ran. He fell to the ground, forgetting the wound to his leg. With the adrenaline flowing in his veins, he couldn't feel much pain. Thomas looked down and was surprised at the sight of his blood-soaked leg. A strong arm pulled Thomas to his feet. Thomas whipped his sword around to place his point on the man's chest.

"Oh, John, thank God it's you," Thomas said gasping for breath. "Ya hurt bad?"

"Don' know; that'll have t' wait. The prisoners safe?" asked Thomas.

"Think so; got Pumroy guardin' 'em."

"The other woman ran over that way; let's go after 'er," ordered Thomas.

"Wait a minute! Lemme bind ya up," ordered John as he ripped a strip of cloth off his shirt tail.

Thomas yielded as John bent down to tie the cloth around Thomas's lower leg. Then the two men headed off in search of Alice. Both men paused twenty yards beyond the camp. They didn't know which way to go. They crouched down and listened. After several minutes, a woman cried out loudly, and then made muffled sounds before all returned to quiet. Thomas and John headed out toward the cry. They walked cautiously with sword and pistol at the ready, respectively.

After walking about fifty yards they stopped to listen again. They weren't sure if they were still headed in the right direction. Thomas examined the ground, yet the moon failed to yield enough light to find tracks. The thickly packed trees strained out most of the moonlight anyways. The men couldn't see much away from the light of the campfire, and felt blind while they awaited the return of their night vision. They had to rely on hearing and instinct. Immediately Thomas and John heard voices to the right of them.

"What was that?"

"What was what?"

"I heard somethin', o'er that way."

"Doubt it; too early for 'em to come lookin' for 'er. Gotta still be fightin'."

"I tell ya I heard somethin'!"

"Shut up! If ya keep yellin' they will be on us."

"Both o' ya keep it down. Just listen an' keep alert. Truth is we don't know when they comin'."

Then the quiet of the night resumed. John and Thomas tried to gauge the distance of the voices. They crouched as they walked, paying closer attention to what they treaded upon. From a crouching position a faint outline of the terrain could be discerned.

Soon they came upon a clearing in the wood. They stopped behind two trees and peered intently into the night. The clearing allowed more moonlight with which to see. They dared not enter the unprotected open space. In spite of the additional light, they caught no sign of their prey. They waited. Then a low voice emerged out of the far side of the clearing at about ten o'clock.

"Hold onto 'er; I'm gonna check the muskets."

Thomas made out the dim outline of a man at the edge of the clearing. He paused in the shadows, and then moved forward two steps. He held two muskets and turned each one up to the light to check their loads. Satisfied, he returned to the others.

"They both loaded all right."

Thomas and John exchanged hand signals, and then moved around the clearing counterclockwise. They paused after every step and listened. About halfway around the clearing, Thomas stepped on some dried leaves that crinkled under his boot. Both men froze.

"I heard it 'gain."

"That time I did too."

"Alright, you two take the muskets an' check it out. I'll keep an eye on her."

Thomas signaled John to move to the right side of the wide tree, while Thomas took up position on the left. They heard almost indiscernible rustling, as though a gentle breeze moved the leaves. But there was no wind tonight. Thomas switched his sword to his left hand while he wiped the sweat from his right hand on his pants. Then he cleaned off the sword hilt with his sleeve. Both men peered out from behind the tree and strained to see. They waited.

Soon Thomas was able to make out a vague silhouette of a man, walking with a musket at the ready. He walked slowly and panned his head from side to side. Thomas couldn't see the other man. He searched for any sign of the other Yorker, and a wave of nerves rippled through Thomas as he failed to find him. As the visible Yorker neared their tree, Thomas leaned back further behind the tree. He turned back to John and raised two fingers with a question mark on his face. John signaled that another approached on his side of the tree.

Thomas could feel his sword hand pulsing with his heart beat. Sweat trickled down his forehead. He wiped it away to keep his vision clear. Thomas deliberately slowed his breathing, and waited. Not seeing the man appear after what seemed like an hour, Thomas was tempted to look again; however, only through discipline did he restrain himself. He feared the whites of his eyes would give him away.

Thomas started as a musket muzzle pierced the darkness barely two strides from where Thomas hid. For a moment the muzzle didn't move, and Thomas feared he'd been seen. Thomas reminded himself to breath shallow and slow; he knew he must keep his nerves in check. Finally arms attached to the muzzle slowly appeared. Then a leg emerged beneath the arms. Thomas felt an impulse to lunge at the man right away, but again held himself in check. Once the man walked completely beyond the tree Thomas signaled John. On the silent count of three both men leapt out from behind the tree. John pistol-whipped his man on the back of the head; he collapsed without a sound from his mouth. Thomas hit his man on the back of the head with his sword hilt. Thomas's man cried out before losing consciousness.

Thomas turned back around as he heard retreating footsteps. He strained his eyes to catch sight of them, but saw nothing. John picked up both muskets and unloaded them. Then he searched the unconscious men for their powder and ball and found they had none. John pulled off and tore up one of the men's shirts and bound them both with long shirt strips, hand and foot.

John suggested they spread out a few yards to make a smaller profile, and then they headed out after the retreating footsteps. At first they heard nothing, but then a gentle gurgling arose from down to the left. A moment later, Thomas and John came upon a small creek. While John stood guard, Thomas bent down to examine the creek's edge for any signs of tracks. Thomas didn't find any markings at first, and moved up and down the creek, widening his search.

After thirty minutes he came across two sets of footprints entering the creek. He signaled John to come look. As soon as John bent down to examine the tracks, they heard a muffled cry. They looked up and immediately saw a woman tied to a tree across the creek. It was the Litchfield woman. But was she alone? They didn't see anyone else around. Thomas and John backtracked and conferred in whispers.

Thomas remained back in the trees lining the near side of the creek. John forded the shallow creek and cautiously approached the woman. John kept scanning back and forth for an abductor. The woman shook her head and became more agitated once John had reached her. She tried to say something, but the gag allowed only muffled groans. John reached for her bindings, only to find her protest. Puzzled, John took a step back, pondering her agitation. He walked around behind the tree that held the woman fast, but only made it halfway. John heard footsteps and turned just as the Yorker slashed across his left arm with a knife. The Yorker slashed again but John stepped out of the way, holding his arm. John dodged another swing of the knife, but the backhand caught him across the chest. John felt searing pain, yet maintained his wits and jumped out of the way of the next attack. Then the man lunged forward to thrust into his chest, yet strangely stopped short and cried out. He fell to the ground dead.

Thomas had heard John cry out and leapt from his hiding place. He ran around the tree as fast as his leg would allow, seeing the Yorker slash John across the chest. Thomas immediately cut deeply into the man's back, severing his spine and ending his life. Thomas knelt down to make sure the man was dead.

"Hey, how deep 're ya cut?" asked Thomas.

"Don' know for sure. My chest don' seem too bad, but my arm hurts pretty good; can't move it," said John as he winced.

"Lemme help ya out in the light so I can git a look at that arm," suggested Thomas.

Thomas took a look at John's arm and grimaced. He went back to the fallen Yorker and cut a length of his shirt, which he used to bind up John's arm to stop the bleeding. He cut a second bandage and tied it around John's chest. Satisfied with his work, Thomas turned to the woman. He first removed her gag.

"Ma'am, I'm Captain Thomas Chittenden, an' this here's Lt. John Jackson. We're with the Salisbury Militia, sent to come after ya. There's no more Yorkers out here?"

Alice wept in response, and then shook her head from side to side. Thomas went behind the tree and untied her bindings. She fell to her knees as the ropes dropped to the ground.

"Oh, thank God; thank ya God," was all she got out between sobs.

"Are ya hurt anywheres? Ma'am," asked John. Alice continued to weep and looked puzzled at the question. Thomas helped her to her feet. She fell into his arms.

"Okay, it's over now," soothed Thomas. "Can only imagine what you folk been through."

Suddenly Alice stepped back with a look of fear. "Is my family alright?" she asked. Thomas and John exchanged a glance.

"Truth is, we don' know for sure," answered Thomas.

"But we think so," interjected John. "We left to come after ya afore it was over."

"Dear God, let 'em be okay," Alice prayed. "Let's go find my family."

Right as they set out for camp, Thomas noticed his leg throbbing. With each step it seemed to hurt more. By the time they were halfway back, Thomas began to feel light-headed. He stopped and rested on a rock. Thomas walked the rest of the way leaning on John as his limp became more pronounced and his energy evaporated. Alice leaned on the other side of John.

As they neared the Yorker camp, they heard shouts and much excitement. They paused as they reached the edge of the clearing. The Yorkers still alive had their hands bound behind their backs. The six Yorkers were wide-eyed, with some pleading and others demanding their release. Scout looked on with crossed arms as Hugh led the first Yorker to a thick tree, roughly pushed him against the tree and tied three ropes around the prisoner and tree as though one. He did the same to the remaining Yorkers. Hugh stepped back to examine his work. He smiled with satisfaction. Then Hugh tied ropes around each of their necks, cutting into their skin and preventing them from moving their heads at all. At this point John started toward the Yorkers, only to be stopped by Thomas's firm grip on his arm.

"Wait for now," said Thomas.

"How can you..."

"Trust me," Thomas replied simply.

John and Thomas watched as the Yorkers faces reddened. A couple of them began gasping for air. John stood to intervene and looked at Thomas with palms upheld. Thomas put his hand on John's arm to restrain him. Thomas reexamined the Yorker faces and decided they couldn't breath. He stepped out into the clearing and strode to the trees as quickly as his leg allowed.

"It is enough! They have received enough for now," shouted Thomas as he cut each of the ropes binding the Yorkers' necks.

Just then a shot rang out, and one of the Yorkers slumped to the ground. Thomas's eyes darted across the clearing to see a man standing behind the black smoke of a discharged musket.

"Who in God's name fired that shot?" demanded Thomas.

"Ya din't think I'd let ya have all the fun, did ya Cap? Oh, I'm sorry ya thought them ropes an' a green guard gonna keep me outta this. Takes a whole hell o' a lot more 'an that to keep me from doin' my job!"

By now the smoke had cleared enough for Thomas to discern a smirking Haskins. Haskins went down on one knee to reload his musket.

"Damn you, Haskins! Scout, disarm him and retake him prisoner!" shouted Thomas as he staggered.

Thomas could feel his strength failing him and his head became dizzy. By strength of will, he ordered his mind to clear for a moment longer and turned to John.

"Lieutenant, see that order is restored and that no other punishment is given out except under my order," commanded Thomas. At this Thomas collapsed in a faint. John caught him before he struck the ground, and carried him over to Dr. Dickens.

Summer 1749 - Salisbury, Connecticut Colony

Thomas and Ben worked side by side in the barn. Ben was cleaning out the old straw and bringing in fresh, while Thomas fed the animals. Thomas had thought all morning about what he liked about Liz, and why he might want to marry her. He found himself curious about Ben and his relationship with Anna, especially now that they were married.

"So Ben, how be the married life?"

"Why do ya ask?" wondered Ben.

"I'm just wonderin' how ya like being married?"

"Oh, its okay," said Ben.

"Well, can ya tell me a bit more? I'm tryin' t' decide 'bout gettin' married myself," confessed Thomas.

"Oh, so that's what this is 'bout? Okay, so ya lookin' for a little big brother advice then?" Ben continued on, not waiting for an answer.

"Well, I tell ya, little brother, marryin' Anna was the best thing I ever did. I made myself a man, an' I've got my own woman, little brother. It's been great."

"So, what's great 'bout it?" asked Thomas.

Ben laughed scornfully. "Look little brother, ya gotta look at the big picture. When a boy comes to the right age, he's gotta learn that it's time to be a man a' take a wife; otherwise you're gonna be a boy your whole life. How long have ya been courtin' Liz?"

"More 'an a year," answered Thomas.

"Come now, little brother, what're ya waitin' for? If ya been courtin' that long, ya oughta know if she' the right one or not. Maybe it's time ya stepped up an' took on your duties as a man. So what're ya waitin' for anyways?"

"I wanna make sure Liz an' me are the right match," answered Thomas simply.

"What kinda foolish talk is that? All ya need to figure is if Liz be the right girl. We already know you been courtin' the right amount o' time. So, is she or isn't she the right girl?"

"I don' know, Ben; I'm not sure it's that simple for me. I'm not sure I wanna get married for the same reasons as you. I wanna take my time and make sure, at least as best I can, if Liz and me..."

"What do ya mean it isn't that simple? Don't make it harder than it has t' be, little brother. You're thinkin' way too much. Ya been courtin' for a good year, an' if ya aren't havin' no fights then she's the right one. Okay, ya got it?"

"Ya make it sound so easy," replied Thomas; "I'm not sure..."

"Not sure o' what? It is that easy, Thomas. Let me put it this way; how do ya know when it's time to harvest the crops?"

"Well, mostly by lookin' at 'em," answered Thomas.

"That's right, little brother; it's not that hard to tell when to harvest, an' it don' have t' be hard to know when to marry. If the girl looks right and it's the right time, ya just do it!"

"I don' think that way works for me."

"Oh, Thomas, ya hopeless. With that attitude o' yours, ya likely to never marry. If ya won't take it from me, ask Father; he'll tell ya the same thing."

Thomas realized there was nothing else to say at this point. He nodded to Ben and returned to his work. Thomas wondered why he'd bothered to ask Ben about his marriage. By now Thomas had heard Ben's views of marriage many times. Maybe he was hoping for a different response this time.

Thomas finished up his work and wearily headed for the house; it had been a long day of both physical labor on the farm and mental labor trying to sort out things with him and Liz. As Thomas walked through the door, he saw Ben and Father whispering back and forth. They looked up as Thomas walked into the room.

"Hey, Thomas," said Father, "when you're done washin' up, come over here a minute."

Thomas nodded his assent and washed up. He wondered what Father and Ben wanted with him. Thomas figured it had something to do with his conversation with Ben earlier in the day. A discussion with Father regarding a possible wedding was hardly an appealing possibility for Thomas. He dreaded feeling pressured by Father to get married. He took a bit longer washing up so as to give himself more time to think through how he might respond. He slowly walked over to the table.

"So, Thomas, Ben tells me ya thinkin' o' marryin' that gal o' yours," began Father.

"Ya, I'm thinkin' on it," replied Thomas.

"That's good," said Father. Father paused expecting Thomas to volunteer more. Father gave up waiting when Thomas didn't quickly continue.

"An' what's holdin' ya up?"

"I don' know that anythin's holdin' me up; I just need time to think on it a bit more," said Thomas.

"What's there to think on?" asked Father.

"Don't ya think gettin' married's a big enough deal to give it time to think on?" asked Thomas.

Father laughed condescendingly. "Well, I s'pose ya may wanna think some, but there really ain't much to think on, Thomas," said Father. "I think Ben here's got a good point, and I don't want ya to confuse yaself by makin' it too complicated. There's only a few questions that be important, an' let me lay it out for ya real plain; is your girl nice to look at, does she keep her talkin' to a tolerable amount, is she o' strong constitution an' able to bear ya offspring, an' does she seem fit for farm work? That's all ya need to know, son."

"I don' know, Father, it don't seem that simple to me," said Thomas. "I wanna ..."

"Damn it, son, 'course it's that simple!" countered Father. "Don't go talkin' no foolish talk an' makin' this more than it has to be!"

"Maybe it's that simple to you, but maybe it ain't that simple to me!" returned an angry Thomas.

Father looked incredulous. He had little experience with anybody disagreeing with him, at least disagreeing with him openly, and even less experience with anyone expressing anger with him. Father shook his head in disbelief of what he was hearing. "I don't believe what I'm hearin'. Am I hearin' ya talk back to me? That can't be what I'm hearin'!"

"Father, don't ya care 'bout anythin' else with Mama? Don't ya ever just wanna talk with her?" asked Thomas.

"'Course we talk; we talk 'bout the farm an' what needs be done an' if somethin' needs tendin'.'"

"That's not what I mean," countered Thomas. "I mean don't ya ever wanna tell Mama 'bout your day, or how you're doin'? Don't ya ever wanna know 'bout Mama an' her day?"

"What sort o' fool talk is that? That's the sort of damn fool talk o' busybodies that ain't got nothin' better to do with their time! I'm a farmer; I ain't got no time to waste on woman's talk!"

"Well, not for me!" said Thomas. "I think what ya call 'fool talk' be the best kinda talk; maybe the only kinda talk that really matters! The rest o' it don't amount to a hill o' beans!"

Father and Ben had never seen Thomas angry like this. They were now worried. They looked at Thomas with stunned looks of amusement, as if he was the village idiot.

"See, Father," cried Ben, "I told ya he don' get it! Thomas has lost it! I don' know what's gotten into him. He's talkin' jibberish that don't make no sense!"

At this point Father was more concerned than angry. "Thomas, who ya been talkin' to? Ya been talkin' with some women folk in town, or where ya gettin' these fool ideas o' yours?"

"I'm finally beginnin' to think for myself, that's what!" said Thomas. "Nobody tells me how to think. I'm thinkin' for myself at last."

"Oh, I get it," said Father. "That girl o' yours is fillin' ya head with these fool ideas. You be careful son, women folk will get ya thinkin' all kinda crazy thoughts if ya give 'em half a chance."

"Don't put this on Liz," retorted Thomas. "These ideas be my own, an' it's 'bout time I did my own thinkin'. I won't have nobody be tellin' me what to do no more - it's time I did some decidin' on my own!"

"Now ya listen here, son. As long as ya be livin' on my land, ya damn will better listen to me!"

"Well then maybe it's 'bout time I thought 'bout gettin' a place o' my own," said Thomas.

"A place o' your own?" repeated Father.

"That's right," said Thomas.

Father's jaw dropped. He couldn't imagine what had possessed his son to consider such a thing. It had been long decided that Thomas and Ben would take over the Chittenden family land when they came of age. As a matter of fact, the two young men ran the farm right alongside Father, as he groomed them to take over after his passing. Father couldn't fathom what would induce Thomas to reconsider the family plans. Father took several steps back and sat down in a chair, as if absorbing a blow. He'd never considered that any of his offspring might have other plans than his.

"Thomas, I don' know where ya gettin' these crazy ideas o' yours, but I hope ya come to ya senses an' don't do nothin' foolish. I think its right time we ended this conversation afore somebody say somethin' they gonna regret. You think on what I said, boy."

"I think I know where he's gettin' them foolish ideas," interjected Ben. "He's gettin' 'em from that ole man MacDonald. That ole fool is fillin' his head with these damn fool ideas."

"The feed seller? No. Thomas wouldn't waste his time talkin' with him. I don' know where he's gettin' his ideas, but ya worryin' me, son. Ya best just think on what I say before ya go off on some cockamamie idea; ya hear me?"

Father walked out of the room, not waiting for a reply. He was feeling less certain than he sounded. The truth is that Father didn't know what to say to Thomas. He didn't understand Thomas. Ben followed right on his heels, after giving Thomas one last look of exasperation and disdain.

Thomas stood his ground without moving until after Ben and Father had left the room. He took a deep breath and slowly exhaled, surprised at himself. He was unsure of what had just happened. Not having planned what he was going to say, he too felt stunned at the words that came out of his mouth, almost as if they came from someone else.

Thomas walked outside. He looked around, and then rubbed the sides of his head with both hands. He began wandering around, at first in circles. Thomas walked aimlessly as a ship that has lost its anchor in a storm and doesn't know in which direction land lay. He couldn't have said where he'd been during those hours, nor did it occur to Thomas that he'd missed supper. It wasn't until the next morning before he felt his hunger and realized he hadn't eaten since the midday meal the day before.

At first Thomas had trouble thinking clearly; he felt confused, even mildly disoriented. He seemed unable to form any clear thoughts about what had just happened. His mind merely spun and spun without catching, like a phonograph that gets stuck in a scratch. After struggling with his thoughts for time untold, all he could make of it was that something important had just happened, exactly what he couldn't say. Thomas felt worried. He wondered how things would be with Father. Would things continue to be the same, or would he and Father somehow be different? He didn't know what to expect. Thomas feared a change, and yet he didn't wanted things to stay the same.

The only thing that seemed clear was that Thomas needed to see MacDonald as soon as possible. Ben had been right about one thing: Thomas had been talking with MacDonald, and was greatly the better for it. Thomas hoped MacDonald could help him make sense out of what had just happened.

The family anxiously looked up as Thomas entered the house. Mama ran over to Thomas and put her arms around him, relieved he was safe. Between sobs, Mama questioned her son. "Where were ya, Thomas?"

Thomas didn't know how to answer her question. "I, uh, I was walking 'bout," Thomas simply said.

"Whatever for?" asked Mama.

"I, uh, I mean, I needed some fresh air," said Thomas.

Mama searched her son's face, hoping it would provide answers that his words did not. It wasn't like Thomas to be out after dark, and especially alone. She'd heard her husband's and son's animated voices earlier, but hadn't heard the particulars of what was said. All Father would say when asked was something vague about Thomas having some damn fool ideas in his head. Understandably, this didn't clear up Mama's concern over Thomas missing supper and being out after dark; actually it raised her worry. Although she pressed him, Father would say no more about it. Mama was left to wait until Thomas returned. Not finding any answers on his face, Mama pressed Thomas for more.

"Now, Thomas, when do ya ever miss your supper an' stay out this late?"

Thomas wasn't sure how much to say, especially with Father and Ben listening in. "Ya might o' heard that Father an' me had some words, an' I guess I just needed to think on 'em some," said Thomas.

Mama stared into his eyes, and then decided to leave it at that for now. Neither Mama nor Thomas wanted to provoke Father to attempt to resume the conversation. When Mama released Thomas from her embrace, he walked over to Sally and placed a hand on her shoulder. She smiled weakly at him. Thomas could see that Sally had been crying and immediately felt for her. He gently reached down for her hand and led her to her room in the old house so they could talk privately. Thomas took his usual place sitting on the ground with his back against the wall. Sally began crying softly.

"Hey, Sal, did I scare ya?" asked Thomas.

Sally looked up at Thomas with tear-filled eyes, but uttered no verbal reply. She appeared to reflect on her brother's question, yet came up with little to say in response. Sally had overheard the passionate words between Father and Thomas too, although she couldn't hear much of the conversation.

"I don' know... I worried when ya was gone so long, an' I din't know what happened with you an' Father."

Upon further reflection Sally had another thought. "Also, maybe I was afraid ya weren't comin' home."

"Oh, Sally, I'm so sorry I scared ya. I had no thought o' leavin' ya. I just needed a little time alone to think," said Thomas.

Sally nodded. "What happened with Father?" asked Sally.

"Well, I don' rightly know," said Thomas. "We had some angry words... I don' know, I guess I don' want him tellin' me what to do no more... I don' know, I'm still tryin' to figure what just happened... I never talked with Father like that... I figure I'll go an' talk with Mr. MacDonald; maybe he can help me figure it."

"You'd tell me if ya was goin' away, wouldn't ya?" asked Sally.

"Oh, Sally, I don' figure to be goin' no wheres. I'm not leavin' ya, little sis."

"Ya better not; or I'm liable to follow an' track ya down till I find ya," said a mischievously smiling Sally. Thomas laughed and gave Sally a playful pat on her head.

Thomas didn't sleep well that night. He woke every hour or two, replaying his fight with Father. Although he tried not to think about it, it kept coming back to his mind again and again. Thomas kept trying to figure out what he might have said differently, but he couldn't reach any conclusions. Two hours before dawn, he finally arose and walked about the house in his stocking feet. He paced the house for thirty minutes, then finally dressed and went outside to begin his day.

Thomas was in the barn when Father and Ben came in, and Thomas tensed when he heard them. Father merely wished him "good morning," and said nothing more. He felt relieved when Father didn't bring up yesterday's quarrel; he didn't know what he'd say to Father.

Thomas made a point of telling Sally where he was going and then saddled up his horse and headed off to see his old friend. It had been a long night and morning waiting to see MacDonald. Thomas still couldn't make heads or tails of the quarrel, but he was sure that he and Father had never before had that kind of fight. Thomas had certainly been angry with Father before, and even hazarded a word or two in the past; however, he couldn't remember firing back at Father quite like that. At times he doubted whether he'd actually challenged the way Father talked with Mama, not to mention the threat of finding another place to live. Could he have actually said those things, or did he merely imagine them?

Thomas breathed a sigh of relief when he saw MacDonald's cart standing behind the Feed 'n Seed. By now he'd long since learned that if the cart is there so is MacDonald, and if the cart is gone so is its master. MacDonald looked up with a welcoming smile as Thomas entered the back room.

"Weel lad, 'tis been a fine number o' days since ye last visited. 'Tis truly good t' see ye."

"I'm so relieved ya here, Mr. MacDonald. There ain't nobody else I could talk with right 'bout now," responded Thomas.

"That right, lad?"

MacDonald looked with curiosity and concern on his young friend. He knew Thomas well enough to know such a statement foretold his young friend's distress. "Weel then, by all means hae yerself a seat, lad."

Thomas sat down and took several deep breaths. "Guess I don't rightly know what to tell ya. I'm not really sure where to start..." Thomas glanced up at MacDonald, who merely waited. "I guess I'll just tell ya what happened," began Thomas. MacDonald nodded for Thomas to continue.

"Ben an' me was talkin', an' he was pressurin' me to hurry an' make a marriage proposal to Liz. 'Course I told Ben I'd have no one pressurin' me, an' so he goes an' says somethin' to Father 'bout it. Next thing I know, Father's pressurin' me to make a marriage

330

proposal an' be quick 'bout it. I figure I told Father 'bout the same I told Ben, that I'd have nobody tellin' me when to make a proposal an' that I wanted t' think on it. Well, Father din't take too well to me tellin' him such, an' I guess he got angry an' tried pressurin' me all the more. I figure I got a good bit angry an' tried to back him off even more, an' the next thing I know we're talkin' 'bout me maybe findin' another place to live! Damn, Mr. MacDonald, I don' rightly know how we got to that! I don't think I wanna find another place to live."

MacDonald nodded with gravity and rubbed his forehead. "Hoots, lad, that be a big day fo' ye," said MacDonald. "I can see why ye be upset." Thomas nodded and looked at the floor.

"I don' remember ye tellin' me 'bout somethin' like that with yer father afore," MacDonald said.

Thomas thought for a moment. "I don' think I ever stood up to Father quite like that before."

"That be quite a milestone, lad."

"Ya think so?"

"Sure thing, lad, an' why do ye think ye stood up to 'im this time?"

Thomas reflected a minute before responding. "I don' know, I guess I'm just tired o' him tellin' me what to do. I figure I'd just had enough. It makes me mad that he always seems to think he knows what's best for me!"

"There ye go, lad," said MacDonald.

Thomas tilted his head sideways as he gazed up at MacDonald. "I don't get it; where am I goin'?"

MacDonald laughed merrily. "'Tis truly a great day when a boy 'comes a man an' take himself from underneath 'is father's authority. Yer tree's growin' t' be a man's tree, no longer a young sapling. No boy becomes a man withoot pushin' up against those who hae been in authority o'er 'im."

"But how does me gettin' mad at Father make me a man?" asked Thomas.

"'Tis not enough t' be angry t' make ye a man, lad; ye hae t' be ready t' allow yerself t' hate yer father a wee bit so ye can be free with 'im. A boy who can't hate 'is father in moments can never be free with 'im. Ye see, lad, the boy who never frees 'imself t' hate

331

remains forever under 'is father's thumb. It be the only way for ye to take hold o' yer strength."

Thomas stood and walked about the store room. "So, what do I do with my hate now?" asked Thomas.

"I think ye already begun t' do wi' it!"

"How's that?"

"Weel lad, ye done some wi' yer hate last night', an' yer doin' something wi' it right now," answered MacDonald.

Thomas paused to think. His face brightened. The idea that last night was a step toward manhood seemed strange, and yet felt good. The seed of a sense of satisfaction began to shed some light on the fog within his mind. He hadn't considered that something good might have come out of his argument with Father. Thomas had thought he'd done something wrong. He felt like he'd hurt his father; maybe even hurt him real badly.

Thomas spontaneously laughed. He laughed more and more. MacDonald looked curiously at him as a grin emerged on his own face. "Ya know, I never woulda thought it be a good thing to hate, an' I'm still not so sure 'bout it. Some o' the things ya tell me seem the rightest things I ever heard, an' at the same time, 'bout the craziest things I ever heard," said Thomas.

MacDonald nodded and laughed as well. He enjoyed hearing his comments characterized that way.

"So, what do I do now?" asked Thomas.

"What do ye mean, lad?"

"I mean, what 'bout last night? Am I s'posed t' say somethin' to Father?" asked Thomas.

"I think ye said 'nough, lad. Be there somethin' more ye want t' say t' yer father?"

"Uh, no, not really," answered Thomas.

"Then there may not be a thing for ye t' do, lad."

"Ya mean I just act like nothin' happened?" asked Thomas.

"Nae lad, I said nothing o' the kind. Somethin' happened that might change ye forever an' there's no point in denyin' it, but there may be nothing else t' say t' yer father for now."

Thomas looked out the open back door as his thoughts drifted to Liz. He found himself pondering asking her to marry him, strange as that seemed after he'd just finished telling his father and brother he wasn't ready. Oddly enough, he felt more ready to pursue marriage with Liz.

"Ya know, Mr. MacDonald, I feel a bit crazy sayin' as much, but I think I wanna ask Liz to marry me," said Thomas.

"An' do ye feel pressure t' make a proposal t' yer lass?"

"I don' think so," answered Thomas. "I think I kinda want to now."

"Weel lad, 'magine that," said MacDonald. MacDonald slapped his young friend on the shoulder.

Thomas walked his horse slowly up the road toward home. He kicked at the dirt with his boots the way he used to as a boy. In no hurry to get home, Thomas strolled at a leisurely pace while pondering the events of last night and MacDonald's strange response. Before long the Salisbury mill appeared on the horizon. Thomas had not been intentionally heading there, yet somehow had been impelled to go there. His good friend John Jackson lived at the mill along with his family. John and Thomas had known each other since their first year at the town schoolhouse years ago; they started school the same year. Besides his brother Ben, John had become Thomas's best friend soon after starting school. Thomas couldn't have put words to it back then, but he'd immediately been drawn to the quiet John. Although John didn't say much, there was a sense about him that somebody was home.

Thomas talked more and more with John, while less and less with Ben. It saddened Thomas that he and Ben had drifted apart the last couple years. At first he didn't want to admit it to himself that something was changing between him and his older brother. It just seemed like they were becoming more and more different, yet it used to seem to Thomas that they were alike. At times Thomas had considered Ben like his twin brother. Now Thomas felt so different from Ben, it was as though they were from two different families.

As Thomas approached, he noticed John working the mill. Water flowed from the river through the mill race and into the mill, creating a soothing sound of fast running water. Thomas had always loved the sound of running water. He dismounted and washed his hands and face in the tail race, which flowed back into the river. Refreshed from the water, Thomas stood up and made his way up the stairs into the mill. John looked up as he heard approaching footsteps and smiled. John waved Thomas over as he working the millstones.

"Hey, John," Thomas greeted his friend.

"Hi there." Thomas sat down on a nearby bench as he watched John work.

"How ya be?" asked Thomas.

"I'm right fine; an' you?"

"Got somethin' on my mind. Ya gotta minute?" asked Thomas.

"Yeah sure, just lemme finish up with this one real quick."

Thomas nodded. John finished grinding the wheat grain, bagged it up, and sat down on a stump.

"Okay, my friend, shoot," invited John.

"Well, I guess I'm fixin' to, uh, well I'm thinkin' o' askin' Liz to marry me."

"Really? That's great! I din't know you were even considerin' that yet," said John.

"I din't really know I was considerin' it neither."

John laughed. "How could ya not know?" asked John.

"I don' know," answered a laughing Thomas. "Anyways, John, ya know me 'bout as good as most, an' I wanna know what ya think 'bout it."

"Ho boy, what do I think; what do I think 'bout what?"

"I don' know; I guess I wanna know what ya think o' Liz, an' if ya think me an' Liz be a good match."

"Shoot, Thomas, I ain't been 'round Liz much. What I seen o' Liz I like, but I ain't seen much. I s'pose I know more 'bout you an' Liz from what you have told me yaself. I don't know if I got any concerns 'bout the match, but maybe a concern 'bout Liz."

"What's that?" asked Thomas.

"Well, shoot, Thomas, I don't wanna go shakin' bushes that ain't got nothin' in 'em."

"Come on, John, say what ya gotta say. If ya got a concern, I wanna hear it. There ain't nobody but MacDonald that knows me better 'n you."

"Alright," said John. "Well it's like this; I know Liz lost her pa a bit ago, right?"

"Yeah."

"Well, I just wonder if she be ready to marry so soon after," said John.

"What's that got to do with anything?" asked Thomas.

"Well, maybe nothin', but...I don' know, Thomas, maybe it's not a good idea me bringin' this up."

"No, no, if ya gotta concern I wanna hear it out; maybe I don't sound so open," suggested Thomas.

"Well, now that ya mention it, ya do sound a bit protective o' Liz."

"Yeah, probably I am. No really, John, I wanna hear this; I'll try an' be open-minded."

"I don' know, Thomas. Liz din't lose her pa too long ago, an' I 'magine she misses 'im somethin' terrible. Maybe it's got somethin' to do with her wantin' to marry so soon after. I don' know, Thomas; it may have nothin' to do with it. Now din't ya tell me you was feelin' pressured by Liz?"

"Yeah," said Thoma. "Well, I hate t' admit it, but ya probably got a point there. I s'pose it be somethin' t' think on; I 'preciate your honest thoughts, John."

"You bet. Maybe I'm off base here, but see where it takes ya."

The next day Thomas went to see Liz. Thomas had decided to ask Liz about her reasons for wanting to marry him, having determined that John brought up something well worth considering. Liz and Thomas had discussed marriage a few times, yet Thomas wasn't sure he knew the reasons for Liz wanting to marry him. Thomas arrived at the Lewis farm well into the afternoon.

Liz put her foot in the stirrup and jumped up behind Thomas. Thomas walked his mare while they talked, catching up with each other. Liz talked about her difficulty with her depressed mother; Thomas discussed his angry argument with Father. Both found their burden a bit lighter after. Once they reached town, Thomas and Liz went into the tavern and sat down in the far corner. They ordered a simple meal. After the food came, Thomas decided to broach the concern on his mind.

"So, Liz, I been thinkin' more 'bout gettin' married," began Thomas.

"You have?" said an excited Liz.

"Yeah. Ya know, I been thinkin' over my own reasons for wantin' to marry ya, an' when the right time be."

"Yes," said Liz.

"Anyways, I been wonderin' some 'bout your reasons too," continued Thomas. "I guess I'm wonderin' why ya think ya wanna marry me?"

"You really don't know?" asked a surprised Liz. "Thomas, it's because I love you! Don't you know that by now?"

Thomas reached for Liz's hand and squeezed it. He knew she loved him, as he loved her, but it felt good to hear her say it again.

"Yeah, I figure I know that by now. I guess I was wonderin' 'bout somethin' else... This might be hard to talk 'bout. Liz, I know ya losin' ya father cut ya real deep..."

"What does that have to do with anything?" interrupted an angry Liz. Liz stiffened and let go of Thomas's hand.

"Wait. Give me a chance to finish, an' please don' be mad. I need t' ask ya 'bout this, an' I know it be a sore subject for ya," said Thomas.

Liz nodded her agreement to hear him out. "Let me go 'bout this from a different direction," continued Thomas. "I've given quite a bit o' thought t' my own reasons for waitin' to ask ya t' marry me. I figure I been takin' my slow, sweet time partly 'cause I wanna be sure ain't nobody else pressurin' me t' marry - not Father, not Ben, an' not you. I figure that be a thing for me, that I gotta be sure I'm decidin' for myself. I don' know, maybe I waited longer 'n I needed to. God knows I loved ya for a long time now. I guess what I'm tryin' t' git at is if ya think ya might wanna marry me partly 'cause ya miss your father so bad."

At first Liz felt her anger rise again at the mention of her father, but after hearing Thomas out she softened. She could now hear the spirit of concern in his words, and it helped that Liz could hear that Thomas pondered his own reasons as well as hers. Liz looked up at Thomas and smiled weakly. Thomas picked up and squeezed her hand and waited.

"Yes, I do miss Papa," began Liz, "and I still think about him almost every day. I hadn't thought about that having anything to do with me wanting to marry you, but maybe it is related. I guess I'd have to give it some thought. Right now I'm struggling with being angry with you for bringing Papa into this."

Thomas nodded and continued to hold Liz's hand while she wiped her eyes. "Ya know, Liz, I think ya already gave me what I'm lookin' for from ya." Liz looked at Thomas quizzically.

"Just ya bein' open to considerin' that ya losin' your father might be related tell me all I need to know," continued Thomas.

"I don't understand," said Liz. "I said I didn't know if Papa was related to me wanting to marry you."

"I know, but 'tis enough for me that ya open to lookin' at that part o' your tree. Ya see, that's part o' what I love 'bout ya, Liz. I love ya for bein' the kind o' person that looks at her own tree an' faces whatever ya see. I don' know many that're willin' t' do that."

Liz smiled as understanding dawned upon her. It felt strange to her to be valued for such a thing. Aunt Hannah and Thomas were the only two people she knew who seemed to value self reflection.

"Well, I think I'm satisfied," said Thomas. "How do you feel 'bout gettin' married?"

"Thomas, I'm ready. You're the kind of person I want to be with. I respect your character and love the man I know you to be. You know, as much as you angered me by bringing up Papa, I like that you're the kind of person that asks hard questions. I like how hard you work at your own tree; you dig around in the roots, surround yourself with some people who will tell you straight what they see, and you work at giving your tree good food to eat," said Liz.

It was Thomas's turn to smile. He felt known by Liz. The more they talked, the less it seemed like they were about to marry because of any external reasons. He couldn't have said exactly why, but the time did seem right to move forward, and the fit seemed good. They seemed to fertilize one another's trees, helping each other to grow.

"Liz, let's go t' the cave."

"Alright."

Thomas led Liz to the cave. Thomas thought of Ben as he ducked to enter, and couldn't remember the last time he and Ben had gone to the cave together. Ben said the cave was for kids and that he was too old for that now. Thomas now enjoyed visiting the cave with Liz or Sally. Ben seemed too much like an adult now.

Liz waited outside while Thomas went inside first, as he explained that he wanted to get it ready before she came in. A minute or two later he popped his head out and invited her in. Thomas seated Liz in his chair and knelt before her on one knee.

Thomas gently took her smooth hand in his rough hand. Thomas paused a moment, and then spoke.

"Elizabeth Cranfield, will ya agree t' be my wife?" said Thomas.

"Oh yes, yes, yes!" Liz jumped up in her excitement.

"Okay, now sit yaself back down," said Thomas with a smile.

Liz sat and Thomas pulled a handkerchief out of his pocket. When Thomas unfolded the handkerchief, a small wooden box emerged. The box was of deep brown grain, held together by a brass hinge.

Thomas opened the box and offered Liz the ring it contained. The ring sparkled in the candlelight as soon as the box opened, the silver brightly reflecting the candle flame into Liz's eyes. Liz squealed in delight as she saw it, reflexively putting her hands to her mouth. Liz took the ring from Thomas and slipped it onto her ring finger. She carefully examined the simple silver band.

"Thank you, Thomas. It's beautiful! Where did you get it?"

"Look inside it," suggested Thomas.

Liz pulled the ring back off to inspect the inside, and noticed an engraving in small, worn letters. She squinted to read the name - Mary.

"Who's Mary?"

"Mary Chittenden's my great-grandmother who moved t' the colonies from England. My grandmother gave it to me when I was small. I guess I was kinda her favorite," said Thomas with an embarrassed grin. "I guess I been savin' it for when I met somebody."

Liz threw her arms around Thomas and cried. She'd feared this day might never come after the last few difficult weeks they'd had. She'd tried to be patient as Aunt Hannah had urged many times, and now she was grateful that she hadn't given up.

Ever since he and Liz had begun courting, Thomas had fantasized about proposing to Liz inside his secret cave. For some reason he couldn't put words to, it seemed like the fitting location to have such an important encounter with Liz. Thomas held Liz and enjoyed the moment, as tears slowly welled up in his eyes. Thomas too had not known if he and Liz would get this far, having seriously doubted it the last few weeks. Thomas picked Liz up and set her down in his lap as he sat down in his favorite chair. They sat for a long time holding one another and talking softly in the candlelight, neither of them wanting the moment to end.

May 23, 1753 - Hampshire Grants

Thomas opened his eyes and at first stared blankly. He lay on his back. His eyes refused to focus, and all he could make out appeared vaguely brown and indistinct. Thomas blinked several times - still nothing. He rubbed his eyes with both hands and looked again. The brown object slowly came into focus, yet he didn't know where he was. He massaged his eyes again and only then could discern his familiar canvas tent. Thomas stared blankly without thoughts forming. He felt a cold dampness on his forehead. Then he noticed a dull pain in his leg. He reached down and felt his heavily bandaged leg. His head felt light. Then thoughts began to come to him.

"How'd I git in my tent?"

Glancing to the left, he noticed the familiar objects within: his saddlebags, pistols, hat, and sword. Thomas looked to the right and saw Dr. Dickens entering the tent and then he kneeled next to him.

"Welcome back, Captain. Ya been out a long time," said Dr. Dickens. "Ya gave us quite a worry."

"I'm all in a sweat," said Thomas.

"Yep. Ya fever just broke," said Dr. Dickens.

"How long I been out?"

"Let's see; thirty or thirty-two hours."

"I have?" said a surprised Thomas.

"Yep. Ya fainted right when ya got back to camp, an' been out since," explained Dr. Dickens.

"How'd I sleep through the whole o' the next day?"

"Ya nearly bled to death! The musket shot ya took in the leg ain't too bad an' don't normally cause that kinda blood loss if ya stay put. But ya lost much o' ya blood stayin' on it and runnin' 'round like ya did," said Dr. Dickens.

Thomas turned his head and thought in silence. "What 'bout them prisoners; they all right?" asked Thomas.

"They in pretty fair shape, considerin' what they been through. All o' 'em are malnourished, an' with bruises on their wrists an' necks."

"None o' 'em hurt in the fight?" Thomas inquired.

"Just one o' the men; bandaged up a couple knife wounds he took during the battle."

"I gotta go see Lt. Jackson," Thomas said. Thomas attempted to raise himself up, but felt dizzy and laid back down.

"Captain, you ain't goin' anywhere just yet," instructed Dr. Dickens. "I'll bring Jackson to you."

John pulled back the tent flat to see Thomas with his eyes closed, and thought he was asleep again. He turned to go when he heard Thomas's weak voice.

"Come on in here, John. What happened to ya arm?" said Thomas as he noticed John's heavily bandaged arm.

"Ya don' remember?" Thomas stared blankly, and then shook his head.

"Got that from the Yorker that had Alice," explained John.

"Alice?"

"That be the woman we rescued the other night. Yorker was 'bout to slice me up good, afore you came 'round the tree an' finished him off," continued John.

Thomas frowned as his memories yielded vague and porous fragments. "I think I remember that. So we got her back okay?"

"Yeah. All the Litchfield folk 're alright. They shaken up pretty good, but they gonna be alright," said John. They eatin' like they ain't seen food in awhile."

"All the men okay?" John hesitated and looked away.

"Who did we lose?" asked an anxious Thomas.

"Just one... uh, Morse din't make it. He took a musket ball when we was takin' out the guards. Bled to death afore the doc could git to 'im," said John sadly.

Thomas turned his face away. "Damn! That gonna be hard on 'is young wife," Thomas lamented.... "Nobody else hurt then?"

"Dr. Dickens patched up a number o' us, but everybody else gonna make it. You were the one that worried us," said John.

"So what happened after we got back from gettin' Alice?"

"Ya don't remember the tree lynchin'?"

Thomas looked blankly at first. "Oh, yeah, we came back just in time," said Thomas.

"Well, ya fainted right after. Ya gave me quite a fright," admitted John.

"Any Yorkers dead?" asked Thomas.

"Six. The Yorker captain an' three others din't make it through the fight; plus the one ya kilt savin' my hide, plus the one Haskins's kilt."

"Really? I wonder if the captain mighta been my doin'," said Thomas.

"Yeah, Scout said he saw ya cut 'im up pretty good. Dr. Dickens figures he bled to death afore he could get to 'im. Said he din't think he coulda done much for 'im anyways."

"Who's in charge o' the Yorkers now?"

"Lt. Bill Deeters. Turns out he's the brother o' the dead captain. They together had a New York grant to the same plot as the Litchfields."

Thomas sat up slowly as he took in all that had happened during his unconsciousness. He felt an urge to meet with the Litchfield folk, as well as the Yorkers. "Guess we'll have to talk 'bout what to do next," said Thomas.

"That'll have to wait till ya feelin' better," said John.

"Naw. I been restin' long enough. Help me up," asked Thomas.

John helped Thomas to his feet. He was too weak to walk on his own, so John lent himself as a crutch. John led Thomas over to where the Litchfield folks sat eating their breakfast. They were talking energetically amongst themselves. When Alice saw Thomas, she lept to her feet and threw her arms around Thomas, almost knocking him to the ground.

"Ya'll have to excuse me, Ma'am. I still ain't got my strength," said Thomas as he recovered his balance.

"I'm so sorry," offered Alice as tears welled up in her eyes. "I don't know how to tell ya how grateful I am that you an' the Lieutenant here rescued me. To think o' what might of...."

"Thank God we came in time. Thank God we was in time for all o' ya," said Thomas as he looked to the rest of the freed prisoners.

By now Daniel had stood up and came over to Thomas. "Name's Daniel, an' Alice here's my wife; thank ya kindly for bringin' her back alive. That Bull was an evil man. Can't say I'm sorry he's gone," said Daniel.

"Ya welcome, all o' ya. All o' ya done well to just survive out here. I can't even 'magine what ya all been through. Ya outta be proud o' yaself for not givin' up. We'll talk later 'bout what's gonna happen next. I ain't got much energy for more 'an sayin' hello."

Then Thomas turned to John. "John, I wanna talk to the Yorker in charge," said Thomas.

John offered Thomas his shoulder to lean on and led him over to the Yorkers. They sat around the campfire with their hands bound in front. One leg of each Yorker was tied on a common rope that bound them all together. Pumroy and Peterson stood nearby guarding them. Most of them bore a defeated countenance. One or two appeared defiant. Three of them lay on blankets nearby, too wounded to be a threat and were not bound. All of them evidenced bruised necks.

"Which one is he?" asked Thomas.

John pointed to Lt. Bill Deeters. Thomas whispered something to John, and then limped slowly to a nearby tree and waited, leaning up against the tree. John motioned for Deeters to be untied, and John led him over to where Thomas waited.

"Lt. Deeters, I'm Captain Chittenden of the fourteenth regiment of the Colony of Connecticut," Thomas began. "Are you an' ya men bein' treated fairly?" Deeters thought for a moment and then slowly nodded his head.

"Good. So I figure this all been over a land dispute then," summed Thomas.

Deeters stared off in the distance and shrugged his shoulders before responding. "Them damn Connecticut folk was squatters on our land. We was tryin' to reason with 'em to git off our land."

"What do ya mean, your land?" asked Thomas.

"I mean we gotta legal land grant from the Governor o' New York, an' we found these damn Connecticut boys pokin' 'bout on our land when we went t' claim it."

"Who's we?"

"My brother an' me," answered Deeters as he pointed to one of the freshly dug graves just outside the camp. He then continued

343

sadly. "Well, he's gone now; died in the fight the other night. Never thought anybody'd be able to git him.... I still can't believe he's gone."

Deeters averted his face for a moment. Then Deeters's face suddenly changed, as if he flipped a switch. "Them damn Connecticut boys had no right to be on our land, an' they would listen to no reason 'bout gittin' off. So we had to be real convincin', know what I mean?"

"Takin' 'em prisoner was the answer then?" asked Thomas.

"That's right, Connecticut boy. They wunt listen t' nothin' else," retorted Deeters.

"Well, we'll talk 'bout what else later; I ain't got the energy right now," answered Thomas.

Thomas nodded to Pumroy and then went back to his tent with John's assistance. On the way back, a loud voice called out.

"Hey, there be the yella-bellied, green horn captain! When ya gonna be man 'nough to face me man-to-man?"

"I ain't got the energy t' deal with ya now, Haskins."

Chambers brought Thomas some food. His hunger increased each moment he remained awake. Once he finished eating, he went back to sleep. He intended to nap for a couple of hours. The next thing he knew, the morning sun backlit his tent. He awoke disoriented. He thought it was late afternoon, but the sun was in the wrong location. After pulling back the tent flat, he figured out he'd slept through the whole night.

Before even trying to think or talk meaningfully to anyone, he needed a cup of coffee. Thomas was able to get up on his own strength, feeling a bit stronger. He stumbled at his first step, having forgotten his leg. He strapped on his sword and left the tent. John already had the fire rebuilt and a pot warming over it.

"Mornin', John."

"Mornin'."

"Don't believe I can think till I get some o' that in me," said Thomas.

John just nodded and gave Thomas a groggy grin. He untucked his shirt and held the tail in his hand in order to be able to hold the hot coffee pot, pouring himself a generous cup.

"I wasn't woke up, so I guess the rest o' the night went okay?" asked Thomas.

"Well, I wasn't woke neither, so I guess so. I checked on the Yorkers; they mostly still sleepin'. I haven't seen the Litchfield folk yet."

"I think I'll stretch my legs a bit an' clear my thoughts; I'll be back in a bit," said Thomas.

Thomas sipped his coffee and limped off to be alone with his thoughts. Along the way he found a suitable branch to serve as a makeshift crutch. Thomas had much more energy than yesterday, and was ready to do some thinking. He felt greatly relieved to have accomplished the mission. The prisoners were free. Thomas's relief was short-lived as he pondered what to do now. Nothing came to mind.

"Do we jist pack up an' leave? Do we arrest them Yorkers an' bring 'em back for justice? An' what 'bout them Litchfields - do we jist leave 'em free to go out here in the wilds? Or do we escort 'em back safely to Litchfield? Or is there somethin' I ain't even thinkin' of? What would ya do here, my ole friend?" wondered Thomas aloud. "What would ya tell me if ya sat right here, Robert MacDonald?"

It wasn't too long before Thomas found himself remembering his conversation with MacDonald the day before he left on the mission. After meeting with Lt. Chambers to discuss supplies, Thomas stopped by the Feed 'n Seed. He remembered MacDonald's words clearly.

"Mr. MacDonald, I don' know if I'm ready for somethin' like this. I ain't never been on a mission afore. What am I gonna do?"

"Aye, lad, ye don't have much military experience t' draw 'pon. At the same time ye have plenty experience o' another kind. There be few others that I've met that be able to read a man or woman's tree the way ye can. Ye've learnt well t' hear when yer own tree needs tendin', an' likewise ye can hear it in 'nother. There be more t' leadin' men than knowing how t' set 'em for battle. That's fine 'n all, but ye have an ability t' read men that 'tis more rare than ye give yerself the credit for. Ye're no longer a boy. Ye be a man now, lad. Ye're men'll need a captain that can read 'em an' know how t' respond."

Thomas smiled as he savored his old friend's words again. His heart warmed. As he thought more about what MacDonald had said, he recalled that Liz had said something similar the night before he'd left. He longed to see Liz again, and reached into his pocket for her locket. It calmed him to see her image.

His mind seemed a bit clearer now, but he still didn't know exactly what he'd do. However, he now knew where to begin. Once he got a feel for the Yorkers' and the Litchfields' trees, he'd talk things over with John. Thomas headed back to the camp and found John still by the morning fire.

"Why don' we head over an' talk with the Litchfield folk?" suggested Thomas.

The two men found the freed prisoners just awakening and rubbing their wrists and ankles. Thomas winced as his eyes focused on the raw red marks on their ankles and wrists. Dr. Dickens treated some of their ankles that evidenced infection, and now were covered in bandages.

"How'd you folk sleep?" John inquired.

"Best we slept in many days, sir," answered Alice.

"Glad to hear it," said John.

"Everybody got what they need - food, water, anything else?" asked Thomas.

After looking at one another, Daniel answered for the newly freed prisoners. "We been taken pretty good care o'. Lt. Jackson and Lt. Chambers taken right good care o' us. Though we ain't ate this mornin' yet."

"Well go on an' reacquaint yourself with Chambers, and after ya get some food in ya we'll talk 'bout what we gonna do next," said Thomas.

At this the Litchfield folk followed Thomas over to Chambers, who was bent over a fire cooking breakfast for everyone. Chambers had constructed a stone oven at the edge of the fire. Smells of freshly baking bread streamed out between rocks. On a pan nearby, bacon sizzled.

"Lieutenant, look an' see what the Yorkers got for supplies if ya ain't already done so, an' take whatever food looks useful. I want you t' feed the Yorkers after everyone else been fed."

"I figured that, Captain, and already helped myself to them Yorkers' food. Thank goodness they had plenty; must o' recently resupplied. I figured ya'd expect me to feed 'em anyways, knowin' how ya are 'bout fair treatment an' all."

Thomas and John grabbed some grub and talked privately while the others ate their breakfast. "I been so focused on freein' them Litchfield folk, I'm not sure what to do with 'em now," said Thomas.

"While you sleepin' I been wonderin' the same thing. An' what're we gonna do with them Yorkers?"

Thomas paused while he stuffed another strip of bacon in his mouth. "Don' know yet; any ideas?"

"Did the Gov'nor say anythin' 'bout what t' do after?" asked John.

"No. All he said was to free them prisoners," said Thomas.

"We can't jist let 'em go. If I was them Yorkers, I'd just take 'em Litchfields prisoner again soon as we gone," said John between bites of biscuit.

"Agreed, we can't jist pack up an' leave."

"So do we take them Yorkers back to the magistrate in Connecticut, or maybe in the New York colony? Whose authority they under anyways?" asked John.

"That's the whole problem: there ain't no clear authority out here in the Grants. The first crime was committed in the Colony of Connecticut, but we caught 'em out here in the Grants."

"I figure we ain't gonna get no help from anybody else; we gonna have to figure out what to do with 'em on our own," said John.

Thomas nodded. "Sure would be easier to jist turn 'em over to somebody, but there ain't nobody to give 'em to. Well, we gotta do somethin' with 'em Yorkers ourself. We can't let 'em take them poor Litchfields again. An' the Litchfields - do we escort 'em back to their home? An' I don' wanna be lookin' over my shoulder neither - do we leave them Yorkers with any kind o' weapon? Maybe we oughta start by askin' them Litchfields what they want now."

Thomas and John finished their breakfast, handed their plates to Chambers, and walked over to where the Litchfields sat.

"In all honesty folks, our official mission be over now that ya all are free," began Thomas. "At the same time, I hate to just leave ya here. Is there somethin' else we might do for ya?"

The four looked at each other. Hugh spoke. "Well, we was hopin' you would make them Yorkers leave us be with our land grant. Ya see, we got a New Hampshire grant from the Governor himself, legal an' everything."

"What do ya mean, make 'em leave ya be?" asked John.

"We want them Yorkers to realize the land's ours an' not theirs," said Hugh.

"I don' know if it's as easy as that; ya see, the Yorkers believe they got a legal land grant too," said John.

"Don't you believe us?" asked May. "Our grant is for real!"

"We believe you, Ma'am, an' we also believe them Yorkers think they got a legit grant from the Governor of New York," Thomas said.

"You sayin' ya think our grant is no good?" asked an angry Hugh.

"No, that's not what I'm sayin'," answered Thomas. "I'm sayin' I understand there's quite a problem out here in the Grants. New York grantin' land, New Hampshire grantin' land, an' in your case, both grantin' the same land."

"What we're sayin' is that you Connecticut folk probably still gotta problem. Ya no longer tied up, but seein' as you both got legal grants to the same land, it ain't over," interjected John.

"So what're you suggestin' we do?" asked Daniel.

"Look, if ya want us to escort ya home, we will. But have ya considered workin' somethin' out with them Yorkers?" suggested Thomas.

"I don't wanna work out nothin' with bad men that take folk prisoner," said an angry Alice.

"Yeah, they bad men, an' we don't want nothin' to do with 'em," said May. May's words were angry, but she said them with a surprising lack of emotion. Her voice sounded flat.

"Hey, we ain't sayin' what them Yorkers did was right; no question they did you folk wrong takin' ya prisoner," began John. "But jist the same, you folks..."

"Wait a damn minute! That's our land an' we intend to live on it!" retorted Alice. "Them Yorkers will just have to go somewhere's else!"

"Do ya think them Yorkers are just gonna go away an' give ya the land?" asked Thomas. "Ya gonna spend the rest o' ya lives lookin' over your shoulders if ya don't work somethin' out with 'em."

"Now you listen here..." This was all Alice got out before Daniel intervened.

"Now hold on there! These men 're right. I hate to admit it, but if we don't work out some kinda deal with the Yorkers, we'll always be wonderin' when they comin' back. Do you wanna risk being takin' prisoner again, or worse? Think o' the children. No, we gotta work somethin' out. I ain't gonna live like that."

At this point silence reigned. The wisdom of Daniel's words sunk into the minds of the other three. None of them wanted to spend the rest of their lives wondering if their children were safe. In all fairness to the newly freed prisoners, negotiating a business deal with the men who threatened their lives amounted to a tall order. John and Thomas gave them time to think over their options. They didn't want to force the Litchfield folk to do anything, but they also didn't want to leave them to the whim of the Yorkers. After several minutes, Hugh spoke.

"Alright, alright, I git it. We have to make some kind o' deal. I can't live like that neither, always lookin' out for 'em."

"I hate the idea of agreein' to anything with those evil men!" simmered Alice.

"I know, Alice, believe me - I'd rather kill 'em than give 'em anythin', but think o' the other choice!" said Hugh.

Alice sighed deeply. "I know ya right; I just don't know if I can do it. What 'bout you, May?"

"What 'bout what?" said May flatly. She was making a statement here, not truly asking a question.

"I know, May, I know. I wish there was another way, I really do. What if Daniel an' I did all the negotiatin'?" suggested Hugh.

May looked at him blankly. Alice realized she wasn't there again and came to her aid. Alice understood Hugh probably didn't understand how May went away to cope. "Okay, you an' Daniel work it out with those animals. I don't wanna have nothin' to do with them, an' I don't think May can have nothin' to do with 'em neither."

Hugh and Daniel looked at each other and nodded. "Alright, we'll talk with 'em, but we gonna need you boys to help make sure things don't git ugly," said Daniel.

"That's why we still here," agreed Thomas.

Thomas and John decided to talk privately with the Yorker lieutenant. Deeters initially resisted the idea of negotiating with the Connecticut folk, insisting they'd already made them a fair offer. Upon further reflection, Deeters reluctantly agreed to meet with the Connecticut boys and see what they had to say. Although it didn't sound promising, Thomas accepted his reluctant participation as good enough for a first step.

Thomas and John left Deeters and walked far enough to talk privately. "What'd ya think, John?" asked Thomas.

"I don't know; I don't trust 'em."

"No. There's no reason to trust 'em yet," answered Thomas.

Thomas glanced up and noticed Hugh walking over to where the Yorkers were tied up. Hugh's behavior seemed strange, and Thomas instinctively kept an eye on him. Then Hugh charged the Yorker lieutenant, knocking him off the rock he sat on. Hugh got two good blows in before John knocked Hugh to the ground. Hugh made an attempt to get up and reengage the Yorker until he felt the steel of Thomas's blade across his neck.

"Whadda ya think ya doin'?" demanded Thomas.

"Do ya think I'm gonna let them damned Yorkers go unpunished for what they done to us?" Hugh growled.

"Not on my watch. An' do ya think this be the way to work somethin' out with 'em?"

"Whadda ya mean? You think they ain't deservin' o' punishment?" asked an incredulous Hugh.

"Even if I thought that be true, I won't allow ya to attack a bound an' unarmed man," insisted Thomas.

"Oh, so untie 'em so I can give 'em what he's got comin'."

"No. I won't allow that neither," said Thomas.

Hugh's face reddened with anger. He wasn't used to being thwarted in his plans. He slowly stood up, mindful of the blade that still pointed in his direction. Thomas had removed the blade from Hugh's neck but kept it trained in his direction so as to discourage further attack.

"Well, then ya must be plannin' t' give them damn Yorkers their due yourself," concluded Hugh.

"Don't ya figure that already been done? Look at his neck, an' look at the fresh graves," said Thomas.

"That ain't enough! Ya ought to lemme finish the job! Ya damn well better give 'em their due if you gonna deny me the pleasure!"

"Who made me judge over you an' them?" asked Thomas. "That ain't my place."

"Then if you ain't gonna punish 'em damn Yorkers proper, what good 're you?"

At this point John inserted himself in the conversation. "Listen here," John began, "we ain't gonna let you abuse them Yorkers any more than we gonna let them Yorkers abuse you!"

"Ya mighty late on our account!" retorted Hugh.

"Which I regret," said Thomas.

"Ain't it right for me to give 'em what he gave us?"

"An eye for an eye, then. Is that it? Our job is t' stop an' prevent any foul play," said Thomas.

"Ya mean t' say ya puttin' them damn Yorkers on the same level as us?" asked an incredulous Hugh.

"As far as preventin' foul play, that's exactly what I be sayin'," said Thomas.

"I git ya dilemma there, Connecticut boy, this here yella-bellied captain ain't got no stomach to give out proper punishment," yelled out Haskins. "If it be up to me...."

"Damn it, Scout, shut him up!" shouted Thomas.

"Now come off it, Scout, ya ain't gonna..." But that was as much as Haskins got out before Scout gagged him.

At this point Hugh kicked at the dirt in disgust and wandered back to his family in a huff. John and Thomas watched him kick a nearby tree as he cursed angrily.

"I'll instruct the men t' keep an eye on Hugh," said John.

"An' what 'bout Haskins? Do I keep 'im gagged all the time?" wondered Thomas.

"Damn if I know. He sure is a pain in the arse."

As John went off to inform the men of the risk to the Yorkers, Thomas turned to see to the Yorker lieutenant. "Ya hurt?" asked Thomas.

"Not much, thanks t' you," said the Yorker. "Why did ya stop 'im? I thought ya was on their side?"

"Like I said, I be on the side o' fair play," said Thomas.

Deeters gave Thomas a look of surprise and respect, mingled with the confusion of still not understanding Thomas. He wondered if Thomas was setting him up. Deeters made a mental note to keep an especially keen eye on Thomas.

"Look, I'll do my part t' see t' fair play, an' you see t' your part," said Thomas.

"Them Connecticut boys should've done their part when they had the chance back when," said Deeters.

"When they had the chance?" asked Thomas.

"That's right; you ask them Connecticut boys what happened back on the grant before."

"What happened?" pressed Thomas.

"Naw, I said enough. Ya ask them damn Connecticut boys 'bout that."

While Thomas talked with Deeters, John decided to have a conversation with Hugh. John worried that the situation might get out of control if any further incidents broke out. It seemed strange to John that the Yorkers they'd tracked for weeks were now the prisoners they protected. John waited until the grumbling settled down amongst the Litchfield folk, wanting to let Hugh have a little time. John thought he might do better to talk with Hugh and Daniel at the same time, having observed Daniel the steadier of the two. John found the two men talking quietly as he approached.

"Gentlemen, might I have a word?" asked John.

"'Bout what?" grumbled Hugh.

"We're not ya enemy," said John calmly.

"I'll be the judge o' that," simmered Hugh.

"Now hold on, Hugh," soothed Daniel. "Let's hear 'im out."

"Seems t' me that we can best be o' service by keepin' the peace while you boys work somethin' out with them Yorkers," explained John.

"We'll work it out with our fists!" growled Hugh.

"Now hold on, hear 'im out," insisted Daniel.

John paused to allow the effect of Daniel's words to sink into the easily angered Hugh. "Like the captain explained, we mean t' keep the peace no matter who starts the trouble," continued John. "Now, I get ya wantin' to pay back them Yorkers for what they done t' ya; I'd probably try somethin' myself if I was you. But startin' fights with 'em ain't gonna fix nothing for sure, an' it might take away any chance ya have t' work somethin' out. I suggest ya think over real good what's ya best course."

At this John stood up and walked away before Hugh had a chance to say something he might later regret. Just then Thomas walked up, waving John to rejoin him with the Litchfield men.

"Gentlemen, a word please," asked Thomas.

Daniel nodded his assent while Hugh merely glared, still flushed with anger. Thomas looked to see that John had joined him before he began; he wanted John to hear this.

"Tell us what happened before," said Thomas.

"What else do ya wanna know; we already told ya everything them damn Yorkers done to us," returned Hugh.

"That's not what I'm askin'. I wanna know what happened before you was taken prisoner," pressed Thomas.

Hugh and Daniel exchanged a knowing look. Hugh started to respond before being cut off by Daniel. "That ain't none o' your..."

"Save it Hugh; the least we can give these Salisbury folk is the truth," interjected Daniel.

"But these Salibury boys ain't even on our side. I told ya what they just done, they be on the side o' them damn Yorkers and I..."

"Stop it Hugh! Just stop it!" said Daniel. "Don't ya get it? These Salisbury boys ain't on nobody's side, they just tryin' t' do right by us an' them damn Yorkers."

Then Daniel looked at Thomas and John. "Alright then, I tell ya what happened before," said Daniel. "Me an' Hugh an' May was out here staking out our grant land. Ya know, we was figurin' how we might lay out the land and all. The second or third day, we was approached by them Yorker boys; well, at least one of 'em. At first he was askin' what we was doin' on their land. Well, calm words turned t' angry words turned t' angry fists bein' throwed. Truth is, Hugh here gave that Yorker lieutenant a pretty good whippin'. Next day, them Yorker boys come back to talk some more; they thought we might work somethin' out on the land. That Yorker lieutenant said maybe we could
split up the land between us somehow. Well, truth is me and Hugh wouldn't hear nothin' 'bout splittin' up the land. We come out t' the grants for more land. We already sharin' the land plenty back in Litchfield, and we ain't about to split it up. Well, I s'pose calm words turned t' angry words again, an' that's how it was left. That Yorker captain just 'bout kilt us, afore his brother stopped 'em. 'Bout then Hugh and me an' May come back t' Litchfield. I figure

353

'bout a couple weeks later them damn Yorkers turn up an' take us prisoner. I guess that 'bout says it," concluded Daniel.

Thomas looked over and noted the surprise on John's face. "You boys figure all that's got anything t' do with what happened after?" asked Thomas.

"What exactly you tryin' t' say Salisbury..."

Again Daniel cut off Hugh. "Yeah. I'm sure them Yorker boys were pretty worked up that we wouldn't just give up our grant."

"Anything else?" asked Thomas.

"I can't think o' nothing else," replied Daniel.

"I think there be a bit more to it," began Thomas. "Them Yorker boys gave ya a chance t' work somethin' out with 'em back when, an' you boys turned 'em down."

"What exactly you sayin', Salisbury boy?" interjected Hugh.

"What I'm sayin' is that maybe you boys helped make this whole mess more of a problem than it might o' been if you boys had tried t' work somethin' out right off," concluded Thomas.

"You tellin' us we brought all this down on ourself?" fumed Hugh.

"No, 'course I wouldn't go that far. I certainly ain't excusin' them Yorkers for what they done t' you. But I am sayin' you boys might o' helped make a different outcome. You Litchfield folk an' the Yorkers both had some part in all this," said Thomas.

"Of all the damned insultin' things I ever heard," began Hugh. "Ya might as well accuse us o' tyin' ourself up an' draggin' ourself all over the damn country! You damn sure are on the Yorker side!"

Thomas decided it didn't seem helpful to say any more for now. He could see Daniel puzzling over his words and wanted to give him time to think them over. Hugh would get nothing out of his words and only become angrier. Thomas slapped John on the shoulder and turned to head back to their camp and leave the Litchfield folk to their thoughts.

Thomas found Scout and pulled him aside. "I had jist 'bout 'nough o'
Haskins's lip. Ya got any idears? All I can think o' be to keep 'im gagged."

"Don't know what else you can do if you want him quiet. It don't seem quite fair to Haskins though."

"Fair, Scout? I can't have 'im messin' with my dealin's with them Litchfields or them Yorkers. You will keep 'im gagged, except for meal time," ordered Thomas.

The next morning Thomas was enjoying his second cup of coffee when Deeters asked to talk with him. Deeters was untied and led to Thomas. The look on his face concerned Thomas, although he couldn't quite put his finger on what he saw.

"What can I do ya for?" invited Thomas.

"I figured what you militia boys're up to," said Deeters.

"An' what would that be?" asked Thomas.

"We figure you militia boys're fixin' t' make us sign somethin' with them damn Connecticut boys by puttin' a gun t' my head," concluded Deeters.

At first Thomas started with the surprise of being misunderstood by such a wide margin. The Yorker lieutenant had missed the entire target. As he gave himself a moment to gather his thoughts, it occurred to Thomas that the Yorkers probably figured he would do the same thing they had done. In the mind of the bully, all that exists are bullies and people to bully.

"An' why would I wanna do that?" asked Thomas.

"Come on, I ain't stupid," Deeters retorted. "You militia boys're on the side o' them Connecticut boys!"

Thomas took a deep breath and exhaled slowly. "Let's assume for the sake o' argument that ya right 'bout that," began Thomas. "If I put a gun t' your head an' ya signed the agreement, then what?"

Deeters screwed up his face and looked at Thomas sideways. "What, is that some kinda trick question? Then ya got your agreement an' ya be on your way, I s'pose."

"Then what?" asked Thomas.

"Then you militia boys go home an' everything's over, that's what," said Deeters.

"You tellin' me that ya just gonna forget 'bout the whole thing an' go on with ya lives then?" challenged Thomas.

Deeters's face softened while he paused to think. "Well, I don't figure we just forget the whole thing."

"No, I wouldn't 'spect so," began Thomas. "That be precisely the reason why I have no intention o' puttin' a gun t' anybody's head - it

Eventually Alice broke the silence. "Did ya see 'im takin' money?" asked Alice.

"Well, I din't exactly see him take money, but ain't it obvious he musta?" countered Hugh. "I did see 'im talkin' with that damn Yorker lieutenant."

"I s'pose that would explain the change in the captain, but I don't know if the captain could be bought off like that," said Daniel.

"Ya damn right he can! They don't pay them militia boys much, ya know. He gotta git his money any ways he can," answered Hugh.

Hugh looked at Daniel, who merely shook his head slowly. While Hugh waited, Daniel stared at the ground a moment and then rubbed his face like he was washing it with soap and water. "I just hate t' think the captain's in them Yorkers' pay. And if he is, we in a heap o' trouble," said Daniel.

Hugh and Alice nodded their heads affirmatively, while May stared off into the trees. She brushed her hair with a two-pronged stick that she'd found.

"Well, ya better git used t' the idea, cause that exactly what happened," concluded Hugh.

"I don't know, Hugh," said Daniel, "ya might be right but we don't know yet."

"Maybe you don't know for sure, but I do. An' the sooner you figure that out, the sooner we can figure out what t' do 'bout it," reasoned Hugh.

Thomas sat outside his tent on a rock smoking his pipe when John walked up. Thomas looked up and nodded as John sat down on a nearby rock. "Ya think both sides 're gonna work somethin' out?" asked John.

"Don' know; it ain't lookin' so good now," answered Thomas.

"I s'pose we'll find out soon enough," concluded John.

Thomas and John looked up as Deeters approached them, walking in front of his guards. Thomas and John waited to hear what he wanted. Deeters had a resolute look about him. "Alright then, I'm ready," said Deeters.

"Ready for what?" asked Thomas.

"I'm ready to try an' work somethin' out with them Connecticut boys."

"What changed ya mind?" asked Thomas.

"Don't know that anything changed," said Deeters as he turned to walk away.

Thomas turned to John. "Lieutenant, find out if the Litchfield folk 're ready to negotiate. The sooner we begin, the better."

"Yes sir."

And with that John set off to find the Litchfields. They were still scratching their heads as John walked up. The conversation abruptly came to a halt when John approached. "Litchfield folk," said John, "I'm here to see if ya decided to negotiate with the Yorkers. They willin'."

"Yes, we have," Daniel responded quickly. "We ready to begin any time."

Hugh and Alice looked at Daniel with surprise, but didn't say anything to the contrary. Daniel privately decided to go along with the negotiations when he saw John approaching them.

"Good enough," said John, "we begin in an hour."

As soon as John was out of earshot, Hugh and Alice jumped on Daniel. Alice made an attempt to keep her voice low, while Hugh bellowed out his dismay. "What do ya think ya doin' agreein' to negotiate?" asked Alice.

"Of all the stupid things to say," began Hugh. "I thought we agreed the captain's in the pocket of them damn Yorkers!"

"I din't agree to nothing," answered Daniel. "I agree that it's a possibility we have to be ready for, but we don' know yet. An' keep ya voice down."

"Well, I know," retorted Hugh, "an' the sooner you git it, the better for us all."

"Even if you're right, what's the harm in agreein' to negotiate? We don't have to agree to nothin' if we don't wanna," reasoned Daniel.

"The harm is goin' along with somethin' we're being suckered into," said Hugh. "The harm is that we might be playin' the fool."

"Exactly!" agreed May

The others were surprised at her comment; it was the first she'd contributed to the conversation. "Well, I have to admit ya got a point there," admitted Daniel, "we might be played for fools. But what other choice do we have?"

"We can pack up an' get back home," suggested Hugh. "No use in stickin' round here."

The others nodded their heads. It had been such an ordeal, everybody wanted to go home. Daniel had to admit going home sounded appealing, but he wasn't sure it was the best thing to do. He didn't want to walk away from what might be a legitimate opportunity to work this conflict out permanently. "I want ya both to trust me on this. Hugh an' me hear out the Yorker an' see what he got in mind. If we bein' played the fool, then we pack up an' go."

Hugh and Daniel sat inside one of the tents opposite the Yorker lieutenant. Thomas had placed four of his most reliable men outside the tent in case trouble erupted. Thomas and John discussed at length the placement of the men, finally deciding to put them outside the tent. Although there was more of a risk of a fight breaking out with just the three of them inside, in the end Thomas and John thought it best to make a clear statement that the Yorkers and the Litchfields were alone to work things out between themselves. Thomas was most concerned about Hugh. As a safety measure, the three negotiators were searched for weapons before entering the tent. Thomas was tempted to try to listen outside the tent, but fortunately his better judgment prevailed.

Thomas paced back and forth in view of the negotiating tent. Seeing his anxious friend, John suggested they go for a walk and leave the negotiators alone. Thomas reluctantly agreed. He wanted to be there if trouble broke out, but had to admit that Scout and the others were at least as well equipped to handle any trouble as he and John would be.

Not walking in any direction intentionally, the two men found themselves at the top of the hill above their camp. The view from the top of the hill was breathtaking. To the north and west they could see many miles in both directions. Off in the distance was a large lake with a river flowing out of it to the south. They were looking at Lake Champlain. The water shimmered blue in the midday sunlight. Neither man had seen a lake of that size before.

"Dear God, this place is beautiful," said John.

"Unbelievable!" agreed Thomas. "An' there appears to be almost nobody out here."

"As much land as a man could want," said John.

"Ya know, John, I've half a mind to git some o' this land for myself. I've never seen anything so amazing as this place. I had no idea the Grants were this beautiful."

"That so? Ya mean ya might leave Salibury an' ya family?"

"Maybe," pondered Thomas; "when ya put it that way I'm not so sure.... I wonder how much the land cost. I don' know if I could come up with enough to buy a nice sized plot."

"I have no idea," answered John, "but it might be worth inquirin' 'bout."

Both men enjoyed the view in silence. They found their gaze kept going back to the grand lake, as it drew their eyes as if magnetically charged. Thomas forgot all about the important negotiations happening down below. He was transfixed by the view.

"Boy, it'd be great to have land by that lake. I could stand here and look at it for hours.... I was jist thinkin', them Litchfields sure gone through hell tryin' to get their own land. I wonder if it be worth it. Don' know if I could do it. Sure don' seem worth the hell them Litchfields been through," said Thomas.

Thomas then recalled the important happenings down below. "Well, I'd like to stay up here all day," began Thomas, "but I s'pose we oughta be gettin' back."

As they neared the camp, they were jolted out of their dreams by angry shouts coming from the direction of the negotiating tent. Both men hurried to the scene. As they ran up to the tent, the Litchfield men were storming off as both sides gave parting shots. Scout stood between Hugh and Deeters with a hand on each of their chests. John hurried up to the Litchfield men to ask what happened, while Thomas approached Scout. Hugh was only too glad to offer his summary.

"You an' ya Yorker-paid captain ain't gettin' no agreement outta us!" Hugh spat the words. "I know he's deep in their pocket; maybe you are too, an' we done with bein' played the fool!"

A bewildered John looked to Daniel for clarification, but only received a glaring look. Daniel offered no comment. At this point John joined Thomas and Scout.

"Like I was saying, Captain, words got angry all of the sudden, and the next thing we know them Litchfield folk are storming out of the tent," Scout explained. "Then Hugh went after Deeters, and it was only me keeping them from coming to blows. That's really all I can tell you." Thomas nodded his head.

"Damn. All I could get outta the Litchfield folk was somethin' 'bout not bein' played the fool no more," said John.

"Damn! My only hope is that neither side gives up," replied Thomas. "A rough start's to be expected."

"I don' know if the Litchfields 're gonna stay at it; they seemed pretty angry," said John.

"Ya think I oughta go talk with 'em?" asked Thomas.

"I don' know, they din't seem much like talkin' a minute ago. Ya might wanna let 'em cool off first."

An hour later Thomas and John headed over to the Litchfield camp. Their faces were solemn and their steps slow as they approached the Litchfield folk. Both of them dreaded what they'd hear. Whatever hope they nursed slipped away as the Litchfield folk appeared to be packing.

"You folks breakin' camp?" asked Thomas.

Hugh only glared at Thomas and continued what he was doing. Fortunately, Daniel set down what he was doing and walked over.

"That's right, Captain, we had enough. We headin' home, probably should o' done that right off."

"I see," said Thomas, "an' then what?"

"Well, an' then we go back to our lives. We gonna pack our belongin's an' move out to our land grant like we planned all along."

"An' you expectin' them Yorkers to just leave ya be?"

"Right now I don't give a damn what them Yorkers do! I want nothin' t' do with 'em no more. We headin' back to Litchfield, an' don't try an' talk us out o' it!" said Daniel.

Thomas paused to think, rubbing his beard. "I wanna let you know that I'll remain here with the Yorkers till this time tomorrow. At that time we will return the Yorkers their weapons an' supplies an' break camp ourselves."

Daniel merely nodded his understanding and returned to his packing. Hugh continued to glare at Thomas. Thomas and John walked back to their own tents. It was clear there was no point watching them pack, and a risk that their presence might further aggravate the Litchfield folk. Thomas waited till they were out of earshot before he spoke.

"What'd ya think, John?"

"Don' know what more we can do for 'em," said John. "They makin' their own beds, and if they wanna take their chances, well that's their business. It's sad really."

"I figure the only hope is for 'em to cool off some an' reconsider before they leave," said Thomas.

"I wouldn't count on that after what I just saw on their faces," replied John. Thomas just nodded mournfully. He had to agree there wasn't much reason for hope at this point.

Just as John had predicted, the Litchfields did no discernable reconsidering before they left. Flanked by Hugh, Daniel walked up to Thomas and John and informed them that they were leaving. Daniel set his jaw firmly and his face had no trace of indecision. Thomas accepted their decision with a grim nod. He made no attempt to convince them to reconsider. Thomas reached out his hand. Hugh and Daniel just looked at it, and then walked away.

"Chambers, send them Litchfields a horse an' supplies for the trip back," ordered Thomas.

John explained the Litchfields' decision to Deeters. He seemed to take pleasure in their leaving, and heaped many verbal abuses upon the Litchfields. John informed him they'd be free to leave with all their remaining supplies at sundown tomorrow. Thomas decided to give the Litchfields an extra couple hours. Thomas held out some hope they would yet reconsider the folly of their decision, though without logical reason.

The rest of the day passed uneventfully, and the men retired to their tents shortly after sundown, except for those who walked guard duty. The Salisbury militia eagerly anticipated heading home soon. Some of them celebrated that night with their beer rations. Thomas understood their relief and desire to return home, but he did not share their celebration. Nor did he share a sense of the mission being accomplished.

Thomas wasn't sure they had accomplished anything. Thomas and John talked quietly over their supper. They both felt heavyhearted at the Litchfields' departure, but it weighed more on Thomas. He didn't know what else he could have done, yet he still had a nagging sense of having failed in his mission.

The next morning dawned grey and overcast. Thomas took his time getting up and out of his tent. He found less energy than usual for such mundane tasks as dressing. Without conscious thought, Thomas slid his trusted sword into place beneath his belt. Chambers already had coffee brewing as Thomas found him and John at the fire.

"No sign o' them Litchfield folk?" asked Thomas.

"Naw, nothing," replied John with little enthusiasm.

Thomas nodded. He still wished for a sighting of the Litchfields, but he now knew there was no reason for hope. Although they can appear the same, hoping and wishing are quite different. We all wish for many things, often times with little reason for hope.

"The Yorkers itchin' t' go?" Thomas inquired.

"Yeah. Scout mentioned something 'bout them Yorkers givin' him some jaw 'bout keepin' them here unlawfully."

"Don't expect 'em to like it, but they'll have t' wait jist the same," Thomas mused.

John and Thomas mostly sat in silence with their own ponderings as they worked on their coffee and breakfast. Chambers cooked a second helping of bacon and grits over the nearby fire.

Thomas walked slowly about the camp. Some of the men whittled stout branches into poles about three feet long. A couple of men dug two holes in the ground about fifteen paces apart. Pumroy scavenged four discarded horseshoes, and a handful of the men enjoyed a game of horseshoes. Pumroy invited his captain to join them, but Thomas turned away and wandered off by himself. He wanted to be alone with his thoughts. He ended up on the top of that same hill overlooking camp and the whole valley that included Lake Champlain. Slowly thoughts of the Litchfield folk faded and his attention was drawn to the lake. Thomas found himself staring at the lake and the beautiful tree-lined hills surrounding it. His eyes then rested on the silver river that ran out of the lake to the south. Thomas couldn't take in enough of the beauty of the area. His spirits lifted some, but not much. Thoughts of living out this way emerged anew.

Thomas pictured himself and John building their houses along the lake. He saw unending land and plentiful harvests, with many young ones running around playfully. At first he discarded his dreaming as foolish wishing. However, the fantasy returned again and again, as if unwilling to be discarded. The more he thought, the more he found himself drawn to the idea of living here. Thomas slowly warmed to his longings. It also provided a welcomed reprieve after spending so much time and energy trying to broker a deal between the warring parties.

After what seemed like hours, Thomas sighed and tore his eyes from the lake and river and walked back down the hill to camp. The men were giddy. With the promise of home on their minds, they were like kids waiting for school to finally let them out to play. The horseshoe game continued with more men involved than before. Thomas smiled to himself. It actually cheered him some to see the men playing like boys. Thomas wandered over to Lt. Chambers to discuss supplies and figure out how soon they would need hunting parties to resupply them on their trek home.

Thomas finished talking with Chambers and noticed John talking with a familiar face. At first Thomas couldn't quite place the man, but
he knew he should be able to. Then it dawned on him who it was - Daniel had returned! Thomas quickened his step and in a moment was taking in Daniel's sheepish accounting.

"Well, Captain, like I was tellin' the Lieutenant here, we gotta half day's walk from here an' stopped for the night. I got to thinkin' what was gonna happen now. I don't know, maybe I wadn't so mad no more. Anyways, I got to thinkin' that we ain't much better off than we were. I mean, maybe we ain't tied up no more, but we might be again soon. So I talked things over with Alice, an' she reluctantly agreed. It turns out she been turning things over in her mind all day as well. Alice's a good woman, with a good head on her shoulders; often she thinks more clearly 'an me. Anyways, we had a rough time convincin' Hugh. Matter o' fact, he only agreed to resumin' the negotiations with them Yorkers if it din't involve him. 'Course May din't have no opinion on the matter. Anyways, Hugh an' May an' Alice 're takin' all the young 'uns on back towards Litchfield while I try an' work somethin' out with them Yorker folk."

"Well, I think ya made a wise decision," said Thomas. "Truth is I din't have much hope left ya'd reconsider. Sure would hate to see ya leave things as they are."

"Yeah, well, that's 'bout what Alice an' me figured."

"Well, I'll inform Deeters the negotiatin' tent's back in business," interjected a smiling John.

The Yorkers sat idly, waiting to be freed. Their hands were still bound, which limited how they spent their time. As John walked up, many of the men slept, yet Deeters talked quietly with two of his men. Deeters looked up warily as he noted John's approach.

"Daniel's back," said John simply.

"That right?" replied Deeters. "What's he want?"

"He's back to try an' make some kind o' deal," answered John.

"He din't seem too eager to work nothin' out before," said an angry Deeters. "An' what 'bout that other Connecticut boy - he back too?"

"No, just Daniel."

"Well, don't hold ya breathe, Lieutenant, but I'll hear 'im out," offered Deeters.

John untied his hands and led him to the tent. Thomas stood waiting outside the tent, and went in with Deeters. He'd decided to approach the negotiations differently. Both men looked up as he entered, surprised to see him. "Gentlemen, a word please. I'd like t' sit in on the meetin', with both o' ya permission. Might be that I can help.

Ya both 're havin' trouble findin' an agreement, an' maybe I can be that neutral person that moves things along. I hope by now ya both know that I don't be on neither one o' yer sides," said Thomas.

"I don't 'spect we'll reach no agreement with ya involved o' not," began Deeters. "The Connecticut folk ain't showed no signs o' bein' willing to work nothin' out. But, it don't make no difference to me whether ya here o' not."

Daniel momentarily shot fiery eyes at Deeters, then seemed to change his mind and turned to Thomas. "I don't mind if ya sit in," said Daniel.

"Good, it's settled then," said Thomas as he took a seat.

The two men just stared at each other for a minute. Both men appeared to be trying not to blink. Then Deeters broke the silence.

"Well, what ya got in mind?"

"Now hold on there, don't put this whole thing on me. We gots to work this out the two o' us," retorted Daniel.

"Hey, you the one that walked out o' the meetin', not me!" countered Deeters.

"Wait a minute, the both o' ya," interjected Thomas. "Pointin' fingers ain't gonna solve nothin'. I ain't much interested in who din't work it out before, but I am interested in who's gonna do somethin' now."

Both negotiators averted their eyes. They sat in silence. Daniel rubbed the sides of his head, while Deeters folded his arms across his chest.

"Alright then, the trouble be with what to do with the land we both hold claim to. The rest o' the land ain't no problem," started Daniel.

"Wait, lemme understand then," interrupted Thomas. "How much o' ya grants be in common?"

"'Bout a third," answered Daniel. "We gotta fifty acre grant, an' 'bout fifteen o' it be the same land Deeters here has a grant for."

"That seem 'bout right to you?" Thomas asked Deeters.

"Yep. We got forty-four acre grant, an' fifteen o' it be the same as the Connecticut folk."

Thomas gestured for Daniel to continue. "We still don't wanna sell, but maybe we could offer ya a bit more to buy ya out," offered Daniel.

"Naw. I ain't gonna sell neither. My wife got 'er heart set on that land. I only gonna settle for buyin' you out," responded Deeters.

Daniel turned to Thomas. "Ya see, Captain, that's where we stuck. Nobody wants to sell. That's 'bout where we left off last time."

"Have ya considered dividin' up the fifteen acres?" asked Thomas.

"Naw. Then we'd have to live next to 'em," complained Deeters.

"We don' wanna live that way neither," agreed Daniel.

"Why not?" asked Thomas.

Both men grew wide-eyed, wondering if Thomas were stupid.

"Have ya forgot already? These men took us prisoner, molested our wives, an' threatened our lives!" Daniel yelled.

"Yeah, they did," Thomas agreed. "An' none o' that was right. An' Deeters's brother paid with his life, an' Bill here's got a mark on his neck, just like you. An' none o' that got neither one o' ya anywhere."

Now both negotiators sat with arms folded. The sullen glares had disappeared, replaced by indecisiveness. "I don' know. I gotta think on it," conceded Daniel.

Deeters sat wordless, yet his firmly set jaw had loosened a bit. Thomas examined one man's face and then the other's. "Well, you boys think on it then. But lemme leave ya with somethin' to think on. Startin' out on new land in the wilderness ain't no cherry pickin' day. When my folks started out in Salisbury, they almost gave up many a time. Not only did they have t' learn t' work the land, they had to fight off predators. Wolves an' snakes kept comin' an' attackin' the livestock an' eatin' the crops. In the end, they finally banded together with a couple o' neighbors, or they probably woulda just moved back to East Guilford. Hey, I get that ya got pleny o' reason to hate the other, an' ya don' have t' be friends. But ya might need a neighbor t' help to make ya farm work an' be able to support ya families. I don' know, maybe that be too much o' me to ask, but you boys think on it some. We'll stop for some grub, an' then see where we are."

After dinner Daniel and Deeters reentered the tent. Thomas allowed them some time alone before he joined them, although guards were posted outside the tent. When Thomas entered the tent, the two men were poring over a site map. Thomas peered over Deeters's shoulder but didn't say anything.

"What if we give ya eight o' the fifteen acres, since it makes a more natural boundary atween the two properties," suggested Daniel.

"Yeah, that do make the boundary line a bit more straight," Deeters agreed.

"Alright, so we'll draw the boundary line right here then," said Daniel as he drew on the map.

"An' I wanna good strong fence built right along that line then," said Deeters.

"Yep. The first thing we'll do, after buildin' a house that is," said Daniel.

Deeters looked up at Thomas. "I think we got it worked out, but don't 'spect us to be all neighborly. That ain't gonna happen." Thomas laughed.

With a verbal understanding in place, Thomas and John helped the two parties put their agreement in writing. John did the actual writing, while Thomas helped craft the wording in concert with Deeters and Daniel. Of course some conflict arose over the exact wording of the document, but eventually they created an acceptable document. John wrote out an exact copy of the document so that both parties would have it in writing.

With the ink dry on the deal, the Yorkers decided to leave immediately. Several hours of sunlight remained, and the Yorkers wanted no more society with present company. The six of them packed up their belongings quickly, taking what they wanted from their dead comrades' supplies. Deeters approached Thomas as the Yorkers were ready to take to the trail.

"Alright, Captain, it be 'bout time you were givin' us back our munitions," said Deeters.

"S'pose ya will be needin' something to protect yourself with," agreed Thomas.

"Somethin'? I want all our weapons back," demanded Deeters.

Thomas paused a moment before responding. "No, I don't think ya need 'em all," disagreed Thomas.

"Now wait a damn minute..."

But Thomas had turned to Scout and wasn't listening. "Scout, a word in private," Thomas said as he waved Scout to follow.

They talked quietly a few minutes, and then Thomas nodded and walked away. Scout returned and addressed Deeters. "We decided you can have all o' your weapons, but only one ball and powder per man," Scout announced.

"Now see here, we ain't children ya can tell what we can an' can't have. I want all our supplies back, includin' the ammunition!"

"I'm afraid we can't take the chance of giving you more than that," answered Scout. "I won't follow you all the way back to New York to make sure you don't harass the Litchfields again. Like it or not, that's
the way it's going to be. Even at that, I'll have to follow you a good ways to make sure you don't double back and retake them folk."

"Damn you an' your captain," cursed Deeters as he turned back to his men.

Thomas ordered Scout and Pumroy to follow the Yorkers a few miles to guard against any foul play. You never know what might grow within men's souls, even in such a short time. Thomas wanted to take no chances and maintained guard duty as before. Daniel remained with the Salisbury militia after Thomas offered to escort him back to his family.

While the men made final preparations to depart, Thomas wandered back up the hill for one last look at the Lake Champlain Valley. Thomas exhaled out the stress and worries of the warring parties and began to relax for the first time in weeks. His body and mind would need days to fully let go of the burden and stress of the rescue and negotiations. For the moment, the Champlain Valley drew his attention. Again fantasies of living out in this land came to mind. Thomas allowed himself to indulge in his fantasy without a care for the happenings he'd left below. After a long drink of the view and his dreams, Thomas withdrew back down to the camp.

On the walk down the hill, Thomas began to feel excited to see Liz. He reached inside his pocket to finger the familiar locket Liz had given him. He longed to hold her. Her touch was amongst the things he most missed. Thomas also had so much to tell her. In spite of a few hastily written letters along the way, she knew very little of his happenings since leaving Salisbury three weeks ago. The three weeks apart felt like half of a lifetime to be away from the woman he loved. Now that their mission had been accomplished, he allowed himself to leisurely ponder his reunion with Liz. Many times he'd thought of their first night back together, but he hadn't felt free to linger in such fantasies before now. The demands of the mission had virtually taken up all the space in his mind.

Thomas had been gone long enough that the men were wondering where he was. Of course the men were anxious to get on the trail toward home. Thomas checked with John to see that forward and rear guard duty had been established for the trail, and then gave the order to move out back the way they had come. Cheers sounded from most of the men, smiles from the rest. All were eager to return home to loved ones and the comforts of home.

John and Thomas waited for the train to parade past them and took their place at the rear. Thomas had sent a man to inform the scouts to track the Yorkers until they camped for the night and to then rejoin them. Without the benefit of the scouts' skills, they had to rely on Daniel's memory to retrace his steps back to where he'd left his family. Not that his family would still be where he left them, but Thomas figured that the scouts could track them from there.

Hugh, Alice, and May couldn't move fast on foot, especially with the children.

Once on the trail, Thomas's thoughts turned to MacDonald and Sally. Thomas had often thought of MacDonald, wondering what he might say in this situation or that. Even beyond such advice, Thomas simply longed to see his good friend. Over the past four or five years, Sally had grown more and more dear to Thomas, not only because she was his little sister, but because of the bond they'd developed shortly after Thomas got to know MacDonald. Thomas had enclosed brief notes to both Sally and MacDonald in his letters to Liz; he hoped she'd passed on the scant news to them both. These three faces kept coming to his mind.

Once the scouts rejoined the regiment, Daniel's family proved easy enough to track. They hadn't made it much further since Daniel had left them, maybe a day's walk. Thomas made sure the families were adequately supplied and then bade them farewell. As the Yorkers had shown no signs of returning this way, they seemed safe enough to leave behind. Scout gave Daniel a musket and plenty of the Yorker's ball and powder with which to protect them.

The regiment watched the Litchfields turn and wave just before they disappeared behind trees. Thomas breathed a deep sigh of relief, as he exhaled the burden of their safety. A moment later he was reminded of another burden.

"Hey, Captain," barked Haskins, "you man enough to challenge me to hand t' hand yet? 'Cause if ya too yellow, then damn it lemme go! God almighty know you be a coward to keep me bound like a horse thief."

Thomas groaned. He was weary of Haskins's bellyaching. Then a thought came to him. "Scout, over here for a word. I want you to deal with Haskins."

"What do you want me to do with him?" asked Scout.

"I trust 'im to you. Do whatever ya think best. Ya know, I think it's time ya did somethin' a bit different with 'im anyways."

"What does that mean?" asked Scout.

Thomas merely grinned and walked away. Scout watched him go and searched his mind for what Thomas could have meant. Then he shrugged his shoulders and looked at Haskins. Haskins caught his eye and nodded for Scout to come over.

"Hey, Scout, lemme go while the fool captain ain't lookin'," whispered Haskins.

"Naw. It's not going to be like that. It's up to me to figure out what to do about you."

"To you! How's that?"

"Because the 'fool captain,' as you call him, left it to me to deal with you."

"Well, now that's the best news I heard for days. So cut me loose." Haskins held up his bounds toward Scout. Scout started to reach for his knife, and then stopped. Then he put his knife back in its sheath. "No. I don't know if that's best just yet. I'm going to think on it some," said Scout.

"Damn it, Scout. What kind o' nonsense ya talkin'? Ya startin' to sound as bad as that damn, fool captain."

"Maybe that's not such a bad thing, might even be an improvement. Yeah, I'm going to leave you be for now."

"You yellow-bellied son of a bitch! An' I thought you was a friend and..."

This was all Scout heard, as he walked away to prepare to move out on the trail.

The next morning broke sunny and bright. Scout had thought enough. He walked over to where Haskins lay, already awake. His ankles and hands were bound in front. Pumroy sat on the ground with his back against a nearby tree keeping guard over Haskins, as per Scout's instructions. He wouldn't underestimate Haskins's skill.

"Okay, Pumroy, why don't you go get yourself some grub," suggested Scout.

A relieved Pumroy didn't need to be asked twice, and quickly went in search of coffee and biscuits. Scout knelt down next to Haskins and cut the ropes at both ankles and hands. Then he set down a pistol, a musket, a short knife and a long hunting knife on the dirt next to Haskins. Haskins eyed him suspiciously and with contempt. He looked from the weapons to Scout, and then to the weapons again.

"Alright, Haskins, you are free to go," Scout said simply.

"Well, it's 'bout time ya come to your senses."

Haskins put away his weapons in their proper places on his person, all except for the musket. Scout tossed him a bag of ball and a horn of powder.

"Your belongings are already packed on your horse, and you can see Lt. Chambers for four days' supply of grub and water," offered Scout.

"An' where's my pay?"

"Your pay? The captain already paid you for three weeks of service, and you'll receive no more than that - and that's my decision," said Scout.

"So ya relieve me o' my duties, tie me up like a common horse thief, and now ya intend to cheat me outta my pay, pay that was already less than I normally git for my services. I never been so damn unappreciated for what I do! An' more than that, Scout, you a fool for throwin' away the best friend ya ever had. It's once in a life ya come 'cross a friend like me!"

"Yeah, I've played the fool. I've been a fool for placing you on a pedestal, and it's long overdue for me to fix that," admitted Scout.

"Come now, Scout; who else can track like me? Who else can better defend the rights o' common folk? Who do ya know that can take me in hand t' hand combat? Call it a pedestal if ya like, but we both know I live up to my reputation!"

Scout looked at Haskins with a mixture of irritation and sadness. Scout looked away for a moment. "Well, I figure you see yourself the way you need to," said Scout.

"I see myself the way I am!" insisted Haskins.

"I suppose there ain't much more to say then," said Scout sadly. "I figure I can only fix the way I see you. You have to fix your own mind, or not."

All trace of irritation had left his face. He beheld Haskins with sadness and pity. Scout saw the brittle mask on Haskins's face for the first time, and he realized he really didn't know the man before him. He took one last look at Haskins and then turned to leave.

"I wish you well," Scout said quietly.

At first Haskins watched in disbelief as Scout turned his back on him. He was used to men seeking his company, not turning away from him. "Don't turn ya back on me, Scout! You come back here an' finish this like a man."

Scout stopped in his tracks for a second without turning, and then continued back to the other men.

"I said don't turn ya back on me, damn it! This is ya last chance," yelled Haskins.

Seeing Scout continue to leave him, Haskins became enraged and pulled out his short knife and threw it at Scout. The knife embedded itself on the left side of Scout's lower back. Fortunately, Scout wore his animal hide coat and the knife only penetrated half an inch. In one motion Scout turned and went down on one knee, pulling the knife out of his back and pointing his pistol at Haskins's chest.

"I never thought you'd stoop to throw at a man's back!"

"But you made me..."

"Save it - I don't want to hear it! You get your horse and leave - now!"

"But what 'bout the supplies?" asked Haskins.

"You just gave them up. If you stay one more second, I'll supply you with lead."

Haskins face fell and gave the impression of cracked glass; cracked yet barely held together as if by some magic. Then a moment later he recovered, resuming his determined mixture of defiance and arrogance. Haskins picked up his musket and quickly strode to his horse and was gone. That was the last Scout saw of Haskins.

Haskins rode out of camp with his head high and his chin back, grinning at the men who watched him leave. All of the camp had heard the loud confrontation between the two scouts. Once out of sight of the camp, Haskins exhaled and lost his pose, the voices quickly sounding off in his head.

"Damn it all, Scout! Why did ya make me throw at ya? I didn't wanna do that, but ya brought it on yourself. You a damn fool! Why did ya make me teach you a lesson like that? I've a mind to go back and teach ya real good. Ah well, maybe I'll let ya off this time, seeing as ya more o' fool than even I'd realized."

Thomas stood beside Scout and as they watched Haskins ride off. Thomas said, "Do ya think he'll leave us be?"

"I don't ever want to see him again," said Scout.

June 2, 1753 - Salisbury, Connecticutt

Noah joined the Chittendens for supper. He had continued calling on Sally, and their relationship had become more serious. Father and Mama received Noah initially with indifference, and then later with coldness. They had hoped their cold reception would discourage him from visiting. At first their coolness had hurt Noah, and he'd wondered if he'd offended them. However, Noah knew that Sally welcomed him, and he had grown attached to her and thus remained determined to court her anyway.

After supper Liz walked back to the old house, leaving Sally and Noah back at the new house. Liz was cleaning the house when Sally came into the house crying. Liz dropped what she was doing and rushed into the house after Sally.

"Sally, what is it? Why are you crying?"

Sally lay on her bed with her face in her folded arms. She looked up at Liz, and then put her face back in her arms and continued crying. Her shoulders heaved. Liz sat down on the bed next to her and put her hand on Sally's back.

"Father sent Noah away!" Sally sobbed.

"Why did he do that?" asked Liz.

At first Sally just shook her head. Then her sobbing ebbed, and she sat up and wiped her eyes with a handkerchief. "After ya left, Father asked me an' Noah to stay an' talk. Father nodded to Ben an' he got up an' left. Mama stayed. Then Father said he an' Mama been talkin', an' they was happy us children was havin' fun together, but they wonderin' what Noah's intentions be. Well, Noah an' me both said we started talkin' 'bout gettin' married. Oh, Liz, ya woulda thought we said we was gonna become bank robbers. Mama looked up at the roof like she was prayin'. An' Father shook his head slow with that smile like ya have when young children say somethin' silly. Then Father looks at Noah an' says, 'Son, I don't think ya 'preciate what ya gettin' yaself into. Sally here's a sweet child, but she's gotta be looked after real close. I don't think ya can give 'er the care she requires. Now it ain't ya fault, cause you don' know 'bout her leg an' what ya dealin' with here. Now Mama an' me are all for you children havin' fun together, but we gotta draw the line now that things is gettin' outta hand. Now ya can keep callin' if ya like, son, but don' get no idears 'bout marryin' Sally.' Then nobody said nothing for a bit till Mama said, 'Ya seem like a nice boy, but ya in way over ya head on this one. Only Father an' me knows how to watch over Sally proper.' Then Noah said somethin' 'bout it being atween him an' me, an' that he knew 'bout my leg. They laughed an' Father said, 'As long as Sally be livin' under our roof, she'll do as we say, an' we say ya ain't prepared to look out for 'er.' Then Noah got mad an' left."

"Oh Sally, that's awful," Liz said.

"I'm afraid Father an' Mama scared 'im off an' I'll never see 'im again. An' Thomas ain't back yet. What if I never see Thomas or Noah again?"

At this Liz's face grew tense and her lips tightened. It had been over four weeks since Thomas left. Liz put two of her fingertips in her mouth and chewed on them. "I know, Sally. I've had the same horrible thought myself. How long has it been since we heard from him - two or three weeks?"

Sally nodded emphatically. "Do ya think he's alright?"

"Dear God, I hope so!" answered Liz.

Being emotionally exhausted, Sally fell asleep almost immediately. However, Liz tossed and turned for hours, struggling to push away thoughts of what may have befallen her husband. She lay awake staring out the window at the crescent moon. Her reverie broke when she thought she heard a sound.

"Was that the gate closing?" she thought.

Liz got up and went to the window and surveyed the yard. She noticed the weather vane spinning. "Oh, it's probably just the wind blowing the gate shut," she said to herself.

Just as Liz pulled the covers back over her, she heard light footsteps on the front porch. She realized in fear that the wind doesn't make that sound. Liz sat up in bed and listened carefully.

Then a rap on the door rang out. Liz felt fear rush up from within her. She couldn't remember a time when someone came to the door after she'd been in bed. Liz climbed out of bed and headed to the door, when she bumped into someone and fell.

"Who's that?"

"I'm sorry, Liz, it jist me," apologized Sally. "I heard a knock on the door."

"Oh, thank God it's only you."

Sally and Liz embraced and looked at each other with wide eyes. For a moment they both froze, not sure what to do. They looked at each other, and then to the door. Both women remained still as if frozen in place. Finally Sally went to the window and tried to see who was there. The dim light revealed a silhouette of a man.

"Who is it?" blurted out Sally. "That you, Noah?"

Liz stood behind Sally at the window and almost lost her balance again when Sally bumped into her as she turned to the door. Sally pulled the musket off the wall above the door. They kept it loaded.

"You open it an' I'll hold the gun," whispered Sally.

Liz opened the door a crack and Sally looked out with one eye and the barrel of the musket. Someone leaned on the railing of the porch, and turned around as the door opened. She could see it was a man, but couldn't make out much else at that distance in the dark.

"Yeah, what'd ya want?" Sally demanded. "An' I got a musket right here."

"Well, I woulda hoped for a li'l better welcome than that, 'specially from my own daughter," admonished Father as he approached the door.

"Oh Father, it be you! You gave us quite a start!" said Sally.

"I jist wanted to make sure you girls be alright. Oldman tell me there be some wolf sightin's today."

"We be alright. We ain't seen nothin'," said Sally.

"Well alrighty then, I figure I'll git on back to bed. Goodnight girls."

They watched as Father walked back up the hill. "It seem strange to me that Father came down to check on us," said Sally.

"He did seem a bit jittery," said Liz.

Sally moved as though weary, yet what weighed her down was not fatigue but a burdened mind. Her hands and arms automatically hung up the clean and wet laundry to line dry. Her hands felt without feeling, her eyes saw without seeing, glazed over with reflection. She didn't notice the slow approach of steps behind her. Sally was taken completely by surprise when suddenly enveloped by a wet sheet, and held tight by strong arms.

"Stop it, ya makin' me all wet!" shouted Sally.

The arms released her, and she easily pulled the sheet off her. "Guess ye ain't in a playful way today, aye lass?" said Rachel.

"Oh, it be you; I figure it be Ben," said Sally sheepishly. "Yeah, I s'pose I ain't feelin' so playful; got somethin' on my mind."

"Really, lass. Well, ye wanna tell Rachel 'bout it?"

"Yeah, it might help me to talk 'bout it. It be 'bout Noah. After Mama an' Father scared 'im off couple nights ago, he ain't been back since. Guess I'm afraid he ain't comin' back at all. I already miss 'im so."

"What scared the lad off then?" asked Rachel.

"Oh, it was terrible! Father an' Mama painted me like a child that need her mama to look out for her, an' that Noah oughta just go an' find a grown up girl."

"Ain't that 'bout how they always treated ye?" suggested Rachel.

"Yeah, I s'pose so. But they ain't never said nothin' 'bout it to Noah afore."

"An' ye be attached to the lad."

"Oh yeah, I think I'm fallin' for Noah. We just started talkin' 'bout maybe gettin' married someday," explained Sally. "I jist don' know what to do 'bout it. I keep wonderin' if I oughta just wait longer to see if Noah comes back."

"Have ye thought o' goin' an' talkin' wi' the lad yerself?"

"Yeah, but..."

"Well, then what be keepin' ye fro' doin' so?" asked Rachel.

"I don' know. Ain't it the man that s'posed to court the woman?"

"Is that so?"

"Well, ain't it?" asked Sally.

"Allow me t' ask ye a question, lass; be it what's proper that keep ye from goin' t' yer man, or be it somethin' else?"

"What else could it be?"

"I wonder if ye be treatin' yerself the same as yer folks, as though ye be a young lassie needin' to have her hand held?" suggested Rachel.

376

"Naw, it can't be that; could it? Why would I wanna do that to myself?"

"I don't know, but it be a fine question to ask yerself," said Rachel.

"So how am I treatin' myself young; I don't understand that?"

"By only allowin' yerself one course o' action, which be waitin' for someone else t' take the bull by the horns. Seem t' me that wee lassies wait for someone bigger t' step in," explained Rachel.

Sally looked away and scratched her arm absentmindedly. "So what do ya think I oughta do then?" asked Sally.

"Well, what do ye think a grown lass would do in yer shoes?"

Sally folded her arms and paused to think. "I guess they'd do somethin' 'bout it themself," suggested Sally.

"That be my way o' thinkin' as weel."

"I s'pose I have been waitin' on Noah to do somethin'," pondered Sally aloud.

"Aye, lass."

"Maybe ya right. I'm gonna go see 'im right now!"

"There ye go, lass!"

"Rachel, will ya come with me, please? I'll do the talkin' myself, but I want ya by my side."

"'Course I'll come wi' ye."

Noah's folks owned the general store in Salisbury, and he helped out like everyone else in the family. Noah was the youngest of three, with an older brother and sister. His brother made regular trips to New Haven to keep the store supplied, while Noah and his sister worked in the store tending to customers and other odd jobs.

He was behind the counter wearing an apron when the two ladies walked in. Noah noticed them right away and smiled with a hint of blushing in his cheeks. He signaled for them to wait a minute, and went outside to help a customer load her groceries into her cart. Noah came back in and took off his apron and hung it on a hook sticking out of the wall.

"Hey, Pa, I'm gonna step out for a bit; be back soon," Noah said.

Noah nodded for the ladies to follow him outside. "Ye go ahead, lass; I'll just look 'round the store while ye an' the lad talk on yer own then," said Rachel.

Sally embraced Rachel and smiled nervously, and then joined Noah at the door. "So are ya here to tell me to stop callin'?" asked Noah.

"Huh? Be that what ya think I want?"

"Guess I figured ya folks were just speakin' ya own wishes the other night," admitted Noah.

"Oh no! I'm here 'cause I wanna let ya know my folks don' speak for me. Only I speak for me."

"Alright then, an' what do ya say on ya own behalf then?" asked Noah.

"I wanna say I ain't a child that needs to have her nose wiped. I can tie my own boots an' take care o' myself!"

A smile slowly dawned on Noah, broadening more and more. "Well, that be good news, real good news," Noah replied. "I was thinkin' for a good while that ya're the type o' lady that I want, but after the other night I wadn't so sure. I never thought o' ya as a child, but after what ya folks said, I had my doubts."

"That's why I'm here, to talk over the other night an' prove to myself an' to you that I can do for myself," said Sally firmly.

"Well, alright then; just next time don't go gettin' ya folks to do ya dirty work," said Noah with a gleam in his eye and a grin on his face.

Sally feigned being hurt and put her hands on his neck and began to choke him lightly. "Don' ya go runnin' off the next time my folks say somethin' foolish," Sally said as she played along.

"So, now that we got that straight, would ya like to stay for dinner?" asked Noah.

"What 'bout Rachel?"

"She welcome to stay if she likes," invited Noah.

May 27, 1753 - Hampshire Grants

Thomas smelled the welcomed and familiar scent of coffee as he sat up and rubbed his eyes. The smell of coffee had become his wake up call on the mission. He attached his sword to his side and stepped out of his tent. Chambers had the coffee brewed and poured Thomas a cup. "We all out of meat, Captain, We gonna have to git more real soon like," said Chambers.

"Damn! I'd hoped we'd make it back without havin' to hunt no more," said Thomas. "Alright then, I'll send out a team."

Thomas walked over to find John and Scout conferring over a map. "So how long till you figure we be back to Litchfield, Scout?"

"Me and John was jist talking that over. I figure we have four or five days to go yet."

"Damn, we will need to git more meat then. We can't go that long without it," said Thomas. "John, send out two hunters. I want 'em to leave as quick as they can. Pick somebody ya trust. And have 'em git with Scout, so they knows where to find us later on." John nodded as he stood.

While it was still early in the morning the regiment was back on the trail. The men laughed and talked constantly as the militia escorted the Litchfield folk back to their home. Thomas had helped himself to four of the Yorker horses, so the Litchfield folk rode alongside them. Each of the adults rode a horse, with a child or two behind them.

The regiment stopped for a midday meal. John grabbed a plate of food and sat down next to Thomas. Thomas glanced up at John and said, "What be on your mind, John?"

"I wonderin' 'bout the hunters," said John.

"They ain't back yet?" John shook his head.

"Damn! They long past due," said Thomas.

Thomas turned to Scout and said, "Hey Scout, them hunters ain't back yet. I figure they late."

"They're definitely late. I'll go after 'em," said Scout.

"Hold on, I'm comin' with you," said Thomas. "John, get the regiment back on the road. Stay on the planned trail, an' we catch up with ya later." John nodded.

Thomas wolfed down the rest of his food, fetched his pistols and mounted his horse. He and Scout took off at a gallop. Scout took the lead, as he knew about where the hunters ought to be. At first they followed the trail back the way they'd come. Scout stopped to take a closer look at the trail every mile or so.

Just before they reached last night's camp, Scout turned off the trail to the East. This trail proved narrower, and Thomas slipped back behind Scout. Scout slowed, as the terrain became more rugged.

After being scratched in the forearms by numerous low hanging tree branches and brush, the trail opened up at a narrow creek. Scout dismounted and tied his horse to a tree. Thomas followed his lead. The two men knelt at the creek's edge. Scout examined the soft ground near the water. "This is about where the hunters were headed, but I don't...wait a minute, over there are their tracks," said Scout as he pointed across the creek.

Thomas and Scout remounted and followed the tracks, keeping the horses to a walk. The men continued on another mile until Scout suddenly stopped and held up his hand. Scout signaled that he'd heard something. They quietly dismounted and proceeded with caution. Then Thomas heard it too- a low moaning sound.

They crouched down and proceeded forward. Then they saw Pumroy. He sat on the ground with his back to the tree, securely bound to the trunk of the tree. Pumroy's mouth was bound, and he had a gash on his forehead. Thomas scampered forward and quickly untied Pumroy and asked him what happened.

Pumroy rubbed his wrists and said, "It be Haskins."

"Haskins? Ya sure 'bout that?" asked Thomas.

"I'm positive it was him. Haskins even said, 'tell that fool o' a captain o' yours that he cost hisself a life. That be the price I decided on for his fool behavior.' That be jist as he said it," said Pumroy.

"What do that mean?" asked Thomas.

"Damn if I know."

"An' where be Johnson?" asked Thomas.

"Haskins took 'em. I don' know where. I ain't seen him since Haskins knocked me in the head and tied me up, jist like ya found me."

"Then let's find 'em," said Thomas. Thomas turned to look for Scout. He didn't see him. Thomas gave Pumroy one of his pistols and waved for him to follow. They crept forward and searched the brush on both sides of the trail, searching for signs of Johnson. Thomas heard the sound of running water and moved more quickly to find its source. The trail swept around to the left and there they found the creek. And face down in the creek was Johnson.

When Thomas and Pumroy knelt beside him, they found he'd been shot dead through the chest. Thomas pulled him from the water.

"Well now, ya won't be findin' Johnson quite like his ole self," said a familiar voice.

Thomas exhaled deeply and slowly turned as he unsheathed his sword. Haskins stood twelve feet away with a pistol trained at Thomas. "An' that fancy sword o' yours ain't gonna help you none this time, boy captain."

Thomas measured the distance with his eyes. He realized he had no chance of reaching Haskins with his sword before Haskins would fire on him. "That be right, boy captain, I keepin' my distance this time. This time I be killin' you. An' there ain't nothin' you can do to stop me." Haskins grinned leisurely. He was enjoying this moment and in no hurry. "Well captain, be there anything ya wanna say before I send ya to the devil?"

Thomas merely held Haskins' gaze. "Alright then, here we go. Hold on tight to the reigns for the ride down to hell," said Haskins as the raised his pistol and extended his arm. Thomas remained planted in his spot. There was nothing to do but wait for the pistol to explode.

A moment later came the dreaded explosion. Thomas started, and was surprised that he still stood, and that he felt no pain. "Maybe I be stunned," he thought.

Haskins turned his head to the left, and then slumped to the ground. Thomas turned to look behind him. There stood Scout. Black smoke rose from the end of Scout's pistol.

"Thank God for ya, Scout!" said Thomas. "How did ya..."

"Something told me to hold back and wait," said Scout.

"Well, I be damn glad o' that," said Thomas.

Scout stared at the fallen Haskins.

Thomas knelt down next to Haskins. He was dead. Scout removed the pistol from Haskins hand, and slipped it into his own belt. Then Scout stood. "Sometimes the enemy ain't who you think he is," said Scout.

"Sometimes the enemy be one o' us," said Thomas.

June 6, 1753 - Salisbury, Connecticutt

Sally hung up the clean laundry that she and Liz had just finished washing. She hung the second sheet on the line when she heard footsteps behind her. Ben had been talking with Sally and Liz a moment ago, and Sally figured that he wanted something else. Sally waited for Ben to speak, and grew impatient when he didn't. Sally said, "Well Ben, ain't ya gonna say nothin'?"

"Well, I do be ya brother, but I ain't that one," said Thomas.

"Thomas!"

Sally put her hands up to her mouth, dropped the sheet in the dirt, and her legs buckled sending her down on her knees. Thomas quickly filled the distance between them and picked her up into his arms. The instant Liz heard his voice she ran to him and threw her arms around both Thomas and Sally in a bear hug, jumping onto both of them. All three collapsed to the ground, laughing all the way.

"Oh, thank God you're all right!" cried Liz.

Sally cried tears of joy. Thomas grinned from ear to ear as he hugged his two favorite women. They were in no hurry to get up and remained on the ground for awhile, laughing and crying.

Thomas slept well past dawn the next day. His bed felt luxurious and strange after sleeping on the ground for four weeks. He quietly dressed and went outside without waking Liz. Thomas sat down on the well and breathed deeply. Something about sitting in this spot made Thomas feel as though he were truly at home. He never tired of looking out on the sea of trees, taking into his lungs the fresh, rural air. The low eastern sun lit up the whole country before him. Countless times he'd sat in this very spot, drinking in the view as he drank of the well's cool water. Thomas heard soft footsteps and turned to see Liz approaching. She sat beside him, leaning against his shoulder.

"What are you thinking about?" asked Liz.

"Oh, I was just sittin' in my spot here," began Thomas, "lookin' out at the trees. Ya know, it reminds me o' a hill I liked t' look out 'n the Grants. Oh, Liz, 'twas truly the most unbelievable country. There's the biggest lake I ever saw, an' more blue than any water I seen in these parts. I wish ya coulda seen it."

Liz merely nodded. Thomas's face became serious. "Liz, what would ya think 'bout gettin' some land o' our own out 'n the Grants?"

"What? You mean and leave our home here?" asked Liz.

"We'd make a new home for ourselves out 'n the Grants, with land o' our own!" said an excited Thomas.

"I don't know, Thomas," said Liz doubtfully. "Have you thought of all the work it would take to move us that far away, and to land without a home on it?"

"Oh, Liz, if ya could only see it for yourself."

Liz looked unconvinced. She fidgeted with her hands and crossed her legs at the ankles. She started to say something several times, only to stop herself.

"Well, maybe 'tis a bad idear," said Thomas.

At this point the image in Thomas's mind began to fade. He wondered why he'd thought of moving out to the Grants in the first place. Maybe he'd just been caught up in the euphoria of the mission being accomplished. Maybe he'd been caught up in the beauty of the land and had not thought of all it would take to get there. Maybe he wasn't appreciating what he did have here in Salisbury.

By now Liz knew Thomas well enough that she knew she'd helped let the air out of his balloon. "Wait, Thomas, maybe we can think about your idea some," she suggested.

"Maybe. I guess I hadn't really thought it out much. I s'pose there would be quite a few obstacles. I don' know, maybe we oughta just stay put."

"Maybe. I don't want to say 'no' too quickly. Give me some time to think it over, and let's talk more about it, okay?" Thomas nodded.

After breakfasting with Liz and Sally, Thomas headed out to see Father and Ben and Mama. Thomas found Ben tending to the hay in the barn. Ben's routine rarely changed and was familiar enough to Thomas that he knew where to find him this time of the morning.

"Hey, Ben, what 're ya up to?" greeted Thomas. Thomas embraced his brother.

"Hey, little brother, so ya back then."

"Yep, got in late yesterday," answered Thomas.

"Guess ya din't get yaself kilt then?" said Ben.

"Yep. An' got them prisoners freed alright."

"Did ya have t' kill the rascal that took 'em?" asked Ben with a twinkle in his eye.

"Yeah, I did. But I wish it hadn't come to that," Thomas said honestly.

"Oh, so did ya string 'em up or just shoot 'em?"

Thomas gave Ben a curious look. He wasn't sure if Ben were playing with him. "Ya serious, Ben?"

"'Course I'm serious," answered Ben. "Tell me it wadn't just a accident."

"No, it wadn't a accident. I had to kill two men that din't surrender," Thomas confirmed.

"Ya pullin' my leg. Tell me ya ain't serious, little brother. Ya mean you were just gonna let 'em go?"

"Ben, the mission be to free prisoners, not kill folk! I don't get no pleasure outta killin' folk when I don't have to!" said Thomas.

"Hey, them Yorkers took folk prisoner; they deserve to die. Woulda been a crime if ya woulda let 'em go after all that," pushed back Ben.

Ben had expressed enough similar views that Thomas had a pretty good idea where this conversation was going, and decided to let it be. Thomas knew he wouldn't change Ben's mind on such matters, nor would Ben change Thomas's views.

"Hey Ben, ya shoulda seen the country out 'n the Grants; most beautiful country I ever saw!"

"That right?" said Ben reluctantly.

"Yeah, land as far as ya can see, hills an' trees untouched, an' the biggest lake I ever did see. I'm even thinkin' on gettin' me some land out 'n the Grants."

"Why would ya wanna do that?" asked Ben incredulously.

"Why? 'Cause I want some land o' my own some day, that's why."

"What do ya mean? Ya got your own land here," said Ben.

"Naw, that ain't the same. This land belong to Father; at least until he passes."

"No, it don't," retorted Ben. "He gave us this land fifty-fifty when ya got married; don't ya remember him splittin' the land atween us?"

"Yeah, maybe officially he did, but it don't seem like our land to me," answered Thomas.

"'Course it's our land. What a minute, is that what that old fool told ya? Is that old man fillin' your head with more crazy idears? Come on, Thomas, some day ya gotta grow up an' learn to think for yaself!"

"Nobody's tellin' me how to think. Matter o' fact I'm thinkin' more on my own than I ever have," Thomas replied.

"If you was thinkin' clear-like, ya wouldn't even be considerin' such a damn fool move as that," retorted Ben.

"Well, I figure we just see it different," summed Thomas.

"Naw, I figure you just don't see it," said Ben.

Once again Thomas could see that this conversation had reached a dead end with nowhere to go, nowhere good to go anyway. Thomas changed the conversation to matters of the farm, and Ben updated him on its management and condition. Ben tried to reengage Thomas on the matter of the Grants, but Thomas politely refused to discuss it further. Thomas left Ben in the barn and went to look for Mama and Father.

MacDonald walked slowly back to the Feed 'n Seed with his mail. He thumbed through the usual things as he entered his store. He set the mail down on the counter when he noticed a letter had fallen to the floor. MacDonald recognized the handwriting immediately, but couldn't place it right away. Bending down to retrieve it, he noted the return address and realized the familiar hand was his brother Ian's. Since Ian and MacDonald infrequently wrote to one another, this correspondence piqued his curiosity. Inside was a brief note in his brother's hand wrapped around a second letter. MacDonald read Ian's note first.

Robert,

Sit yerself down afore ye read the enclosed letter, as ye may find it quite a shock. As best I can know, the letter was found amongst father's things when his landlady was clearing out his belongings from his garret room in the attic o' her house. I figure Father rented a room from her. The letter was sent to oor home town, an' must o' sat in the post office a good while, till some worthy soul forwarded it on to ole George McGrady, who knew where to find me. I can't be sure, but I'm thinkin' Father died more 'n twenty years past. Can't say that I be surprised the ole man be dead. But I'm still trying to get my own mind around it. Let me know what ye think.

Yer brother,
    Ian

Robert's hands were shaking, making it difficult to carefully unfold the letter. It was yellowed and brittle with tears on the edges. He handled it as though it were a precious newborn baby. His eyes first went to the signature at the bottom of the letter. Seeing his father's name gave him a start. Robert looked away for a moment, blinking a few times as he tried to figure out whether his eyes were playing tricks on him. As the rest of his store appeared as it usually did, he turned back to the letter and took a deep breath, exhaled slowly, and read.

Edinburn, 1730

Ian an Robert,

387

Lads, if ye be readin this note, that likely means I be passed on from this life to the next. Many a time I sat down to write ye both to explain me whereabouts. Each time I failed to bring meself to finish the letter. The day I walked out o' yer lives, I almost turned about many a time. I don't know what kept me fro doing so. I just know that I couldn't turn back. I suppose I couln't face yer mither being taken fro me. Oh lads, I failed ye both as a father, leaving ye to others' care. I don't know quite what to say, but I want ye to know that I thought o' ye often an wondered how ye fared. Many o' time I sat in me room figuring how old ye might be an' what ye might be about.

I couldn't admit it to meself until now, but I can now see that I never recovered meself from losin yer mither. I figure I pretty well wasted away the rest o' me life. Lads, if ye let me say one thing to ye, don't let yer losin me cause ye to ruin the rest of yer lives! And don't let yerself turn to the bottle. I pray to God that this reach ye in time. I don't ask ye to forgive me for me own sake, but for yer own. Bitterness be a mighty fine disease. Oh aye, there be so much more I wish to tell ye, but I don't know how to. I figure I'll jist hae to let this short note be enough for now.

Although I hae not seemed to be,

Father

MacDonald dropped the letter. The next thing he knew, Rachel was calling his name. At first her voice seemed far away, and then as she touched his arm, he realized she spoke to him from his side. He looked at her face, yet needed several moments to focus clearly.

"Papa, Papa, can ye hear me!" shouted Rachel.

"Aye, it be me Rachel," answered MacDonald slowly.

"What happened to ye, Papa?"

MacDonald looked around the back room of his store, his eyes landing on the lone window. "Be it near dusk, lass?"

"Huh? Aye, Papa; it be closin' time. I came back to look for ye an' found ye starin' at nothin' an' lookin' to be a statue. What happened to ye?" pleaded Rachel.

MacDonald searched his mind a moment in vain, and then remembered the letter. He looked down at the ground and found his father's letter where he'd dropped it.

"Aye, lass, me father wrote a few lines t' me brither an' me."

Rachel took the offered letter and read it with eyes like saucers. "Oh, Papa, can this truly be fro' ye father?"

In answer MacDonald looked up at her, his face as that of a child. "I used to run down t' town almost e'ry day an' see if there be any letters fro' the carrier. I hoped there be somethin' fro' me father sayin' he was comin' home. Oh, Rachel, it be many a year since I stopped lookin' for such a note as ye find in yer hand; an' here it be."

"Oh, Papa!" Rachel sat down and put her arms around her father. Father and daughter embraced wordlessly.

Just as Rachel and MacDonald stood to leave for home, a knock came at the front door. A moment later Rachel returned with Thomas behind her. By this time MacDonald had recovered most of his usual clear state of mind.

"Well, hello there, lad! It be good t' see yer friendly face. So ye made it back in one piece then."

"So good to see ya, Mr. MacDonald!" said Thomas as he embraced his old friend.

"Now, lad, I think it be 'bout time yer done with the 'Mr. MacDonald.' Yer a man now an' it be time t' call me by me given name."

"Ya mean I'm t' call ya Robert?"

"That's 'xactly what I mean."

"But I've always called ya Mr. MacDonald," said Thomas.

"Aye, lad, an' there come a time for a man to put away the terms o' lads. An' not just 'cause ye be a man by years, lad, 'cause yer tree 'as grown to the point that ye be a man now from ye inside oot."

"I don' know, Mr. Mac... I don' know what to call ya. I'm not so sure I feel ready to call ya by ya given name."

"An' why not, lad?" inquired MacDonald.

"I don' know. I figure 'cause it puts me on the same level as you," said Thomas.

"That be 'xactly the point, lad. Ye be on the same level as me now. An' it 'bout right time for ye t' be thinkin' o' yerself as such."

"I don't figure I ever thought 'bout it this way, but I guess I always thought o' myself like the boy an' you the man," answered Thomas.

"I know, lad, an' there was a time when that be right. But now that time hae past. Ye been changin' fo' the better the years I known ye. I think ye know yer tree hae grown greatly in the years since I come to know ye."

Thomas pondered MacDonald's comment a few moments. "Well, I s'pose I have grown some," reflected Thomas.

"Hoots, lad, an' maybe more than ye hae given yerself the credit for."

"Well, I figure I'll have to think on it some," asked Thomas.

"'Course, lad. By the way, word 'round town is that ye be somethin' o' a hero," said MacDonald good-naturedly.

"I don' know 'bout that, but the mission did end well."

"Hoots - that be great, lad."

"Yeah. I'm glad for the freed prisoners," answered Thomas. "Looks like them Litchfield folk 're gonna move on out t' the Grants. Ya know, I was thinkin' on gettin' me some land out there too."

"Really, lad?"

"Yeah. When I was out 'n the Grants, I couldn't wait to get back home an' buy me a plot. The land out there be so beautiful an' open, with hardly a soul for miles. There be as much land as a man could want. At first I thought it be jist the beauty o' the land, but now I think mostly I want land o' my own. The Chittenden farm has never felt like mine, an' probably never will."

MacDonald nodded as Thomas continued. "When I first got back an' told Liz 'bout wantin' a grant, she wadn't so sure. Later I got to talkin' t' Ben 'bout the Grants, an' he was tellin' me how stupid such an idea be. Strange thing is after talkin' to Liz I doubted myself, but after talkin' to Ben I knew what I wanted even more clearly 'an before. Now I know I want land o' my own."

Thomas looked up to see a tear or two slowly making their way down MacDonald's face. At first he was surprised, and then all of a sudden the implication of moving to the Grants struck him. MacDonald had made the connection before Thomas had. "Dear God, that means I'd be leavin' you!" Thomas almost shouted. "Oh my... I can't believe I din't think o' that afore now. How did I... Maybe I wouldn't let myself think...."

MacDonald nodded sadly. "That be right, lad."

"Oh no, then I can't do it. There's no way I can move away from ya!"

"Oh lad, I'd like nothin' more than t' hae ye stay here in Salisbury, an' for me to watch ye live oot yer life. But I'd hate t' see ye give up on yer dream so quick on account o' me. Yer a bit young t' be givin' up on yer dreams so quick, don' ye think?" said MacDonald.

Thomas began to fight back the tears he could feel pushing their way up from his soul to his eyes. He didn't want to break down and weep, at least not yet. He shook his head, partly to push away the tears and partly to say "no" to MacDonald.

"No. I'm not ready to give ya up, Mr. MacDonald."

"Oh, lad, I s'pose yer jist beginnin' t' come t' grips wi' all the loss leavin' Salisbury would mean for ye. Ye need time t' let the impact come t' the core o' yer tree, lad. I don' wan' t' push ye too much. I be jist startin' t' come to terms with it meself."

Thomas paused as he pondered MacDonald's words as well as the new emotions flying around within him. Maybe it was MacDonald's invitation to feel, as Thomas then filled with emotion as though the flood gates of the dam had just been released. His shoulders heaved as the emotion came as it might. Neither of them said anything.

After Thomas took his leave, MacDonald was left with his own thoughts and feelings. MacDonald went to find Rachel in the front room. She'd been waiting for him. "Rachel, can ye give an ole father a few more minutes o' yer time lass?" MacDonald asked.

"'Course Papa, le'me just close up the store again so we won' be disturbed," said Rachel.

Rachel walked to the front door and locked up. As she walked back to sit down with her father, she noticed his tear-stained face.

"Papa, ye've been sheddin' tears again; be it yer father?"

"Aye, lass; well, aye an' nae. Thomas just came fro' givin' me sad news - the lad's thinkin' on moving oot t' the Grants."

"Oh, Papa, I'm so sorry," lamented Rachel. "I hae some idea what he means t' ye."

"It be true, lass, that apart fro' me Rachel, none livin' be nearer me heart than Thomas. Would be a great blow t' me trunk to lose the lad. This on top o' jist receivin' the letter fro' me father; 'tis more than I can take in all at once." Fresh tears began to flow as he said these words.

"I find meself rememberin' Grandfather," began MacDonald anew. "I remember Grandfather comin' alongside me when me father left after mi mither passed on. Grandfather din' allow me t' throw me life away sittin' alone 'n the room. He learnt me t' grieve, an' learnt me t' take notice o' my tree. Grandfather learnt me t' take good care o' my tree. Puts the fear o' God in me t' think o' what might hae come o' me if I'd been allowed t' go me own way withoot help. Grandfather grew me t' be a man - a grown tree. I always be grateful t' me grandfather fo' these. An' I think I been some kind o' grandfather t' Thomas." Here the tears began to flow afresh once again.

"Oh, Papa, I know," Rachel confirmed. "I heard Sally say somethin' o' what ye mean t' Thomas."

MacDonald nodded in acknowledgement. "I think it may even go a bit deeper than I been lettin' meself know. More 'an a grandfather, I feel like I been a wee bit a father t' the lad...maybe more 'an a wee bit... maybe I been the father I never hae meself... 'Tis a bit confusin', but I be grateful t' Grandfather, yet at the same time, it don' take away the sadness that me own father left me. Ye know, Rachel, ye've always been nearest me heart since yer mither died, an' yet maybe Thomas hae been the son I ne'er had. Fro' as long as my ole mind can remember, I always wanted a lassie an' a laddie."

MacDonald glanced at Rachel and saw the water flooding her eyes. "Oh, Papa, I miss me mither," cried Rachel.

"Oh, lass, I'm sorry t' bring 'er up t' ye," apologized MacDonald. "I hadn't thought..." Rachel cried on her father's shoulder. They sat in silence, each with their own loss. After an unhurried time, they left the store and went home arm in arm, both still sad, yet a bit lighter.

When Thomas got back to the house, he found Liz sitting on the porch. She waved him over to sit with her. Thomas took one look at Liz and knew her mind was troubled. Her brow furrowed when her mind worked on something important.

"I've been thinking about the Grants. All day I've thought about Auntie... my God, she's become so important to me...especially after Papa... I'm not sure if I could leave her, Thomas. I just want you to know what I'm thinking."

"I understand... I know she become like a mother to ya."

"Yes," said Liz.

"I jist come from MacDonald's... and I don' know if I can go... unless he come with us."

"Maybe you could invite him and Rachel to come," suggested Liz.

"Maybe... maybe I invite MacDonald an' you invite your aunt."

"I've thought of that, and I'm pretty sure she wouldn't come. They just expanded the ranch and are producing more than they ever have."

"Ya probably right, but ya might wanna ask anyways," said Thomas. Liz nodded and looked away. There was a heaviness about them both. Thomas took Liz's hand, and they sat in silence.

The next day Thomas was up and about his farming, though he hadn't been about his day long before Father approached him to talk. Thomas heard Father's footsteps and looked up. The hurt countenance Father's face belied immediately piqued Thomas's curiosity. Father rarely, if ever, exhibited such an expression.

"Thomas, we need to talk," implored Father.

"Father, what's wrong?"

"Please, walk with me son."

Thomas nodded affirmatively and walked alongside Father, waiting in anticipation. Father didn't speak for many minutes.

Thomas wondered what was going through Father's head for so long. Finally Father spoke. "Son, Ben told me ya thinkin' on headin' outta the Grants," Father began.

"That be right," replied Thomas after a pause.

Father stopped dead in his tracks. Ben had already revealed what Thomas had merely confirmed, but somehow hearing Thomas say it out loud stunned Father. For many years he'd known Thomas walked to the beat of a different drummer, but this seemed well beyond a different beat. This seemed a whole new genre of music. The man who rarely was at a loss for words didn't know what to say. Somehow he'd expected, or maybe hoped, that Ben had misunderstood.

Father had long since planned that his sons would carry on the farm after his passing, and had never given a thought to it being any other way. He'd been fully convinced both of his sons were of the same mind. Short of a death in the family, nothing could have been a greater blow to the older man. It was like one of the things you take for granted - the moon will be up tonight, the sun will be up in the morning, the farm will continue to provide for the family, and my sons will carry on after I'm gone.

"Thomas, I, uh, I don' know what t' say," began Father. "I guess I jist can't understand why ya'd wanna do that. I, uh, I thought you 'n Ben were gonna... Don't ya like the farm?"

Father surprised Thomas with his unusual candor. "Oh, Father, 'course I like the farm. My idea 'bout the Grants got nothin' t' do with not likin' the farm."

"Then what? Is it so bad livin' 'ere with Mama 'n me, Ben 'n Sally?"

"Oh no, it ain't nothin' like that," answered Thomas. "It ain't got nothin' t' do with ya. I jist want my own land an' my own life."

Father looked at Thomas as though trying to read a foreign language. "Ya own life? Don't ya have a good life 'ere?" asked Father.

"'Course I do," answered Thomas.

Thomas wasn't sure what else to say. He'd been ready for an angry father, but he was thrown off balance by a vulnerable father. Thomas searched for words to explain and found none.

"Son, do ya have any idea what this'll do t' ya mother?" Father implored.

When Thomas didn't respond, Father answered his own question. "It'll jist kill 'er, son."

"Oh, Father, I don't want ya to be hurt..."

"I ain't hurt, son."

"I wish there be somethin' I could say that would.... Ya know I hadn't told ya much o' my time out 'n the Grants. I was drawn t' the land like I hadn't been afore. 'Tis truly the most beautiful land I ever saw. There was so much space an' so few folk livin' out there. I wish ya coulda seen it! Anyways, I had plenty o' time t' think out on the trail an' kept thinkin' on gettin' me some o' that land out there. Father, ya made a good life for us here, for which I thank ya. I really do 'preciate all ya done for me. It ain't got nothin' t' do with ya; I jist wanna get land o' my own an' out there in them Grants."

"But ya got land o' your own right here," retorted Father. "I always planned t' give you n' Ben my land when I pass. Half this farm's yours!"

Thomas's shoulders slumped and his eyes searched for ground. He was at a loss as to what to say. Thomas sighed deeply. He glanced at Father, who looked away. "I'm sorry this hurts ya so, Father. I wish I could think o' somthin' else to say."

"Oh, it ain't me; it's ya Mama that's gonna be crushed by ya leavin'."

It saddened Thomas that Father couldn't allow himself his own pain. Thomas looked up at Father, who glanced at him quickly and then looked away. Father shrugged his shoulders, and then walked slowly away.

Later that same day, Thomas and Liz took supper with the rest of the family up at the new house. Even though Thomas, Liz, and Sally still lived in the old house below the barn, they continued to take supper and the midday meal up at the new house most days. After supper Sally decided to stay at the new house a bit longer, leaving Liz and Thomas to walk back to the old house alone. Thomas told Liz of his conversation with Father.

"I'm so sorry, Thomas," began Liz, "I can imagine how hard that conversation must have been."

"I jist wish Father would talk with me him 'bout his hurtin' over this Grant thing."

After a pause Liz said, "Have you given any more thought to whether you want to move out to the Grants?"

"Oh yeah. I think on it all the time," answered Thomas.

"And?"

"I don't think I'm ready t' talk 'bout it with ya tonight," said Thomas. "I think I need a bit more time to think over talkin' with Father; maybe in a day 'r two."

"Okay," said Liz.

Liz was content to give Thomas whatever time he needed, partly for his sake and partly because she hadn't decided herself yet. Aunt Hannah helped Liz understand her reluctance to consider a move to the Grants. Having lost her father tragically, Liz feared losing her mother and her aunt as well. Any move away from Salisbury would greatly limit her contact with both of them. The more she thought about it, the more Liz realized she feared giving up Aunt Hannah even more than her mother. An empty feel pervaded her stomach whenever she thought of leaving Auntie behind.

As Liz faced her fears head on, she began to feel some excitement about the prospect of having their own land out in the Grants; however, it took several days for her to get to this point. Even the adventure of the whole move excited her now.

Liz found herself thinking more and more about designing her own home and the way she might decorate. Living in the Chittenden's old house, Liz was quite aware of not having her own home. Although she'd done some minor redecorating with Sally, that house would never feel like her own. Liz and Thomas had long since started talking about having children. Although Liz wanted children, Aunt Hannah helped her realize she'd been reluctant to have children in the Chittenden house. Liz wasn't actively doing anything to prevent getting pregnant, but perhaps she wasn't allowing it just the same. She wanted children in her own house.

June 9, 1753 - Salisbury, Connecticut

The next evening Thomas invited Liz to take a walk with him. They did their best talking while they walked. They wandered up to the highest point of the property to enjoy the best view.

"Well, I feel ready t' talk 'bout the Grants," began Thomas.

"Okay, shoot," Liz replied.

"After we talked 'bout it when I first got back, I wadn't so sure 'bout the whole thing. I thought maybe I was bein' foolish or somethin'. Then after talkin' with Mr. MacDonald an' now Father, I think I wanna go. Ya know, Liz, I really want our own land. I guess it don't have t' be out in them Grants, but I sure would like t' git our own place," said Thomas.

"Me too!" said an excited Liz. "I understand your wanting your own land. I want my own house. Its great your folks let us live in the old house, but it isn't the same. I want that feeling too. I want to feel like it's my own house that we build together and that I decorate. And I want to have our own kids in our own house. I've never had my own house, and you've never had your own land. Thomas, it's about time for us to make our own lives."

A smile slowly spread over Thomas's face as Liz spoke. He'd been afraid she wouldn't want to move, and the last thing he wanted to do was try to force her to go somewhere she didn't want to go. Thomas felt relief, excitement, and gratitude that he and Liz shared a similar dream. He was thankful that neither wanted to live in the shadow of their parents' wings, and that both of them wanted to make their own way. "That's great!" Thomas exclaimed. "But what 'bout leavin' Auntie?"

Liz's face fell, and she said, "I did invite Auntie to come with us, and she said 'no,' which I expected. I'm still sad about leaving her, but I want to go anyways."

"I'm sorry she won't go," said Thomas. Thomas took Liz's hand and they walked hand in hand. Before they realized it, they stood at the entrance to the cave.

"Well, look where we are," exclaimed Liz. "Were you leading me here all along?"

Thomas chuckled. "I don' know, but now that we here let's go in."

They ducked under the tree limbs and stepped into the cave. Thomas quickly found a candle or two and lit them. Liz became aware of feeling romantic energy toward Thomas. She approached Thomas and took his hands and looked him briefly in the eye. Then she began to gently kiss his lips. Thomas eagerly responded, also feeling physically drawn to Liz. An exciting, intimate physical moment ensued in which they enjoyed each other. They took their time, neither in any hurry. When the climax finally came, they both fell back exhausted and satisfied.

As they lay regaining their breath and energy, a light rain began to fall outside. They could hear it softly falling on the leaves and rocks outside the cave entrance. Unconcerned about getting wet, Thomas and Liz found the rain added to the peaceful afterglow of their intimate moment together. Neither felt any hurry to leave.

Thomas glanced over to the cave entrance and saw that dusk was settling over the farm. If they didn't leave soon, they'd be picking their way in the dark, possible scratching clothes and limbs. Thomas gently suggested they head back to the house, although he did so with some reluctance.

The next night Thomas and Liz talked about some of the particulars they would need to think through. Liz asked Thomas if he'd thought about who they might invite to come with them to the Grants.

"Yeah, actually I have thought some 'bout that," began Thomas. "I'd like to invite John and Samantha."

"Okay," said Liz; "anyone else?"

"Well, I wondered 'bout Sally. I think she an' Noah might wanna come, an' I think she might feel hurt if we din't invite 'er."

"I'd thought about her too," said Liz. "She's become a dear friend to me, and we're going to need some friends out there. We're not going to know anyone out there besides who we take with us."

Liz and Sally had barely known each other when Thomas and Liz married, but since that time they'd become fast friends. It's almost inevitable to come to love or hate the people you live with; sometimes both. Sally had lived with Thomas and Liz since they'd married.

"I've thought 'bout that some too," said Thomas. "I think we need some family to bring with us. Maybe it'll be 'nough for us if those two couples come with us, dependin' on what happens to Sally an' Noah."

"Thomas, I've been thinking about someone else," Liz said cautiously. "I've been thinking about bringing Mother with us. What do you think?"

"Wow, I hadn't thought 'bout her," said Thomas honestly. "I don' know, what do ya think it'd be like to have 'er with us?"

"I think she'd be nervous, difficult, opinionated, and hard to be with. Other than that, she'd be great to have along," laughed Liz.

Thomas laughed along with Liz. He was well aware that neither of them enjoyed Liz's mother and didn't spend much time with her as a result. Mother had never come out of the depression she'd fallen into when her husband died suddenly. It took great energy from Liz to be with her mother, not receiving much in return. Mother continued to live with her sister, Aunt Hannah, where she'd been since her husband died. She'd yet to find a purpose or direction for her life, and seemed to merely exist.

"So, what makes ya wanna bring 'er then?" asked Thomas.

"Mostly for her sake," answered Liz. "I'm pretty sure she'd feel hurt and abandoned if I left her here without inviting her to come. I also have some hope that it might give her a second chance to start a new life in the Grants."

"That's a great gift ya'd be givin' her," said Thomas. "I've an idear what it'd cost ya t' bring 'er along with us."

"Yes. It might cost me greatly," said Liz sadly.

"Ya know, maybe Mother might find some purpose 'n helpin' tend t' our kids," suggested Thomas.

"Maybe," said Liz with some hope in her voice. "So, are you okay with me inviting Mother?"

"Oh sure, Liz. I leave that 'tirely up to you," said Thomas. "I'm pretty sure Mother'll weigh more on you than me."

"Thank you," said a grateful Liz. "I know it's more on me, but it'll cost you some too to have Mother come."

With this Liz hugged her husband in thankfulness, appreciating that Thomas understood what it meant to her to bring her mother with them. After releasing him, Liz noticed something come over Thomas's face.

"Thomas, you look sad."

Thomas nodded. "I guess ya talkin' 'bout Mother got me thinkin' 'bout Mr. MacDonald. I sure wish he'd come with us," said Thomas.

"Oh, Thomas, I know it's going to be hard for you to leave him."

Thomas nodded and looked down. "And it be okay by me if you want to invite John and Samantha," said Liz.

The next day Thomas saddled his horse and headed off for the mill. He found John just finishing his meal and on his way back out to resume his day's work.

"Hey, Captain," said John.

"Drop the captain thing," said a smiling Thomas. "We done with that."

"Thank God for that; sure is good t' be back," said John.

"So, what ya been up to, hero," joked Thomas.

"Mostly been helping Pa catch up on work 'round the mill. He ran a bit behind the weeks we was gone. Also been spending a good bit o' time with Samantha and little Davie," John said with a grin. John and Samantha already had a one-year-old son.

"So, John, looks like Liz an' me decided we gonna head on outta the Grants," announced Thomas.

"That so?" said a surprised John. "Wow, ya decided pretty quick. So Liz wants t' go too?"

"Yeah. Liz's pretty excited 'bout it. Seem like she wants it more 'an me. She had t' think on it some, but she's pretty decided now," answered Thomas. "Hey, John, so have you an' Samantha figured out if ya goin' with us?"

"After you an' me talked on it so much comin' back from the mission, I mentioned it t' Samantha right off. She was excited 'bout it right off. She's so ready t' go, she asked me 'bout it several times since."

"Really?" said Thomas. "What 'bout you?"

"That's just it; I don' know yet. At first I was rearin' to go, an' then it hit me - I'd be leavin' my Pa. Ya know that Pa an' me 're almost best friends. Every time I think on it, I just get so sad; I don' know if I can do it," said John.

"I understand that ya probably need more time to think on it," said Thomas.

"Yeah, I figure I do. I jist don' know yet," said John.

"Well, take ya time, John. God knows 'tis a big decision."

Both men pondered their own thoughts in silence before Thomas spoke again. "Ya know, if I'm honest, sometimes I'm not so sure I wanna go, even if I din't have to leave Mr. MacDonald," began Thomas. "Sometimes I worry 'bout the risks. I mean, what if I don't like... I mean...well, I figure it won't help to think too much 'bout all that."

"There sure 're lots o' risks. I figure ya jist can't know 'bout any o' that right yet," said John.

"That's jist it, John. I can't know an' won't know till after we get there! It's not like we can try it out for a month 'n see. Ya ever think 'bout all that?" asked Thomas.

"Can't say that I have," said John.

Later that afternoon Ben approached as Thomas continued his work out in the fields. Ben looked serious as he walked up to where Thomas worked.

"So, little brother, ya still thinkin' on headin' outta them Grants?" asked Ben.

"Yep," responded Thomas.

"If ya don't mind a little big brother advice, how ya gonna pay for the land?"

"I'm not sure yet. I got some saved from my militia pay, but I don' know if its 'nough," answered Thomas.

"If ya don't got 'nough, where the rest gonna come from?" pressed Ben.

"Like I said, I don' know yet," answered Thomas.

"How can ya move outta the Grants if ya don't have the money? And how're ya gonna feed yourselves afore ya can grow anythin'?" continued Ben.

"Don' have that all worked out yet," responded Thomas.

"An' where ya gonna live when ya first git there? Ya gonna sleep on the ground? An' is Liz gonna sleep on the ground?" asked Ben.

Thomas shrugged his shoulders and began to respond when Ben jumped back in first. "Come now, little brother, don't it seem foolhardy to go out there without 'nough money, no plans t' feeds yaself, an' no place to stay in the meantime when ya got all that here?"

Thomas could feel irritation with Ben rising within. "Some of that I jist can't know yet. I ain't got no crystal ball. Some o' ya questions jist can't be answered till we git there. All I know is that we got us a dream an' we figure to go after it," said Thomas, sounding more sure of himself than he felt.

"Ya got a fool's dream with no certain plans, little brother. Ya gotta dream right here; don't ya see that? Why go chasin' some fool's gold out in the hills that jist might end in nothin'?" said Ben.

"I know ya happy here, Ben, an' I'm glad for ya. I have a good life here too, but me an' Liz have a dream for somethin' different. Sometimes ya jist gotta follow ya dreams. Ya can't have everythin' worked out afore or it wun't be a true dream!"

"What if ya dream gits Liz kilt? What if ya dream lands ya flat broke with nothin' to eat? What if ya dream leaves ya with nowhere t' lay ya head?" argued Ben.

"What if ya wake up one day with gray hair an' find out ya never went for ya dreams?" Thomas pushed back.

Ben started to speak and then stopped. Thomas softened, as it occurred to him that he was hearing Ben's fear, not just brotherly advice. Yet before Thomas could say more, Ben turned on his heels and walked away.

Thomas spent some time thinking over the concerns Ben had brought up. He realized he'd thought about each of those possibilities already. He wondered what MacDonald would say about his fears. It didn't take long before he could almost hear MacDonald's response:

"Lad, any dream worth dreamin' will hae its risks. Be afraid, an' yet don' let yer fear run away with ye. A life wi' noo risks be a life not worth yer livin'."

MacDonald lived inside him now. Thomas often found himself imagining what MacDonald might think about this or say about that.

Most of the time he could imagine accurately what his old friend might say; after all, he'd heard him say so many things that his words did indeed live within Thomas. Thomas took great comfort in drawing on his memory of MacDonald. MacDonald had become a resource that Thomas carried with him wherever he went.

As his thoughts returned to his conversation with Ben, Thomas found himself feeling for his brother. It saddened Thomas that Ben seemed so bound by fear. At one time Thomas would have been angered by Ben's comments, but not today. Thomas felt grateful that he didn't feel as bound by fear as he once did.

After supper Thomas and Liz sat down to talk. Sally was out on the porch with Noah, so the couple had the old home to themselves. Thomas recounted his conversation with Ben and his thoughts about it. Liz told Thomas that she was glad he hadn't allowed Ben's fear to take him over, and that she thought he'd handled the interaction well. Thomas found he was most interested in what happened after the conversation with Ben.

"Ya know, Liz," Thomas began, "afore that kinda thing with Ben woulda knocked me 'round pretty good. But after, I was able t' think it through pretty good. It was like Mr. MacDonald was right 'side my head helpin' me sort it all out. I figure I din't doubt myself much this time, but kept my own mind. Used to be I had t' talk over a conversation like that with Mr. MacDonald to sort things out. This time I did it 'n my own mind like Mr. MacDonald was sittin' right there with me. Maybe the best part is I felt more like a man."

"I so respect you, Thomas Chittenden," returned a smiling Liz. "You've grown more and more into a man in the years I've known you."

"Maybe so, an' I think I owe most o' that to Mr. MacDonald, an' some o' that to you. This may sound kinda silly, but ya bring out a more grown Thomas 'n me."

"Well, I'm sure we've helped each other grow plenty," said Liz. "But I don't want you to get rid of that boy completely; I like playing with him," said Liz with a twinkle in her eye.

Liz went on to telling Thomas about her inviting Mother to the Grants. Liz explained that at first Mother was elated at the idea, and then she had a change of heart. "It was so strange," Liz began; "it was as though Mother took off one of those theatre masks and put on another. The first mask was of excitement, the second of fear and worry. She said she didn't know if she could go that far away. She wasn't sure if she had the energy for such a change. I don't know if she'll go with us, Thomas, but I'm worried about what will come of her if she doesn't."

"I bet she comes 'round 'n the end," said Thomas.

"Oh, I hope you're right. I just hate to think of leaving her here," said Liz.

Sally came in from her time with Noah, leaving him at the door to say goodnight. She found Thomas reading in his favorite chair by the window. Thomas read more now than he used to, and slowly developed his reading skill. Sally came over and sat opposite her brother. Thomas looked up from his reading with a warm smile.

"Hey there, Sally. How're things with that gentlemen friend o' yours?" asked Thomas.

Sally blushed with mild embarrassment. "Well, I think pretty good," Sally responded. "We talkin' more 'bout our future."

"Really? That be excitin'," said Thomas. "I din't know things had gotten that far."

"Yeah, things 're movin' quicker than I thought they would," said Sally.

"Ya think he's a good match for ya?" asked Thomas.

"That's actually what I wanted to talk with ya 'bout. Sometimes it seem like Noah don't care 'bout how I'm feelin', but I'm not quite sure," said Sally.

"What makes ya think that?" asked Thomas.

"Like the other night I was sayin' that I din't like the way he said somethin' to me, an' he said, 'Oh, don't be silly. It was nothin'.' I don't think he meant to be mean-spirited, but I din't feel like he took me serious," explained Sally. "What'd ya think?"

"I can see why that'd cause ya some concern, sis."

"Do ya think I oughta talk to 'im 'bout it?" Sally asked.

"Absolutely I do," Thomas replied. "Ya tryin' to tell ya man somethin' important 'bout ya tree an' he's not gettin' it. 'N all fairness to Noah, he may not know much 'bout trees an' their proper tendin'. The way I see it, ya best give 'im a chance to know. Ya've learnt a good bit 'bout that, while Noah may never heard nothin' o' it. Remember, sis, there was a time when we din't know nothin' 'bout our trees neither."

"I s'pose I forget that most don' know much 'bout that. I figure Noah might just be startin' to know himself," said Sally.

"That be likely," agreed Thomas.

Sally nodded and breathed a sigh of relief, feeling a bit lighter now that she'd talked her concern over with her brother.

"By the way, ya mind if I change the subject?" asked Thomas.

"Naw, go right 'head," returned Sally.

"Don' know if ya've caught wind o' it yet, but me 'n Liz 're thinkin' o' movin' outta the Grants. I hope ya din't hear 'bout it from somebody else yet," said Thomas.

"What? Ya can't be serious!" Sally almost shouted. "Oh, Thomas, ya wunt leave me, would ya?"

Thomas held his tongue, merely returning her question with a look of concern. When Thomas didn't respond immediately, Sally continued. "Ya really are gonna leave me? I can't believe it. What am I gonna do without ya? How can ya do this to me?"

Thomas had thought he'd prepared for her to be upset, but was still unsettled by her emotion.

"I'm jist not ready for ya to leave me yet. I'm not on my own feet good 'nough. Things are jist gettin' serious with Noah, an' ya can't leave me yet. I need ya to walk me through things with 'im still. I got Rachel, but ya takin' away my other two best friends - you an' Liz. It's jist too soon!" It was painful for Thomas to hear the emotion he'd stirred in his sister. He wiped his sweaty palms on his pants.

"I know this don't make sense, but I feel like a child whose parent jist said they gonna go away," said Sally. After a brief pause Sally continued. "I haven't said nothin' like this afore, but I figure ya've been more than a brother to me...really somethin' of a father. Ya taught me how t' talk 'bout my feelin's an' take care o' my tree. Nobody else in our family seemed t' know much 'bout such things. Guess ya taught me important lessons Father an' Mama couldn't help me with," Sally said.

"I know, li'l sister, I know," said Thomas.

Thomas's eyes began to mist as he said these words. "I'm so glad I could help ya begin to blossom. Ya right, nobody in our family knows much 'bout people trees, not t' mention tendin' 'em. I'm so grateful for MacDonald. It scares me to think what'd come o' me without 'im. An' I'm so glad I could be o' help to you."

Sally nodded her head; tears returned to her eyes and remained in his. "I'm jist so thankful for ya, Thomas. Ya've helped me so much. I hate t' think what would've come o' me if I din't have ya. An' at the same time, I hate ya right now."

"At times I wondered who was gettin' more outta this, you or me," began Thomas. "Truly has been a blessin' to me to come alongside ya, li'l sister. An' don't forget that at times I brought my tree t' ya for some tendin'."

"Yeah, I know," said Sally. "Hey, wait a minute! Did ya say ya probably leaving?"

"Yeah, don' know for sure yet. But I figure we goin'."

"An' when would ya be leavin'?"

"Maybe a couple months, maybe more."

"Wow, that sounds so soon, Sally said. "So how did you an' Liz come to consider such a big move?"

Thomas took a moment to gather his thoughts. "Well, I might o' mentioned to ya that the farm has never felt like it was mine. Out on the mission I gotta chance t' see them Grants up close, an' it was like a magnet or somethin' was pullin' me to it. An' I met some folks that 're riskin' everything to make that move. But I figure the main thing is me an' Liz both wants our own home an' our own land an' our own dreams, an' here will never be that...Sally, ya welcome to come with us."

"Oh, yes, o' course I be comin'. An' if Noah an' me work it out, can he come too?"

"O' course he can," said a beaming Thomas.

"Alrighty then!" Sally stood up and grabbed Thomas's hands and they danced them around the floor merrily and with great enthusiasm. All of a sudden Sally stopped dancing. After a brief pause Sally continued. "Hey, I just thought o' somethin'; who have ya told so far?"

"Ya mean in the family?" asked Thomas.

"Yeah."

"I told Ben an' Father. I haven't told Mama yet," said Thomas.

"Why not?"

"I don' know, somethin' in me doesn't wanna tell Mama," began Thomas. "Maybe I'm afraid o' how she'll handle the news."

"Mama do git hurt easy," agreed Sally.

"I'm not sure if her bein' hurt's it. Maybe somethin' worse," pondered Thomas.

"I don' know if Mama's gonna be afraid for ya, but I know she's gonna be afraid for me," said Sally. "Oh, dear God, I don' wanna tell her neither."

"Are ya gonna tell the others?" asked Thomas.

"I s'pose I need to talk it over with Noah. I'd like 'im to come with us. Well, eventually I'm gonna tell Mama, but I don' think I wanna tell anybody jist yet," said Sally. "Truth is, I barely jist told myself!"

Both brother and sister laughed at this. "I s'pose I need time to think over what I wanna say to the family, an' especially to Mama," said Sally.

"I'm not ready to tell Mama neither, but maybe we can tell 'er together later," suggested Thomas. "I might feel more ready to tell 'er once we gots more definite plans." Sally nodded.

Sally, Thomas, and Liz sat at the table of the old house eating the midday meal together when they heard a knock on the door frame. The door stood open, as it usually did during daylight hours. They looked up to see John's large frame filling the doorway.

"Hey there, John, sit down an' join us," invited Thomas.

"Yes, there's plenty for you," seconded Liz.

"Don't mind if I do," said John as he pulled up a chair.

"So, ya here to tell us you be comin' outta the Grants with us?" said Thomas half joking. John's face fell in response.

"Guess not," said Thomas.

"Truth is I came here to tell ya we ain't goin'," John admitted reluctantly. "Damn, it was hard to decide. Samantha an' me went back an' forth on it a good many times. Samantha wanted to go. I'm the one that don't. I figure I just don't wanna leave Pa. With Mama gone, we all he's got. An' not only that, I been noticin' he can't do as much with the mill as he could afore. I don't know what he'd do if we all left. I guess I just can't do that to 'im. I'm sorry, Thomas."

Thomas nodded and looked down at his mostly empty plate. "Damn! I gotta admit I'm disappointed. I was sure hopin' ya'd come. No use pretendin' otherwise. But I figure ya have to make ya own decision, an' I respect that," said Thomas slowly.

"Thomas, my decision ain't got nothin' to do with ya. If it was just between us, I'd be goin'."

"I ain't takin' it personal," Thomas responded.

"If there be anythin' I can do to help ya all make the move, just lemme know," offered John.

That night Thomas and Liz were getting ready to get into bed for the night. Thomas finished washing up at the basin and was drying his face and hands. Liz eyed him as she brushed her hair.

"So, does John's decision make you not want to go?" asked Liz.

"It sure don't help."

"I figured as much. I know you were counting on him and Samantha going."

Thomas nodded. "I just feel all mixed up right now. At times I think I'm ready to go, an' then an hour later I ain't so sure."

Thomas made inquiries and discovered that another auction was scheduled to be held in the Grants in six weeks hence. Thomas, Liz, and Sally had all the more to discuss now that there was a specific timing to consider. If they wanted to participate in this auction, they had to move fast. They decided they wanted to examine any plots of land first, before buying. None of them wanted to blindly bid on plots they hadn't seen. They figured to give themselves about a week to walk the available plots of land. In order to arrive in five weeks' time, they estimated they would have to be on the trail in two or three weeks' time. It all seemed so fast.

Thomas, Liz, and Sally noticed the family meals being more tense than usual. The others didn't know that Sally was planning to leave, so they didn't treat her differently. It was a different story with Thomas and Liz. Father no longer spoke much to Thomas and Liz, but did seem to offer them plenty of angry looks. Of course Father had never spoken much before, but now he spoke even less. Ben didn't appear angry as much as arrogant. Ben basically ignored Liz and gave Thomas a steady diet of knowing, superior expressions as if he knew something that Thomas didn't. Occasionally Ben would look at Thomas and just shake his head, which was even more difficult to tolerate. Thomas and Liz considered declining to eat with the rest of the family; however, on further reflection, they decided to continue bearing the meals as long as they could.

Thomas took a walk on his own, wanting to be alone to think. Now that their possible departure date was fast approaching, there was plenty to think over. He glanced up and saw his old cave. His heart warmed to see his old friend, and he made his way into his cave for one last visit. He lit a candle and sat back in his favorite chair with a view out the opening of the cave. Thomas loved to gaze out at the trees and rocks. He reminisced about many times sitting and enjoying the familiar scene and the feel of the wooden chair. Thomas felt the carvings on the chair with his fingers and looked down to see his and Ben's names scratched into the side of the chair. He smiled at the poor handwriting, and then realized it wouldn't look much different if he scratched the letters today. He sat lost in thought.

Thomas became overwhelmed with the enormity of the decision he was trying to get his mind around. He spontaneously uttered his thoughts aloud. "What am I thinkin'? Now, why am I gonna be leavin' again?"

For the moment he couldn't think of why he wanted to leave his home in Salisbury. Right now the whole thing seemed foolish. He lived with his family and had a farm that was to be half his, a good house to live in, MacDonald in town, and good friends nearby.

Maybe he had been crazy to consider such a wild idea. He spoke aloud again, as if someone were there to listen. "Dear God, what am I doin'? I can't believe I'm 'bout to leave my family. An' even more I can't believe I'm 'bout to leave MacDonald."

No answers came to him. Thomas was able to pull up a vague idea about following a dream; yet the dream seemed as unstable as a wispy cloud that's here for a moment and then blown away by the wind. More questions came to his mind.

"God, where are Ya 'n all this. What do God think o' my plans? Is there even a God? An' if there is, do He concern Himself with me any?" Then a stange thing happened - he heard a response. "Have I not provided you with another father?"

"What? Where did that come from?" asked Thomas aloud.

The words struck Thomas like the dizzying effect of spinning in circles. At first Thomas thought he was imagining the words. He didn't hear an audible voice. The words came to his mind in the form of thoughts, as if spoken wordlessly. However, he was fairly sure the thoughts he had were not entirely his own. As he thought more about it, he decided there would be no harm in answering, even if he was only answering himself.

"Are ya talkin' to me, God? An' if so, how have ya provided me with another father?" Thomas asked.

A picture of MacDonald's face immediately came to mind, yet he heard no words. Thoughts flooded his mind, leaving him confused and disoriented. "Is God actually talkin' with me? Or am I jist makin' it all up? Maybe it jist be what I wanna hear. Am I jist goin' crazy from all the pressure?"

As Thomas tried to make sense of what he'd just experienced, he guessed the strange thoughts couldn't have been his own. The thoughts didn't seem to be self-directed. If they weren't directed by him, then who were they directed by? He wasn't even sure he believed in God. Thomas decided to talk it over with the wisest person he knew.

Thomas hadn't seen him since that first conversation they'd had after his return. The next day Thomas found MacDonald at his store. He'd had to wait a few minutes for MacDonald, and spent the time visiting with Rachel. When MacDonald returned he felt a mixture of joy and sadness at seeing his young friend, and was glad to offer him his ear.

"What be on yer mind, lad?"

"I jist had the strangest experience. I wonderin' if I'm goin' crazy. Somethin' happened to me in my cave."

MacDonald's curiosity was piqued. "Aye, an' what would that be, lad?"

"I was in the cave an' jist thinkin' things over, ya know, with the move an' all. I guess I must o' spoken out loud addressin' God, an' somebody seemed t' answer."

Thomas looked up at MacDonald, expecting to see either alarm or amusement on his old friend's face. However, MacDonald merely held his solemn countenance and waited for Thomas to continue. Then Thomas finished recounting the rest of the experience. Instead of telling Thomas he must be imagining things, MacDonald asked a simple question.

"What did He say, lad?"

"Ya mean, ya mean it really was God?" asked Thomas.

"An' why not, lad?"

"He said He'd provided me with another father," answered Thomas.

MacDonald's eyes misted as he heard the simple reply. He pulled out his hankerchief and wiped his face. His expression was a strange mixture of joy and sadness and pride. "That be jist as I thought all along, lad."

"It is?" said Thomas.

"'Course lad; nothing could be more likely," replied MacDonald. "Has truly been me great joy t' be like a father to ye, lad. An' don' forget what the great Father said: He'd be a 'Father to the fatherless' an' that 'God places the lonely in families.' Well lad, He did jist that for ye. An I be grateful for the privilege t' be like a father to ye."

By now MacDonald's eyes had gone beyond mere misting and were now producing a gentle stream down his well-worn face. Thomas had expected MacDonald to laugh at his experience and comfort him that he wasn't going crazy; this was hardly what he'd expected. The thought seemed too good to be true, as if he were hearing of something from another world. But Thomas so wanted the other world to be true.

"Lad, maybe ye be ready to hear fro' the great Father within' yerself now," said MacDonald. Thomas looked pensively at his old friend. "Ye know, lad, an essential part o' growin' to be a man hae to do with readin' yer own story. A man hae to know 'is own tree. The only way to know yer own tree be to read yer own rings. What I'm tryin' to say, lad, to be a man ye hae to know yer own tree, an' that be to know yer own story. I think ye were tryin' to make sense o' yer own story up in the cave. An' that be o' the greatest importance. Ye see, lad, ye can't write a new endin' to yer story till ye read the story ye got so far. Many try to write new endin's withoot makin' sense o' the story they already wrote."

"Ya mean most don' know themself?"

"Aye, lad, that be precisely what I mean. Oh, many try an' read the chapter summaries o' skim through the story, but few actually study their stories 'nough to make good sense o' 'em. Ye an' yer lass can only write meaningful new endin's if ye know the story that came first. How can ye write a new story if ye don't know the old one?"

As Thomas sat silently with his thoughts, MacDonald realized this was a good time for what he'd planned. "Come t' the back wi' me, lad."

Thomas followed MacDonald to the back room and sat in his familiar spot on top of the sacks of flour, wondering what his old friend had in mind. He watched MacDonald walk over to his shelf and take down the familiar box that contained MacDonald's prized sword - the sword that belonged to his father. MacDonald pulled the sword out of the dusty box and sat down next to Thomas with the black sword across his lap. Thomas eagerly awaited what new adventure the sword might bring. MacDonald rarely took it out of its box.

"Ye know, lad, we ne'er spoke o' such, but I hae long since thought o' ye as a grandson. I often said as much to meself an' t' me Rachel. Truth be that I long since knew ye to be like a son t' me, but I wouldn't let meself think as much."

"How could ya know that if ya never thought it?" asked Thomas.

"There be much that we all know, but can't let oorselves think yet. I knew it lad, but i' took me t' a place o' great pain t' remember me own father leavin'. I s'pose I din' wanna go t' such a place in me tree. Maybe ye bein' 'n great need o' fatherin' drew me t' ye fro' the beginnin'. Ye see, lad, I know too weel what 'tis t' be in need o' more fatherin'. I received a letter fro' me father the other day. It got me thinkin' 'bout me own father. Anyways, I been holdin' father's sword t' pass on t' me own son. Now I know that to be none other than ye, lad."

Here MacDonald paused. He gave himself a few minutes to gather himself before continuing. "Lad, I want ye t' hae me father's sword." At this MacDonald held the prized sword out for Thomas to receive. Thomas didn't move; it was as though he were paralyzed. He felt stunned, having had no thought that MacDonald would intend to give him such a gift. That his old friend might bless him with the sword in some sort of ceremony was the most for which he'd allowed himself to hope.

After several silent moments, Thomas was finally able to speak. "I don' know, Mr., uh, I just dunno if I can take such a ..." stammered Thomas.

"I'm not askin' ye t' take nothin', lad. I want ye to allow me t' pass this on from father t' son t' son. Ye're t' be the guardian o' the MacDonald sword till the day yer son be ready to wield it."

Thomas reluctantly took the sword from MacDonald. He slowly turned it over in his hands, trying to get his mind around the gift.

He didn't know what to say. The enormity of the gift was too much for him to take in all at once. MacDonald figured that Thomas needed time to digest what he'd given him and waited.

"Mr. Mac, uh, Robert, can I leave it here until we ready to leave for the Grants?" Thomas asked.

"'Course ye can, lad, an' I heard ye call me by me given name."

Thomas laughed nervously at first, and then nodded his head. "Yeah, I s'pose I might be finally ready to call ya Robert," answered Thomas; "but don't count on me never throwin' in a Mr. MacDonald or two. One more thing...come with me to the Grants!"

When Thomas arrived back at the house, his sister had been waiting for him. Sally had already cleaned up for supper, but wanted to talk with Thomas before heading over to the new house. "Thomas, can I have a moment afore we go to supper?" asked Sally.

Still pondering his conversation with MacDonald, Thomas took a moment to process her question. "Oh, 'course ya can," he said. "What be on ya mind?"

"Thomas, I fear we done wrong by Mama," Sally began. "We maybe leavin' in less than a fortnight, an' we yet to tell Mama."

"Oh my... I fear ya right," Thomas responded. "I figure I been puttin' off tellin' her as long as I could get 'way with. Oh Sally, I still jist dread tellin' her."

"I know, I dread tellin' 'er too; but we have to do it," remonstrated Sally.

"Ya know, li'l sister, I can't say exactly why, but I have a real bad feelin' 'bout tellin' her. Proably this sounds crazy, but I'm 'fraid it gonna kill 'er," said Thomas.

Sally put her head down and nodded. Thomas sighed, exhaling deeply. "Okay, when do ya wanna tell 'er?"

"Tonight after supper," said Sally firmly.

"Wow! I guess ya ready t' go then."

"I don' know how ready I am, but I jist know we have to do it," said Sally. "I was talkin' it over with Rachel, an' I jist see that we makin' it harder by puttin' it off."

"Alright then, tonight it is then."

Thomas, Sally, and Liz walked up to the new house. On the way it was decided that Liz would walk back to the old house on her own, while Thomas and Sally stayed behind to talk with Mama after supper. Liz readily agreed to miss that conversation.

The usual tension of recent family meals continued tonight. Few words were exchanged, and those that were either seemed awkward or a poor attempt to pretend that everything was as it should be. Thomas and Sally felt nervous throughout the meal, eating little; neither had much of an appetite. At this point they just wanted to get it over with. Finally the meal came to an end and Thomas asked Mama if he could have a word with her. Father and Ben probably figured what was on his mind and immediately agreed to go outside to smoke their pipes. Neither of them wanted to be present when Mama learned the news.

Mama and Sally cleared off the dishes from the table and set them soaking in water before sitting back down at the table. Thomas remained where he'd been and fidgeted. Mama sat down wordlessly, with mouth pursed and eyes darting back and forth. Mama was well aware that Thomas rarely asked to speak with her.

"Mama, we have some news," began Thomas. "I'm not quite sure how best to tell ya, so I figure I jist come right out with it. Liz, Sally, an' me 're figurin' to move on outta the Grants."

Mama instantly put her hand to her mouth with such an expression of terror that she might not have looked more startled if she'd seen a ghost. At first she seemed frozen in that position, and stared at Thomas as if trying to make sense of his pronouncement. She next looked to Sally, searching her face for what she couldn't find in Thomas's. At last she broke the silence and spoke.

"I can't figure it out," Mama began. "I can't figure what I done."

Thomas and Sally exchanged puzzled glances. Sally responded. "What do ya mean, what ya've done?" Sally asked.

At first Mama didn't respond, merely shaking her head slowly back and forth. She seemed to be trying to decipher a hidden message that she couldn't quite decode. "I just can't figure what I done," Mama continued.

Sally and Thomas stole another glance. "Ya haven't done nothin', Mama," said Thomas.

"It must be somethin'," said Mama. "Ya wouldn't be leavin' me if there wadn't somethin' I done. I'm turnin'it over in my head an' I still jist can't figure it."

"Mama, there ain't nothin'," Sally said. "This ain't got nothin' to do with anythin' ya done. This is 'bout what me an' Thomas want for ourself!"

Mama stared blankly at Sally, as though her words were spoken in coded language and had no meaning to her. Suddenly Mama's eyes brightened. "That it! There must be somethin' ya waitin' for me to apologize 'bout," Mama said. "This be a test to see if I apologize! 'Course I'll apologize, just tell me what I gotta apologize for."

"It ain't nothin' like that!" said Thomas. "This be 'bout me an' Sally an' Liz wantin' a new life for ourselves. It ain't got nothin' to do with what ya done!"

"Oh, so I have to figure it out on my own then," said Mama. "I see, ya ain't gonna tell Mama. I have t' figure it myself."

Thomas looked to Sally with growing alarm. "Mama, din't ya hear what Thomas said?" asked Sally. "This ain't 'bout nothin' ya done."

"No, my hearin' is just fine," responded Mama. "I heard just fine that ya ain't gonna tell me, an' I gotta figure it myself. It's all a test. The apology's no good 'less I figure it myself."

"What?" cried Sally.

Sally hadn't intended to say this aloud, but it came out spontaneously. Mama's initial pleading for her crimes turned to growing anger as the specifics she sought were not forthcoming. Now Sally and Thomas were really worried.

Thomas was tempted to emphatically deny what Mama was saying and try to convince her otherwise. Fortunately, his alarm hadn't turned to panic and he was able to think with some clarity. While Sally tried to convince Mama otherwise, Thomas had time to think. Thomas imagined what MacDonald might say in a situation like this. He could imagine MacDonald asking why he feared telling Mama about the move. The reason for Thomas's dread of this conversation became clear to him - Thomas had known somehow that Mama would take their move personal. Next, Thomas could almost hear MacDonald asking if it would be helpful to try and convince her otherwise. Thomas could answer that one quickly. He'd never been able to talk Mama out of anything when she'd decided something was because of her.

Thomas refocused on what was being said between his sister and his mother. Sally had stopped trying to explain, perhaps realizing her attempts were futile. Mama continued searching about the room for clues to her crime, as though she inspected a crime scene. Sally and Thomas listened with the helplessness of knowing there was nothing to do but keep their tongues from throwing further fuel onto an already blazing fire. Sally reached out and held Thomas's hand under the table.

Years ago neither Thomas nor Sally would have been able to restrain themselves. Thomas kept thinking of MacDonald's words. Sally kept holding onto Thomas to restrain herself. Thomas had given up trying to convince her. Sadness came over him. He spoke slowly. "Mama, I can see that ya hurt by our decision an' all, an' I'm sorry 'bout that. I also wish I'd told ya sooner, so ya'd have more time. I figure I was scared o' how ya'd take the news. I s'pose what's happenin' now is 'bout what I'd feared," said Thomas.

Mama merely stared heatedly at Thomas, then Sally. "I want ya to know we might leave in a fortnight, but we don't know exactly," added Sally.

As Sally uttered the final news of their departure day, Mama rose and ran tearfully from the room, yelling something about the unprecedented cruelty of her son and daughter.

Sally and Thomas walked back to the old house with heavy hearts. It saddened them that Mama could not hear what the move meant to them. They also felt for Mama; she was clearly deeply shaken by the news. Thomas went straight for Liz when they got back. "I don' know if I can do this," said Thomas.

"What do you mean?" asked Liz.

"I don' know 'bout leavin'."

"I guess it didn't go so well with Mama then," suggested Liz.

"Naw. She took it real bad. She took it like we was punishin' her somehow."

"So you can't leave Mama?" asked Liz.

"I don' know what it is."

"You seem pretty shaken, Thomas. You've got to be upset after a rough go with Mama," offered Liz.

"Yeah, but I think I can leave her; I jist don' know if I can leave Mr. MacDonald."

Liz glanced up at Thomas and saw that he was as white as a ghost. His hands shook, even though he held them together.

"I don' know, maybe talkin' with Mama reminded me o' how she and Father just don' know me none. They never did. I never knew what it was like to be known 'till I met Mr. MacDonald. I just can't give 'im up right yet... I asked him to come with us, but..."

Thomas put his head in his hands, yet in spite of his efforts he continued to shake. Liz put her arm around his shoulders and gently rubbed his arm. "I'm reluctant to say anything with you upset and all, but I'm scared you may decide not to go. I really want to go!"

"I know, Liz. I so hate puttin' ya through this," said Thomas.

Liz stood up and walked out of the room; she stopped at the doorway and turned back. She opened her mouth to speak, and then closed it and left the room. Thomas got up, felt woozy, and grabbed onto the wall for support. When he regained his balance, he went out for a walk.

When Thomas came back, Liz was waiting up for him. She looked up expectantly as he entered their bedroom. Thomas returned her look with his steady gaze. His face still appeared pale as though he'd seen a ghost; maybe he had.

"I still can't figure which way's up. I figure I be a good bit confused." Liz nodded and slipped into bed. Thomas took off his boots and went into the outer room and sat and thought.

The next morning Liz awoke to find Thomas already gone. She went outside and looked around, but couldn't find him. She shrugged her shoulders and then went about her day as best she could. Liz hoped Thomas had gone to see MacDonald. It was what he needed. At least every half hour Liz looked up the road.

About midday Liz was finally rewarded for her efforts by seeing Thomas walking up to the Chittenden gate. He walked slowly with shuffling feet. His eyes were on the ground and his shoulders slumped. He carried a long, black box under his left arm. When Thomas's head finally came up to unlatch the gate, his face appeared as though it were under a double dose of gravity.

"Oh no, He doesn't look good," Liz thought.

Liz straightened her apron, and then straightened it again. She wrung her fingers, doing anything to fill the few minutes until Thomas made his way to the house. Liz turned to go back into the house, but changing her mind, she returned to stand at the door. She decided not to hide her anxious waiting from Thomas. He knew anyways.

Thomas finally made his way up to Liz, and gave her a long hug with one arm. He still held the box. He looked her in the eye and motioned for them to sit. Thomas sat down and put one hand on Liz's knee and the other on the box in his lap. A hint of water shone from both eyes. He smiled weakly and nodded his chin up and down. Liz's hands flew to her mouth, and then she threw her arms around Thomas in a grateful embrace.

"Oh, thank God!" said Liz.

References

Blackwell, E. (1734). A Complete System of Fencing. Williamsburg: Parke.

Crockett, W.h. (Ed). (1932). Vermonter: A Book of Biographies. Brattleboro: Stephen Daye Press.

Jelsoft Enterprises Ltd. (2004). Weapons That Went Away. http://boards1.wizards.com/archive/index.php/t-302862.html

Smallwood, F. (1997). Thomas Chittenden: Vermont's First Statesman. Shelburne: The New England Press.

www.ingramcontent.com/pod-product-compliance
Lightning Source LLC
Chambersburg PA
CBHW070349260626

47161CB00001B/80